Tea Cooper is an established Australian author of contemporary and historical fiction. In a past life she was a teacher, a journalist and a farmer. These days she haunts museums and indulges her passion for storytelling. She is the bestselling author of *The Horse Thief*, published by Harlequin in 2015.

www.teacooperauthor.com

Also by Tea Cooper

The Horse Thief

Available in ebook

Matilda's Freedom
Lily's Leap
Jazz Baby
Forgotten Fragrance

The CEDAR CUTTER

TEA COOPER

HARLEQUIN® MIRA®

First Published 2016
First Australian Paperback Edition 2016
ISBN 9781489211576

Published by
Harlequin Mira
An imprint of Harlequin Enterprises (Australia) Pty Ltd.
Level 13, 201 Elizabeth St
SYDNEY NSW 2000
AUSTRALIA

Cataloguing-in-Publication details are available from the National Library of Australia
www.librariesaustralia.nla.gov.au

Printed and bound in Australia by Griffin Press

Jo, Ann, Kew and Sarah
this one's for you!

Even if time heals all wounds,
you still bear the scars…

Wollombi, 1855

One

The road widened from a track to a well-worn thoroughfare and the chill afternoon air blended with the rank odour of civilisation, signalling the end of their long journey. The dray swayed past carts laden with goods and vendors hawking their wares. Women dressed in their Sunday best picked and pored over ribbons and gewgaws, everything from sweet baked delights to rabbit-skin hats, and layered beneath it all was the pungent scent of freshly cut timber.

Drawn by the spectacle, the driver eased to a halt and stood, shading his eyes from the sun. A mighty roar rose up, drowning out the catcalls and cheers, and the crowd stopped and turned, their fevered excitement palpable as they elbowed and jostled their way to a front-row spot.

Curiosity and her son's wriggling body won out and Roisin dragged herself to her feet. Beyond the walls of the inn a seething crowd blanketed the bright stretch of grass, heads craning to catch a glimpse. Silence fell and the sea of bodies parted.

Balanced on the shoulders of two enormous giants, a man sat brandishing an axe above his head, acknowledging the roar of adulation with a cocky grin before brushing aside the shock of damp black curls clinging around his lean, raw-boned face.

'As if I couldn't guess. Carrick's done it again.' The dray driver raised his clenched fist in a salute. 'Good on him.'

'What is it? What has he done?' Roisin deposited the squirming body of her son back onto the seat with a thump.

'Won. Won again. Champion.'

'What's he won?' Something very noteworthy and highly prized, judging by the reaction of the crowd and the look akin to worship on the dray driver's face.

'Won the Woodchop. Best cedar cutter in the district, probably the country.'

'Cedar cutter?' Roisin turned away from the dirty champion clad in a stained, sleeveless vest and thigh-hugging moleskins.

'Good God, woman! Don't you know nuffink? Where you been all your life?'

'Sydney.' She straightened her shoulders and lifted her nose. Sydney was hardly beyond the black stump. It was the largest and most advanced city in the country.

'Right.' The driver gave a dismissive snort. 'City girl born and bred. I'd forgotten.' He hawked his displeasure into the dirt before edging the dray through the press of people. 'Town's on the up and up now the convict gangs have moved on. You won't find the likes of Sydney here. Much as the new settlers pretend otherwise.' He eased alongside another wagon. 'Get your belongings off here and I'll move on. Can't block the road. The show's as good as over.'

The procession of men bore the cedar cutter closer, the slanting sunlight dancing on his sweat-soaked skin, and when he turned his muscles rippled like water over sand. The resounding cheers rent the air, then all sound receded as he fixed her with an intense stare and the strangest shiver tiptoed down her spine.

'Oi! I'm talking to you.'

Roisin blinked as the raucous parade swarmed on its way and the cedar cutter disappeared in a sea of jubilation.

'I said stay there while I get your bags down.' The driver climbed out into the hurrying throng that wavered this way and that, a tide swelling, rising and falling. 'There you are.' He reached out his hand and she balanced on the wheel before scrambling down and landing with a thud on the dusty road.

Stretching up, he grabbed Ruan then deposited him and their bags beside her amidst the swirling chaos. With a wave of his hand he drew away, leaving her perched on the side of the road, Ruan's hand clasped firmly and two carpetbags languishing at her feet.

Her stomach turned three neat summersaults then righted itself. In the safety of Sydney Aunt Lil's plan had seemed like such a good idea. Put the past behind her, make an end of the fear, the constant over-the-shoulder glances, and strike out on her own. A new life—all she thought she wanted and all she knew Ruan needed.

The enormity of her decision sat as heavy as her carpetbags. Snatching a breath of the sticky, fetid air, she pulled Ruan closer, more for her own comfort than his. Now the whole prospect seemed the most foolish idea. If only she'd taken time to think it through instead of packing her bags and fleeing. It was too late for recriminations. She must find a room for the night then tomorrow … tomorrow she'd take the next step.

Ruan squirmed from her grip, jiggling with pent-up energy, and dodged into the road.

'Stop!' One of the bags crashed against her shin as she grabbed at his arm and searched the crowd. No one offered any assistance; they were far too busy going about their business, making their way home. Perhaps if she took Ruan inside the inn she could leave him there and come back for the bags, maybe find someone to help.

'You're hurting me,' Ruan moaned, as she made an instant decision, left the bags and dragged him across the road.

'Hurry up.' Holding her chin high, she marched the poor child towards the sign proudly proclaiming the Harp of Erin. It might be unseemly, a woman alone entering a place like this, but she had no option. She shouldered open the door and stepped over the threshold into the dim interior. Dust motes hung in the thin shafts of light illuminating the sultry gazes and appreciative stares of the gang of sweaty, half-dressed men lounging around the fire.

The woman behind the bar wiped her hands on a filthy apron and looked her up and down. 'What can I do you for you, love?' Her wrinkled face creased into the semblance of something that could have been a smile.

'A room for the night, if you please. For myself and my son.'

Her son, Ruan, dangled from her hand, twirling around, his eyes as round as buttons as he took in the packed room.

'Ruan, stay right beside me, here.' She stamped on the floor to emphasise the spot.

'Just for the one night will it be, love?'

'Yes, that's all.' It wouldn't even be one night except for the fact they'd been travelling for longer than she could remember and they needed food and sleep.

'Come on Davy's dray, did you? From St Albans?'

The stares and the woman's questions set Roisin's teeth on edge. 'Ruan, stay still.' She sucked in a deep breath of rum-drenched air and willed herself to relax.

After hours of bumping along the rutted road, the boy had ants in his pants. Roisin could understand his impatience, every one of her bones seemed dislocated by the buffeting they'd received. The dray had rattled and banged all the way from St Albans, falling into every single one of the potholes lining the road. What she wouldn't give for a cup of tea.

'Only got one left, it's round the back. Got a few people in town. The Woodchop, you know.'

'I'll take it.' She didn't care how small the room was or where as long as it was dry and they could find something to eat. If the wretched driver hadn't taken so long gawking at the crowds she'd have been inside ages ago and with her bags. Who knew how many light-fingered, dubious characters lurked in the shadows. There were enough in the cramped room of the inn to populate Hyde Park Barracks.

She glanced over her shoulder. 'Ruan?'

'The man's got our bags.'

Roisin whipped around. The man in question, the woodcutter with the broad grin, had both her bags balanced on his shoulders, as though they weighed no more than a flimsy bolt of silk.

'Where do you think you're going with those?' She took a couple of measured steps towards him, schooling the scowl on her face, hoping it would be enough to stall him in his tracks.

'Depends where you'd be liking them.' His intense blue eyes twinkled at her from under black-winged brows as he tossed the mess of curls off his forehead.

A man had no right to hair that beautiful. A man had no right to her bags, either. 'Just put them down here, thank you.'

One eyebrow quirked and the corner of his mouth twisted into a slow mocking grin that would have done the devil proud.

'The lady'd probably like them in her room—out the back.' The woman tipped her head in the direction of a closed door behind the bar.

'Right you are.'

'Just a moment I …'

Unable to do anything but gape, she stood stock-still as his broad shoulders edged through the doorway into the dark recesses of the inn and disappeared. Scrambling to follow, she nudged Ruan in front of her, intent on keeping their possessions in sight.

'Woah! Not so fast, Missus. That'll be a shilling each for the bed and same again for a bowl of my very best Irish stew. And as much tea and damper as you can handle.'

'Oh yes, of course.' She rummaged in the small drawstring reticule hung around her wrist while Ruan vanished through the door after the man. 'Ruan, wait for me. You'll get lost.' She slid the coins across the bar.

'He'll be right. Carrick knows his way around the place.'

'Carrick? The woodcutter?'

'Carrick, the 'andsome bloke you couldn't take your eyes off, carrying those bags of yours.'

'Oh, Carrick,' she stammered, batting down the flush scalding her cheeks. Something about the man, even in his sweat-stained clothes stirred a heated confusion in her. 'Ruan, come back here.' Her brain seethed. How could she find a man like that even remotely attractive? Most likely he was some ticket of leaver employed at the inn when he wasn't showing off with an axe.

'Off you go, and don't worry. Your little boy won't come to any harm unless Carrick sits him down and starts recounting his far-fetched yarns. He's got the gift of the gab, that scoundrel.'

'Yarns,' Roisin echoed. She spun around, managing to catch her foot in the hem of her travelling skirt, before scuttling after Ruan's retreating back. The lack of light hit her the moment she passed under the timber lintel into the passageway. 'Ruan!'

'Down here, Mam.'

Following the sound of Ruan's high-pitched giggle and a burst of deeper laughter, she edged her way through the half-open door and stopped dead. 'Excuse me!'

'Just testing the bed.' Carrick slammed the palms of his big hands down on the coverlet, making Ruan bounce in the cloud of ensuing dust.

More shrieks of laughter from Ruan reverberated around the crowded room and Roisin smothered a sneeze, then groped in the pocket of her jacket for a handkerchief.

''Tis a very fine colour on you. Brings out the green in your eyes. Emerald like the green grass of home, enough to tweak a poor man's heartstrings.'

'Come along, Ruan. Now.' Roisin grasped at her son's hand. As much as she longed to, she didn't dare make eye contact with the owner of the dulcet tones. Not again. What man noticed the colour of a woman's clothes? Even more, appreciated the fact she'd chosen the colour because it was an exact match to her eyes. It served her right, payment for a foolish moment of vanity.

'That will be all, thank you.'

In a flash the cutter was on his feet. His lopsided grin made a mockery of her cold words and his wretched eyes sparkled with amusement. 'The pleasure's mine, ma'am.' He tugged his forelock and winked at Ruan, before striding through the door, whistling some tune that reminded her of swirling skirts and madcap dancing.

'Get off that bed. I need to put the bags there. Where are they?'

Ruan struggled off the mattress and landed on the floor with a bump. 'Carrick put them down over there so they'd be out of the way.' He pointed into the back corner of the room where both bags sat in a forlorn heap.

'I hope you said thank you to Mr … Carrick.'

'Yes. And he said mates didn't thank each other.' Ruan gave a delighted jump. 'I'm going to like it here.'

'Ruan, darling,' she sighed, 'you really must be a bit more sensible. You can't just go off with anyone who comes along. It's not the right thing to do.' Roisin couldn't bring herself to look into his eyes. Warnings like that belonged in Sydney, yet she couldn't shake her concerns. They'd become second nature after two years of looking over her shoulder every time she and Ruan set foot outside the house.

'I wasn't following *just anyone*. I was following our blasted bags.' He slammed his hands on his hips and pouted.

'What is the matter with you? I shall scrub your mouth out with carbolic if I hear words like that again. And for that matter they're not *blasted bags*, they contain our livelihood, our possessions.' Her most precious possession, the pocket sewing machine Aunt Lil had given her, bought for a song from a gold digger's wife when the woman and her husband had run short. 'I'll have you remember …' Roisin sucked in a deep breath and glared at Ruan, a mirror image standing hands on hips scowling back at her. Her shoulders sank. 'Oh, darling, I'm sorry. I'm tired after the long journey and you must be exhausted, too. I was worried. Come along, let's wash your face and hands and then we'll go and find some food.'

A jug and bowl sat atop the single corner cabinet. 'You're big enough to do this yourself.'

While Ruan threw handfuls of water across his face and the floor, she rummaged through their bags until her fingers touched the tasselled silk shawl covering her pocket machine. It was there, safe, just as Ruan was.

Ruan scrubbed at his face, then his green eyes met hers over the top of the cloth and her heart hitched. She hadn't made a mistake. Leaving Sydney was the right, no … the *only* thing to do.

'My turn and then we'll find something to eat.'

'I'm not putting my coat back on.'

Roisin nodded into the damp cloth as she patted her face, thankful to remove the grime from the journey. None of the raggle-taggle bunch hanging around the inn wore a jacket. She'd never seen such a collection of brawny arms and muscled shoulders. What she needed was a decent night's sleep and some food, then with a bit of luck, this time tomorrow they would be in their new home.

She patted the envelope tucked into the pocket of her skirt, relishing the reassuring crinkle of paper; a letter of introduction to the Reverend Benson, who would provide the key to the house. The owner, Mr Martin, had assured her there would be no problem, saying he was pleased the property could be used and the women in the town would more than welcome Roisin's services. She couldn't wait. This would mark the end to all of the uncertainty and the beginning of a lifelong dream. Every penny she'd saved, she'd gambled on this venture, and she had every intention of making it a success. The idea had grown from the moment Aunt Lil had told her half the businesses in Sydney were run by women, some of them even ex-convicts. That was when she began to think that perhaps her plan wasn't as far-fetched as she'd originally believed.

'Come on.' She smoothed Ruan's tousled hair behind his ears and opened the door. At least she didn't have the stigma of *convict* hanging over her head. She was as free as the day her mam had birthed her. If convict women could make a go of a business, then so could she.

When they entered the front room of the inn the woman behind the bar tipped her head towards a small table tucked against the wall. 'There's room for you over there, lovey.'

'Thank you, Mrs …'

'Me name's Maisie. And you'd be?'

'Roisin, Roisin Ogilvie.' She swallowed, praying Ruan didn't overhear her lie. 'And my son, Ruan.' He was too busy staring around the room, wide-eyed. Her stomach rumbled in anticipation when Maisie pushed two huge helpings of stew across the counter.

'And you take this.' She leant across the bar and handed Ruan a basket full of sweet-smelling damper.

Roisin glanced across at the rough-looking men sprawled in front of the smoking fire, hogging the best spot.

'Don't worry about them. Just a bit rowdy. Celebrating Carrick's win.'

That confirmed it, as if she'd been in any doubt. Carrick was the *good-looking bloke she couldn't take her eyes off.* Her face flushed. Had she really made it so obvious? Nodding her thanks, she edged her way to an empty table tucked into the corner. The conversation lulled and then a large guffaw filled the room. Determined not to be intimidated, she concentrated on the task at hand, crossed the room and set the plates down and turned back to Ruan to take the damper.

The chair was whisked back from the table and she stared up, transfixed by the intent expression on the cutter's face. His eyes were an even deeper blue in the dim light, almost black, the colour intensified by his thick lashes. For the second time they stared at each other amidst the clatter and chaos for a long moment, the impact of his glance warming her skin and scoring a path deep down into her belly. 'I can manage, thank you.'

'Ah, you'd not be depriving a man of a bit of pleasure, would you?'

Pleasure? That wasn't a word to be discussing right now. Not in front of Ruan, not in connection with this man. 'Thank you Mr …'

'Carrick, Carrick O'Connor at your service.' He wiped a stained, roughened hand down his trousers then shook his head. 'Maybe not. Cutter's hands.' He laughed and settled her into the chair. 'And now for you, me lad.'

Before Roisin could speak, he swung Ruan onto the chair next to her. She turned aside, determined not to notice the muscles bunching in his arms, or the way his broad shoulders strained the seams of his stained shirt.

He pushed Ruan's stool up to the table. 'Maisie does a rare mutton stew.'

'Are you going to have some?' Ruan gazed up at the big man with a look suspiciously like adoration.

Oh, for goodness sake. The prospect of having to spend another moment in his company set her heart rate scampering. She'd never experienced anything quite like it before. It had to stop. 'No, Ruan, the gentleman is busy with his friends. Now eat up and then it's time to sleep.'

'Your mam's right. Eat up, won't you?' With a wink at Ruan he strode back to his cronies by the fire, picking up an oversized tankard from Maisie on his way.

'Has Carrick eaten?' Ruan asked.

'I have no idea.' Roisin pushed her spoon through the mutton stew in an attempt to set Ruan an example, but her appetite had vanished.

For a moment there he'd believed his sanity had deserted him. He rubbed at the cold fingers of fate still prickling the hairs on the back of his neck. When he'd first caught sight of them standing on the side of the road, it was as though the very angels had answered his prayers. Now, even in the half-light of the inn, he could see his mistake.

Where was she going and why? Meeting up with a husband or a lover? The child was hers, no doubt about that. He shared her eyes and she made no attempt to hide the fact he belonged to her. And why was she travelling alone?

He sneaked a glance at her over his shoulder. She reminded him of days gone by, hair somewhere between the spun gold of the sunshine and the pure new cedar in the forest after the first axe stroke. And those eyes, flaming emeralds heightened by the artifice of her outrageous green jacket, the colour of new leaves, love and home. Certainly not a widow. He hadn't seen a woman dressed in a colour that bright since … since ever.

Tossing back the last of his drink, he dragged his attention to the timber cutters' stories growing taller by the second as the free-flowing rum lubricated their imagination. Let them have their fun before they headed back to the forest for another bout of hard labour. The possibility of crossing the path of the delightful Miss … he didn't even know her name. That wasn't good enough.

'Who's for another, for the road?' Clasping the eager, outstretched tankards, he made his way to the bar. 'Fill 'em up, Maisie. There's a girl.' His gaze strayed to the table in the corner, where they sat, heads close. Her hair was shades darker than the strawberry blond of the boy's.

'She's a sweet young thing, is she not?'

'Aye. And you needn't grin at me like that, you scheming old witch. I'm back to the forests tomorrow.' Back where he wanted to be, in the company of men relying on strength, nothing more. He'd not have his heart ripped out again, though it couldn't hurt to know her name. 'Has the sweet young thing got a name?'

'What would that be to you if you're going back to your timber cutting?'

He shrugged his shoulders. 'Just curious. The boy's Ruan. That's a good Irish name. Little red one.'

'And she's Roisin, another good Irish name.' Maisie winked one of her I-told-you-so looks. 'Though there's not much poor Irish about her, dressed like that. That jacket would be worth as much as one of your cedar trees.'

'I'd be doubting that.' He picked up the drinks and made his way back. Full to the brim, the tankards slopped rum across the back of his hands and down his fingers. He plonked them onto the table and licked away the sticky mess. He'd be needing every drop tonight to keep the ghosts at bay. It didn't do for the boss to be heard thrashing and screaming. His cutters were hard men and it took an even harder one to keep them in line, to make them pull together in the forest and keep them safe. Complain as they did, they were happy enough when they divided the profits; better than slaving for the bleeding government.

'Give us a tune, Slinger.'

'Where's your fiddle?'

'Something from the old country. A taste of home.'

And so it all began again, the simple pattern of the last night free of the forest. Slinger caressed the old fiddle as a man would a woman. Perhaps it reminded him of someone he loved. Carrick had never asked. They'd cut together for years, from the days when they both wore the irons, and never asked questions. Rarely did a man tell of what went before. That was the realm of dreams, the land of what if and one day. So long as there was something to return to.

Slinger cut to a jig, fast, furious and snappy, making the men's feet stamp and the floor reverberate. Carrick rested his back against the warm chimneybreast, his ears ringing with the raucous shouts of encouragement. The increasing beat of the music soared and filled the four walls of the inn.

If he ducked his head just so, he could see Roisin. A good Irish name, as Maisie said. Her foot tapped in time to the music, her face now flushed with the warmth and a decent dollop of Maisie's stew. She wiped a trace of gravy from the lad's face with her finger and gave him a loving smile. They'd be off before long, tucked up for the night, though they'd need plugs for their ears if the cutters' shouting and carrying on took its usual path. Why was she travelling alone? There'd have to be a man waiting somewhere, a man with Irish blood if the child's looks were anything to go by. Not all of that came from his mam. His eyes were as wide and green as hers, but his skin was so pale, as if it had never seen the light of day, never run under a summer sky. A washed-out imitation of his mother, and thin. The boy had no meat on his long, ribbon-like bones. He had the look of the Irish immigrants running from the

Famine. But *her* voice—that was pure English, not a lilt of Irish in it.

She pushed back her chair and stood, encouraging the lad to leave. He didn't want to go and glanced in Carrick's direction. Carrick started to rise, then sank back against the heat of the chimney stones. The lad needed his sleep; even from across the room the blue bruises under his eyes stood out.

She scooped him into her arms and sat him on her hip. A low whistle skimmed across his lips. Holy Mary, Mother of God. With that tilt of her hip she was enough to turn a man away from his rum. Tall, very tall. He narrowed his eyes and took another slug of the sticky drink and the penny dropped. Cornstalk. She was a cornstalk, born and bred right here in Australia. Never seen the verdant grass of home. Not Irish. Poor lass didn't know what she was missing.

Not that Ireland was worth seeing these days. The bloody English had seen to that with their laws and taxes. Bled the country dry. The irony in the fact so many Irish were making a place in Australia went some way to easing the pain. Beating the English at their game. They'd be a force to reckon with, given half a chance. Unruly, difficult to handle, struggling for independence for their homeland, even from across the seas. Seas he'd cross again soon enough. Scores he'd see settled.

Two

Silence wrapped the village, low as the mist hovering in the valley. Roisin shivered and pulled the blanket up over Ruan's shoulders. It was much colder than she'd expected away from the coast and the whole of winter stretched out ahead of them. If their new home didn't have a fireplace, they'd be in trouble.

After the thrill and furore of yesterday, the enormity of the task ahead sat heavily on Roisin's shoulders. Not so Ruan. It had taken hours to get him to settle last night and now he looked as though he'd sleep the day through. She ran her hand over his forehead. Cool to the touch. His chest rose and fell in a steady rhythm with not a sign of the breathing sickness that had plagued him in Sydney, despite all the cold fresh air of the last few days.

Easing up from their bed, she tucked her shawl around him. Today was the beginning of their new life. She shook back her hair and the past, determined to dwell only on the promise of the future.

Armed with her letter, she felt her way along the dark corridor and pushed through into the taproom. The smell hit her with the force of a sledgehammer. Stale rum, sour beer, rancid sweat and the greasy overtones of last night's stew. Had she eaten that? Her stomach roiled and she clamped her mouth closed.

'You'll be wanting some breakfast, then?' Maisie eased upright, rubbing the small of her back and grimacing. 'Bloody mess they leave, though I can't complain. They pay their dues. Still 'n all I'm glad it's over until next time.'

'Don't worry about breakfast. I couldn't.' Roisin edged towards the door, seeking some fresh air. 'I have a letter. I need to find the Reverend Benson.'

'He won't be up and about just yet. Not judging by the state of him when he left here last night.'

'I have to collect my key.'

'Now what would you be wanting with a key?'

'The key to my premises. I have an arrangement with Mr Martin. I'm to rent the house behind the General Store.'

'Oh you are, are you?'

What was the matter with the woman? Sticking her nose in. Checking up. Wanting to know it all. It wouldn't hurt to be a little more helpful. Roisin drew herself up to her full height. 'I'd appreciate your assistance and then I'll be on my way.'

'With no breakfast.'

God no. No breakfast.

'And what about your boy? He'll be needing something.'

He could have one of the apples left in her bag until she had the key. Curiosity would get the better of her long before Ruan suffered from starvation.

'And where would all your belongings be if you're planning on staying here?'

For goodness sake. 'My trunks will be delivered to Morpeth at a later date.' No need to explain it was all part of the intricate plan she and Aunt Lil had devised to ensure her destination remained a secret. Until she wrote and told Aunt Lil she was settled, the rest of her belongings would remain in Sydney.

'Well, then. Show us your letter. You're in luck. I have the key.' Like some ancient chatelaine, Maisie lifted the massive bunch of keys dangling around her waist and shuffled through them, tutting loudly. 'Can't be seeing a thing in there. Come outside.' She elbowed her way through the door and stood in a patch of frail sunlight. 'Right. Key to the girls' house.'

'Girls' house?'

'That's what it's been known as. Don't be bothering yourself.'

She didn't care what it was called. 'I was told there was a house, and the parlour would suit my business.'

'That there is. There's rooms out the back that'll make a fine place to live after a decent scrub and the parlour has a window onto the street, with glass even. You'd have noticed that when you arrived.'

Roisin shook her head. With the throngs of people lining the streets and all the noise and carry-on from Mr O'Connor and his loud-mouthed, bumptious cutters she'd hardly noticed anything. They'd passed a couple of fine houses on the outskirts of town, one belonging to the magistrate, according to the dray driver, and some small farm holdings; other than that she hadn't seen much more.

'No. Maybe not. Not yesterday with all the hullaballoo. Here it is.' Maisie handed over a large ornate key.

Roisin clasped it in her palm, hefting the unexpected weight, and then traced the intricate swirls and patterns with her forefinger. The idea of the lock it belonged to and the prospects set her pulse racing.

'Down the street, past the General Store. If you get as far as the millpond and the cemetery you've gone too far. We'll be as good as neighbours. See the verandah of the General Store? It's just the other side. Stick your head in and introduce yourself to old Elsie, that way she won't attack you with her broomstick. She can be a bit territorial.'

Old Elsie sounded more like one of the dogs that guarded the Sydney Barracks than the local shop owner. It didn't bode well.

'If you follow the footpath past the store, you'll see a narrow alley on your left, cut down through the timber gate and you're there.'

'I'll go and wake Ruan and bring our bags down.'

'Leave the wee mite sleeping. I'll keep an eye on him. You go and check out your new home.'

Leave Ruan? It went against every fibre of her being. 'No, thank you. I'll wake him and …'

'Off you go.' Maisie's hand landed firmly in the small of her back and propelled her across the road. 'You're not in the big city anymore. We take care of our own in Wollombi. You go and have a look-see and by the time you come back your boy'll be up and breakfasted. I'll make sure he doesn't get into any trouble.'

She gulped back another refusal. Wasn't that the very reason she'd fled Sydney? It was time to put the past behind them, just as Aunt Lil had said. The road outside was as quiet as anything, as though the chaos of yesterday was nothing more than the tendrils of another frantic dream. She'd run down the road and be back in no time.

'Thank you. I won't be a moment.'

Lifting her skirts she took off down the street, past the church and the courthouse. When she reached the shadow the awning of the General Store threw across the flagstone footpath, she slowed before pushing open the door.

The air was rife with the smell of onions, their skins crackling like tissue paper as an apple-faced woman with flyaway, greying hair bustled around sorting them into bins.

'Good morning.'

The woman's shrewd eyes scanned her from top to toe, making Roisin smooth her skirt and straighten her collar. 'I'm the new tenant of the house and shop at the back. Maisie said I should introduce myself.' She held up the key to prove her point.

'You are, are you?' The woman dropped the last remaining onions into the barrel and thumped her hands onto her ample hips. 'I won't be standing for no competition, I'm telling you.'

Roisin sketched a look around the well-stocked store. 'I don't think we will be in competition. I intend to open a dressmaking business. More likely I'll improve your business buying my supplies here.'

The woman's head snapped up. 'So you'll not be setting up a general store?'

Roisin shook her head and offered a tentative smile.

The light returned to the woman's eyes and she wiped her hands down her apron, and then stuck out her hand. 'Name's Elsie.' When Roisin took her hand she pumped it up and down like a recalcitrant water pump. 'Come on, then, I'll show you through.'

'My name's Roisin, Roisin Ogilvie.' There, the second time she'd used Aunt Lil's name and it wasn't difficult.

'Pleased to meet you, Roisin. We don't stand on ceremony here.' Elsie led her out of the door back into the street. 'See this alley here? Your place is just at the end. Bit narrow. It opens up once you get inside the gate. Or you can use the entrance around the back and come in by the brook.'

Before they'd made it as far as the garden gate, Ruan's voice, ten times louder than she'd ever heard it before, echoed down the street. 'Wait for us!' Perched on the woodcutter's broad shoulders, he threw her a cocky grin and waved like a mad thing.

Her stomach turned over and her knees sagged. 'Get down from there before you fall.' She shouldn't have left him with Maisie, she should have woken him up. What was the man doing with him?

'Now that's no way to greet a jockey in training.' Carrick O'Connor's voice boomed out as big as the rest of him. Huge. He swung Ruan over his head and deposited him at her feet.

Would nothing turn out the way she expected? Maisie said she'd keep Ruan out of trouble and here he was careering down the street balanced on the wretched cutter's shoulders.

She drew herself to her full height and glared up at him. 'Thank you, Mr O'Connor. Ruan, come here.' Grabbing Ruan's hand, she pulled him close to her skirts.

Whatever was happening? Maisie promised to keep an eye on him, not hand him over to the first person that crossed his path. And anyway what was O'Connor doing here? Hadn't Maisie said the timber cutters would be leaving for their camp at first light? The whole idea of leaving Sydney was to keep Ruan safe, not to expose him to strangers who picked him up and carried him around without a second thought.

The cheeky wretch winked at her as though he could read her thoughts. 'Fear not. Yer lad's as safe as houses. We'll be leaving soon.' He turned on his heel and strode back down the street to the inn.

The corners of Ruan's mouth tipped down in disappointment as his newfound friend disappeared. 'Bye, Carrick.'

O'Connor turned and grinned over his shoulder. 'Back in two shakes of a lamb's tail, me little mate.'

That brought the smile to Ruan's face again. 'He's gone to get our bags, I bet.'

'Come with me. I've got the key to our new house.' With any luck it would divert Ruan's attention. She didn't like the way O'Connor had taken possession of him, treated him like long-lost family.

She towed Ruan behind her down the narrow alley to a timber gate hanging crooked on its hinges.

Elsie pattered behind, huffing and puffing. 'Been a while since the last lot left and they didn't spend too much time on house keepin', I can tell you.'

Roisin lifted the gate, propped it open and stepped into the overgrown garden. Wild grass almost as high as Ruan's head edged the path, and pull as he might she refused to let go of his hand. 'Stay with me.' This wasn't like the city. There'd be snakes lurking in grass that long and heavens knew what beyond the door.

'There we are,' Elsie wheezed, her apple cheeks blooming with the exertion.

The door sported a hefty lock and Roisin inserted the key and jiggled it a few times until with a creak and groan the door swung open. Catching a breath, she stepped over the threshold. For a moment she wanted to do nothing more than turn on her heel and run, run back to anything that was familiar. In the last few days since they'd left Sydney, she'd covered more miles and seen more than ever before in her lifetime. Gritting her teeth she stepped further inside. 'Come on, Ruan. Let's explore our new home.'

The smell hit her first, dusty but not damp, as though the house had lain waiting for her to slip the key into the lock. A beam of sunlight infiltrated the narrow hall and she stepped inside where flecks floated in the stale air and her heels clicked on the wide timber floorboards. She eased open the first door on her left and peered inside. The front room, the parlour, was largish with a good-sized mullioned window facing the street; it would make a perfect place to conduct her business. At least it would when she'd given it a decent clean. The glass in the window was an unexpected bonus. She ran her hand along the mantle above the fire, thick with dust and ancient soot, and a shiver of recognition darted up her spine.

'Someone dance on your grave, did they?' Elsie asked with a smile. 'It happens to me all the time. I put it down to all the history in these walls. All those stories aching to be told. This place has been here since the convict road gangs first came to build the road from Sydney.'

What nonsense. It's the last thing Ruan needed to hear, that their new home was haunted by an itinerant band of convicts. 'No, just a little cold. I'll be fine in the sunshine.' Dark and musty, the air was redolent with the smell of vermin, and strangely, an overtone of something flowery.

'You've got no kitchen as such. The room at the back's big with a good fireplace. There's a scullery outside, a privy and a woodshed. It's pretty mucky. No one's lived here for a long while. Not since the girls got sent packing.' Elsie smothered a sneeze with her apron.

'Sent packing?'

Elsie cleared her throat, a long, drawn-out kind of snort. 'It wasn't the best sort of place.' She wrung her apron in her hands and shot a quick glance at Ruan. 'A place the men liked to visit.' She raised her eyebrows and bobbed her head up and down. 'That's why you've got that window at the front. Not many can afford glass like that.'

A bubble of laughter rose in Roisin's throat and she swallowed it down. She'd leased a house of ill repute. She'd come full circle. The irony of it made her grin and all her fears floated away, scented by the familiar ghosts of the past.

'I'll leave you. I need to get back and mind the store. There's no stove, just a camp oven, a billy and some old furniture out the back in the woodshed, couple of padded chairs and a few other bits 'n pieces you might be able to make use of. Sing out if you need anything.' Elsie bustled out, leaving a gaping silence.

Ruan tugged at her hand. 'Come on.' He clattered down the hallway, which opened into a bigger room and off that a door. 'This is the bedroom. See, Mam?'

In one corner stood a large stringed bed with a rolled ticking-covered mattress, big enough for both of them. Moth-eaten curtains dangled in one corner forming a cupboard next to a shuttered window. Only the front window of the building merited glass, its face on the world. Good enough. She pushed the hinged timber shutter wide and light flooded in.

'A ladder, Mam, a ladder.' Ruan pulled away and scampered up the rungs.

'Take care …'

His head disappeared into the small, shadowed hole. 'It's dark.' He gave a loud sniff. 'Argh! And smelly.'

'Come down. We'll look later.'

Taking no notice of her, he clambered up the ladder, his body disappearing until only the scuffed soles of his boots remained, staring at her like upturned palms. 'There's another bed. Come and see.' The ceiling creaked, marking his progress, and she scuttled up after him.

The attic lay beneath the sharpest point of the roof, the steep pitch below head height for anyone except a small boy.

'Got it.' With a bump and a whine the shutter opened and Ruan turned his pale face, wreathed in a huge smile. 'I shall have my own room. This is mine.'

'No, Ruan. We'll sleep downstairs.'

'Mam. I'm not a baby. I've never had my own bed. Look.' He crossed the floor and sank onto the bed, nothing more than a series of branches held together by rope ties, the lumpy, straw-filled mattress already unrolled. 'They knew I was coming. See—they've left me a present.' He waved three black-and-orange feathers bound with dried grass.

The hairs on the back of her neck rose. 'Put them down.' It was all fanciful childish nonsense. There'd be a dead bird somewhere to account for the feathers and putrid smell.

'They're clean, Mam. All cleaned.' He gave a bounce on the bed, swung his legs up and lay back with the feathers fanned out in front of his face. 'My own room.'

What could she say? Of course it could be his, though not until it had been scrubbed within an inch of its life, the same as the rest of the place. She pushed her sleeves above her elbows and tucked up the corners of her skirt. 'Come downstairs and let's see what else we have.' She backed down the ladder. 'Come on now. We'll fix it later.'

'But this can be my room. My very own.'

'Yes, my darling. We'll make it yours.'

Satisfied, Ruan clattered down the ladder, the three feathers tucked into his back pocket, dark against his cord trousers. 'What else have we got in our house?'

The back room was the width of the house with a large, sooty walk-in fireplace. A huge black pot on three legs sat over the dusty remains of a fire. A far cry from the immaculate range Aunt Lil had installed a couple of years ago in Sydney. Never mind. She'd work it out and no doubt Elsie would be more than happy to offer advice.

The walls were lime-washed, and bundled in one corner behind the rectangular table and a couple of mismatched chairs lay a pile of grubby rag rugs. She grimaced, lifting them with her toe, her flesh creeping at the thought of the rats' nest she might unearth.

A dresser stood in the niche between the fireplace and the back door, and around the knob a key hung on a piece of twine. She pushed it into the lock. It squeaked and complained and when she delivered a hefty wrench the door swung free. Two steps led down to a flagstone path and a small yard framed by the scullery and privy.

Ruan gave a cursory glance and skipped outside. 'There's another house at the back.'

By the time she'd left the kitchen and negotiated the sandstone steps Ruan had vanished.

'Blah, it smells!'

'Mind your manners and come here. Away!'

'It's a woodshed.' His muffled voice drifted out of the dilapidated slab hut. 'There's wood and some old junk, chairs and stuff. We can light the fire and make our dinner.'

'We'll do nothing until this place is spotless. Now let's go and get our bags and bring them in. There's work to do.'

A loud thump and a clatter echoed through the house, sending her back up the steps at a gallop.

'Where would ye be liking these?' Carrick grinned, her two carpetbags clamped in his enormous paws. With his shoulders as good as touching the walls he eased his way down the hallway and kicked the bedroom door open.

'Oh, anywhere. Just anywhere.'

He deposited them just inside the door. 'Anything else I can do?'

'Carrick!' Ruan barrelled up the back steps and into the house. 'Come and see my bedroom and you were right, there's a woodshed, and wood.'

'That's men's work, me boy. Come along.'

Roisin opened her mouth to object, and then closed it with a snap at the sight of the pride beaming from Ruan's face. He'd had so little contact with men, lived all his life within a tight circle of women, cosseted, pampered and hidden away from prying eyes. Perhaps it was time to set aside her fears. 'You stay right here and don't leave while I go and speak with Elsie. We need brooms, buckets and cloths.'

'And that's women's work.' Carrick threw the words over his shoulder and tossed another of his audacious winks, before walking away with Ruan clinging to his hand as though he'd evaporate.

Standing in the middle of the room, Roisin held her breath and listened to the sighing of the house. This would be their home.

Nothing as elaborate as she'd find in Sydney but she could relax, free of the constant need to guard Ruan's every move.

Clean first and then unpack. It would take several days, but what did it matter? She had all the time in the world. No need to look over her shoulder anymore. No need to worry that she'd turn and Ruan would be gone. No problems soap and sunlight wouldn't cure.

Armed with mops and a bucket, soap, brushes, cloths and most importantly tea, Roisin nudged her way back through the front door. She'd begin in the bedroom and work her way through, leaving the parlour until last. Until her trunks arrived from Morpeth she couldn't even start to think about setting up shop; making a home for Ruan was more important. But first she needed water.

She dumped everything onto the kitchen table and peered outside into the garden, where Ruan was busy stacking a pile of freshly chopped logs against the wall.

Carrick, shirtsleeves rolled up revealing his strong, pale forearms, raised the axe as though it weighed nothing more than one of Ruan's black-and-orange feathers, and brought it down, splitting the log into two neat pieces. Ruan waited for Carrick's nod and rushed in, picked one up and deposited it on the growing pile. Grasping the bucket, she set off in search of the water pump.

'We've made a wood pile here.' Ruan pointed to the rows of wood stacked against the woodshed wall just inside the door. 'Then we can light the fire and make some tea.'

She ran her hand over his head. 'I'd love a cup of tea and I expect Mr O'Connor would, too, but first I have to find some water.'

'It's over here.' Ruan led her to the side of the woodshed and sure enough, lurching against the lopsided timber wall, stood a hand pump. She placed the bucket underneath and lifted the handle. The pump wheezed and coughed its belligerent response.

'Let me.' Carrick's big hand came down on her shoulder, easing her aside. 'I should have thought to check it.'

'It's fine, I'm sure I can do it.' She heaved the handle again. 'I think something might be blocked, or maybe it's just because it hasn't been used.' She wiped at her forehead with her arm.

Carrick stepped closer. 'Move away.' He lifted his booted foot and slammed it against the casing, making the whole woodshed rock and groan and threaten to topple.

'Stand back.' Using both hands, he raised the lever then slammed it down, not once, three times in rapid succession. The pump coughed, spluttered and finally a few desultory drops hit the dirt. The dribble grew until a rusty stream of foul-smelling water ran and puddled at their feet.

'Water's been sitting for a while. Give it time to clear then I'll fill the bucket. We need to be lighting the fire before we can put the billy on.'

'Thank you. And thank you for chopping the wood, too.'

'You don't have to keep up with the thanks. I've time to do the work. And I've got a good little helper.' He slapped his hands together and wiped them down the back of his trousers before retrieving his vest from the log pile and shrugging it over his chequered shirt.

'Mam?' Ruan's head appeared in the doorway of the shed, his hair standing up like a cocky's crest. 'Can I stay outside?' She nodded, wiping a smudge of dirt from the bridge of his upturned nose and he was off like a shot. 'He's a good lad.'

'He's only six.'

'He'll grow up fine and strong. Guard him well.' Carrick walked into the kitchen carrying an armful of logs.

Guard him well. She had every intention of doing that. Ruan was the reason she got up each morning, the binding that held her together.

Within moments Carrick had smoke billowing from the fireplace, filling the room. She threw open the shutters and the doors. 'Oh dear. I think I may have taken on more than I bargained for.'

'We'll have it spick and span in no time. Don't you worry.'

'I can't impose on you any longer, Mr O'Connor.'

'Just Carrick'll do. And like I said, it's my pleasure. We'll be heading off later this afternoon. Until then me time is yours.'

'You're too kind.'

'You can repay me with a cup of tea. I'll sort out the chimney and bring in some water for you. It'll be running clear by now. You've got a decent pile of logs. Should keep you going for a few weeks, until I get back.'

In a matter of moments a cheery fire burned in the fire place and Carrick had set the billy to boil. Roisin opened the bag of tea from the store, added a handful to the billy and took two cracked cups down from the mantelpiece and rinsed them in the bucket.

'Tell me about these trunks Maisie's on about. Coming to Morpeth, she said.' He righted the two wooden chairs stacked in the corner and brought them to the table.

Maisie hadn't wasted much time in broadcasting the chitchat. 'Yes.' Roisin swallowed and looked away. Being without all their belongings still made her feel something of a fugitive. She'd write to Aunt Lil tomorrow and ask her to forward them on as soon as possible.

'They'll be wanting collection, then?' He lifted the billy from the fire and banged it against the side of the table then poured the tea into the cups.

'I have to arrange it.'

'You let me know if I can help.'

The man made everything sound so simple, yet there was something about his familiarity that made her uneasy. She sipped the scalding tea, sneaking a look at him over the rim of the cup. He appeared so relaxed, so at home with his long legs stretched out in front of him as he rested against the table. 'I'll manage. Thank you for the offer.' Her taut tone sounded stiff and unfriendly, although he didn't seem to mind. He just grinned, downed the rest of his tea and stood up.

'Thanks. I better be off.'

Ruan appeared and his face crumpled when he realised Carrick was leaving. He propped his elbows on the table and groaned, a picture of abject misery. 'Can I come with you?' His voice caught in his throat, a familiar precursor to tears.

'You must stay here with your mam and protect her. She needs a man about the place.'

Why did Carrick always manage to say the right thing? Just the words to keep Ruan happy, more than happy, puffed up and full of pride.

'I'll be seeing you both next time I'm coming through town.'

And with that the cedar cutter was gone.

The room seemed suddenly empty and Roisin swirled the remains of her tea in her cup. Ruan sighed heavily and pulled the three feathers from his pocket and smoothed them. 'They're black cockatoo feathers, you know.'

'No, I didn't. You're a very clever boy.'

He mumbled something under his breath that sounded suspiciously like *man*. 'Carrick told me.'

'I might need some help.'

Ruan stomped his way outside and slammed the door behind him. She picked up the teacups and put them in the bucket for later. She didn't seem to have the right words to keep Ruan happy, not like the cedar cutter.

Three

Slinger's abusive shouts bounced down the street, telling Carrick it was time to leave. He'd sorted most of the lass's problems. The rest she'd manage herself. Despite her fragile looks and fey face, she was stronger and more capable than he'd given her credit for.

'We sure as shit gave those Paterson boys a run for their money.' Slinger sniffed dismissively and slumped down next to Carrick, reeking of stale rum and something he'd rather not dwell on.

'Took all their money, cleaned them out. And you won fair and square.'

'They can have the title next year. We'll be out of the Hunter by then.' For the first time Carrick could remember, he didn't relish returning to the Yarramalong. The job was as good as finished and once they'd cleared the last trees he'd call it quits. He'd long become used to the festering damp and incessant insect attack of the forest, it was not seeing the sky for weeks on end that caused him grief.

The heavy canopy of vines, some thicker than a man's wrist, clung to the treetops and blotted out most of the light. They turned day to a miserable twilight and left a man's skin pale and wan. After a time the touch of the sun on his face meant more than any stand of cedar trees. 'Red gold' they called the cedar; he preferred the warmth of the sun. Was it too great a price to pay? No. The red gold was worth the days of sacrifice and soon they'd be finished.

And he'd be on his way home. There had to be a decent sum sitting in the pile of drafts at the bank in Sydney. Almost enough for his passage back to Ireland.

Carrick resisted the urge to hurry the bullocky—there was little point. The animals set the pace regardless of the weight they were carrying on the dray. It would take them the best part of five days no matter how much he complained. And that was without rain. He leant back as the incline increased and a thud echoed. He didn't need to turn to know who it was. 'G'day, Billy Boy.'

'Boss.' The man hung over the back of the seat between him and the bullocky.

Carrick reached into his pocket and dragged out a plug of tobacco and tossed it back with a grin.

'Thanks, boss.'

'How's the old man?'

'Old. He get lazy. Sit by the brook and dream his stories.'

'You give him my best.'

'Will do, boss. You go cutting?'

'Yep.'

'Be seeing youse.' As quickly as he had appeared, the native left, his narrow, agile limbs blending into the tangled bush lining the road.

'I don't know why you bother with 'em,' Slinger grumbled, hoicking a glob of spit onto the road to emphasise his displeasure.

'They're men, all men.'

'Bloody bunch of savages. Ain't no more than animals.'

'We owe them. Without them you'd not be earning enough to keep your rum-soaked blood flowing, so quit your whingeing.'

'Yeah, yeah. Yarr-a-ma-long.' Slinger drew out the words with a dismissive curl of his lip. 'Place of cedars. Won't be for much longer. There's not a lot left. I'll be heading north with the others as soon as we're done here. Cedar's not gone there. Plenty of teams'll take me on.'

Carrick nodded in agreement. He'd be needing a bit more help for a little longer and as a cutter Slinger was one of the best. If Carrick could convince him to stay he'd be more than happy. *King Polai.* He had every intention of cutting it before they left. With that and the money he had saved he'd have plenty to seek out the godforsaken maggot who'd started all this.

He let out a long sigh. If it hadn't been for Billy Boy's old man, he'd not have his pot of gold. The old native had spotted King Polai from miles away, before they took to the Yarramalong. His eyes, which were good then, attuned to the way the light fell from the treetops, had picked out the subtle shades of colour, the pink of the new leaves.

King Polai was all he'd said, pointing his long, thin finger towards the setting sun. It had taken them days to travel deep into the valley and find it and Carrick had kept the secret spot. King Polai was his. He'd have it and he'd have it soon, with or without Slinger.

After five mind-numbing days they reached the canvas lean-tos on the edge of the stand of timber as the twilight fell. In the strange grey-brown light of the forest the camp seemed almost welcoming. The stacked barrels of Bengal rum, tea and sugar formed a backdrop to the campfire and the billy bubbled away, Smokey doing his job and keeping the men out of the rum until they finished and called it a night.

Carrick gazed around, checking the crew. Blue, Sampson and Will. It would be their turn for the next run to Morpeth. Slinger, Jojo and Goose would stay behind with him. That's the way it worked best. Two weeks full on, a bit of a break, then back for another stint. Good and regular.

He studied the shady recess of the forest beside the cool stony creek. They'd tumble the last remaining trees in the next month and then head back to town. He'd lay them off, send them up the coast. The boys would pick up more work quick as a wink. They made a great team and as long as they got a decent feed and plenty of rum they were happy. Most of them couldn't see further than the next barrel. No boss cutter asked any questions about why they sought refuge in the forest just so long as they did a decent day's work and pulled their weight. Slinger, he was different, he thought a bit further ahead.

Maybe he would tell Slinger about King Polai. See if he wanted in. He couldn't bring it down alone. They'd have to cut above the buttress roots, at least thirty feet around. It'd take a good while. The tree had to be close to two hundred feet. If the two of them could manage it, they'd be able to keep it quiet.

The days ran together in a never-ending cycle. They took a break at noon for dinner and, on a good day, a quick stop for a billy of tea in the afternoon. Today Carrick would sell his soul for a swig of rum, but he couldn't flaunt his own rule of no grog until they'd finished for the day. When the light went and they called it quits they could hit the rum.

Carrick stood astride the pit and sucked in a deep breath before forcing the crosscut saw down towards Slinger. Sweat dripped onto the red timber, turning it dark in the fading light. Slinger took the slack and yanked on it, pulling it down, a shower of sawdust peppering his head.

'Go.' Slinger pushed back and Carrick pulled up, not needing to think about the rhythm they'd established over the years. It was better than the mines. A living hell three hundred feet beneath the surface. Dark, damp tunnels, the miners' blackened skin and their inability to catch a decent breath. It was no life for a man. The day he'd first wielded the crosscut saw and felt it sink into his hands like an old friend was a blessing, as was the soldier who'd noticed his natural skill and claimed him for the cutters' team along with Slinger.

With a final tug the saw released and Slinger bounced back against the dirt wall out of harm's way. One wrong move and a falling log would flatten him; break every bone in his body. 'She's a big bugger.'

Not as big as King Polai, probably only half the size. Carrick set down the saw and wiped his arm across his forehead. 'We'll call it a day. Finish your cuts.' The hum of the saws and the groans of the men ceased, returning the forest to its natural silence.

Slinger clambered out of the pit, wiping the sawdust and woodchip from his blackened face. 'We're close to another dray load. When's the bullocky back?'

'Another three days.' Carrick turned to the other men working the pits. 'You done?'

'Done! Me stomach thinks me throat's been cut.' A sinewy redhead clutched at his non-existent belly and elbowed his way down the track.

'Back to camp, then. Smokey'll have tea sorted.'

Smokey's pickled pork and damper stuck to the roof of his mouth and even a huge mouthful of scalding tea wouldn't dislodge it. Perhaps the rum would work its magic. The nights were the worst, when the velvety blackness encompassed the forest, reminding him of the hell of the solitary cells. There was no starlight and rarely even a shaft of moonlight beneath the thick canopy, just moths and insects swarming around the campfire drawn to the only light for miles around.

He'd taken to sleeping away from the fire, away from the canvas lean-tos where the cutters threw their swags at night, since the dreams had returned. No one would witness his agony, his cries and sweating, his pathetic trembling. If he closed his eyes he could see their faces pushed to the window as they hammered against a backdrop of licking flames while he stood shackled, unable to move. He'd watched, watched to the very end, even when they'd tried to drag him away. Only now it wasn't his darlings' faces he saw, it was the lass and her little lad hammering against the glass of the window in Wollombi. He tossed back the remains of his rum and pushed to his feet, staggering to the dray out of the light of the fire.

Slinger dragged off his hat and wiped the back of his hand over his mouth, before refilling his mug from the barrel on the back of the dray. 'Once the bullocky takes this lot I'd say we've got one more load and we'll be finished.' He tossed back the entire contents of the enamelled mug and reached for some more. 'Where's Smokey? I'm hungry.'

Carrick flicked his head in the direction of the fire. 'Damper's done and there's the last of the pork over there.'

'I'd give all of the pork for some of Maisie's Irish stew. Sick to death of these rations. I need a break.'

'I need you here. I'll be going with the bullock dray.'

'You'll be doing what? It's not your run.'

'You heard me. Going with the dray. Got business in Morpeth.'

The way Slinger raised his bushy eyebrows told him his lie had failed, but right now he wasn't about to go into his reasons. He couldn't get the lass out of his mind, or the lad for that matter. They'd haunted his dreams for the last two weeks and a cold dread clutched at the pit of his stomach as he imagined them coming to harm.

It was a load of nonsense, but there was only one way to get rid of the fug in his brain. While he'd been locked in the forest,

Roisin and Ruan had merged in his imagination, become one and the same with Liam and Brigid. He had to clear his head. Leave it sit and he'd make a mistake. A slip with the blade, a miscalculation and he'd be doing someone harm. Cutting demanded concentration and with his head full of Roisin and Ruan, he was a danger to them all.

Just so long as he could see them and make sure they'd settled and the townsfolk were treating them well and hadn't decided that because she'd moved into the old cathouse, she was setting up in the trade. They'd run the last lot out of town. He knew only too well the way strangers to the small town could be treated. No one deserved that.

'Tonight you sleep with me and tomorrow you can sleep in the attic.'

Exhausted by the day's events, Ruan grunted his acceptance and snuggled under the covers. His soft hair tickled Roisin's face as she spooned him close, secure away from prying eyes. Aunt Lil had known. Known that only when they were out of Sydney could she truly relax. She waited for his leering face to appear and fill her vision. Instead, there was only the night sky, peppered with stars, the call of a mopoke owl somewhere in the distance, and the settling of the old house as it accustomed itself to new inhabitants.

They slept together, snug beneath her cloak and the old blankets, and when the grey-gold light pooled on the bed, she rose to peer out into the tiny plot behind the house. Yes, this place would do well, very well.

Leaving Ruan sleeping, she pattered down the hallway to the parlour. Even with her nose pressed right up against the panes she could see nothing. Rubbing the glass with the heel of her hand, she cleared a spot and peered out into the street.

Life beyond the city moved at a different pace. Would she find enough customers to patronise her business? Seeing no sign of the cutters' dray outside the inn took the shine out of the morning. In some strange way she missed the outrageous smile of the cedar cutter.

Outside Elsie worked her way across the front verandah with tight, determined sweeps of her broom. A couple of chickens picked lazily in the middle of the road as Maisie ambled across from the inn. Elsie ceased her sweeping and together they edged down the alley to the house, their heads together, trying to peer through the filthy glass into her parlour. Roisin stepped back from the window and flattened herself against the wall.

'I've never heard of a woman running her own business.'

'That's a load of old rubbish for a start. Look at you. You run the General Store. And I run the inn.'

'It's not the same. Our men hold the licences, own the business.'

'And they're lazy buggers. Who does all the work?'

'This is her business. Her own. Not anyone else's. She hasn't got a man. And she's got that child. Now where did he come from? Where's her husband, I'd like to know.'

'Maybe she hasn't got one.'

'Oh, right. And the child's an immaculate conception, is he? Touch of the Virgin Mary. The boy's a darling, I'll grant you that, but not quite that good.'

'There's only one thing to do. Ask her. Put an end to all this nonsense once and for all.'

Roisin ducked down the hallway, back to the kitchen. Being caught eavesdropping wouldn't endear her to her new neighbours. Besides, if they were going to chatter about her, better they got the facts straight. She'd got her story sorted. Had gone over it so many times even she'd forgotten where the truth ended and the lies began.

Sucking in a deep breath, she marched back and threw open the front door. 'Morning, Elsie. Morning, Maisie. How kind of you to come and visit. Come through to the kitchen. The billy's on the boil.' She pressed her lips together and took no notice of the guilty glance passing between the two women. That would teach them.

By the time they'd settled at the kitchen table with their cups of tea in front of them, her mind was made up. Stick to the truth as closely as possible, only lie when absolutely necessary, and hope Ruan stayed upstairs fast asleep.

She drew up a chair and offered her sweetest smile. 'Now, ladies to what do I owe the pleasure of your visit? I'm not open for business yet; however, I'm happy to discuss any needs you might have.'

'Needs? Us?' Elsie spluttered her tea back into her cup. 'We ain't got no need for a dressmaker. We're working women.'

'Oh, stop beating around the bush, Elsie Sullivan. You know your curiosity's killing you.' Maisie plonked her teacup back into the saucer. 'We was just wondering if you'd care to answer a few questions.'

Here it came. 'Questions?' She cocked her head to one side with studied innocence.

'There's rumours round town already.' Maisie sat back, her hands laced over her ample stomach. 'It's better to put an early end to it before it gets out of hand. You just turning up out of the blue. And from Sydney.'

The scuttlebutt around town could only have been stoked by these two; she'd hardly had anything to do with anyone else. 'I see. What would you like to know?'

'It's about your business, see.' Elsie rested her elbows on the table, her tea forgotten. 'We've never known a woman to have her own business afore. It's men that set up the business. We just work for 'em.'

Was that all they were anxious about? Far, far easier to sort that out. And all the time she'd worried they'd grill her about

Ruan's father. Talk about jumping to conclusions. 'This is my business. No one else's. In Sydney lots of women own their own business. Why in Pitt Street women run every kind.' She held up her thumb. 'For starters, there's Matilda Cox's fruit shop, Elizabeth Hudson's music rooms, mind you her husband gives piano lessons.'

Maisie let out a snort of amusement and relaxed back in the chair. 'He gives music lessons? Nah, that's a woman's job.'

'Mrs White's oyster bar. And then there's Madame de Lolle's business.' She ticked off each one on her fingers to prove the point.

'Madame de Lolle! What sort of business does she run?' Elsie dug her elbow into the space where Maisie's ribs lay buried. 'As if we couldn't guess.'

Right. Now was the time. 'A millinery and costume business called Maison Français.'

'Oh. She'd be a Frenchie, would she? Well, that accounts for that.' Elsie folded her arms and rocked back in the chair and huffed 'Frenchie' as though the word denoted some abomination responsible for the world's ills.

'I worked for her, in fact. That's where I learned my trade.' First observing the women at their work while she cleaned and later as one of them.

'Thought you said you were a dressmaker, not a hat maker.'

Both women narrowed their eyes and studied her for a moment, while she willed the flush back down below her collar. 'I learned how to make all kinds of things. Hats, dresses, coats.' And the most stunning corsets, the like of which would send both Maisie and Elsie into a flat spin, and have her drummed out of town before she'd even unpacked her trunks.

Elsie pursed her lips and glanced at Maisie as if asking for permission. 'Hmmm. All well and good, I suppose.'

Now the questions about Ruan's father would come. Only to be expected, and once the lies were told, she could rest easy.

'So what happened to your husband, young Ruan's father?'

Her cheeks reddened and she gritted her teeth, fingering the worn grooves in the scarred tabletop. 'He's dead.' She covered her face with her hands, more to hide the flaming colour than from despair. If only she was a better liar and wasn't cursed with a pale complexion that showed her every thought.

A hand came down on her shoulder, sending her heart pitter-pattering nineteen to the dozen. She wrenched her head up and peered into Maisie's sympathetic face, then hid behind her hands again.

'There, there, dear. Don't you fret. The good ones are always taken young.'

Little did Maisie know. Roisin sniffed behind her hands and lifted her face, mopping her dry eyes with her handkerchief. 'I needed a fresh start, somewhere new. I want Ruan to grow up away from the city, away from trouble.' And that much was completely true.

'What about the rest of your family? Your ma and pa, brothers and sisters.' Maisie's hand patted Roisin's shoulder in a rhythmic beat that echoed in her head. 'Haven't you got no one?'

'My mam was a seamstress.' When she wasn't working flat on her back in one of Aunt Lil's best rooms. That wasn't exactly an untruth. More of a half-truth really. Not an outright lie. 'That's why she sent me to work for Madame de Lolle.' To keep her out of trouble and away from the groping hands and licentious leers. Lot of good that had done. 'When Mam died there was a little money left after her funeral.' And the other amount that Aunt Lil had slipped her, though she better not mention that. 'I came here. Everyone needs a seamstress now and again and my work is, well my work is said to be good, very fine.' So fine even the best of Sydney's courtesans would scratch each other's eyes out for one of her corsets.

'There, there, dearie. Don't you worry now. Elsie and I'll take care of it. Put pay to all this silly nonsense once and for all. If a reputable widow can't take care of herself and her son without a bunch of bored old women sticking their beaks into her business, I don't know who can. We'll sort them out for you. So long as we know your story.'

Oh, God. Were they going to ask more questions? She'd thought saying she was a widow would be enough. Had she got away with it?

'Mam, Mam.' Her heart lifted as Ruan appeared in the doorway, his hair poking up at all angles and his eyes still blurred with sleep. Maybe his presence would end this inquisition.

'Mam, look at this treasure.'

'Come here and greet Mrs Sullivan and Mrs Kidd.' She wiped the hair back from his eyes, wanting to cover him in kisses as thanks for his timely appearance.

Ruan leant against her knee and peered up at Maisie and Elsie through his long lashes. 'Good morning.'

'He's a bonny lad. What have you got there?'

Ruan opened his clenched fist. 'It's a skeleton, I think.'

'Lord alive. A skeleton, you say. Now where would you be finding that?'

He shrugged his shoulder and smoothed the small skull cradled in his hand.

'Ouch. Nasty thing. I wouldn't be touching it too much.' Maisie wrinkled her nose and pushed back her chair.

Ruan lowered his hand to the table. 'What do you think it is? A little person?'

'No. I don't think so.'

'More like one of them rats that live out the back, I'd say.' Elsie's face wrinkled in distaste.

'It's not dirty.' He stretched out his palm across the table. 'It's clean and sort of polished.' He ran his little finger over the skull. 'See it's smooth, real smooth.'

'I expect your skull's smooth under all that hair.' Roisin lifted the fall of his hair and raked her fingers through his silky locks. Paler than hers, more like his father's. 'Off you go, Ruan. Upstairs and put your treasure in your box.'

Maisie heaved her bulk out of the chair and brushed her hands down her apron. 'Can't be sitting around here all day looking at skulls and skeletons. I've got live bodies to deal with. Me stew'll be burning.'

'And I've got deliveries to sort. Thanks for the tea, love. We'll leave you to your business now. You'll be setting up shop in the parlour, will you?'

Roisin nodded, still incapable of framing any words, as the relief of having survived their examination turned her legs to jelly.

'Those windows will need a clean.'

'Yes. I've still got a lot to do. I have three trunks to collect from Morpeth. They're coming on the steamer. I have to arrange someone to pick them up. All my materials and cottons and silks.'

'Silk you say—well we'll be calling this Maison Wollombi at this rate.'

'Silk! No silk for the likes of me. I'm lucky if I can keep me pinny clean.' A faraway look drifted across Elsie's face. 'Though when I was a girl I had a red flannel petticoat. Always wanted another one. Some bugger nabbed it at the female factory and I never saw it again.'

'Get away with you—red flannel petticoat.' Maisie chuckled. 'I'll put the word out and see if anyone's going Morpeth way. Save you a bit if someone can pick those trunks up for you.' She bustled out with Elsie following close on her heels.

Roisin stood by the door swirling the tea leaves in her cup, as the two women strolled down the alley, heads close together.

'See. I told you. Pure as the driven snow—sweet love. Widowed and so young and that boy he's a pretty thing. Must have been a corker, her husband.'

Letting her lashes fall, Roisin rested her head against the wall. At some stage she'd need to have a longer talk with Ruan and make sure they came up with the same story. No one had ever asked him about his father and he'd never questioned it. It would happen one day soon. Lies—that was the trouble; after the first one the net dragged deeper and deeper.

Four

Carrick made his way into the offices on the Queen's Wharf at Morpeth, the last of the cedar unloaded from the dray, marked and ready for shipment to Sydney.

He pushed open the office door and frowned at the clerk, who threw him an officious glance, then buried his head. 'Next load's in the yard ready for shipment to Sydney. Have you got the paperwork for me to sign?'

The clerk peered over the top of his fine round spectacles. 'Mr O'Connor. That was quick. Another load already. My paperwork says not to expect you until next month.'

'Well your paperwork's wrong.'

'I can assure you it is not. I do not make mistakes.' He inserted a new nib into the penholder and toyed with the totals on the white pad of paper. 'You must have found an impressive stand.'

Carrick grunted in response, his hand outstretched for the reckoning. He wasn't falling for that. No bragging about the size of the stand, where or when it would run out. It was none of the bugger's business. Knowledge like that was worth money and could cause a brawl. They were cutting on unallocated ground without a licence and there was a fifty-pound fine or the threat of the entire cargo being seized, which would make a God-awful hole in his profits. All he wanted was the signed bill of sale.

The system worked, always had. Didn't need some officious little rat, too full of his own self-importance, sticking his nose in. The regulations favoured a few wealthy merchants in Sydney who thought they had the trade in their pockets. Carrick wanted the timber shipped down to Sydney same as always, straight into the hands of his agent, no matter how long it was between shipments. He trusted Brinkworth. He'd dealt with him for the last five years, trusted that his money would be tied up tight in his account in the Bank of New South Wales, right there on George Street in Sydney. Trusted him to keep his mouth shut, too. Brinkworth got the cedar cheap because he didn't ask any questions about licences and he made a nice tidy sum on the side. 'And there'll be more in the next month, too.'

'Must be a big stand, then? Where did you say it was?'

'Hunter cedar. It's good quality and not for you to judge. Just give me the receipts and I'll be on my way.'

After a great deal of shuffling and sorting, all designed to make the job appear hard, the clerk handed over the paperwork.

Carrick ran his eye down the neat list of figures, totalling them as he went. 'You'll be checking the addition on these totals before I sign it.'

'I assure you, Mr O'Connor it's all correct.'

Lazy sod, and a cheater, too. 'Check it. The total should read five pounds six shillings at twenty-two shillings per hundred foot. We just offloaded three hundred. That's not what's on the receipt.'

'The conditions for purchase have altered, Mr O'Connor. Let me read the new conditions to you.'

Carrick snatched back the bill of sale. 'There'll be no need to read anything. It says here that Brinkworth's paying twenty-two shillings.' He stabbed at the piece of paper.

The clerk flushed and pushed his glasses up above the bulbous lump on the bridge of his nose.

Carrick took a step closer, his shadow falling across the desk. 'You'd be new around here, would you?' And thinking him blinded by the sawdust or the rum. Well, he was wrong. Idiot thought he was onto a good thing. The sooner they learned that just because men worked the forests didn't mean they were all rum-swilling halfwits, the better he'd get on.

The clerk flinched and cleared his throat. 'There does seem to be a slight error here.' He adjusted the totals. 'If you'd like to make your mark we'll confirm the transaction.'

Carrick signed his full name with a flourish and dropped the pen back onto the desk. A blob of ink spluttered from the nib and landed on the clerk's cuff. His face darkened. Serve the bugger right. Messing him about. 'Now if you'd be telling me where I might find the luggage storage, I'd be obliged. I have some trunks from Sydney to collect.'

'Passenger trunks?' The thin eyebrows disappeared up into a moth-eaten fall of hair thick with pomade or some other affectation.

'That's what I said.'

'They'll be stowed at the Rose, Shamrock and Thistle. You will of course require some proof of identity to collect them.'

'Rose, Shamrock and Thistle, you say.' Carrick winked at the clerk. 'Then I'll be having a word with the lovely Nell. I'm sure she'll not have a problem with me picking anything up. G'day to you.' He rammed his hat back on his head and let the door slam behind him. Jumped-up little rat. The bigger and busier Morpeth got, the more like Sydney it became with its airs, graces and narrowed eyes that peered down on a working man.

He waved at the bullocky and gestured across the road to the inn, nestled next to the quay, then whistling some long-forgotten tune he struck off up the street. Now wouldn't it be a lovely surprise for the bonny Roisin Ogilvie if he were to turn up with all her chattels collected and nothing for her to worry about. That'd make those emerald eyes sparkle. He chuckled to himself as he swung through the door and into the taproom.

'Well, Nell me darlin' girl, just look at you. Lighten any man's heart you would.'

'Oh get away with you.' The old woman's face flushed, stripping away the years of hard work and disappointment, giving a glimpse of the lass she'd once been. 'You and your Irish blarney. Now what can I do for you? I don't want any of your roughhousing here. All my rooms are full and they're paying guests, so no nonsense from you and your cutters.'

'Ah, Nellie me girl, would you not be having a bit of fun with us?'

'No, I wouldn't, as you very well know. What do you want?'

'A favour if you please. A favour.'

'Why would I be granting you any favours?' A blush spread across her wrinkled cheeks as Carrick leant across the countertop. 'Get away with you.'

'A little bird told me you had some trunks here waiting to be collected. Belonging to a Mrs Roisin Ogilvie.' A bit of a gamble, though with luck they might have arrived.

'And what if I have?'

'I'm here to collect them.' He stood back from the counter and folded his arms.

'And how would I know that's the truth? Have you got a letter authorising you?'

'Come on, Nell. I'd be doing the lady a favour. You wouldn't want to be spoiling a surprise now, would you?'

'I can't let them go without something to show.'

'I'll tell you what we'll do. You give me a piece of paper and I'll be signing it to say I've received the trunks. If there's a problem you know where to find me.'

'If you think I'm crawling through some forest with all them snakes and spiders and the like to find you, you're mistaken.'

'You won't need to and you know it. Come on.' He reached across the desk and took a piece of paper and pen and scribbled a few words, then folded it and sealed it with a quick kiss. 'There.'

She opened the paper and scanned him up and down. 'You could charm the birds from the sky, Carrick O'Connor.' She unclipped a key from the bunch around her waist and held it out. 'They're in the luggage room. Three fine blue trunks. You can't miss them.'

Grand. 'Thanks, Nell. You won't be sorry.'

'Get along with you.'

A little bit of romance always found its way to a woman's heart. Carrick grinned and swung the door to the luggage room. As Nell said, he couldn't miss the three trunks, and they were very fine. Two good-sized travelling trunks and one smaller one. Leather and studded with brass rivets. The sort that belonged to an uptown lady, not a widow setting up business in an out-of-the-way township. He picked up the largest and shouldered open the back door. Good to his word the bullocky sat round the back, waiting. 'Two more after this. Reckon we got room for them?'

The bullocky eyed the empty dray and took a swig from the flagon of rum clasped in his hand. 'Tie 'em up tight and we might manage to fit 'em in. Want a hand?'

'Nay. The other two are smaller. Got to drop the key into Nell. Back in a tick.'

Once Carrick had fastened the three trunks he swung up beside the bullocky. 'Let's be getting along, then.' The sooner they got to Wollombi the happier he'd be. Even the thought of them, the boy and Roisin, brought a smile to his face and set his heart thumping.

'You're sounding bloody chirpy. All that whistling, 'nough to drive a man to drink. Here.' The bullocky thrust the flagon into

Carrick's hand. 'Have a swig of that and calm yourself. You've got a day or four to wait.'

Carrick shook his head; the lure of the rum had paled. He didn't want to see the world through the haze of oblivion. Today he wanted to see it in all its glory. The winter sky was as blue as a parrot's wing and the grass, after the rain, as green as ... the eyes of the lad and his mam. It had been a long time since a woman had caught his fancy, and for the first time since he'd left Ireland, his heart didn't ache with sorrow. Little Ruan reminded him of Liam sure enough. In daylight hours it was a bittersweet memory and not the agonising pain that burned his gut and rendered him half a man.

After five days on the road Carrick's patience had worn to a thin, taut string. 'I'll be spending the night in Wollombi and then we'll head back to the Yarramalong bright and early on the morrow. Does that suit?'

'Whatever you say, boss. I'm not going to knock back a plate of Maisie's stew and a decent night's sleep free of the bugs and biters for the sake of a few hours. Missed it on the way to Morpeth.'

With any luck he'd not be eating a plate of Maisie's stew, he'd be sharing a mug of tea with a beautiful lass, making those green eyes sparkle and her pretty cheeks dimple. She'd cut a mighty fine figure when she'd stepped off Davy's dray in that dazzling green jacket. There couldn't have been a man there who'd missed her.

The sun was still high, it wouldn't be much longer. Maybe if there was a bit of light left he'd take Ruan down to the brook and show him that fishing hole. A boy needed to learn to fish, and then he'd never go hungry.

'You'd think these animals of yours would move a bit faster without a load.'

'They'll get there in their own time. Patience, man.'

'Give me a crack of the whip, that'll get them moving.' He reached across the bullocky and got a clip around the ears for his trouble. The bullocky rarely used his whip; his charges responded to the tone of his voice.

'You'll do no such thing. My bullocks, my dray. Settle down.'

Carrick slouched on the seat and gazed up at the sky, drumming his foot. The trip never took this long, least not in his memory. He let out a long sigh and took to counting the bullocks' steps.

It took another godforsaken two hours before they reached the outlying farms. Already the tall eucalypts cast long shadows across the track. There was at least another mile or two to go. His feet just wouldn't keep still. Maybe he'd get out and walk.

'When we get there pull up outside the General Store.'

'That's not going to please Elsie. She'll be shouting about bullock crap on the road and her customers' shoes.'

'It'll only take a moment. Just tell your bullocks to keep their legs crossed. Promise them something fine for their tea.'

Finally the trees cleared, the track widened and the flourmill on the pond came into view. The dray slowed as it passed the cemetery and Carrick swung down well before it came to a halt outside the General Store. He jumped up onto the back and hefted the largest trunk onto his shoulders ready to leap off as soon as the bullocky brought the animals to a standstill.

He hit the ground running. 'Just leave the other two outside the store. Won't be long.'

With a careless toss the bullocky dumped the two smaller trunks onto the flagged footpath.

'Gently does it. They're not a length of timber.'

The bullocky wiped his hand across his face and winked. 'Wouldn't be wanting to upset your lady friend, then?'

'Get off with you. I'll be catching you later.'

'Unless you get lucky.' The bullocky let out a belly laugh and clambered back onto the dray, cracked his whip at Carrick and moved off.

'Bugger off.' Carrick grinned and turned sideways to ease down the alley to the gate, his heart beating a tattoo inside his chest. Ahead of him the door stood open and a pool of light shone right down to the back of the house. The smell of baking scones made his stomach growl and he lowered the trunk to the floor. 'Anyone home?'

'I'm in here.'

Through the front window the sight of Roisin with her head half up the chimney and her backside stuck up in the air made him want to laugh aloud. She was as right as rain and all his worries had been for naught. Stepping over the trunk he ducked inside.

'And a very good afternoon to you, 'tis a lovely sight to greet a man.'

She whipped around, as good as flying to her feet, and then wiped her hand across her face, leaving a sooty streak from the end of her upturned nose to her right ear.

Her cheeks pinked and she tugged at the piece of green material she'd wrapped around her head and her glorious mass of red-gold curls tumbled down below her shoulders. His heart gave a thundering hammer and his mouth dried.

'I look a fright. I'm trying to get the chimney to draw. It's …'

She held her arms wide, palms up, a picture of dishevelled loveliness. In three swift strides he covered the space between them and she was in his arms. Soft and supple beneath his hands. For a fleeting second she relaxed against him, then her body stiffened and she uttered a sharp cry and jerked away from him. Holy Mother of God, what had possessed him?

'Mr O'Connor …' She turned her back on him, her shoulders lifting and falling as though she couldn't get enough air into her lungs.

He couldn't either. Couldn't even get his tongue to work, couldn't say a thing. He shook his head to clear the fog. 'I've got your trunks for you, from Morpeth.' Would that make up for the outrageous liberty he'd taken? Not that he hadn't enjoyed it, hadn't wanted to feel her in his arms. He could still smell the scent of her—baking and beeswax, lavender and linen.

She spun around with the grandest smile, as though the sun had come out from behind a cloud. It warmed his very heart.

'My trunks.' She clapped her sooty hands together. 'How did you know they had arrived?'

He tapped the side of his nose and wriggled his eyebrows, trying to make a joke of it all. 'Just a lucky guess. The big one's on the doorstep and the others are sitting on the footpath outside the store. If you'll be telling me where you want them I'll fetch them in before some bugger does a runner.' He let the breath trickle out between his lips. She'd recovered faster than he had, and the trunks—well, that was his best move. From the look on her face he might have presented her with a fistful of jewels—emeralds they'd be, to match the sparkle in those eyes.

'The big one in here. In here will do just fine. And the smaller ones in my … I can sort the smaller ones. Can you take them down to the kitchen? How can I thank you?'

'We'll worry about that when I've got them all inside.' He could think of a thousand ways, though none that a lady like Roisin Ogilvie would relish. 'A mug of tea and one of those scones wouldn't go amiss.' He settled the trunk in the centre of the room. 'And where's the lad?'

'He's out the back collecting things for his treasure box. I'll tell him you're here and go and put the billy on.'

Carrick as good as ran back to the street, whistling with the sheer pleasure of the reception he'd received. Her reaction had whisked away his foolish concerns. She and the boy were as fine as fine. The expression on her face and that smile when she'd seen her trunk had given him more of a kick than dropping the biggest cedar. He'd forgotten such simple pleasures.

'And what would you be up to, I'd like to know?' Elsie glared at him, hands on hips, guarding the two trunks. 'These don't belong to you. Sure as eggs is eggs.'

'No they don't, you're right there. They're Roisin's. I picked them up in Morpeth.'

'Did you indeed, and what would she be saying about that?'

'Not sure it's any of your business, Elsie. For the record, she's asked me in for tea and scones, so she can't be too bothered.' Interfering old biddy. What business was it of hers? Just the reason he'd wanted to come and check, make sure Roisin wasn't suffering any nonsense from the meddling old bags around town. He grabbed a leather strap in each hand and swung the two trunks up onto his shoulders. 'Now, if you'll excuse me I'll be on me way.'

Spluttered mumbles drifted after him as he walked back down the alley. The townsfolk barely tolerated the wild ways of the cedar cutters. Branded them a bunch of lawless fools addicted to bushranging and cattle stealing in their spare time. Chance would be a fine thing. They slaved away from dawn to dusk and only hit the town when they received their pay. Damn Elsie and her squinty-eyed gaze. She was happy to take their money when it suited her, though if anything went wrong the blame was always laid squarely at their feet. Stupid fools, most of them owed their heritage to a trip in a transporter, so why should they put on airs and graces? He kicked the door wide, dumped the trunks down and dusted off his hands. He'd not be letting some dragon shopkeeper spoil the afternoon. And besides, Roisin had promised tea and scones.

Deep in thought, his feet as good as went from under him as his knees were clasped in a firm hug. 'Carrick, Carrick. I've been waiting for you to come.'

He swept the boy up, closing his eyes and inhaling the smell of little boy and memories. His heart twisted and he clamped his teeth against the shaft of pain. He was so like Liam with his pale hair and freckled face. He even smelled the same. If it hadn't been for what he'd witnessed with his own eyes, he'd almost believe the angels had carried his boy away unharmed and dropped him here in his arms.

Ruan wriggled his way down to the floor and grasped Carrick's hand. 'Come with me. You've got to see my room. Quickly.'

He let himself be dragged down the hallway. Roisin had worked miracles in the past weeks. A cheerful fire burned in the kitchen grate and a table and chairs were in the middle of the room. She'd somehow managed to find two soft chairs and had placed them on either side of the fireplace and above it a clothes rack hung scenting the air with the smell of clean, fresh washing. 'This is a far cry from the hovel I was seeing last time.' And a far cry from the hovel he'd subjected poor Brigid and Liam to back home.

She put her hands on her hips, sending his eyes to the swell of muscles beneath her honeyed skin, and then she laughed. The pure joy of the sound made him want to catch her up in his arms and twirl her around and around. 'I'll have you know, Ruan and I have worked really hard these past weeks. We're pretty happy with our new home. Aren't we?' She ruffled the lad's hair and rearranged her sleeves, her cheeks flushing in embarrassment. 'I wasn't expecting visitors.' And he wasn't expecting to be as taken with the lovely lass. If his heart kept performing backflips this way he'd never catch a decent breath of air.

'Shall I bring the other two trunks down here?'

'That would be wonderful. I'd like them in there.' She pointed to the open door off the kitchen. The bedroom. So that was why she'd paused earlier. She must have come to some decision and was happy about him entering her bedroom. He strolled along the corridor and brought back the two trunks, Ruan leaping and skipping behind him as though he'd really missed him.

'My bed's up there.' The lad pointed to the ladder running up to the roof in the corner of the bedroom.

'That'll be a fine place to sleep. Nice and cosy with the chimney, I don't doubt.' He placed the trunks on the floor, snatching a peep at the cosy bed. A picture of Roisin with her hair fanned across the pillows sent his pulse skittering again and a ball of heat slammed into his guts. It had to stop. He pushed the trunks against the wall and the bed from his line of vision.

'Do you want to come and see?' Ruan sat perched on the ladder in the corner of the room, his grin as wide as his mam's. No doubting who the child belonged to.

'Later, Ruan. Let Mr O'Connor have his cup of tea.' Roisin held back one of the chairs and invited Carrick to sit. The snug kitchen even had curtains at the window and the contents of shelves beneath the dresser were covered in a matching pair.

'Can I swing the billy? Please, Mam.'

'If you're very careful.'

She grimaced and mouthed 'sorry'. Why should she be sorry? Because his tea was taking too long? He'd happily sit for the rest of the night watching her move around the room. The homeliness of it all made him ache. How long had it been since he'd sat before a fire enjoying a woman's company? Close on ten years. Way too long.

'Now be careful, Ruan, remember to swing it gently just to settle the tea leaves.'

'Only townsfolk swing the billy.' The words flew out of his mouth and he clapped his hand across his face.

Ruan peered up at him and frowned. 'What do you do, then?'

'Well I'll be needing to go outside and get meself a stick. Just hold everything right there.'

The cold wind hit him as he stepped outside the door. It was so snug and comfortable inside. Better than a dripping canvas tent in the depths of the forest. He bent down to pick up a stick from the kindling just inside the woodshed door. Atop the pile a perfectly formed pale-blue egg sat. Just the gift for a young lad. Cradling it in the palm of his hand, he tucked the stick under his arm.

'Now take the stick and slap it on the side of the billy, just once, a sharp rap. That's right and then let your mam pour the tea and we'll see which way's best. The townsfolks' way or the cutters' way. And while we're waiting I've got something for you.' He squatted down and opened his palm.

Ruan's squeal of delight was a pleasure in itself. He stretched out his fingers.

'Be careful now it's very fragile.'

The lad took the egg and held it up to the light. His mouth turned down. 'It's empty. There's no baby bird inside.'

'Here give it to me.' Carrick pinned the egg between his forefinger and thumb and held it up to the window. The afternoon sun shone through the almost translucent shell as he turned it over in his fingers. Then he spotted the two tiny holes, one on the top and the other at the bottom. 'Ah, you tricked me. You've blown the egg.'

'Blown it? What's that?'

Carrick lent down again, his finger pointing to the tiny pinhole in the top of the egg. 'See here, there's the hole you made and there'll be another in the bottom.' He turned the egg over and pointed to the other tiny hole. 'Now, who taught you how to do that?'

Ruan reached out and took the egg. 'No one. I didn't do it. Look, Mam. It's another treasure from the woodshed.'

'Sit down and drink your tea while it's hot, Mr O'Connor.' She picked up a scone and spread it with butter and jam before handing it to Ruan. 'And you sit down, too, young man and no more of your funny stories.'

'It's not a funny story. It was in the woodshed. Carrick found it this time. Not me. It's another treasure.'

A frown played across her smooth forehead and her eyes darted to the back door then to the window as if she was checking to make sure everything was closed. 'A scone, Mr O'Connor?'

'Thank you.' He bit into the scone and chewed. What was bothering her? One minute laughing and happy, the next cold and uncomfortable. She looked like a startled roo. 'What else have you found, Ruan?'

'He's forever finding bits and pieces. His treasures, he calls them.' Her voice held a tremor and her gaze flicked to the window again.

'I've got feathers and a skeleton, well not really a skeleton, just a skull. It's polished, and a snakeskin. A real, live snakeskin, but dead. A butterfly. And more feathers. The three black ones I found on my bed and a blue and brown one and now this.' He picked up the egg and held it up to the light again. 'Can I go and put it in my treasure box?'

Roisin nodded, her cup cradled in her hands as she blew a stream of air across the top of the scalding tea. 'I don't know where he finds all these things. They keep turning up.'

'Boys like to collect things. I'll keep my eyes open in case I see anything he might like.' It didn't explain how the blown egg had come to be in the woodshed and sure as shite it hadn't got there by itself. He pushed back his chair. 'Is there anything else I can be doing? Have a look at that chimney in the front perhaps?'

'Oh, would you? Now I've got the trunks I can set up shop, and if I'm going to use the room for fittings it mustn't be cold.' A hint of colour stole across her cheeks, no doubt at the thought she might be discussing ladies' business in front of a man.

'I expect it'll be something else for young Ruan's treasure box hiding up the chimney.'

She raised her head and locked eyes with him. A flash of fear, at least he thought it was fear, traced her eyes, but in the next moment it had gone. 'A possum nest would be my guess. The chimney hasn't been used for a few years and they've moved in. Let me go and have a look.'

Five

Roisin cleared the table and swept up the crumbs from the scones, then carried them outside to throw to the birds. No wonder Ruan found eggs and feathers everywhere for his treasure box. She attracted the birds by feeding them. They must have made a nest inside the woodshed. She pushed the door wide and peered into the gloomy depths, pausing to allow her eyes to adjust to the dimness. Since Carrick had cleared the old timber and chopped new pieces, the pungent smell had dissipated, replaced by the clean, sweet smell of fresh wood. Surely a bird wouldn't nest in the dark and it didn't account for the egg being blown. Someone had done it. Maybe Carrick hadn't found it, maybe he'd brought it with him as a little surprise for Ruan. He was full of tricks and treats like that.

Shaking her head at her own foolishness, she returned to the house. Ruan sat at the kitchen table, his box of treasures in front of him, sorting the strange assortment of bits and pieces. It kept him amused, but he needed more of her time and attention. Before they left Sydney he had already begun to learn his letters, though she'd paid him scant attention since they'd arrived in Wollombi. He lined up a group of stones then added a few more and muttered twelve.

'It's all sorted now.' Carrick appeared, dwarfing the doorway, thick black curls in a messy disarray hanging almost to his shoulders, and those eyes, as indigo as the night sky, above a mouth that just wouldn't stop grinning. 'No possum nest, just a lot of leaves, sticks and soot. Shall I be lighting the fire?' He ruffled Ruan's hair and pulled up a chair, peering into the box with fierce concentration. He sat down next to him and laid his arm along the back of his chair.

Something about his familiarity made her skin prickle, a reminder of Sydney, the lascivious look on Dankworth's face as he'd recognised his own blood. The fear that had clutched at her throat as he'd reached out for Ruan.

'So these are your treasures?' Carrick plucked a dried gum nut out of the box and twisted it in his fingers.

Ruan nodded and continued to line up the stones in the base.

'You'll be needing a new box soon. This one's as good as full now you've got the eggshell.'

Had he really found the eggshell in the woodshed? She caught the expression on Carrick's face as he tousled Ruan's hair. A far-away look in his eyes, almost as though he wanted her son for himself. It made her want to scoop Ruan up and hug him close. Thoughts like that belonged in Sydney, not here, not where they were meant to be out of harm's way.

All of a sudden she wanted Carrick gone, out of the house. What if he took her in his arms again? What if his attentions were simply a way of getting to Ruan? 'I'm going to start unpacking my trunks. I must get my business up and running.' Did he expect some sort of reward for his favours, for bringing the trunks, chopping the wood, clearing the chimney? She stopped stock-still. Heavens above, she'd never thought of that. How naïve could she be? The way he'd pulled her to him when he'd arrived. Did he think she'd be happy to exchange her favours for his?

Carrick didn't respond, didn't even glance at her, instead he concentrated on Ruan. 'What's this here?'

'It's a skull. I thought it was a skeleton, but it's only the head. See here where his eyes went.' Ruan smoothed his finger across the polished bone, making her shudder.

'And where were you finding it?'

'On my window when I woke up.'

'On your window. How would it be getting up there? Did the fairies leave it?'

Ruan stared at him with complete disdain and Carrick winked and elbowed him in the ribs. He squirmed and squealed and threw himself across the big man's lap. Carrick tucked him under his arm and stood, lifting Ruan high in the air, spinning him around until she was dizzy with watching. Her bright-eyed, towheaded boy laughing as she'd never heard before and Carrick's deep rumbling chuckle filling the room. The next minute he took off with Ruan clasped in his big hands.

The door slammed behind them and her heart started to hammer, one blow after the next, pulsing with fear. She flew to the door and wrenched it open. The garden was empty, the door to the woodshed swung in the breeze. *No!* It couldn't be happening, she shouldn't have let her guard down, begun to relax. She scooted down the path out to the brook.

Cavorting on the grassy bank, Carrick and Ruan performed some strange sort of dance involving yelping and screaming and carrying on. Her legs turned to jelly, her knees wobbly and she sank onto the damp grass.

Before she could steady herself, Ruan threw himself down next to her. 'Mam, Mam. Save me.'

Because she needed it more than he did, she lifted him into her arms for a ferocious hug. 'It's time you came inside now.' Her breath heaved and her voice sounded breathless and wavering, more from her vivid imagination than her flight from the house.

A shadow fell over them. Carrick. His face grinned down at her, as flushed and excited as Ruan's. Her heart started thumping again. He had to leave. Now. She couldn't let him into the house again. She struggled to her feet, ignoring his outstretched hand offering assistance. 'Thank you. I really can't impose on your time any longer. You've been too kind.' And too terrifying. Taking Ruan and running outside, frightening her half to death.

'You're not imposing. I've got nothing on me plate until early tomorrow morning when I'll head to the Yarramalong. I won't be back for another while. You'll be needing some more wood, the shed's as good as empty.'

'I can arrange the delivery of some wood myself, Mr O'Connor.' She clasped Ruan tightly by the hand and made her way back to the house, praying he wouldn't follow. She knew she was being rude. Now the thought that he might take Ruan had invaded her mind she couldn't get rid of the man fast enough. 'Thank you.' She repeated. He frowned at her, he must have noticed the change in her behaviour. No matter how attractive or amusing she found him this was not a good idea. Ruan's attachment to him was bad enough without admitting to her own.

He nodded and the corner of his mouth quirked in disappointment. 'I'll be seeing you, then. Goodbye, young man.'

'Goodbye, Mr O'Connor,' she chimed before Ruan had a chance to respond.

Ruan tossed a quick, fleeting grin over his shoulder before he turned and ran inside, unaware of the ridiculous heart-wrenching fear gripping her.

As she locked the door a wave of relief swept over her. Ruan buried his head in his treasure box, oblivious to her churning emotions. In her trunk she had some pattern paper and charcoal. She'd find them and give them to him. They should keep him amused while she unpacked the trunks and soothed her befuddled brain. Their clothes could remain in the smaller trunks in the bedroom and the lid would serve as a dressing table. The sooner she set up her business and started work the better. Then she wouldn't need help from anyone.

Carrick had pushed the largest of her three trunks up against the wall in the parlour. She sat on it, running her hand over the studded surface, fighting a pang of homesickness. How she and Aunt Lil had laughed when they'd packed it, imagining all the customers who would flock to her door and the flurry of business she'd have. Well, that was to be seen. She could hardly remember what they'd put inside now. It had been forgotten in the mad rush when that wretched man had started hounding her, following her every time she left the house, demanding to see Ruan, shouting about rights and records. How he could imagine that she'd hand over her son, out of the blue, just like that. He hadn't even known of his existence until that chance meeting on the street. She'd seen the flash of recognition in his eyes the moment Ruan had gazed up at him. Why would a man like that, an upper-class toff, be interested in his by-blow, the result of his filthy attack?

Goosebumps flecked her arms and she rubbed her hands up and down, forcing away the thoughts. She had to forget, put the past behind her, otherwise what was the point of leaving Sydney? She wouldn't let anyone have Ruan, not now, not ever. Ruan was her son. No one else's.

Jumping to her feet, she pushed her tumbled hair away from her face and bent to the padlock on the trunk. The key slipped in and turned without complaint and she lifted the lid. Spread across the top was her patchwork quilt. She pulled it out and held it to her cheek, inhaling the flowery scent, such a reminder of her mam, Aunt Lil and all her friends. Each scrap of material had a story to tell. Ruan's first nightdress, pieces of her mother's favourite silk shawl, scraps from the first sampler she'd made. Bunching it into her arms, she carried it down the hallway to the bedroom. She shook it high, each little piece of colour sparkling with memories as it floated down, and covered the bed. She let out a long, slow breath. Now the house felt like home.

Disgruntled, Carrick kicked the stone along the path running alongside the brook. What had happened? Why had she closed him out like that? He belted the stone and it swung off the bank and into the water. Too fast, too strong a kick, just like he'd behaved with Roisin. A woman needed to take things slow, he'd forgotten about that.

He found the bullocky down by the brook, the campfire raging and the billy boiling, the ever-present flagon of rum at his feet.

'Wasn't expecting to see you back here. Lady friend turn you down, did she?'

More than turned him down, as good as kicked him out. 'No. She's got things to do. Unpacking those trunks. She was pleased to get them though.' Just not so pleased to see him and have him in her home.

'Sounds like you've been given the heave-ho to me. Here.' He passed up the flagon of rum.

'Thanks.' The rum burned a path down his throat, dousing the memories and the pain in his heart. He was better staying away, the lad reminded him too much of Liam. Thoughts like that would make him soft and he hadn't the time. The stand was as good as cleared. He needed to move on. His deposits in the bank were mounting.

He tipped the flagon and drained it. 'Let's go see what's for tea. I want to make an early start in the morning.'

The inn was crowded, the start of another round for the cutters. Familiar faces, same old rivalries, tall tales and free-flowing rum. The noise was enough to make a man long for the forest. Carrick knocked back another tankard then weaved his way to the bar. 'Whass for tea, Maisie?'

'You'll want to be quick.' She tossed her head in the direction of the crowd clustered around the fireplace. 'The cutters are in from Paterson. Reckon they'll drink me dry, never mind the food.'

'Good job Slinger's tucked up in the forest, then. Had a run-in with the bastards last time.'

'They're a rough bunch and making the most of it. I'll give you a hoy when your tea's ready.' She pushed a full tankard across the bar.

The reputation of the Paterson crew preceded them. A large group of hard-drinking, hard-fighting men who liked nothing more than a barney once the grog took 'em. Crowded around the fire in a tight semi-circle, the cutters packed the small room, fists thumping as a hefty bloke tossed a couple of cartwheel pennies from a cedar chip. All eyes followed the coins as they twisted and fell to the ground. Cries of outrage from the losers rent the air and serious money changed hands.

The Paterson bullocky called for bets and Carrick eased his way to the front of the group.

'Heads.' He reached into his pocket and handed over a shilling.

The coins twirled and fell and he pocketed his winnings, ignoring the mumbled discontent. The ringie handed him the kip with a sly grin. He shook his head. The Paterson boys liked control of the game. What were they up to? He tossed back the remains of his rum. Why the hell not? Slinger wasn't around; perhaps it was their way of making peace.

He gave a curt nod and took the cedar chip. The ringie placed the coins tails up on the kip, balancing the pennies on the slim piece of wood, the shiny, polished heads down, the dark tail side up.

Carrick settled the coins and gauged the distance around the small circle. If the coins fell outside the circle the toss wouldn't count. If he tossed it too low they'd call foul. If he didn't toss heads his chance was over. The circle closed in. The heat from the fire singed the backs of his legs. He flicked the kip and the coins circled high, almost as high as the roof, then twirled and fell.

'Foul.'

'Goin' to have to try a bit harder than that.'

'Only good with an axe, are you?'

He tossed again, the coins glittered and twisted in the light from the fire and landed with a soft thud on the mat.

'Tails.'

Carrick shrugged his shoulders and handed back the kip. He'd stick with a few more bets then call it quits. He picked up his tankard and staggered over to the bar. 'Fill 'er up, Maisie.'

'How much did you have afore you got 'ere? What's got your goat?'

He slouched against the bar. None of her business if he wanted to drown his sorrows. Better do it here than in the forest, where he had to keep his wits about him. The lass had got to him with her bright eyes and soft smile and the lad …

'Here, wrap your face around that.' Maisie pushed the tankard across the bar. 'Food's coming. You need it.'

'Later. A couple more bets to cover me costs.'

'Don't give me that rubbish. I know what those trees are worth. You're raking it in.'

All the money in the world couldn't replace what he'd lost. Jesus, he was maudlin tonight. He'd be crying in his drink before long, propped in the corner like some old-timer with nothing more than memories. He downed the rum, wiped his mouth and elbowed his way to the game once more, pulling a handful of coins out of his pocket, holding his hand high. A decent win always cheered a man. 'Tails.'

'Reckon you're goin' to win this one, do you?' The burly beef-steak ringie pushed his way to the front of the circle and stood next to him. 'I'll take your bet.'

Carrick handed over his money. The two coins flew straight and high, twinkling in the firelight before landing with a soft thud, dark side up.

'Heads,' the ringie called.

Heads? It wasn't heads. It was tails. A blind man could see that. If they'd landed heads the firelight would pick up the shiny side of the coin. 'Tails. It was tails.' He bent down to point at the pennies and found himself spread-eagled on the mat. He was on his feet before he'd caught his breath, facing the leering crowd through a red mist. The men began stamping and the circle closed in as they sized him up. He spun around, sucking in a breath of the close air. The ringie's fist flew, filled his vision and hit bone. Blood gushed from his nose, salty and thick, spraying his face. He shook away the coppery tang wetting his chin, sticky against his teeth, and lowered his head, ready to charge. Hands grabbed his arms and held him firm.

'Don't be an idiot.' The bullocky's voice hissed in his ear. 'Call it quits. You haven't got a hope in hell.'

Carrick never gambled unless he knew he'd win, never fought unless he had to. Somehow events had spiralled out of control. 'I'll give those cheatin' bastards …' He struggled. He'd flatten them, every one of them. Whatever happened to the luck of the Irish?

'No you won't.' His feet lifted from the ground as the bullocky spun him around and away from the crowd. 'Give it up. You can't take 'em all on.'

Beyond the heat of the fire the dull-red mist cleared and Carrick let his shoulders drop. The crowd around the game closed ranks and the coins flew again. 'I'd like to.'

'Yeah well sometimes it's better to step back. You've had too much to pack a decent punch.'

The cold air hit him as they stumbled outside. 'Where's the rest of the crew when I needed them? Could have done with some backup in there.' He yanked down his shirt and staggered a step or two, blinking owlishly, trying to make out the camp. Christ, how much had he drunk? The rum whirled in his head, clouding it, churning in his belly and sickening him.

'There's food down at the camp.'

'Thought you were after Maisie's stew.'

'Got our own. Scored some corned beef while you were busy with your lady friend.'

He couldn't remember when he'd last eaten, save for the scones the lovely Roisin had made before she'd kicked him out. He took a swipe at an overhanging branch. The young lad had brought back the pain, sharpened it. The loss cut worse than before. When he went home to Ireland he'd search out that maggot and give him a dose of his own medicine, even if it meant a trip back in irons. Who the hell cared?

Carrick woke with his head splitting fit to bust and a mouth parched as the brook in drought. Lying in the back of the bullock dray, the banging and crashing over the rough track turned to anvils in his head, thumping like the very demons of hell. He squinted up. Glimpsed through the treetops the sky was nothing more than a narrow shard of blue, no horizon, yet the light still scored his eyeballs. He'd not be touching the rum for a while—the drink of the devil. The bullocky flicked the tip of his whip in the air. 'Gee up lads.' The dray lurched, turning off the road back into the forest, while Carrick sat nursing a sore head full of maudlin thoughts of a life once lived.

Clouds appeared without warning, billowing, bringing the damp scent of the forest. More than anything else the smell and the pungent sweetness of the cedar mixed with damp earth, rotting leaves and campfire smoke told Carrick they'd arrived. The deep glistening green of damp ferns and creepers, the dusty grey and blue of the eucalypts and the raw crimson of the split and bleeding cedar heart. He'd like to crawl into one of the dark gullies and crevices where the sun never shone. The wind thrummed through the trees, drowning the babble of the creek and the thump of the wallabies and roos as they swept through the undergrowth.

A rumbling groan and an ear-splitting crack signalled the fall of a tree, then the hush followed as though the world mourned the loss of another giant. He mourned the loss of a brief and tantalising gander of another life, not populated by rum, sweat and muscle-grinding agony, but clean linen, scones and tea, and most especially the smile of an Irish beauty and a little lad who'd captured his heart.

Stuck in the forest he laboured from dawn to dusk, chopping and sawing until his body screamed for rest and he collapsed under a canvas strung in some scooped-out clearing. Despite the hardship, the leeches, mosquitoes and ticks, he'd found a kind of peace mixing with resilient men. Men like Slinger. They'd formed a team long before either of them had been granted freedom, their axe blows timed in perfect rhythm and their bodies balanced against the huge crosscut saws alternating in the pits.

The hard-living cutters drank more, swore more and fought more than most, but they measured themselves against the giant trees, not against each other when they collected around the campfire at night. None of the drunken shenanigans that pitted crew against crew down at the inn.

He eased closer to the light of the fire and rubbed the handful of sand from the creek bed over a piece of cedar.

Slinger squatted down beside him. 'Here, just use another piece of cedar. Rub 'em together. It'll work as well if not better.'

Carrick took the offered cedar chip and rubbed it against the wood block that would form the base of the box he had in mind.

'What're you making?'

'A box—a treasure box.' He picked up an identically sized piece and balanced it on the first. 'There's the lid.' Beside him the pile of smoothed-off cuts lay like jigsaw pieces. This box would have compartments and lids and all the things that might take the fancy of someone keen on collecting treasures.

'You're planning on taking to the high seas, become a pirate? I'd have pegged you for a bushranger first.'

'Nah! It's for the lad.' Although with a bit of imagination it would make a fine pirate's chest.

'The lad—ah. The lad that belongs to the lovely lady who's caught your fancy. The quickest way to a woman's heart is through her children.'

And the quickest way to shrivel a man's heart was to lose a child and the darling of his heart. 'And how would you be knowing that?'

Slinger threw him a wink. 'Here, give me the other piece, I'll do it for you. Then you'll need some beeswax. Make the colour shine through. And if this is a success maybe we'll be chippies when we give up the cutting.'

'You might get your wish sooner than you think. There's not much left around here worth cutting.'

He rubbed the beeswax into the timber and watched the colour change until it was almost as though he was running his fingers through her hair.

Six

Roisin's needle dipped and bobbed through the material, the stitches forming a pleasing, fine straight line. The comfort of the repetitive movements and the knowledge they would result in something worthwhile gave her enormous pleasure. This would be her first piece of work in Wollombi.

As pleased as she was with her new home, she missed the safety and security of Aunt Lil's, the companionship. The incessant banter and babble of the girls as they prepared for the night and their raucous, outrageous jokes. Their descriptions of the men who crossed the threshold always made her laugh. Sharp and accurate character sketches summed up in a single sentence or even simply a word. What would they make of Carrick? A smile flitted across her face. There would be no complaint about his physical prowess, his laughing eyes and playful manner, yet there was the tender, caring side; they wouldn't see that, and overlying it all the lingering sadness in his eyes that spoke of pain and loss. She shouldn't have sent him on his way. It was a foolish overreaction that had spoiled Ruan's fun. Not only that, she'd have to ask Maisie to find someone to deliver timber.

It had been the egg in the woodshed that had raised her hackles, or was it her reaction to the comfort of his arms, so strong and secure. Ruan continued to find all kinds of bits and pieces as though they'd been left deliberately as a gift. How did they get there? Carrick was the only person she could imagine doing such a thing, but he was long gone back to his forest and the lure of the giant cedars.

The log spat and sent a flurry of orange-and-red stars chasing their way up the chimney. Roisin lowered her sewing and stared into the flames. Carrick had seen loss, great loss, someone close to him. That she knew with a deep certainty. The sadness that welled in his eyes when he looked at Ruan made her heart twist. She blew out the candle and sat in the dwindling light of the fire, tears burning her eyes. She'd never get over the ache of losing her mother. Nigh on eight years might be long enough for some, but not for her. Strange that Ruan should be the result of that dreadful night. If anything happened to Ruan it would destroy her. Hadn't that very fear started her on this mad journey? To live with such pain would be worse than death itself.

Leaving the fire she climbed the ladder, sticking her head through the trapdoor into the attic. From her perch on the top rung, Ruan's face in the shaft of moonlight was serene and peaceful, a slight smile tilting his lips as he cradled the fragile blue egg to his chest. His gentle breathing proving her fears were groundless, unfounded. His days brimmed with adventures and exploration. His incessant questions, his ever-growing box of treasures that he studied, polished and rearranged. Seeing his head bent in concentration over the table brought a tug to her heart. When the new year came and he turned seven, she'd send him to school.

Not yet. The thought of letting him out of her sight still made her blood run cold. At first she'd believed he'd need no more than his letters and his numbers and she could teach him those just the way Aunt Lil had taught her. But this sudden, almost academic interest in things and his growing questions were at times beyond her knowledge. Why did snakes shed their skins? She'd no idea. In a moment of fanciful imagination, she'd told him it was because they wore out and the snake tailors made new ones. Six months ago he'd have nodded his head and accepted her every word as the truth. Not anymore. With a sense of patent disapproval he'd rolled his eyes and turned back to his detailed drawings.

Sighing, she edged down the ladder and made her way to bed.

With the window at the front of the house cleaned and polished, Roisin had no trouble spotting Elsie when she made her morning check. Like clockwork every morning. A broom in one hand and her eyes darting to and fro. 'Elsie would you like to come in?'

Elsie's face flushed and she chewed on her lip before taking a deep, shuddering breath. 'Morning. I didn't expect to see you here. I was just sweeping up, cleaning the alley. I expect you'll be having visitors soon and we want it all to look neat and tidy.'

Roisin drifted back to the window. 'Would you like to come inside, Elsie?' The woman shook her head, although it wasn't what she meant. Her currant eyes darted back and forth, taking in the transformation.

'Come and see what I've done so far, I'm rather proud of it.'

Elsie set foot slowly, one step at a time, and as she turned into the parlour her face became a picture, her mouth gaping open, her surprise evident. 'You've been working, very hard. Goodness me, look at those windows. And the fireplace is as good as new.' Her eyes danced from one side of the room to the other. 'Ah.' She pointed to the trunk sitting against the wall. 'That'll be the trunk Carrick collected for you. He and that nasty bullocky man delivered them. Threw the other two on the footpath, I'll have you know.'

'Yes. They did deliver them for me. It was very kind. I've unpacked everything. Would you like to see some of my work?' She held up a soft white nightdress and smoothed the pleats down the front. With the little pearl buttons in a perfect line down the centre and such fine cotton, it was as light as a feather. Perfect for the hot summer nights. 'What you think about this, Elsie?'

'It's very fine for a chemise.'

She smiled gently and held out the whisper-fine cotton. 'It's not a chemise, it's a nightgown. A dress to wear while you're sleeping.'

'You'd wear something like that to bed? I sleep in me chemise. No fuss. Quick in the morning. Haven't got time for fancies like that and what would Alfie say? He'd think I was givin' him the come-on.'

'I like to wear a nightgown. It's comfortable and soft and cool on a hot night.'

Elsie's frown said it all. The idea of something worn for anything except practicality was far beyond her understanding. Perhaps Roisin's idea was a pipe dream. Something for the ladies of the night in Sydney, not for the likes of Elsie and Maisie.

Elsie dropped the nightgown onto the table as though it might infect her with licentious thoughts. 'If you sleep in something like that you'll get a chill. And goodness only knows what else.'

Now was the moment. She'd planned it. Sat every night in front of the fire after Ruan was asleep, sewing. Not just for Elsie, but also because it calmed her, soothed her. 'What do you think of this?' She held up a bright red flannel petticoat.

Elsie's eyes lit up. 'Oh my. It's a petticoat.' She as good as snatched it from Roisin's hands, running her work-worn fingers over the soft flannel, then held it against her cheek and let out a long, low sigh. 'I'd give my eye teeth, if I had any, for something like that.'

'It's for you.'

She smoothed it like a pet cat. 'For me?'

'Yes, for you. A present. A thankyou for all you've done for me and Ruan.'

'I can't be taking it. Not as a gift like. It's not right.'

'I'd like you to take it. I couldn't have settled in without your help and I owe you money for everything I've bought in the shop.'

'Tut-tut! I know you're good for the money. You keep it and sell it to one of your customers.' Elsie peered furtively around, giving the petticoat a loving pat as though she couldn't bear to part with it despite her best intentions. Then she thrust it into Roisin's hands, her face blanching. 'There's Maisie. She's 'eading this way. Quick, put it away. I don't want 'er to see it.'

'I've got one for Maisie, too.'

'You got one for Maisie?' Elsie frowned.

What a silly mistake. 'The one I have for Maisie is nothing like yours. It's a blue check. Not red.'

'You think I'm the kind of person who would wear red unmentionables?' Her face flushed as she struggled to regain her composure. 'And she's not?'

When Maisie rapped on the door Roisin slid the red petticoat under the cushion on the chair. Just as well because Maisie marched straight in. 'So when is the grand opening?'

'I'm not planning on a grand opening. I was going to ask if I could put a sign up in the shop window and down at the inn.' Roisin held up the sign she'd worked on last night while Ruan was asleep. The charcoal had smudged a little, though it was still readable and the elegant woman she'd drawn with her large-brimmed hat and tightly fitting pelisse looked all the better for the softening of the lines.

Maisie and Elsie peered at it. 'What does it say?'

'The undersigned, Roisin Ogilvie, is prepared to do dressmaking and all kinds of needlework to suit ladies at moderate charges.'

'So it's not just alterations. You'll be making things from scratch?'

Roisin nodded. 'If someone would like them. If you'd put the sign up in your window, Elsie, and I'd like to ask you if you could please tell everybody who comes into the shop that they're very welcome to come and have a look and see what I can make.'

'Will you be thinking I should be showing my petticoat? I could twitch my skirt a little bit.' Elsie clapped her hand over her mouth.

Roisin laughed and drew out the petticoat from under the cushion. 'The petticoat is for you, no matter what. I hope you like it.'

Maisie let out a shocked gasp, her eyes wide and her gaze darting between the red petticoat and Elsie's outstretched hands. 'I have one for you, too, Maisie. If you'd do me the honour of taking it.'

'For me? You wouldn't catch me wearing anything that colour, I can tell you.' She folded her arms across her bosom as if to defy the audacity of the bright red flannel.

Roisin eased the blue-checked petticoat, trimmed with white lace, from the trunk. 'I thought this might be more your style.'

Maisie's face softened and her lower lip trembled. 'I love it. You wait till Harry sees it. Next thing you know I'll have another baby on my hands and I'm too old for that.'

'I didn't think that was how you make babies.'

'That shows you how much you know.'

Roisin smiled. They'd helped her so much, it was the least she could do to repay their kindness. 'So you'll both be taking the petticoats, then?'

The two women exchanged glances. 'Wouldn't want to upset you. Tell you what,' Maisie glanced at Elsie to check she was in agreement, 'suppose we take 'em as payment for displaying your advertisement and spreading the word like. Means you'll have to do up a few more of them signs.'

'I'll give 'em to the women when they come in to the store.'

'And I'll give 'em to the men …'

Elsie gave an outraged shriek. 'You will not, Maisie Kidd.'

'Well maybe not. I'll keep 'em under the counter for when the travellers come through and give 'em to the ladies. Never know who wants what.'

'Are you sure you don't mind?' Roisin asked.

'Doing you a favour, so I don't feel so bad about taking your gift.' Elsie grinned. 'Do you think I've got time to put it on now before my Alfie gets home?'

Roisin held back the curtain she'd hung across the corner. 'Madam, if you'd like to step this way.'

'Oh, no one can see. It's very clever.' Elsie disappeared and after a lot of huffing and puffing reappeared a few minutes later with cheeks as red as her new petticoat. She twitched the bottom of her skirt. There was a flash of colour and a little bit of lace. 'Your turn now, Maisie. Go on.'

Maisie frowned and scowled a bit, then held out her hand for the petticoat and disappeared behind the screen.

'You should be putting something in *The Maitland Mercury*, too. That's where they have advertisements for important things. Then you'll be attracting some of the high-fliers around town. The Winchesters and their fancy friends.'

Seven

My dear Aunt Lil,

I am sorry it has taken me so long to write at any length, but the days have been busy. My trunks arrived and now the place is beginning to feel like home. Ruan has settled in well and he has his own room in the attic. He is busy collecting treasures, which he constantly finds around the place. I am keeping up with his lessons.

Chewing the end of the pencil Roisin stared into the fire. Should she mention the cedar cutter and the strange friendship they'd struck up? Probably not. In a way she longed for Carrick's return as much as Ruan did and regretted having told him to leave. She shook her head and sketched a quick drawing of the two petticoats she'd made. She'd remedy that when he returned. She licked the end of her pencil.

Business is beginning to come my way. I have made two petticoats, one red and one with the pretty blue check I had in the trunk. Several local women have sought my advice on matters and I hope it will lead to commissions.

A slight deviation from the truth as the petticoats had been gifts, though they had led to several visits from local women, or maybe the advertisements had. More out of curiosity than anything else.

Nothing she could imagine leading to any great result. Some advice on buttonholes and a badly fitting sleeve, turning a frayed collar and repairing a snag in a lace pelerine. However, the money Aunt Lil had given her was holding up and she and Ruan wanted for nothing.

The house is very cosy and with much washing and scrubbing many of the existing furnishings are quite satisfactory.

That part was at least true. The pile of rag rugs and curtains she'd found in the corner of the kitchen had cleaned up a treat and made the house more comfortable, and the two soft chairs she'd discovered in the woodshed had pride of place by the fire.

As always I miss your company and that of the girls, but I am not dissatisfied with my life and believe we have made the right decision. Ruan is so much stronger. The fresh air and freedom is seeing him grow. He hasn't had one single bout of the breathing sickness since we left.

Please write to me soon and let me know how life is in Sydney.

She wouldn't, couldn't mention his name, wouldn't tempt fate.

I miss you all and long to hear your news.

With all my love

Roisin let out a huge sigh and pushed the paper across the table. She was doing no more than marking time, and no matter how hard she tried to convince herself, being in Wollombi was the best outcome for Ruan. There were days when she missed home, missed the only other life she'd ever known.

She drifted into the bedroom and sank down on the edge of the bed, running her fingers over the complicated patchwork of the quilt. Pieces of the past all neatly sewn together, a map of her life. She stroked the silken offcuts of the first corset she'd ever made and Ruan's first dress. It was to have been his baptismal gown, but the priest had refused to mark the father as unknown despite Aunt Lil's insistence, and poor Ruan had never been baptised.

'Roisin.' Elsie's eager tone roused her.

She shook her head and straightened her skirt. Such maudlin thoughts. Maybe it was a customer coming to order a ball gown. The idea made her laugh aloud. Who in Wollombi would ever need a ball gown?

'I have a letter for you.'

Almost as good as a ball gown. She threw open the door.

'Mr Sullivan picked it up for you in Morpeth when he went for the mail.'

'Oh, Elsie, thank you.' She took the envelope and turned it over, her heart lifting as she saw the familiar handwriting. 'It's from my aunt in Sydney.'

A flicker of confusion crossed Elsie's face. 'I thought you said you had no family.'

'She's not my real aunt. A friend of my mother's.' That was a foolish slip. She'd have to be more careful. 'Thank you so much for delivering it. I shall make a cup of tea and go and read it in the sunshine.'

'Suppose I better be getting back to my work, then. Can't be hanging around here all day.' Obviously the prospect of sharing news, good or bad, had brightened her day and she felt owed since Mr Sullivan had picked up the letter and she'd delivered it with her own hand.

'Thank you, Elsie and please thank Mr Sullivan, it'll be lovely to get news of home.'

'Thought this was home.'

'Of course it's home now, Elsie.' Aunt Lil must have known she was missing her and written, just as she'd been framing a letter herself. She ran her finger under the seal and the single piece of paper fell out of the envelope before she was back through the front door.

Sinking down at the table, she unfolded the paper and immediately inhaled the exotic waft of perfume that took her back to the house in Sydney.

My dear Roisin,

Forgive my earlier silence. I thought it would be better to wait. I have good news. The gentleman in question did call on several occasions and was disappointed to discover you were no longer in Sydney.

Disappointed, that was an understatement. She could imagine him thumping through Aunt Lil's rooms, questioning the girls and generally being aggressive and obnoxious. There was little he could do. He couldn't prove Ruan was his child. It was only that first chance meeting on the street that had sparked his curiosity. He'd known instantly. She'd seen it in his eyes, but he couldn't prove it no matter how much he dogged her footsteps and made her life a misery. It could never be more than his word against hers, although his word would undoubtedly carry more weight, bearing in mind his associations in the colony. Why would he want to acknowledge a bastard child?

We were pleased to discover he was married and so I feel that his interest in Ruan was nothing but a passing fancy. However, do not allow yourself to be lulled into a false sense of security. Plan as we always have to remain in Wollombi and hopefully the time will come when we can put all of this behind us and welcome your return.

Perhaps his wife had absorbed his interest. Maybe she was with child and he had no inclination to seek out Ruan. She folded the letter and pushed it deep into her pocket. Aunt Lil's words had set her mind at rest and she couldn't wait to read the rest and respond. If only she had some better news about business. Patience, she schooled herself. Patience.

For the next few days Roisin buried herself in her work, determined to have some samples available if any customers ever turned up. The parlour at the front of the house was all arranged and a fire burned in the grate. Her materials, ribbons, lace and cottons were stored in her trunk, and scissors, needles and silks tidily arranged and close at hand.

The knock on the door took her by surprise. She put down her sewing and peered through the window. A man dressed in a long black frock coat and a stern expression stood on the doorstep.

'Mrs Ogilvie?' His face showed no movement, no sign of a smile. A cold, hard lump settled in her stomach. Who was he? He seemed so officious, a little scary. Rather as she'd imagined Father Benson, except he was round, red-faced and smiling. This man was the exact opposite. Surely Aunt Lil's cheerful message wasn't going to be slapped away so quickly. She wanted more time to bask in the warm glow of success and the knowledge that leaving Sydney had been the right thing to do.

'My name is Blackmore, madam, Mr Blackmore. I'm the schoolmaster. You may have heard of me.'

Oh yes, she had. She let out a breath of relief and then gasped. Was he going to try to make her send Ruan to school? He couldn't do that. She'd kept up his lessons. She wasn't ready to let him go just yet. Despite Aunt Lil's assurances, she still needed to know he was close. And besides, she hadn't enough money to throw away on tuition. At six Ruan was too young for school.

'I think you should consider sending your boy to school.'

She squared her shoulders, ready to do battle. 'I teach Ruan myself. His education is not lacking.' Ruan lacked for nothing. Ruan was young but he was in no way behind with his letters and numbers. At least not at present, but he would be if she continued to let him spend the days down by the brook hunting for treasures. She was proud that everyone had so much time for him and thought him older than his age. He'd grown taller in the last month, was quick-witted and spoke well, so many people thought him eight or nine.

'No, madam his education is not lacking, of that I'm certain. You've done a remarkable job. I was lucky enough to bump into him down at the brook the other afternoon and I had a little chat with him.'

Ruan had said nothing about a chat. Why didn't she know? Perhaps she'd been neglecting him. 'Ruan! Come here, please.'

She ushered Mr Blackmore into the parlour. 'Please come and sit down.' She indicated the single chair in front of the fire.

'Madam, there is nowhere for you to sit. I couldn't.'

'Please, Mr Blackmore I'm quite content sitting here.' She perched on the edge of her trunk. 'Please excuse me. This is my work room, my shop, it's the most suitable place for me to receive you.' Turning away slightly, she called Ruan again.

Mr Blackmore cleared his throat. 'Before Ruan arrives I'd like to inquire whether you are opposed to sending him to school. I have it on very good authority that you intend to develop your little business and I thought …' He waved one long, thin hand in the air and left his sentence hanging.

Such a double-edged sword. It was good to know people were talking about her business, but not Ruan, not her private life. Was it going to be impossible to keep the two separate?

The corner of his mouth quirked and for the first time she saw a glimmer of emotion in his face. 'My wife has many friends in the area.'

And there was the answer. His wife and her friends had been jabbering. Hopefully they would all like new dresses.

'I'd like to teach Ruan. I believe he has a good mind and would benefit from some formal instruction.'

Of course he had a *good* mind, surely a mother would know that. His mind was not the problem, her purse was. 'Mr Blackmore, I agree with you and I'd love to see Ruan spend time with children of his own age and benefit from your experience.' There, that should set his mind to rest. Praise a man and he always became more amenable. Another of Aunt Lil's gems which seemed to be holding her in very good stead, despite the difference in their businesses. 'I'll be honest with you, Mr Blackmore. I simply can't afford the school fees until my business turns a profit.' There, it was said.

'Why don't we ask Ruan his thoughts on the matter? Ruan!'

Immediately, Ruan appeared. What was it about him and these men? One word, whether from cedar cutter or schoolteacher, and he was as good as gold.

'Ruan, my boy.'

'Good morning, Mr Blackmore.' Ruan stood next to her cool, calm and detached. He was growing up and she'd hardly noticed. He needed a new pair of breeches and his shirt strained across the shoulders. Being out of Sydney and having the space to run must have made the difference.

'Ruan, would you like to go to school?' Mr Blackmore asked the question straight out and simply. No specially prepared speeches. Just directly. She admired him for that.

'Yes, I would. Mam?'

'I'd love you to go to school, too.' She turned to Mr Blackmore. 'Ruan is only six. Maybe next year when we have a little more money?'

Ruan nodded his head, his disappointment obvious. 'I told you, Mr Blackmore. I can't go to school just yet. Maybe next year.'

'I might have a solution to that problem, Mrs Ogilvie. I've been talking to my wife—her brother's daughter is getting married next month and we'll be travelling to Sydney for the wedding. She would dearly love a new outfit for the occasion. There'll be insufficient time to arrange this when we arrive in Sydney and we can't leave earlier because of my commitments to my pupils.'

Was this to be her first commission? A dress for a wedding. Mrs Blackmore, who was she? What did she look like? What would she require? A bubble of anticipation lodged in her chest and she clasped her hands tight and craned forward.

Mr Blackmore cleared his throat. 'She wondered if perhaps you could make over one of her dresses? If you would be prepared to assist her I would waive Ruan's school fees for the remainder of the term. How does that sound?'

It sounded … not as good as she'd hoped. There would be no money in the job, but Ruan could go to school. Did she want him to? She'd never been to school, but Aunt Lil's instructions had stood her in good stead, all those elocution lessons, account books and totalling numbers, reading the newspapers to the girls.

'Mam. How does that sound?' Ruan tugged at her sleeve, his eyes pleading. 'You can do it, can't you, Mam? I know you can. Aunt Lil says you have magic in your fingers.'

Roisin gulped back a smile. Hopefully, Ruan hadn't discussed Aunt Lil in too much detail with Mr Blackmore. How could she refuse him? His little face shone. 'Why don't you ask your wife to call on me, Mr Blackmore? I'm sure we can come to a suitable arrangement. I'd be very happy to pay for Ruan's fees in that manner. It's very kind of you.'

'Excellent.' He towered over her as he rubbed his hands together, the dry skin making a rasping sound. 'I shall send her to call on you at say, ten on Monday?'

'That would be perfect. Ten o'clock it is.'

'And I shall expect to see Ruan at school at nine-thirty sharp.'

'Ruan, would you please show Mr Blackmore out.'

How in heaven's name had that happened? Roisin stood and stared out of the window as Ruan and the schoolteacher sauntered down the alley, deep in conversation. He barely came up to the man's hips, yet they were chatting away like old friends. Events had moved so quickly. Well, it was what she'd wanted, wasn't it? Freedom for her son.

'Thanks, Mam.' He barrelled back through the door, a huge grin plastered across his face. 'Carrick said you'd agree.'

Carrick! What had Carrick got to do with it? 'He did, did he? And how does Carrick know about Mr Blackmore and school?' Carrick seemed to be behind too many things.

'He said it was important I went to school. In Ireland all the children go to school but not in houses. They go to hedge schools. Can you imagine that? A school in a hedge.' He shook his head in wonder.

She couldn't. More importantly, how and when had Carrick and Ruan had this discussion? She wouldn't have to wait long for the answer. Ruan's face was beaming and he was almost tripping over his words in excitement.

'Carrick said that Mr Blackmore liked to go fishing at the brook and if I went down there in the afternoon after he'd finished at school I'd meet him. If he thought I should go to school he might ask me.' He scratched at his head. 'He didn't tell me you would have to do work for it though, Mam. Do you mind making a dress for Mrs Blackmore? You're very good at it.'

She hugged him tight. 'No, darling,' she whispered into his hair. 'I don't mind at all. In fact, I think school is a wonderful idea.'

And she did, she truly did. Not only would Ruan get to learn and be with other children, it would free her to spend more time working, if and only if, she had something to work on. Well, she'd soon know. What kind of a makeover would Mrs Blackmore require?

'Carrick will be back soon.'

'And how do you know that?'

Ruan rolled his eyes and tipped his head to one side, looking for all the world as though he was dealing with someone of limited intelligence. 'Because it's four weeks since the last time he was here and the bullocky comes through every four weeks.'

'He also said that he didn't always come with the bullocky. And that he thought it would be at least six weeks before he was through again.' She hadn't forgotten. The date sat lodged in her mind because she was planning to ask him if he'd eat with them. An apology for her ridiculous overreaction the last time he was here. She'd even planned a mutton pie and pickled cabbage. 'We'll just have to wait and see. If you're going to be at school you might not have as much time to spend with Carrick.'

'Oh.' His eyes widened. 'I didn't think of that. Am I allowed to have a holiday from school?'

'Only when it's holiday time. Mr Blackmore said he and his wife were going to Sydney for a wedding so I expect there might be a day off here or there.'

Ruan edged towards the door.

'Where do you think you're going?'

'To ask Mr Blackmore.'

'You can't go chasing after him. He's a busy man. Wait until I speak to Mrs Blackmore about her dress. I'll ask her then or you can ask Mr Blackmore when you're at school.' Her stomach clutched in anticipation. This might be the beginning. Mr Blackmore had said his wife had many friends in the area. It wasn't what she'd have asked for, remodelling an old dress, but if she did a decent job surely word would spread.

'I'll tell you what. Why don't we walk along the brook and call in and see Maisie. She might know when Carrick is next expected through town.'

Roisin's heart caught as she waved from the school gate. In his new corduroy breeches with matching cap perched on his head Ruan seemed so grown up striding towards his future. She wiped the tear trickling down her cheek and smiled at her foolishness as she strolled back up the road. Mrs Blackmore would be calling and she wanted one last chance to check the parlour to make sure she'd left everything in place. A nonsense really because if she'd organised the room once she'd done it a million times. Still, first impressions counted and so did first customers.

'Morning, Elsie.' She slowed as she approached the General Store, itching to get back inside, but not wanting to appear rude.

'Taken my boy off to school, have you?'

She nodded. 'I'm a little miserable. He's not my little boy anymore.'

'Not such a bad thing. Give you a bit more time to concentrate on that business of yours.'

'I have my first real customer coming in a moment or two.'

'Oh, that's exciting. Who would that be?'

'Really, Elsie, I shouldn't tell you. It's a question of confidentiality.'

'Con-fi-den-she-who?' Elsie waggled her head from side to side, a wide grin splitting her face, highlighting the gap between her two front teeth.

'Privacy, Elsie. Have to keep appointments private. My customers might not want everyone in town to know they're calling.'

'Bit like that place in Sydney you were talking about, Maison Frenchess. Oh look! Here's Mrs Blackmore with her dress all parcelled up ready for the alterations. Off you go now, you don't want to be late.'

'How did you know?'

Elsie tapped the side of her nose with her finger. 'It's all a question of con-fi-den-she-who. Get on with you. You have a business to run.'

And didn't she know it. With a quick skip Roisin turned the corner, rushed down the path and yanked open the door. Smoothing her skirt, she cast a glance around the room and then strode back to the door.

'Good morning, Mrs Blackmore.'

With her curls clustered beneath a dilapidated straw bonnet adorned with a bunch of faded artificial cherries, the schoolmaster's wife took in every inch of the room with her shrewd dark eyes.

'Good morning, my dear. Mr Blackmore said you were willing to help me out.'

'I hope I shall be able to do that. Would you like to come inside?'

Mrs Blackmore eased her way through the small front door and into the parlour. 'Why this is delightful.' Her gaze darted around the room. 'Mr Blackmore said you had settled in well.'

'Please, take a seat.' Roisin gestured to the chair by the fire. The small padded seat had seemed quite adequate when Mr Blackmore had visited. As his wife lowered her bulk, Roisin's lips twitched and she sent up a silent prayer that the woman wouldn't end up flat on her back and her legs in the air. She pushed the picture to the back of her mind. 'Is this the dress you'd like me to look at?'

Mrs Blackmore offered a very large parcel wrapped in brown paper and tied with string. 'Yes this is my gown. I fear it is somewhat outdated and I simply don't have the time to have a new one made. We can be in Sydney for only two days. Mr Blackmore can't leave his charges for any longer. A dress for an occasion such as this is way beyond my limited skills.'

Roisin placed the parcel on the table and unwrapped the brown paper with a strange mixture of apprehension and elation. If she could make a success of this, then more work might follow. Fail and she'd be lucky to see another customer.

The paper fell away to reveal a mound of murky-brown satin. She swallowed and lifted the dress from the shoulders and shook it out. With a rustle of displeasure it settled to reveal wide full sleeves, a scooped neckline and not much else to recommend it.

A small sigh escaped her lips. It would take every ounce of her imagination to make this dated day dress into something suitable for a Sydney wedding.

'Too difficult, my dear? I wouldn't be at all surprised.' Mrs Blackmore's face flushed ember red. 'A Wollombi schoolteacher's wife has very little need of anything sophisticated.'

It would certainly stretch her imagination; however, she'd no intention of giving up this early in the piece. 'No, no I have an idea or two. Would you mind slipping the dress on?'

Mrs Blackmore's hand rose to her chest, and her gaze searched the room, and then settled on the glass window.

'I can draw the curtains and wait outside if you would like some privacy.'

More colour infused the poor woman's cheeks as she checked for any lurking observers.

'I can also lock the door.' She sent up a silent prayer, thanking Carrick for his help. 'There's a curtain in the corner there and I could help you with any lacing.'

'Just tell me what you have in mind, I'm not sure Mr Blackmore would approve of me removing my clothing in your parlour.'

No, he probably wouldn't. This was something that hadn't crossed her mind. Her clients in Sydney were more than happy—used to, in fact—slipping in and out of any garments when they came for a fitting. Perhaps in the country she'd have to consider an alternative.

Instead, Roisin spread the dress out on the table. 'I could alter the sleeves, make them smaller, even remove them. If you'll be wearing the dress in the evening it would be more suitable. And …' She paused, her mind racing through the options. 'One moment.'

Inside the trunk there was a length of blushing apricot silk. Placing it against the brown as an overskirt with some ribbon roses, or even bows made from the material in the sleeves … She delved into her trunk.

'There.' She held the lustrous material aloft. 'I think perhaps with a drape and a fichu of lace adorned with some roses like these.' She dropped a ribbon rose she'd made for a very pretty corset for one of Aunt Lil's girls into Mrs Blackmore's hand. The possibility of Mrs Blackmore coming into contact with one of Aunt Lil's girls, never mind her corset, was highly unlikely, so no one would be any the wiser.

The colour heightened in Mrs Blackmore's cheeks as she twirled the rose, then fingered the gossamer silk, before clearing her throat and huffing out a sigh. 'It is very pretty, too pretty for someone like me. Mutton dressed up as lamb.'

'Not at all, Mrs Blackmore, please, trust me, I wouldn't suggest it if I didn't think you could carry it off.' The woman was big, more statuesque than oversized. She carried herself well. If only she could get her to put the dress on.

'Let me show you.' She bunched up the shimmering fabric and held it against the satin, then folded the sleeves away from sight. 'I think it would be very attractive, especially with your colouring.' The coppery highlights in her hair would lift the dress and the apricot would bring out the bloom in her complexion.

'What would Mr Blackmore say? I wear colours a little more sedate, befitting a matron of my standing in the community.'

'I think he'd say you look ravishing. This is for a wedding, Mrs Blackmore, a time for celebration. It is definitely your colour.' What now? What could she do to convince the woman otherwise? If she didn't get the job, then Ruan's schooling would be in the balance and her credibility shot to ribbons.

She picked up her charcoal and sketched a quick design of the dress with the silk overskirt and shortened sleeves. Still, Mrs Blackmore's face displayed a mask of total disbelief. How to make the woman see … 'Just one moment.'

Roisin skittered down the passage to her bedroom and flung the smaller of her two trunks open and rummaged through the collection of garments until her fingers closed over the hand mirror Aunt Lil had given her. Why hadn't she thought of it before? Call herself a dressmaker? She'd forgotten the most important item. If Mrs Blackmore could see the apricot silk against her skin she'd be swayed.

When she re-entered the room Mrs Blackmore stood at the window, the material resting against her cheek and a dreamy look in her eyes. She *did* like her ideas. She was simply too unsure of herself to take the risk.

Holding up the mirror Roisin edged closer. 'Mrs Blackmore …'

The piece of material fell from the startled woman's hands and she jumped, her eyes scanning the room as though terrified of being caught with something so frivolous as apricot silk.

'Please, have a look in the mirror. Remove your hat and hold the material against your cheek again.'

Mrs Blackmore removed two ferocious hatpins from her bonnet and laid it on the table. 'Are you certain this is absolutely essential? I think perhaps I should wear the dress as it is.'

Roisin blanched. How could she tell Ruan she'd failed, or worse, bear the ignominy of Mrs Blackmore telling her friends that the new dressmaker harboured outlandish, inappropriate ideas? She sucked in a breath. 'Mr Blackmore will be so disappointed if his wonderful gift to you is a failure.' She held up the mirror.

Mrs Blackmore frowned and took a step closer, held the material to her cheeks and, like the sun coming out after rain, smiled at her reflection. 'It reminds me of when I was a young girl.'

'Oh come now, Mrs Blackmore, you are hardly an old woman.' And with the smile on her face, Roisin realised with a start that Mrs Blackmore was indeed far younger than the first impression her dowdy appearance had conjured.

'Mr Blackmore and I were married eight years ago. I was sixteen. We have four fine children now and I'm well past the age of frivolity.'

'You are barely older than I am.'

'Too old for an apricot dress.'

'This won't be an apricot dress, your dress will simply have some lighter trimming. The contrast of the light and dark materials will be elegant yet refined, an overdress of silk and beneath a skirt of satin. Mrs Blackmore, trust me. If you don't like the alterations I can always put it back to the way it was before. Please.' Now she was beginning to sound desperate. She was desperate.

'Very well, my dear. It seems I have no alternative.'

Hardly a vote of confidence, though Roisin had no doubt her idea would work, and when Mrs Blackmore saw her dress completed she'd fall in love with it, of that she was certain.

'When can you have it ready?'

'This time next week?'

'That will be a week before I leave for Sydney.' A frown creased her brow and then she gave a little shake. 'Ample time to rectify the situation. Mr Blackmore said I should take a gamble, so I will.' She nodded her head and smiled, her brown eyes sparkling.

'Thank you. I'm sure you will be very pleased with the result.' Her words sounded far more certain than she felt. The work was worth it even if it meant she'd be sewing every hour God sent. Thank heavens Ruan would be at school and thank goodness for her portable sewing machine.

Lost in her work, a clatter and a crash followed by the slam of the door made Roisin jump. She lay down the brown satin on the table. 'Ruan, is that you?'

He skidded through the door. 'Yes. It's dinnertime and I'm home. What's to eat? Did you know that the Romans had whole houses just for baths?'

'No, I didn't.' She ruffled Ruan's hair and he shook his head, pulling away.

'Don't. Can we build a bath? I think you'd like one. The Romans had hot water steaming out of the walls. It would be better than standing in front of the fire trying to get clean. I'd like a bath. I'm going to ask Carrick if he thinks he could build one. A washhouse like we had in Sydney, in the scullery. You'd like a bath, wouldn't you?'

'I think it might be …'

'And anyway where is Carrick? It's way past the day he said he'd be here and Maisie said he'd come. I've got so much to tell him. Mr Blackmore says …'

Roisin let Ruan's words wash over her. His mind raced ten to the dozen and there was little point in even trying to keep up with his conversation. As though his brain had expanded overnight, he sucked up every piece of information, digested it at a rapid rate, then applied it to his own life—not just his own, hers as well.

She put the bowl of soup down on the table for him.

'The Romans had big plates of fruit and banquets and they lay down to eat. Can you imagine that?' He toppled sideways in his chair, taking the spoon and a liberal dose of soup with him. 'I'm going to go fishing this afternoon. We could have a fish banquet for tea.'

'Don't go too far away, please.'

'Do you want to come with me?'

'I'm sorry I can't, Ruan. I only have two more days to complete Mrs Blackmore's dress.'

'When you've finished?'

'Maybe.' Though unlikely. True to her word, Mrs Blackmore had spread the news and commissioned new bed linen with lace trim for the bride and groom and she had three other dresses waiting for makeovers. Not exactly what she'd hoped for, nevertheless it was work. And none would be as difficult or as time-consuming as the outdated brown monstrosity Mrs Blackmore had presented. After three fittings, Mrs Blackmore was beginning to panic, convinced her dress would never be completed in time. Tomorrow she'd see it with the additional flounces and she'd love it. She had to.

'I'm going now.' Ruan pushed back his chair.

'Make sure you're back before the light goes. It's cold in the afternoons.'

'Yes, Mam.' He threw the words over his shoulder and disappeared, leaving his jacket hanging over the back of the chair. Thank goodness Aunt Lil couldn't see him. He seemed closer to a street urchin than the restricted, frail little boy who'd first arrived in Wollombi.

Tutting, she cleared away the plates and set the evening meal on the fire, then returned to the parlour. The dress was almost finished and it had come up a treat. Hopefully Mrs Blackmore would agree.

The afternoon passed in a flash as every day had done since Mrs Blackmore's first visit, and when the light began to fade her thoughts turned to Ruan. He hadn't come home.

Leaving the parlour, she headed out of the back door and down the path to the brook. He'd be down there, searching for treasures or fishing, of that she was certain.

As she rounded the bend his head came into view sitting on the side of the brook next to, next to … She lifted her skirts and ran. 'Ruan, come here, come here this minute.'

At the sound of her voice he stood, bending down to say something to the old man sitting under the tree. A black, a native. Oh for goodness sake. There were more dangers here than in Sydney where she'd kept him inside all the time. Whatever had possessed her to leave him to his own devices?

'Goodbye,' he called, lifting his hand before running to her.

'What are you doing? You can't just sit and talk to anyone. The natives can be dangerous.'

'That's Old Pella.'

She studied the hunched old man dressed in a ragged shirt and trousers cut off below the knee and held up at the waist by twine. 'You can't be friends with a native, no one is.'

'Carrick is.'

Carrick again. Would the man always cause problems even when he wasn't in town?

'And Carrick will be back tomorrow.'

'How do you know that?'

'Old Pella told me.'

'And how would he know?'

Ruan shrugged his shoulders. 'He just does. He knows everything and he knows so many stories. Dreaming stories, all about rainbow serpents and evil bunyips.'

'You mustn't talk to him, Ruan. If I can't trust you to go out on your own, you will have to stay at home with me.' She grabbed hold of his hand and towed him back up the path.

Eight

The late-afternoon sun had disappeared behind the hills as the dray weaved its way past the empty cattle yards back to the camp. More than anything Carrick wanted to go and knock on Roisin's door and hope she invited him in for a cup of tea. After two weeks at the camp and the interminable trip he'd a need for her, to see her again, and the lad. She might turn him away, close down on him, but that was a risk he'd willingly run, and besides, he had the box for the lad. Polished bright and ready for a thousand treasures. Maybe that would change her mind.

After all the rain the trip from Morpeth had taken forever. They'd had ten wet, soggy, mud-strewn days. Even the bullocky had complained, giving the poor animals an unusual taste of the whip. When they finally drew up alongside the camp, the flames from the fire sparked high into the night sky, illuminating the motley group collected around and about. The smell of rum and the greasy remains of the mutton they'd roasted for tea stuck in his craw. Slinger's fiddle cut the air with one of his madcap jigs and the clapping and stomping had begun.

He swung down from the dray, his gaze riveted on the lone figure leaping like a demented banshee around the flickering flames. The men's raucous voices grew as they heckled the dancer on. He twisted and turned, arms flailing, leaping over the flames and circling the fire like a decapitated chicken, and then he stumbled and fell to wild applause.

A shiver ran down his spine, turning his skin clammy. This wasn't the usual evening's entertainment. A large figure loomed over the body on the ground and Carrick ran through the drunken audience, pushing them aside. The big bastard from the Paterson crew stood astride the prostrate body, with an upended flagon splashing rum over the crumbled, curled mass of bones huddled on the ground.

Carrick leapt forward, his fingers closing over the frail old man, his stomach roiling at the sour stench of panicked sweat and heated rum. 'What the feck do you think you're doing?' He scooped up the shrivelled body and threw him over his shoulder.

'A bit of entertainment.'

'The old man's half dead.'

'Just a native.' Another cutter shouldered his way through the crowd head down, hands clenched at the end of his long arms. 'What's your problem?'

Carrick wiped away the spittle that peppered his face.

'Just a native dancing for his tea.' The cutter lurched forward. 'Bloody heathens.'

'He's a man and he deserves a bit of respect.' Carrick hefted the limp, rum-soaked body of the old man across his shoulder. He'd worry about the idiots once he had Old Pella out of trouble.

A heavy hand landed on his shoulder, spinning him around. A fist came from nowhere and found his face. Rum took the power out of the bastard's punch but made it more than clear he'd not be walking away. He lowered Old Pella to the ground.

The cutter swayed on his feet, his head down, ready to charge. Carrick raised his arm and pushed hard against the cutter's shoulder, causing him to stagger backwards into Slinger's waiting grasp. Slinger spun him around and belted him. The cutter flew backwards and landed with an earth-shattering thud, the wind knocked out of him. Slinger dusted his hands. 'Who's next?'

Carrick threw him a wry grin. 'What the hell are you doin' here?' Then pain radiated up through his gut, igniting a blast of rage. He swivelled, sucked a breath of air into his parched lungs and lurched. His fist connected with bone with a sickening crunch. The cutter rocked back on his heels and let fly. Carrick ducked, dodged the flaying fists. The bastard was drunker than Old Pella. He'd knock him cold if he could get a decent punch. He stepped closer, blood boiling at the taunts from the other cutters. The old man groaned and curled himself into a tight bundle on the ground.

'Forget it.' The old man needed help. The Paterson cutters could wait. There'd be plenty of time for them later.

He bent down, half expecting to be sent sprawling. Thank God Slinger had his back. The old man cocooned in his smelly possum rug weighed no more than a sack of potatoes. He needed to get him somewhere safe, away from the drunken louts. Let them find another outlet for their sick games.

'Sure you don't want to finish this off?' Slinger followed him away from the fire. 'They've got it in for the pair of us. Time to teach 'em a lesson.'

'They'll not be learning anything from me. Why aren't you in the forest with the boys?'

'Needed a bit of a break. What're you going to do with that bag of bones?'

'Find him somewhere comfortable for the night, let him sleep off the rum.'

Slinger gave a derogatory sniff. 'Got enough trouble with those Paterson cutters, bunch of mongrels, without taking on anyone else's problems.'

'Leave 'em be. They'll be gone in the morning. And so will you.' The old man wriggled and squirmed and Carrick shrugged him higher up onto his shoulder and clasped him firmly around the knees. 'I'll be seeing you later. And thanks.' The sooner he found Old Pella somewhere to sleep, the better. With the mood Slinger was in he'd as likely go back and pick up where they left off.

He cast a glance back to the fire as Slinger made his way through the circle of men, somehow managing not to thump anyone. Old Pella needed somewhere dry to sleep; without the slightest breeze in the cool, crisp night there was a chance of frost. He meandered along the path by the brook until he found himself outside the back of Roisin's cottage. No sign of life, no lamp burning in the kitchen, just the glow from the fire. What he'd not give to bunk down on her kitchen floor. The old man struggled and gave a pitiful moan. He'd have a head and a half tomorrow and he'd be needing somewhere to sleep off the effects.

Following the path of moonlight, Carrick slipped through the lavender bushes and up to the woodshed. The perfect spot. He nudged the door open and carried the old man inside. Tucked in the back corner, he'd be out of harm's way and a darn sight warmer than anywhere else. Carrick lowered him down onto the ground and folded his possum rug around him. The old man grunted and stirred and burrowed down into the loose dirt. 'Sleep the night here, Old Pella. Good and warm.'

'You got rum, boss?'

'No, Old Pella, no rum. Too much is bad. You had too much.'

'Makes troubles go away.'

'No, it brings troubles.' And didn't he know it.

'You staying, Carrick?'

'No, I'm going to go and cut King Polai. You happy with that?'

'Bad land there. Bunyip's there.'

'You sleep and I'll come back later.' Carrick sighed and rubbed his hand through his hair. Bloody cutters. He touched his cheek, flinching as his hand rasped the grazed skin. Why the hell couldn't they live and let live? What harm had Old Pella ever done to them? The woodshed was virtually empty. He'd come back and cut some wood for Roisin tomorrow morning and check on the old man.

Roisin snuggled down beneath her quilt and gave a pleasurable sigh. The house was snug and cosy. She'd even put up the checked curtains at the kitchen windows, framing the view of the backyard, so she could keep half an eye on Ruan while she worked. Soon she'd clear a patch for some herbs. She'd found some old lavender bushes near the pump and with a bit of water they were already showing new growth. She'd plant some vegetables, maybe carrots and beans once the winter frosts had passed.

The sound of splitting wood seeped into her consciousness and she struggled from her bed, pulling her shawl around her shoulders. It would be Carrick. Elsie said the cutters were back and camped down by the brook again. To know Carrick cared enough to ensure their comfort stoked a curl of heat in her belly. She hadn't expected him to come around after she'd packed him off last time. She'd been too harsh on him. Her own insecurities making her jump at shadows.

Pulling her shawl tight, she opened the back door, shivering in the morning chill, her breath puffing out in a fine white cloud. Carrick didn't seem to feel the cold; he'd thrown his shirt and vest down on the dirt behind him. She stood admiring the play of his muscles as the axe rose and fell.

'Carrick.' He didn't respond, didn't hear her, the axe continued to fall, the rhythm a pleasure to watch. She turned inside and made a mug of tea and carried it back outside. When he dropped the axe and threw the last of the splits onto the pile she stepped forward. 'Here's some tea.'

He jumped at her words and turned with a grin. 'Good morning.'

'Good morning to you.' Dark stubble dusted his chin and upper lip and his reddened eyes blinked owlishly at her. 'That should see you through. I'm not going to be in town again for a while.'

She scanned his face, one eye swollen shut, blue and bruised, his skin pale, highlighting the split on his cheekbone and the swelling across the bridge of his nose. 'You've hurt yourself.'

He rubbed his hand over his face and grimaced. 'Busy night. Paterson cutters were in town.'

She held out the mug, their fingers brushing as he took it from her. 'You've been fighting.' The words slipped past her lips before she gave them a second thought.

'Just a bit of rough and tumble around the fire.'

The need to soothe him almost overwhelmed her. She took a step closer, her hand outstretched.

He shook his head and turned his back on her, studying the woodpile. 'No sympathy. My own fault.'

The skin on his upper arms was pale where the sun hadn't reached and the early-morning light highlighted the planes of his muscles. He raised his shoulders as though he could feel her eyes on him and brought the mug to his lips. Across his right shoulder a puckered scar stood out. 'You've hurt your shoulder, too.' Her fingers reached out to soothe the shiny red skin and fell. It wasn't a new injury. 'Whatever is this?'

He flinched and dropped his mug to the ground and gathered up his shirt. When he turned, his face blanched chalky white and the fury blazing from his eyes sent her stepping back.

Shrugging into his shirt, he fumbled at the buttons. 'It's long gone.' His colourless voice did nothing to betray his emotion, yet as if the clouds had covered the sun, his face closed tight. 'A reminder not to tamper with the English.'

'An Englishman did that to you?' She'd never heard of anything so barbaric. She'd grown up in Sydney close to the barracks and the gaol, heard talk of punishments, floggings, even hangings, but the mark on Carrick's shoulder was like a brand. The kind they put on cattle or horses claiming ownership. What had brought Carrick to Australia? He was certainly a freeman now, but maybe he'd been transported as a convict originally. Sydney was teeming with Irish men and women these days, some of them free settlers or assisted passages come to escape the horrors of the Famine, others political prisoners sent out in chains for their defiance against the English—that would be it. He must have been a political prisoner. Now was probably not the moment to ask. His reaction to her question had sparked such a change in his face.

His eyes, bleak pools of emptiness, stared at her. 'Forget it. It was long ago. Not worth the worry.'

'What about your face, does that hurt? Let me clean it and get some arnica.'

'I said, forget it.' He finished buttoning his shirt and tied his neckerchief. 'I'll stack the wood in the woodshed. Then I'll be gone. Is the lad about?'

'Please, stay for a while and have some breakfast.' It was the least she could do, and then maybe she'd have time to apologise for the way she'd sent him away last time. She owed him that.

As though he could read her mind he grinned and reached for her hand. 'Don't worry about me. It's nothing new. I can look after myself. Slinger had me back.'

When their palms touched a fizzy breathlessness seized her, making her legs almost buckle. She left her hand in his for a moment, against his hard, calloused palm. A lingering glow spread through her body, lodging deep in her belly. Fighting to control her breathing she dropped his hand, stepped back and bent down to pick up his mug.

He grabbed the first of the logs and began tossing them through the door into the woodshed. She sank down on the doorstep. The lines on his face softened with the exertion and every now and again he glanced up and threw her a rueful grin. She could have sat all morning watching him, the easy grace of his movements, his perfect balance and the pale morning light touching his dark hair. Maisie had picked it from the beginning—he was a handsome man and she couldn't keep her eyes off him.

When he straightened up he slapped his palms together, sending a fine cloud of sawdust into the air. 'That should keep you going for a while. The lad's been keeping on top of the kindling. That's good to see.' He sat down on the doorstep next to her; the heat radiated from his body and the scent of fresh timber, and something very masculine swirled in the crisp morning air, leaving her short of breath.

He wiped his arm across his forehead. 'So where is he?'

She dragged her eyes away from his thigh muscles, trying to concentrate on his words and not the delicious feelings slipping over her skin like a whispered dream. 'Asleep still. I must get him up for his breakfast soon otherwise he'll be late for school.' Although it would be very pleasant to let Ruan sleep. Sitting here with the scent of the freshly chopped wood and this man beside her made her thoughts turn from the everyday to—well, to thoughts she'd never had before. Strange feelings that she didn't understand and couldn't prevent bubbled in her chest, making her limbs heavy and her skin flush.

'So you sent him, then.'

'I'm sorry?'

'To school.' He smiled, cupped her face in his big hands and stared into her eyes. 'Your eyes are the very colour of the damp Irish grass sparkling with morning dew.'

'Yes.' She swallowed. He'd think her mad. She'd never even set foot in Ireland, how would she know what colour the grass was, damp or otherwise. His eyes were dark, almost black, though when he smiled little flecks of colour danced. She shook her head. Concentrate. She must concentrate. 'Mr Blackmore came to see me. I traded a makeover of his wife's gown for Ruan's school fees. Ruan was very keen to go.'

Carrick grunted and slid his fingers down to her chin, then dropped his hands. His voice lowered into a caress as potent as his hand on her skin. 'A lad needs an education.'

'He said you'd told him that.'

His face broke into an all-encompassing grin and the sparks of amusement danced in his eyes.

'Something about hedge schools.'

He laughed and stood up, holding out a hand to help her to her feet. 'I was telling him about my childhood in Ireland.'

So he wasn't averse to talking about some aspects of his past. How she wanted to know. Know all there was about him. 'Will you tell me about your past?'

As quickly as it had appeared the smile slipped from his face and he let go of her hand. 'Those are stories no woman would want to hear.'

Holy Mary, what had made him say that? The touch of her cool fingers on his shoulder more than not. Even though the pain of the branding had long since gone he kept the scar covered. Easier than having questions asked. He shook his head; at least the boy hadn't seen it. He'd be the last one he'd want to explain the indignity to. Best let it lie. The story belonged in Ireland and that's where it would stay.

Inside the woodshed the pile of kindling stood stacked in the right-hand corner, just where he'd told Ruan to put it. No sign of Old Pella other than a hollowed-out patch in the dirt. The old man must have taken off before the sun came up.

Ruan was a good lad. Would Liam have been like that? He shook away the thought. It was a nonsense. Liam would be a man now—getting close, and a big, strapping lad at that. Ruan was only a young thing. He clenched his teeth, banishing his morbid thoughts.

Did the lad or the woman draw him? He threw the last of the split logs onto the pile at the back of the shed, squinting as he walked out into the sun, ridding himself of the memories.

He closed the woodshed door and saw Roisin still sitting in the same spot. He took her hand in his and lifted her to her feet. She barely reached his shoulder, yet there was strength in her arms and in the tilt of her head, independence and determination. She'd have to have that to make her own way and a life for herself and the lad. The gossip around the town said she'd been widowed, though neither she nor the lad ever mentioned the man.

She nudged the back door open and the smell of the cosy kitchen hit him, warming his heart and making his belly rumble. She'd made the old house into a home for herself and the boy. A home he'd like to dream of sharing.

'I've porridge for Ruan's breakfast. Would you like some, and some cream?' Her eyes held the sheen of tears and the sight bore a hole straight through to his heart. He'd hurt her with his curt dismissal.

'Thank you. I'd like that.' Porridge. Porridge and cream. No one would find the likes of that in Ireland these days. Perhaps Brigid and Liam were in a better place. No suffering where they were.

A frail smile hovered on her lips as she accepted his unspoken apology. Unlike most women, she'd ask the question then leave it be, wouldn't flog it. Wouldn't keep hammering until she got an answer. Just as well.

'Carrick!'

Closing the door behind him, Carrick squatted as the bundle of joy threw himself into his arms.

'I thought I'd missed you. Come on, breakfast is ready. I mustn't be late for school. I'm telling everyone about my snakeskin. Mam says snakes shed their skins because they wear out and the snake tailors make new ones.' He lowered his voice. 'But I don't think that's true. Do you? I'm going to ask Mr Blackmore.'

He chuckled. 'I'm thinking you might be right.'

'And talking about naked snakes is not right in front of a lady.' Ruan nodded his head at his mam.

'Right again.' Carrick swallowed a chuckle and pointed to the kitchen table.

Ruan tugged on his hand, dragging him away. 'Before we have breakfast, can you tell me about the snakes though?'

'We'll leave that for Mr Blackmore. Your mam's waiting for us. Besides, I've got something for you.' He unwrapped the cedar box from his jacket. 'I thought you might be needing this.'

The lad's eyes widened in delight. 'A new treasure box.' He smoothed his little hand over the soft cedar.

The beeswax had brought up the colour a treat, a perfect match for the dark-red streaks in Roisin's hair.

'It's so shiny.' He plucked at the lid. 'Why can't I open the box?'

'Because you need the key. Come on, I'll see what I can do.'

Roisin's eyebrows rose as Ruan swaggered into the kitchen clasping the box close to his chest. When she turned to Carrick, a spontaneous smile lit her face. That in itself was reward enough. Never mind the lad's pleasure. If he'd known she'd look like that he'd have made her one for herself as well. A hundred even. Just a few offcuts and a way to pass the time in the forest.

'I've got a new treasure box.' Ruan placed the cedar chest on the table like an offering in the church.

Roisin ran her long, thin fingers over the smooth timber and a shudder traced his skin. 'You shouldn't have gone to so much trouble.'

'I wanted to.' He grinned back at her. To see the pleasure on their two shining faces was the best gift he'd received.

'Can I have the key, Carrick? Can I? I want to open my treasure box.'

'You sit here and eat your breakfast before it gets cold.'

'Do what your mam says and then we'll open your treasure box before you go to school.'

'Can I take it to school?' Ruan mumbled through a mouthful of porridge.

Roisin shook her head. 'Treasures should be kept at home. Safe.'

He shovelled his breakfast into his mouth and the spoon clattered to the table.

'Have you finished?'

Ruan nodded, leaping down from the chair and depositing his half-full bowl into the bucket by the door.

Before his mam had time to complain, Carrick produced the key from his pocket. 'Well, then in that case.'

Ruan snatched the key from him and turned to the treasure box. The key slipped into the lock and Ruan opened the box, sighing in delight as he ran his fingers over the compartments, lifting the lids on the little boxes. 'It's perfect.'

'Time for school now, Ruan. Say thank you to Carrick.'

'Will you be here when I get home, Carrick?'

'No, I won't. More's the pity. I've got work to do.'

When Ruan's face crumpled he almost changed his plans. 'I should be back soon if you're a good boy and work hard at school.'

'I will, I will.' He threw his arms around Carrick's neck before sprinting down the hallway.

'Ruan, take your cap.' He came flying back and snatched up his jacket, too. 'Bye, Mam. Bye, Carrick. Thank you.' The door slammed behind him, leaving the house quiet and still.

'He's a great lad.' Carrick stretched out his feet and took the tea Roisin put in front of him. How long since he'd enjoyed such simple pleasures?

'So you'll be going away again?'

'Aye. We've pretty much finished up now. It wasn't a big stand. Never expected it to last long. It's too small to be of use to the government contractors and there's no watercourse nearby so it takes longer to get the timber out. Too much like hard work for the lazy sods, but there's been decent money in it for us.' And there was still King Polai.

'Are the trees really as big as they say?'

'Depends how long they've been growing. There's trees over two hundred years old. Two hundred feet tall. A single tree that size could produce enough timber to fill a cedar vessel twice over.'

'It seems almost a shame to cut them down.'

'It's good money for the colony. It's not going to stop. Not for a long time. "Red gold" they call it. After wheat and wool it's what's keeping the colony flourishing. Most of it's going to England. Some say Queen Victoria has all her rooms decked out with fine furniture made from Australian cedar and it's good for building boats and houses.' He'd build a fine house with the cedar from King Polai given half the chance, if the money wasn't earmarked for something else. The very thought of sharing a home with Roisin made his heartstrings vibrate like Slinger's fiddle. 'The insects don't like the smell of the wood. You can build a house that'll last forever.'

She bent her nose to Ruan's box and inhaled. 'It smells like you.' She lifted her flushed face and pushed back a curl.

His fingers itched to draw her close and lay his fingers on the pulse beating below the soft skin on the side of her neck. 'And do you like the smell of the cedar?'

'I do.' Her lips quirked in a smile.

He stood and moved around the table. 'Then you'll be liking me, too.' He couldn't help it, he shouldn't. He leant in and let his lips graze hers.

She didn't move, didn't turn away, just stayed stock-still, a moment locked in time. A moment he'd keep close to his heart. She was lovely, all rose and gold and warmth, her eyes clear and honest. The blood surged through his body and he kept his eyes locked on hers. She lifted her hands and cradled his face.

Sure and if she wasn't the most beautiful sight he'd seen for many a year. He'd bare his heart to her in a moment. He'd lost it already, lost his heart the first moment he'd seen her standing in the road across the sea of faces, bright as a new blade of grass amongst the withered weeds. Who'd have thought he'd still be capable of love?

The break in the misery plaguing him since he'd left Ireland worked its way through his blood, seeping into every corner of his shrivelled soul. He might even believe that one day everything could be right again.

Nestled in the crook of his arm, she lifted her green gaze to scan his face. 'What will you do next?'

He paused. He'd return to Ireland to find and finish the English bastard. That one thought had sustained him, kept him going. The truth was best. 'I'll go to Sydney and buy my passage on a ship back to Ireland. I have unfinished business.'

'Will you return to Australia?' It might have been his imagination, but he'd swear her voice hitched and a tear glistened in the corners of her eyes.

'That'll be God's decision.' Though his work was more of the devil. 'I might well do that.' In chains no doubt, if they didn't hang him first, unless the very luck of the devil stayed with him.

'I'd like that.'

And so would he. The bullocky's irate bellow cut him short, ruining his chances. 'I have to go.' He dropped a kiss on her upturned nose. 'Be staying safe, my darling.' With more strength than it took for the first axe stroke, he turned and left.

She stood silhouetted at the door and when he raised his arm and waved, she did, too, holding her hand high until they rounded the bend in the road and she disappeared from sight.

Roisin dropped her hand and sighed. Carrick breezed in and out of her life and every time he left he took a little more of her heart with him. The thought of him leaving Australia caused an aching hollow inside her, a void no one else would be able to fill. Not even Ruan.

She dabbed at her eyes with her apron and as she turned to go inside caught sight of Mrs Blackmore's dress. It was finished and today, in a matter of moments, she would be here to collect it. She scurried down the hallway into the kitchen and scooped up the remains of Carrick's breakfast and her own then dumped everything into a bucket and took it outside to the scullery. It could stay there until she had time to attend to it. She had a business to run.

Mrs Blackmore's knock came at exactly nine o'clock.

She swung open the door. 'Good morning. Please come in.'

Mrs Blackmore rushed inside and came to an abrupt halt in the middle of the parlour, hands clasped to her bosom and her eyes dancing. 'Oh my dear it's perfect, absolutely perfect. Can I touch it?' The delight in Mrs Blackmore's voice sent a surge of pleasure through Roisin. Without a doubt this was the very best part of her job, seeing the joy on Mrs Blackmore's face and knowing that she'd had a part in it.

'Of course.' Roisin took down the dress and held it across her arms.

With a look of awe Mrs Blackmore ran her fingers over the apricot silk and then touched each one of the ribbon roses and bows. 'I honestly thought you would be unable to finish it in time.'

And on more than one occasion she'd thought the very same.

'It's absolutely perfect.'

'Would you like one final fitting just to make sure you're happy with it?' Roisin moved to the window to pull the curtains closed.

'There's no need. The earlier fittings took care of that.' Mrs Blackmore shook her head in wonder. 'It's so beautiful. I only hope I can do it justice.' Her eyes sparkled as she lifted her gaze. 'I haven't told Mr Blackmore very much at all, in fact I've been quite reticent about the dress. I want to surprise him.'

Roisin lifted the dress to Mrs Blackmore's shoulders and let the skirt fall. 'I do hope there's some dancing because the overskirt is so very light it'll float.'

'There will be dancing, of that I can assure you, and if it's not at the wedding I shall make sure it happens elsewhere.' Her brown eyes twinkled. 'Now package it up for me. Nothing frivolous. I want just a brown paper parcel to take with me.'

Roisin laid the dress on the table and folded it carefully then wrapped it in a length of cotton before covering the whole lot in the very same brown paper the dress had arrived in.

'Excellent.' Mrs Blackmore reached into her reticule and brought out a thick vellum envelope and held it out.

Roisin took the envelope and turned it over. Her name, written across the front in a flowery script and finished with an exaggerated swirl, dominated the small square. 'Mrs Blackmore there's no charge for your dress. I've already discussed the matter with Mr Blackmore. Ruan's school fees …' She didn't want to be paid for the dress. If Mrs Blackmore had come to some decision and the contents of the envelope didn't cover Ruan's school fees she would be in a worse situation than before.

'I'm well aware of the arrangement you and Mr Blackmore came to. Open the envelope.'

Roisin slid two shaking fingers beneath the flap of the envelope and brought out a thick sheet of paper. She unfolded it.

10th July 1855
Wollombi House, Wollombi

Dear Mrs Ogilvie,

I should very much like the opportunity to call on you at your earliest convenience. Would Monday the 24th of July at 9.30 be suitable?

Mrs G. Winchester.

Roisin traced her shaking finger over the signature and snapped her mouth closed to contain the yelp of joy trying to escape. Her heart lifted for the first time since she'd waved goodbye to Carrick. Mrs Grace Winchester, wife of the magistrate, had made an appointment to see her.

Mrs Blackmore patted her arm. 'The opportunity presented itself and I felt it was the least I could do after all your hard work.'

'I … I … I don't know how to thank you.'

'No thanks are needed, just make the most of the occasion. That will be ample reward.' Mrs Blackmore picked up her package and gave it a squeeze. 'You've turned this turkey into a swan. Wish me luck as I sail forth.'

'You won't need any luck, Mrs Blackmore. You'll look absolutely lovely.'

Nine

Two weeks later Roisin bundled Ruan out of the door into the early-morning chill, wrapping a scarf tight around his neck. 'Now take care. Go straight to school. Don't stop and talk to anyone on the way. I don't have time to take you this morning.'

'Why not? Is Carrick coming?'

'No, he's not. I'm expecting a very important client. She wants to talk to me about a new dress.'

'Mrs Blackmore.'

'No, not Mrs Blackmore.' She held Ruan's new jacket out behind him so he could find the sleeves, then lifted it across his shoulders. He had grown so much in the past couple of months, she ought to make him a new one. Maybe today would solve all her problems. Roisin would never be able to thank Mrs Blackmore enough. As much as she appreciated the business her advertisements had brought, a call from Mrs Winchester was an enormous step up. 'Off you go. Be a good boy and come straight home at dinnertime.'

He slammed the front door behind him and she stood at the window watching him race up the street. So much energy and enthusiasm. Such a far cry from the pale, fractious child of Sydney. If nothing else she'd made the right decision for Ruan's future.

Turning to the parlour, she cast her gaze around. Everything was in place, the fire lit and the cushions plumped. The mirror now hung over the trunk and the curtained corner sported a hat stand. Lifting the lid of the trunk, she removed the sheaf of papers. All the drawings and designs she'd worked on. Perhaps one of those would interest Grace Winchester. *Oh!* She lifted her hand to still the pitter-pattering of her heart. Whatever was the matter with her? Just wait and see. Stop trying to second-guess.

She squinted in the mirror and ran her hand over her hair to ensure it was still controlled, then took off her apron and adjusted the collar of her dress. She had to look her best. It was such an important day. Although the wealthy property owners rarely came to town other than to attend church or, in Mr Winchester's situation, the courthouse, there were many on the outlying properties who might use her services if Mrs Winchester deemed her suitable.

On the dot of nine-thirty there was a knock, and with one last glance around the room she opened the door.

'Good morning, Mrs Winchester. Welcome.'

'Good morning.' Dressed in an eggshell-blue walking-out costume, fastened with large buttons, over a skirt of cream trimmed with black ribbon at the hem, Mrs Grace Winchester presented a very elegant picture. She marched in as though she owned the place. She might as well have done. Her husband had been magistrate of the town and surrounding areas since the early days of Wollombi. Her success, the success of her business, rested as firmly in this woman's hands as the immaculate cream leather gloves she so carefully removed.

'Please sit down.' She gestured to the chair by the fire. 'How may I help you?'

'Before we get to that I'd like to see some samples of your work. I believe Mrs Blackmore is very impressed with your efforts on her behalf. What can you show me?'

From the trunk, Roisin extracted the nightgown that had so confounded Elsie, and her drawings, and placed them on the table.

Mrs Winchester ignored the nightgown, and instead inspected each page of her drawings, before placing the paper upside down on the table and turning her attention to the next. After an interminable time she looked up, her blue eyes piercing. 'And these are all your own designs.'

Roisin nodded and a spark flared in the woman's eyes. 'Do you have any ready-made articles you can show me?'

'The nightgown.'

'And what about outer clothing?'

'Only my own.' Mrs Blackmore had taken her dress two weeks ago and the only remaining makeover was a mass of unpicked panels and dangling sleeves. She reached behind the door and took down her green velvet jacket, the one she'd worn when she'd first arrived in town. It was a little out of the ordinary, based upon a riding jacket with a long basque and peplum.

Mrs Winchester took it and ran her hand down the frogging at the front, over the soft velvet, examining each and every stitch in the lining, even turning it inside out. Beads of sweat gathered on Roisin's upper lip and beneath her arms as her stomach churned the remains of her breakfast.

'And what about this?' Mrs Winchester reached out and ran her fingers down the sleeve of Roisin's cream voile blouse. It was tucked and embroidered, adorned with tiny pearl buttons and bottle-green ribbon.

'It's my own work.'

Mrs Winchester turned to the window. 'I've seen enough.'

Disappointment curdling in her stomach, Roisin moved to the door. If she could have interested Mrs Winchester the other women in the district would have flocked to her. Such dreams, but it was not to be. She closed her eyes for a moment and composed her face while she reached for the door handle.

'If you have time now I'd like you to take my measurements.'

Roisin's heart stuttered to a halt and she spun around. The first lady of Wollombi stood smiling and nodding her head. 'Did you think I was unimpressed? On the contrary, I'm thrilled you have decided to bring your business to us. Such a wonderful addition to our small community. The town is on the up and up and we need people with your skills to entice the settlers from Sydney. How else will the town thrive?'

The laugh caught in Roisin's throat and she coughed. 'It would be my pleasure.' She reached for her tape measure from around her neck, resisting the temptation to crow aloud. 'If you'd be so kind as to remove your pelisse, the measurements will be more accurate.'

Oh how she wanted to ask what Mrs Winchester would like made. A blouse, a nightgown? Surely not a corset! She hung the eggshell-blue pelisse on the hat stand, then stretched the tape across Mrs Winchester's shoulders and down to her waist, jotting the measurements onto the back of one of her designs.

Mrs Winchester turned her head. 'I have some broadsheets from Sydney depicting the latest French designs. I'd like you to cast your eye over them and tell me what you think would be suitable and if you would be able to replicate them.'

This was most certainly not a dismissal. The lady had something specific in mind. Roisin gulped back a spark of elation and schooled her voice just as Aunt Lil would have expected. 'I'm able to source most materials in Sydney. I have some contacts, if you tell me what colours and weights you're interested in.' How she'd pay she'd no idea. Perhaps Aunt Lil would arrange for them to be shipped to Morpeth and then maybe Carrick would be coming through and could collect the packages. Alternatively, she could arrange to collect them herself. Her mind galloped while her fingers toyed with the tape measure. Ruan would love a day out. It had been so long since they had taken a trip anywhere. 'Mrs Winchester, I'm so grateful for your custom. I won't let you down.'

'Well that's to be seen. Now, tell me, when is a suitable time to call again?'

'Whenever suits you.' The middle of the night. Now. Tomorrow. As soon as possible.

'In that case we will make it next week. At the same time?'

So long to wait. 'It would be my pleasure.'

Roisin held out the blue woollen pelisse, barely able to suppress the emotion billowing in her chest, as Mrs Winchester slipped her arms into her coat and buttoned it.

'Until next week, Mrs Ogilvie.'

'Indeed. Thank you.' Waiting while Mrs Winchester negotiated the narrow alley, she clutched her skirt tightly in her fingers. Then she shut the door with a firm click and rested her back against the timber.

It took a few long moments for her breathing to calm and then she peered out of the window just to make sure she'd truly not been dreaming, before letting out a huge whoop.

'Ruan!' *Oh!* He was at school. *Elsie!* She'd go and tell Elsie. She had to tell someone. She bolted down the alley, around the corner and skittered to a halt.

Elsie stood waiting in the front of the General Store. 'Well, what happened?' She grabbed Roisin's arm and dragged her inside, then patted the stool next to the malodorous basket of onions.

'She's coming back.'

'Coming back? What for? Didn't she like what she saw?'

'She's coming back because she *did* like what she saw. She's bringing some pictures, fashion papers. She wants to know if I can copy them.'

'Copy them? Why would she want that? Isn't your own work good enough?'

Roisin laughed. Elsie had become such a staunch supporter; however, she didn't understand the fickle nature of ladies and their needs. 'Elsie, everything is wonderful. That's exactly what I wanted her to do.' She rubbed at her temples before pulling the pins from her hair and letting her long, loose curls tumble down. 'The only headache I'm going to have is sourcing the materials. I can write to my aunt and she'll buy them and send them to Morpeth, but the problem is—how am I going to get them from there?'

'If that's your only problem then that's easy fixed. My Alfie goes to Morpeth twice a week to collect the mail and stores for the shop. You know he does, he brought your letter, remember? We'll tie it in.'

'I could ask Carrick next time he's in town.'

'No need for you to be doing that. My Alfie can do it.' Elsie huffed and pursed her lips. 'And he's a darn sight more reliable and quicker. You wouldn't want to be trusting anything to those damn cutters and their filthy bullock dray.'

'He helped me with my trunks and that didn't cause a problem.'

'That was before. You're in business now and you've got patronage. A reputation to keep up. You can't be seen with the likes of cedar cutters.' She waggled a grubby onion-flavoured finger under Roisin's nose. 'Now Mrs Winchester's called, you're going to have all the high and mighties flooding in. They won't want to be left out. You mark my words.'

With a jingle of the shop bell and a flurry of cold air, the door flew open. Elsie jumped to her feet, guilt written all over her face, then subsided onto the stool when Maisie closed the door behind her.

'It's all right. The lady and her carriage has left town. Now, tell me what happened. Mr Winchester was down at the courthouse and I overheard Mrs W telling him about her wonderful find and how lucky Wollombi was. You're putting us on the map, Roisin. Make them toffee-nosed la-di-dah Sydney folks stand up and take notice. Why, Mrs Winchester even took a cup of tea at the inn. I had to dust off me best china. Good job those ne'er-do-well cutters weren't in town lowering the tone.' She gasped a breath and collapsed onto a stool. 'So tell me all about it.'

'There's not a lot to tell that you don't already know.' A giggle slipped from Roisin's lips. It was simply too good to be true. 'Mrs Winchester's coming back next week with some pictures. She wants to know if I can copy them and make suggestions for colours and styles I think will suit her.' She clasped her hands to her chest, her heart almost ready to explode.

As the last of the giant stand of cedars fell beneath the cutters' axes the days became longer. It was time to call it quits. All that remained was King Polai and one question. Should he take it alone or share his nest egg with Slinger? Carrick stared into the dying embers of the fire. 'Tomorrow will see the last of the cutting. The bullocky'll be back and we'll be out of here.'

Slinger nodded. 'I'll miss the forest. I like the hush.'

'You're right. I like to stand at the end of a day's work when the saws are stilled and listen to nothing. Nothing but the stirring of the breeze. Once the sun has set even the animals are quiet.'

'Except for the howls of the dingoes. Never forget the dingoes.' Slinger scratched at a festering bite on his arm. 'Mind you the little biters are a bloody nuisance. The boys are going north, up Bellinger way. They say the trees are big there, bigger than here.'

Perhaps, if the rumours were true. Carrick doubted they'd find anything bigger than King Polai. The last one. His pot of gold at the end of the rainbow. The last figures from Brinkworth in Sydney confirmed his reckonings. It was time to return to Ireland. Make good the agony he'd left behind and raise a stone for Liam and his Brigid. They deserved that. Even after all the years the need burned deep, made worse every time Roisin and the lad tugged at him. A living reminder of how he'd failed. He'd put it right. The bastard would pay. He closed his eyes and let the rum work its magic.

A house built by his own hands. The red cedar walls shining in the lamplight, reflecting Roisin's hair as she bent her head over her sewing. The gentle breathing of the lad while he slept, dreaming of treasures. King Polai would provide that. A fitting end to his life in the forest. Maybe he'd leave the cedar for Roisin and if he didn't come back, she could build a house, a house of her own where she and the lad could thrive. A house no landlord could take away. And if he did return, then they'd build it together.

He jumped to his feet, scattering the sparks from the fire. Slinger blinked lazily at him. 'What's got your goat? Settle, man. For once there's nothing to do.'

That sealed it. 'Slinger can you keep yer gob shut?' He studied the man sprawled at his feet. Although his eyes were blurred from the rum, Carrick knew him and knew him as the finest cutter. Together they'd bring King Polai down faster than he could alone and he'd be one step closer to making an end of it, one step closer to a life worth living.

'Reckon.'

'Want to make some big money? Might mean you never have to cut again.'

'You serious?'

Carrick nodded and sank down onto the ground. 'I've got one more job to do. One more tree.'

'Boys won't be happy about that. They're ready to go.'

'Not the boys. Just you and me.'

The rum left Slinger's eyes in an instant, his muscles tightened and he sat hugging his knees to his chest, rocking towards the last of the fire. 'Tell me.'

'Old Pella showed me. He calls it King Polai, King of the Cedars.'

'Not more of your native nonsense.' The tension leached from Slinger's body as he reached for the rum bottle again.

'Not ten miles from here. Deep, deep in the valley. It's got to be two hundred feet.' He threw another log into the fire, watched the sparks rise and ignite Slinger's interest once more.

'How do you know? How did you find it?'

'Old Pella spotted it that first spring when the tips of the new leaves were pink. You can see them from miles away.'

'He's having a piece of you.'

'He's not. I've seen it with me own eyes. He took me there before I put the team together, before I brought the team into the Yarramalong.'

'And you've kept it to yourself? All this time?'

Carrick nodded, he had no guilt about that. It was never part of the deal he'd struck with the cutters. They signed on for as long as it took to clear a stand, he paid them a decent wage and next time they could stay or go. Only there was no next time now. Just King Polai. But Slinger, Slinger was different. They'd shared too much, far back to the days of the labouring gangs and the mines, back before they'd been picked for the cutters crew. Slinger deserved the chance. He was his mate.

'Why should I help you?'

'I'm not asking for your help. I'm offering you a share. It's the last tree I'll cut. We'll take the boys back to Morpeth, send them on their way. Wish them well. Pay off the bullocky and go in. Just you and me and a couple of horses.'

'Think you can find it again?'

'I can find it.' He could. The memory was etched in his mind as deeply as the bastard's brand on his shoulder.

'And after?'

'We'll cut it. Bring in the bullocky. Once the tree is down it doesn't matter who knows. There's nothing else around there worth taking. The rest is small stuff. I reckon we can do it in a week or two.'

'Strange. You'd think where there was one there'd be many.'

'It's deep in the valley. Fed by a single shaft of sunlight. The rest are spindly, the cedar moth got to them.'

'And what'll you be doing then?'

'Then I'm back to Ireland. I've got business to finish.'

'Oh it's business now, is it?'

'Yeah, mine. Not yours. I'm asking if you want in on the tree, not the rest of me life.' Carrick stood, wanting to distance himself from Slinger. He'd share the tree, not the pain in his heart. Never had. Never would. 'Make up your mind.'

Slinger grunted then grinned and stuck out his hand. Carrick grasped it and hauled him to his feet. 'It's a done deal, then.' He slapped the big man's shoulder and they shook on it, the rough, calloused grasp of a man he'd trust with his life. Then he breathed a sigh. He'd sleep well and tomorrow he'd start making good the mess he'd left behind in Ireland.

The days passed in a flurry of preparation as Roisin scrubbed and dusted the parlour until it sparkled. She rummaged through her trunk and took out her sewing tools, box of cottons and silks, every piece of material and lace, edgings, ribbons and tassels she'd brought with her, even some of the scraps. Three more days until Mrs Winchester returned.

When the moment finally arrived it almost took her by surprise. For some reason she couldn't fathom, Ruan had been particularly fractious, not wanting to go to school, mumbling something about having to go down to the brook and emu eggs. She simply hadn't the time, so she'd bundled him out of the door with strict instructions to come straight home from school at dinnertime and not wait for her.

She changed into one of her voile blouses and attempted to tame her hair into what she hoped resembled a tight chignon. The knock on the door made her jump. Taking one last peep in the mirror, she patted a few stray strands of hair into place, and sucking in a steadying breath made her way to the front door.

'Good morning, Mrs Ogilvie.'

'Good morning, Mrs Winchester.'

The magistrate's wife swept into the parlour, followed by another woman, thin and somewhat peaked, her drab olive-green pelisse buttoned high and her bonnet covering all except her pointy nose.

'May I present my dear friend, Lady Alice.'

Lady Alice. Roisin stumbled a half-hearted curtsy, more of a crooked bob, in fact. She gestured to the chair by the fire. 'Please sit down.' One, only one chair. Why had it never crossed her mind that she might have more than one customer at a time? 'Let me fetch another chair.'

'It's not necessary, Roisin. Why don't you sit down, Alice?'

Lady Alice. Roisin swallowed a squeal and schooled the grin threatening to spill all over her face. 'May I get you some refreshment? A cup of tea?'

'No, thank you, Mrs Ogilvie. We have much to discuss. These are the ladies' fashion papers I promised.' She toyed with the tasselled drawstring on her embroidered reticule then eased it open and withdrew a sheaf of papers, which she spread on the table.

Roisin blinked once, then again. The latest illustrated papers of fashion, not a reprint from one of the Sydney newspapers—the actual papers. She clapped her hand over her mouth to prevent it running away with her. Illustration after illustration of the most beautiful evening gowns she'd ever seen. The sleeves were much smaller, a narrower and more practical silhouette, the necklines lower. How could she remember all of this? The latest fashions. Was there a date? How new were they? It only took a matter of weeks for ships to reach Australia now. The headline read, *Gagelin-Opigez et Cite Paris.* Exquisite shawls and wraps complemented the dresses. 'These are unbelievable. Works of art.' The hushed, reverent tone of her voice startled her.

'Mr Worth. A young Englishman who is making something of a name for himself in Paris. His use of fabrics and exquisite tailoring is causing quite a stir. Can you make me a dress like this, Roisin?' She stabbed at a particularly elegant evening dress covered with white embroidery and silk lace. It represented hours and hours of work even with her sewing machine.

'It's beautiful.' Orange silk and white lace, spider-web fine, accentuating the waist and fall of the skirt.

'Can you copy it? Something similar?'

'I could.' Yes, she could if she could get hold of some suitable fabric and yards of lace. 'What colour did you have in mind?'

'I have brought a small piece with me. My driver could deliver the bolt. I acquired it in Sydney.'

Roisin fingered the rose-coloured piece of silk, her mind swirling as she studied the design, the low scoop neck, the short sleeves. Mrs Winchester had the figure to carry it off. A fine waist and broad shoulders for her narrow frame; however, she'd need a heavily boned corset to set it off to perfection.

When she looked up Mrs Winchester was standing at the window staring out to the street. 'I'd need the dress completed by next month for the Governor's Ball. Is that possible?'

A month, just a month. Could she do it? Of course she could, even if she had to sit up all night, every night.

A large sigh from the depths of the chair by the fire broke into her musings. 'Lady Alice?' She blinked. She'd ignored the woman, forgotten all about her. Been so taken with Mrs Winchester's request she'd daydreamed and overlooked a customer. 'Can I help you with anything?'

'No. Sadly, no.' Lady Alice's thin, humourless face lifted and disappointed eyes met hers, eyes that seemed as though they'd searched for something for so long their brightness had waned.

She'd taken off her bonnet and she sat picking at the ribbons as it rested in her lap. 'I have a dress for the ball. Besides, I could never hope to emulate Grace.' She gave a small derogatory laugh. 'I don't have the …' She sketched a wave in front of her chest. 'The necessary benefits to carry off something so, so revealing.'

For the first time Roisin studied the woman. Next to Mrs Winchester's sparkling assurance, Lady Alice appeared very dowdy, though there was nothing wrong with the quality and cut of her pelisse. It was the colour. The olive green of her walking-out coat was such a poor choice for her pallid skin and hazel eyes. If she introduced some additional colour through ribbon or even trimmings on her bonnet, her complexion would bloom. Nothing that couldn't be fixed with a little bit of artifice. She offered a small smile. 'That is not an insurmountable problem if you would allow me to make some suggestions.'

Lady Alice curled her lips in a polite, somewhat distant smile and pleated the dull ribbons on her bonnet, making no effort to respond. Roisin turned back to Mrs Winchester. 'You would also need certain undergarments to set this dress off to perfection.'

'Undergarments?'

'Yes. Specifically a corset.'

'I have corsets.'

'I would suggest that they would not be suitable for this dress. It will require a much smaller, briefer corset to complement the neckline and pinched waist.' She picked her words carefully, not wanting to cause offence and spoil this unexpected opportunity. How to explain that without the right undergarments the dress would not hang correctly and that she was more than capable of creating both.

She didn't have to.

'Well in that case, if you can make me one I shall have a new corset as well.' Mrs Winchester smoothed her hands over her hips, her eyes sparkling. 'I can't wait. Alice, what about you?'

'As I said, I have a dress for the ball, I had it made in Sydney.' She sighed again. 'I fear you will put me and every other woman to shame.'

'Oh, nonsense, Alice. You have a fine figure.'

'That is exactly the problem, Grace, under-developed, not fine.' She rolled her eyes, attempted a smile and then returned to picking at the now frayed ribbons.

The poor woman. She was not unattractive. Her hair was thick and her eyes were a pretty, flecked colour. It was simply the colours she'd chosen. Worse even than Mrs Blackmore's brown satin, and she at least had the physical attributes to set her dress off. That is what Lady Alice lacked. Her waist was tiny, otherwise she had the figure of a boy.

'Then we are organised. You have my measurements. My driver will deliver the material tomorrow.'

Roisin managed a nod of her head. If she opened her mouth she'd squeal or worse, fall to her knees and cover Mrs Winchester's hands in kisses. What a wonderful opportunity. In a swish of satin and rose water, the ladies departed. Roisin closed the door behind them and collapsed into the chair, clasping the illustration of Mr Worth's evening dress close to her heart as though her very life depended on it.

Ten

There wasn't another place on God's earth Carrick would rather be. He swirled the rum in the enamel mug and leant back against the chimneybreast, enjoying the simple pleasures of being free of the forest. The picture Roisin painted heated him more than the fire. Her body vibrated with excitement, her eyes flashing, her fingers never still.

'I don't know how you keep going. Is it not time for a rest?' The light had long since faded and she'd been at it all day.

'I have to. I have to for myself and for Ruan. And besides, this is such good fortune.'

'Can you be doing all this work alone?'

'I'm not alone. I have my pocket sewing machine, which makes it much faster. I could make you a shirt in about an hour, by hand it would take me a good day.'

'Next time I'm needing a fine suit of clothes I'll be remembering that.'

'Mrs Winchester is coming back for her fitting soon. Then I have just three weeks to have the dress cut and stitched.'

'Ready, as in finished. You'll never have it done.' He'd seen the pictures of the dress. It looked more complicated than anything he'd ever seen. All lacy bits and billowing skirts. Right now all she had was a pile of material sitting in her front parlour, pretty though it was. How it could become a ball gown didn't bear thinking about.

'I intend to. Maybe not all of the embellishments, just ready for Mrs Winchester to try on. I've almost finished sketching the pattern and tomorrow I'll cut the dress. I worry that the smell of food in the kitchen will taint the material. I have a little more stitching to do tonight, but I can't do it in here.'

'In that case I should be lighting the fire in the parlour.'

'Would you?'

He wiped a smudge of charcoal from her cheek.

'Have I got a dirty face? Charcoal makes such a mess.'

'You're spotless now. Perfect.' He tightened the shawl around her shoulders and then clasped her hands in his. 'You're cold. I'll go and light the fire.'

Carrick placed the first log on the fire and then another, moving the kindling aside so the air rushed in and made the flames leap and dance. It wasn't only desire she sparked in him, though there was more than enough of that to keep a man happy, it was a fierce protective urge. Deep down he had a need to see she lacked for nothing.

The chill of the small room would vanish in a moment once the blaze caught. It was a good job he'd kept up the supply of wood for her. This winter was one of the coldest he could remember. The rows of timber ran across the back of the woodshed, three or four deep. It'd be more than enough until he and Slinger got back. He'd not tolerate the thought of any of the local men working for her. He straightened up and turned.

She stood framed in the doorway, a gentle smile of gratitude on her face, reward enough for his paltry efforts. 'Thank you, Carrick, for all your help. It makes my life so much easier.'

She closed the door behind her and sat in the chair by the fire, reaching out her hands to the flames. 'It's colder here than in Sydney and if my hands are cold I find it difficult to sew.' She reached for the silky pool of material on the small table beside her, running her long, pliant fingers across it as she spread it on her lap.

The movement made him shudder and he dragged his eyes away. Instead, he made a show of feeding the fire, poking and prodding, all the while gazing at her out of the corner of his eye as she lifted the thread of silk and held the needle to the light, pulling it through the eye and picking the tiniest spot to insert the point. She caught him watching her and glanced up. 'Is it cold in the forest?'

'Not when we're working, the exertion heats us, and at night there's the fire, rum and exhaustion.' And thoughts of a girl with red-gold hair and the little lad who might have been his own. 'What are you sewing now? It's not the dress.'

Colour stained her cheeks as she eased the needle through the flimsy material and clasped it on her lap beneath her hands. 'Unmentionables.'

The murmured word caused him to sink to the floor at her feet. 'You can't mention it? Is it a secret?'

The sweet peal of her laughter sounded in the small room. 'Unmentionables. A lady's garment to be worn beneath her dress.' She dug the needle into the material then shook it out, her eyes sparkling. 'Promise you won't discuss this with your friends in the forest, or worse down at the inn? They'll think I'm a woman of ill repute and I'll be drummed out of town.'

He doubted anyone would drum her out of Wollombi. The locals were far too pleased with the attention her little business had brought from the Sydney ladies who spent their money in the local store when they came to call upon her.

She pinched the sides of the material between the fingers of both hands and held it high.

The dangling pair of drawers with their satin ribbons and lacy frills made him laugh aloud. 'Unmentionable perhaps but very pretty.'

'Mrs Winchester has ordered a set to match the corset I'm making her. They'll be trimmed with rose embroidery, the same colour as her dress.'

'And this is what these highfalutin ladies are coming here to buy? I imagined dresses, coats perhaps, or hats.'

'Those as well. Just because something isn't on display to the world there's no reason it shouldn't be pretty.'

Pretty they were, yet how much prettier with a body such as hers within them. He shook his head and stretched out his legs, attempting to banish the thoughts playing havoc with his peace of mind. 'Your stitching is very fine.'

She plucked at the silk pooled back in her lap. 'I'd like more lace. I've run out and it's very expensive to order from Sydney.'

'I'm sure the lady will be more than happy, and her husband, too, I don't doubt.'

That brought a delicious flush to her skin and she fanned her face. 'Enough of this talk. Tell me about the forest. I know nothing of it. Have you always worked as a cutter? What brought you to Australia?'

Surely she knew he'd come as a convict. Maisie or Elsie would have told her, along with all the rest of the blathering and blame the town lay at the cutters' feet. Some of it was justified, though he'd not be admitting that unless she pushed him.

'The one good thing the redcoats did for me. The soldier who threw me that first axe and set me chopping has my eternal gratitude. My hands took on a life of their own, as if they had always known how to wield the axe, how to cut the timber. Slinger and I worked the government cutter teams. When I got me ticket of leave I managed the team. By then the red gold was in me blood and even with me freedom I couldn't give it away.' He could have given it away if there had been a quicker or easier way to earn the money for his passage home. Still, it hadn't taken much more than three years and the job was all but done.

The flames jumped and hissed and he prodded a log aside with his foot and reached for another. Soon, soon he'd set foot on Irish soil and even the score. He scrubbed at his shoulder and settled back on the rag rug. Why spoil an evening such as this with dark thoughts and miserable memories?

She let the *unmentionables* fall to her lap and curved towards him, the light from the fire dancing in her hair. 'Australia is my home. I was born here. I can't imagine the thought of being sent away. Leaving Sydney was bad enough. You must long for your homeland, your family.'

'Aye.' He did long for his family, always would, though there was naught he could do about it. The English had taken care of that. 'I've almost enough for my passage home now.'

'You're leaving?'

As soon as he and Slinger had taken King Polai he'd be leaving. He didn't need Brinkworth to tell him the exact amount he had sitting in the Bank of New South Wales. Enough for his passage and enough to buy himself a fine horse and the information he'd need to track the bastard agent down.

'Soon enough. Slinger and I have one more job. It's as much a secret as those unmentionables you're stitching.'

She lowered her needle and tipped her head to one side.

'There's a tree deep in the forest. I've saved it till the last. King Polai. It's as straight and as tall as any I've ever seen. It'll pay more than my passage back to Ireland.'

Her face shadowed and she turned her gaze to the flames. 'When will you leave?'

'We'll be taking the boys to Morpeth and then we'll head off.'

'I shall miss you.'

His heart gave a stumble. Would she? Just the wood in the shed out the back or these quiet moments he'd always cherish?

'Will you return to Australia?' She lifted her head and pinned him with her eyes. Green as the grass of home, yet here in Australia, a million miles from the pain.

He shrugged; she'd asked him this before. Who knew what would happen once he returned to Ireland?

'Could you make your home here?'

Aye that would be the easiest thing in the world to do. And build her a little house down by the brook, maybe take a land grant and settle. A farm that would flourish, not like the miserly plot he'd once called home. No. The promise he'd made he'd fulfil, and then he'd look to the future, once he'd taken his revenge and the devil no longer prowled this earth.

The laughter slipped from his eyes as his defences lowered, and deep anguish scored his face. A face she'd come to know and heaven forbid, like, like a lot. She could love a man like this, a man with poetry in his soul and eyes as dark as the deepest ocean. As she gazed at him the lines she associated with laughter became lines of pain, of stress. The flash of his ravaged shoulder drifted across her mind and she picked up her sewing again. With her hands occupied she found it easier to talk. The man was such a mass of contradictions, soft one minute, as hard as rock the next. 'Tell me about your family in Ireland?'

He didn't answer, just stared into the flames, brooding, full of anger and turmoil, seeing something beyond her understanding. Her needle dipped and bobbed through the silk as she tacked the fine pleating into place, filling the silence, keeping her hands busy while her mind swirled. Perhaps she shouldn't ask about the past.

She was no better than Maisie and Elsie. To see the pain on his face made her want to soothe it away, and sometimes it helped to share.

He poured another mug of rum and lifted the flagon in an unspoken question. She shook her head, not wanting to speak, not wanting to break the fragile silence. He took a swig and rested back against her trunk, his long legs stretched in front of him towards the fire.

'They're long gone.' His jaws clenched as his teeth clamped, making his cheekbones stand out in the flickering shadows of the fire. 'It's a sorry tale, and of my own making. Had I not had my head in the clouds with thoughts of a better world my darlings would be with me today.'

'We all want a better world for those we love.' Wasn't that the very reason she'd left Sydney? So Ruan could run free, go to school and grow without the shadow of his conception hanging over him.

'It's the injustice of it all I couldn't stand, cannot stand.' He slammed his hand down on the floor, making the rum slop up over the brim of the mug, forming a damp spot on his thigh. His eyes flashed and every muscle stretched taut. 'The bloody English landlords bending the laws, hacking away at our lives and our land until we'd barely enough to scrape a living. Me rations on the convict ship were more than I was able to provide for Liam and Brigid.'

Liam and Brigid? Her fingers froze and her heart twisted tight. She dropped her sewing to her lap. 'Your family?'

'Me wife and darling boy they were.'

'I didn't know.' She moistened her lips, her throat tight with unshed tears, tears for this man who'd lost his child and tears for herself. She couldn't imagine … Her stomach clenched. If anything happened to Ruan, she couldn't live. He was her world.

She'd known from the very beginning the sadness in Carrick's eyes when he looked at Ruan held more than he admitted. And his easy familiarity, knowing what to say, how to make Ruan feel good about himself. Oh he'd make a wonderful father. Life was so unfair.

Why had he deserted his family? He didn't seem like a man who would leave his responsibilities. What crime had he committed? She needed to know. Besides, how could she let Ruan alone with the man if she didn't?

'It's the thought of what they must have suffered that still makes me sick to me stomach and breaks me heart.'

'Do you want to tell me? Sometimes it's better to share a sorrow.' Her duplicity twisted in her belly. Why was she asking—to ease his pain or reassure herself that Ruan wasn't in danger? Not for herself, she didn't care, but for Ruan. Oh, God, what if any harm came to Ruan because she'd let down her guard, because of the tall, handsome Irishman with a soul full of memories as black as his unruly hair?

He took another swig of his rum, his eyes still trained on the fire. 'It's a simple story. I wouldn't bow to the landlord's demands. He sent his agents to toss us out, we'd not paid the rent, no crops, no food. They'd come to get the women and children, take them to the Poor House. Some of us thought we could do better. Stop the bloody agent in his tracks. The bastard came with his band of henchmen.' His voice broke and the empty mug toppled from his numb fingers to the ground. 'I thought to waylay them. Kill the agent if necessary. Get rid of the pale-eyed sadist, except they were one step ahead of me, they'd brought dogs, the hounds of hell. We were no match. They set them on us. Like a bunch of scared rabbits, we were. Then when they'd had their sport they made us watch. Watch while the soddin' agent torched the thatch and my darlings burned.' Tears poured freely down his face, dropping to the floor.

She sank down on her knees and cradled his broad shoulders close, trying to ease the shudders racking his body.

'I will have vengeance. I owe them that. Raise a stone for my poor darlings. I'll seek him out, hunt him down. King Polai will give me the money for that. Then and only then can they rest in peace. I'll take his life the same way he took my darlings.' He put her away and stood, scrubbing his hands over his wet face, then picked up a log and threw it into the fire, sending a shower of sparks across the floor. He stamped out the smouldering remains and turned to the window, his shoulders shaking. 'Ignore me. 'Tis the rum speaking. A long-held grudge and nothing that should rest with you. I apologise.'

'Aren't we good enough friends now for you to know that if it has scarred you I carry your pain also?'

Her words didn't register; his eyes were fixed on some far-off place she couldn't reach. 'God says I should forgive.' His lip curled. 'I can't and I'll not. Not until I see the bastard in his grave.'

He picked up the flagon and tipped his head back, his throat moving as he poured down the remains of the rum. 'I'll be leaving.' He swayed, spreading his arm wide to steady himself against the wall, dwarfing the room with his big body and his misery.

She reached up and wiped his hair back from his face. 'Stay a while. I'll make some tea.' She eased him back into the chair, running her hand down his cheek, hoping to soothe his pain. He grasped her hand and pressed her palm to his lips. 'You're a good woman, Roisin. A good woman.' His hand fell limp to the arm of the chair and his eyes closed, his taut body relaxed at last. 'Victim of an unjust system, rioting and aggravated assault,' he murmured as his eyes closed.

Roisin tiptoed to the kitchen and placed the billy on the fire, then climbed the ladder to the attic to check on Ruan. He lay asleep on his side, the snakeskin draped across the blanket, breathing sweetly.

His wife and child. The Irish, Ireland, the Famine. She'd seen the Irish girls lining up outside the Sydney Barracks, riddled with tuberculosis and all manner of disease, their faces drawn and wan, their stick-like figures and sad, hollow eyes.

She lowered herself back down the ladder and dragged the quilt from her bed. She couldn't bear to think of Carrick alone in the crude tent down by the brook with no one for company except Slinger and the ghosts of his past.

By the time she returned to the parlour he was fast asleep. She tucked her quilt around him and picked up the long-forgotten corset and drawers. While she'd played and primped with silk and satin in the relative safety of Aunt Lil's and Madame de Lolle's, this man, the Irish, had suffered more than she could ever imagine—and Australia was the convict colony? She lay her sewing atop the trunk, doused the lamp and closed the door softly. Let him sleep in comfort by the fire before he set off again. How she'd miss the handsome Irishman when he left. He'd worked his way into her heart, into the fibre of her life. Ruan would not be the only one cut to the very quick when he departed.

Eleven

With little time for sleep, Roisin measured, cut and sewed in an anxious blur, her thoughts constantly returning to Carrick. When she'd woken the next morning he'd gone. The bullock dray had left and only the remnants of the fire remained at the campsite down by the brook.

With the aid of her sewing machine, she'd managed to finish the basic dress and today when Mrs Winchester arrived she'd check her measurements before she began the lace overskirt and embellishments. The undergarments, unmentionables—she grinned at the memory of Carrick's face and the twinkle in his eyes when she'd shown him the drawers—had come up a treat. If she hadn't known better he might have been imagining her dressed in them.

A flush of heat washed over her, doused by the memory of their conversation that followed. The horror of his story was more than she could imagine. She tried to force it to the back of her mind; however, in the long evenings while Ruan slept and she sewed, she couldn't help but remember the agony etched deep on his face, as much a scar as the brand on his shoulder.

She shook out the corset. Although as yet unadorned, it would provide Mrs Winchester with sufficient support to show the dress to its best advantage. If only she had some more lace; tatting had never been a skill she'd mastered.

The knock on the door came at nine-thirty sharp and she smoothed her skirt and answered it.

'Good morning, Mrs Winchester, Lady Alice.'

'Good morning, Roisin. I brought Lady Alice with me again as she is to be the first to witness your skill. We are beside ourselves with anticipation, are we not?' She turned to the dour Lady Alice, attired today in a vomit-coloured walking-out coat trimmed with a mustard-yellow stitching. Whoever was responsible for the lady's wardrobe deserved to be taken out and shot. Brushing her uncharitable thoughts aside, she led the way into the parlour.

Mrs Winchester scanned the room. 'Where is it? I'm agog. I simply can't wait.'

'Your dress is hanging behind the curtain. I must ask you to put it on. I can't make the final adjustments without seeing you in it. The corset is also there. I will draw the curtains across the window. Would you like me to lock the door?'

'That won't be necessary.'

Roisin busied herself at the window and Lady Alice dropped into the chair while Mrs Winchester disappeared behind the curtain.

Butterflies peaked and swooped in Roisin's stomach as she waited for the verdict.

'Are you ready for lacing?'

'I am.' Clad in a hooped petticoat, under-linen and the corset, Mrs Winchester stepped from behind the screen into the middle of the room, her eyes closed. 'Please, help me with the dress.'

As the rose silk slipped over her head Mrs Winchester shivered, and when the skirt pooled on the ground Lady Alice let out a gasp. 'It's exquisite. I had no idea you had such skill.' She beamed, her sallow face shiny. 'Would it be possible …? I wonder if you would have the time …'

Roisin's stomach sank. If Lady Alice asked her to make a dress, she'd have to refuse. Not only did she not have any suitable material, she simply hadn't the time. Even if she stayed up all night for the next week she'd never be able to get it finished.

Mrs Winchester smoothed her hands down her dress and stood on the low stool for Roisin to pin the hem. 'Now see what we have started. You will have a constant trail of ladies clamouring for your services.'

'I shall look like an under-stuffed duck,' Lady Alice mourned. 'My dress is nowhere near suitable to stand alongside you.'

How she hated to turn Lady Alice away. Creating a new dress was out of the question, but perhaps … 'I might be able to help you. If you call back tomorrow we could take a look at the dress you intend to wear. Perhaps a little nip and a tuck here and there could make all the difference.'

'And one of your magic corsets,' Mrs Winchester added, smoothing her hands over her hips and turning to show off her new silhouette.

Lady Alice's skin bloomed, an instant improvement. 'Could you?'

Roisin nodded, resisting the grin which wanted to creep across her face. If they only knew what she could do with a corset. Turn a duck into a peacock. Maybe that was the solution to Lady Alice's problems. Some discreet padding to soften her angular shape. An easy fix with some cleverly placed carded lamb's wool and a fichu of lace. 'As I said, there isn't the time to make a new dress, but I'm sure I could fashion a new corset for you. First tell me about your dress.'

Lady Alice's eyes brightened. 'It's a little difficult to describe, the colour is, well, the colour is unusual …'

Please, God let it not be vomit yellow. 'Would you be able to bring it in tomorrow?' She glanced at Mrs Winchester. 'Is that possible?'

'I have a previous engagement; however, I shall arrange for my driver to escort Lady Alice.'

Roisin knelt and pinned up the underskirt of Mrs Winchester's dress. 'I need to hem this for you and attach the overskirt. I could have it delivered as soon as I finish and then I'd be free to spend the next few days assisting Lady Alice.'

Happy with their morning, the two ladies left and Roisin slumped against the front door. Why had she agreed? She'd no idea except the poor woman was such a mouse she tugged at her heart, making her want to help.

She reached up and stretched, circling her neck, soothing her cramped muscles, which were stiff after the long hours of sewing the previous evening. It would have to be a very plain corset for Lady Alice because she'd just about run out of ribbons and lace. She must find the time to write to Aunt Lil and get some more sent. If only she could order another pair of hands at the same time. She certainly needed them.

Pulling the door closed behind her, she strolled into the General Store. Maybe Elsie still had some silks left and she could add some embroidery to Lady Alice's corset in place of lace.

'Elsie, I was wondering if you have any silks, or have I bought them all? Oh. I beg your pardon.' She stopped dead and clamped her hand over her mouth. Elsie hung over a frail woman, patting her back while she slumped on the chair mopping a bucketful of tears. 'I'm sorry, I'll come back later.' The woman sniffed and lifted her head. Roisin's breath caught. One side of her face was the colour of thunderclouds, bruises blossoming across her cheekbone and around her eye.

The woman shook her head. 'Don't go.' She wiped her hand across her nose. 'I've taken up enough of Elsie's time. I'll be on my way.'

'And where exactly are you going to go?' Elsie's look of outrage would have stopped a giant wombat in its tracks.

'Why, home of course.'

'Home for another beating.'

A light flashed in the woman's eyes as she tried to stretch her battered face into the semblance of a smile. 'Yes, home. That's the only good thing to come out of all of this. I have the place to myself. He's gone.'

'And good riddance, miserable sod. If you have any difficulties you come straight to me and we can see you right until you find some way of earning your keep. Go and have a word with Maisie.'

'I'll do that.' She stood, a little wobbly, but with her back straight and her head held high she made her way to the door.

'I apologise for taking your time. Goodbye.'

'Don't. I'm pleased to see the back of him. Good for nothing lout.' Elsie shook her head and tutted. 'Poor woman.'

There was no need for Roisin to ask any questions, she'd seen enough women sporting backhanders to recognise one, although the thought of it happening here, in Wollombi where she'd come to feel so sheltered, sent a shiver down her spine.

'She's well shot of him and lucky the house is hers to keep. Willed to her by her father. He can't touch that since he didn't bother to marry her.'

'What will she do?'

'Find herself a way of making some money. She hasn't any children to worry about. That's why I've sent her down to Maisie. See if she can use her. I'd have her here 'cept my Alfie wouldn't have a bar of it. Says we're not making enough as it is to keep another body.'

Roisin sank down onto the stool, her elbows resting on the counter, her mind turning over and over. Could she employ the woman? Maybe for a few hours. Mrs Winchester's dress would be paid for soon and then there was Lady Alice, and the money from Mrs Blackmore's bed linen and the last of the three makeovers.

A helping hand would give her more time, maybe not permanently, just for an hour here or there. Someone to set the fires, keep the parlour dusted and swept. She rubbed the ends of her fingers, easing the soreness from the use of the needle. 'I might be able to give her some work.'

Elsie's head snapped up. 'What kind of work?'

'Nothing much, a bit of cleaning and work around the house. I came in to tell you that I had to turn down a job for a dress because I hadn't the time to do it—for Lady Alice, Mrs Winchester's friend.' Probably better not to mention the corset. Some things should remain between a lady and her dressmaker.

'Oh, my dear.' Elsie threw her arms around her neck and enveloped her in an onion-flavoured hug. 'I'm so pleased. I knew you would make a go of this.'

'I might make a go of it, but not if I can't find the time to do the work I'm offered. Even Ruan being at school hasn't made a difference. There just aren't enough hours in the day, or the night. What do you think? Is the girl trustworthy? She'd be in the house and I have Ruan to consider. I don't want him to come to any harm.'

'Jane's a lovely girl. Lived in Wollombi all her life. Mother and father got one of the first grants here. When the smallpox took them and the two little ones she struck up with that no-hoper. I'll go and fetch her. It'll save Maisie having to say no. Maisie doesn't like that.'

'I don't know if I can afford to employ her full time, maybe just for an hour or so a day.'

'We'll see. We'll see. You stay here for a while and watch the store for me. Have a look in that box over there. I think there may be a few silks left. Not sure the colours will be right though. You've had all the delicate ones.'

Elsie untied her apron and threw it on the counter.

'Just before you go, Elsie. Can you tell me where I can get some carded fleece?'

'Fleece? You mean sheep's wool? Need to talk to Bob down at the wool store on the other side of the Millpond. What d'you want that for?'

'A little idea I have, that's all.' Elsie had no need to know what she intended to do with the fleece. It would be a secret she'd share only with Lady Alice.

'That all?' Elsie patted down her misshapen curls and adjusted her mob-cap.

'Yes that's all, thank you.'

'Back in a jiffy. You have a gander at them silks.'

The box of Indian silks was nearly empty and the only colours left were bright reds, a black and a blue, the colour of the feathers on a kookaburra's wing. She lifted them out of the box and took them to the door where the light was better. For the kind of work she'd done in Sydney these colours would be perfect. Somehow she couldn't see them suiting the mousey Lady Alice.

Maybe matched with a little lace—if she had some. So frustrating. Opportunities slipping through her fingers. Time. She needed time. Perhaps she could unpick something from one of her own corsets. It would need to match Lady Alice's dress and she wouldn't know until tomorrow what that would be. She'd need the padding without a doubt. Some carded lamb's wool. From Bob at the wool store, Elsie had said.

'Find what you wanted?'

'Elsie, I'm not sure. Possibly. May I take these and let you know tomorrow?'

'Of course, of course. You earned your favour. You've made Jane very happy. She's gone home to change and clean herself up and she'll be back to see you after dinner.'

'I hope I won't disappoint her.'

'You won't. You need to have a bit more faith in yourself, young lady. With customers the likes of the Winchesters and their friends you're going to be in great demand. Only right and proper you should have a bit of help. And Jane's handy with a needle, too.'

With Elsie's words ringing in her ears Roisin went back home. She lifted the lid of the trunk and emptied out every scrap of material, lace, buttons and ribbons she could find and lay them out on the table, grouping them in colours. Creams through to yellows and oranges. Then the deep, deep red of plums to morning sunrises and blues through to the green she loved so much.

Her charcoal flew over the paper as she sketched a corset set with ribbon and pearl buttons. Oh how she needed to see Lady Alice's dress. Why hadn't she asked more about it? The colour was all-important, and the neckline. Her mind was such a mess of ideas, jumbled like the contents of the trunk.

When a knock sounded on the door she straightened her back and stretched. 'Come in. It's open.'

A straw bonnet appeared around the door. 'It's Jane, Mrs Ogilvie. Elsie said I should come and see you after dinner.'

Was it really after dinner? How much time had she wasted sitting here with her knick-knacks and charcoal? She was as bad as Ruan and his treasure box. 'Come in, Jane.' She stood up and gestured at the table. 'I'm sorry about the mess, I've been trying to sort out my materials. I'm running low.'

Jane drifted to the table, her eyes set on the display in front of her. She reached out a tentative hand and smoothed it over a tiny piece of silk lace. 'Oh, this is lovely.' She picked it up and turned it over. 'See how carefully the tatting has been finished. Did you make this?'

'Me?' How she wished. 'No. I bought it in Sydney.'

Jane placed it back on the table with a reverence. 'And this one, see? I like the cotton lace. It looks so very pretty on a blouse, around the neck. Nice and fresh like.'

A stillness came over Roisin as Jane edged around the table, her fingers touching and smoothing, her breath a gentle sigh when she picked up something she liked.

'Jane? Do you know about these materials?'

'Me? No, Miss I've never seen the likes of these ribbons. Mémé, my grandmother, she was French, she taught me the tatting. I never had the time to do much. My pa thought it a waste of time. All right for a lady's pastime, not for the likes of me. I'm sorry, Miss. I'm wasting your time. Elsie said you might have some work for me. I can turn my hand to most things. Cooking. Cleaning. I like gardening, too, me mam said I've got green fingers, and I could keep an eye on the boy.'

'I'll be honest with you, Jane. I won't be able to pay you very much and I don't know how much work I'll need done. It depends on my business and how many orders I have. How busy I am.'

'Yes, I know, Miss. Elsie told me. I'd love to work for you. Better than the pub, and besides, Maisie didn't really want me. Just helping me out because she knew me mam. God rest her soul.' Jane crossed herself. 'And I won't be takin' no charity. I'll earn me keep.'

Roisin found herself taking to the girl. She seemed so free of artifice. She liked her. 'How about we make a deal. Start tomorrow morning. Come early because I have an appointment at nine and I'll show you around.'

'I could stay now, Miss, if you're busy. I haven't anything else to do with Mick gone.'

'Mick? Your husband?'

'As good as, Miss. And between you and me, good riddance.' Her eyes flashed again and she fingered the bruise on her face, her defiance endearing. 'He reckons there's money in the goldfields. Been talking to that Mr Hargreaves. He's gone off and I don't expect to see him back. He went, taking everything with him. Would have taken the house, too if he could've picked it up and carried it.'

'In that case why not stay. I haven't had anything to eat. There's some soup on the stove and a cup of tea would help.'

Sitting in the parlour with the winter sun streaming in the window and the fire glowing in the grate, Roisin let out a sigh of pleasure and took the remaining pins out of the hem of Mrs Winchester's dress. She stood and shook it out, pleased with the result, then hung it in the corner of the room.

'Oh, Miss, that's just lovely.' Jane appeared at the door with a pot of tea and a plate of biscuits. 'I thought you could be doing with a cup of tea. You've been sitting here all afternoon.'

'It's time you went home, Jane. I'm sorry I forgot the time. Ruan will be home soon and …'

'He's already home, Miss. He helped me make the biscuits. He's in the kitchen practising his letters.' Roisin peered out of the window; the sun hung low in the red-tinted sky. How had the time flown by so quickly?

'I've peeled some potatoes and put the bones in with some carrots and onions. You didn't have any.' Jane flushed. 'I nipped back to my garden and brought them from there. Mick took what was in the store but not the things still in the ground. Doesn't like to get his hands dirty. Don't know how he'll manage digging for gold.'

'Jane, you're a godsend.'

'You sit down, Miss, and drink your tea. I also brought something else from home to show you. May I get it?' She set the tray down on the table and poured a cup of tea.

Mystified, Roisin nodded.

'Drink your tea now. I'll be back in a moment.'

Stretching out her legs, Roisin sighed as she sipped at the tea. With Jane's help, she would definitely be able to assist Lady Alice.

If the dress had promise she could do some alterations, and with the help of a corset, improve her stooped figure. The memory of Aunt Lil's girls rose, bringing a smile to her lips. It would be fun to turn the little mouse into a princess. Poor woman. It had been a day for little mice. Jane was nothing like the girl she'd seen this morning. Fate had a strange way of delivering when she least expected it.

At the knock on the door she lifted her head. 'Jane there's no need to knock. Just come in. I have nothing to hide.'

With a black metal box clasped in her hands, Jane approached. 'This belonged to Mémé. I thought maybe you could use some of it for the time being like. I heard what you said to Elsie in the shop about not havin' the colours and things.' She knelt down on the floor and with a caring reverence opened the tin. A cloud of lavender drifted out. Jane waved it away. 'I put the lavender in to keep the bugs out. I was saving it for my glory box. Mick didn't hold with that kind of nonsense. Said there was no point us getting dressed up just to stand in front of Father Benson. Weddings was for rich folk. I'm glad Mémé wasn't alive to hear him say that, she'd worked for years on this.'

Length after length of lace appeared from the tin, creams and whites and the prettiest pale pink of new rose buds.

'Your Mémé made all of this?'

'Not just her. I've added to it over the years. A way to keep her memory fresh in me mind like.'

Roisin ran her fingers over a length the lace. 'You made this?'

Jane nodded, a flush rising to her cheeks. 'I'd not be lying to you, Miss.'

'It's not that I think you're lying. It's delightful. You're very talented. In Sydney people would pay a lot of money for work like this.'

'Oh no, Miss. It's not something I do for money. I just like to keep me hands busy in the evenings.'

Roisin placed the lace back in its tin bed and sat back in the chair.

Jane's flushed face peered at her. 'You don't have to use it, Miss I just thought … I just thought maybe … I'm sorry, Miss.'

The girl tore at her heartstrings. Roisin moved closer to her and lifted her hand. Jane flinched and a rush of pity swept over her. She knew that movement, knew it only too well. Something her mother had done after the beatings she'd received from perverted, drunken patrons. If it hadn't been for Aunt Lil taking her under her wing she might have ended up in the same position, flat on her back.

'Sit up here. I want to talk to you.'

Jane rose from the floor, her eyes wide and perched on the edge of the trunk. 'I have a proposition to put to you, Jane—about the job.'

'I don't need much. I'd be prepared to work for just me meals until you make a bit of money from your customers. I'd count it an honour to …' She wrung her hands together, creasing the linen of her embroidered apron.

'Jane, stop and listen to me.'

The girl bowed her head and clasped her hands tight, the whites of her knuckles showing in the firelight.

'I want you to work for me. Not just cleaning and cooking. I'd like us to work together. We can both handle the household chores and then I'd like to pay you for some of this lace or any more that you would like to make. It might take a little time, but I'm certain we can make a decent business of it.'

'Making dresses, Miss, for the ladies?'

'Yes, dresses. Not just dresses, Jane. Undergarments. Ladies' unmentionables.'

If Jane's eyes were wide before they now almost popped out of her head and her face took on a glow that challenged the fire. She cleared her throat. 'I beg your pardon, Miss?'

'I need to explain something to you, something I'd ask you to keep to yourself. I've told no one else in Wollombi. I haven't been entirely honest.'

'You've lied, Miss?' Jane's face fell as though in that moment Roisin had toppled from some pedestal. A pedestal she had no right to be balancing on.

'Jane, when I lived in Sydney I worked for someone called Madame de Lolle. She trained me to all intents and purposes. She was a dressmaker and milliner and had a shop. She also had a sideline that was far more profitable and much to my amazement, I believe there could be a market for it here in Wollombi. She made corsets and drawers and chemises, ladies' undergarments. Not just functional, also pretty things.'

Jane's eyes lit up as she stifled a giggle behind her hand. 'Their husbands would like that.'

'Not only their husbands. Some of the ladies didn't have husbands, they had another occupation.'

Jane's eyes widened again. 'You mean working ladies.'

'Yes. I mean working ladies.'

'There's none of those in Wollombi. Not since the girls went.'

'No, Jane there aren't; however, there are tricks I learned which many women would benefit from. Take the lady who was here this morning.'

'Lady Alice.'

'We don't mention names, never names when we're discussing undergarments, unmentionables. This lady is disappointed that she doesn't have the figure of, say, Mrs Winchester. The tiny waist, the bosom. To be honest she's more plank than hour glass.'

Jane let out a titter. 'She is, too.'

'I had to tell her I didn't have the time to make her a new dress. I said that if she came back tomorrow I could make her old one a better fit. I intend to make a corset to highlight and add to her attributes. Look at this.' Roisin opened the trunk and withdrew the sample she'd saved, buried deep where no one would see it. A kingfisher-blue silk corset offset with black lace and ribbons.

'Oh, Miss!'

'Jane!' Roisin whipped around. 'I can't stand it a moment longer. Please call me Roisin. If we're to be in business together it's to be a partnership.'

'Yes, Miss. Roisin.'

'Just Roisin. Try it again.'

'Roisin.' Jane's lips quirked in a smile. The girl really was quite pretty and once that bruise faded from her face and she got some life back into her she'd be a force to be reckoned with. Roisin turned back to the trunk and held the corset up against her body.

'I love it. Look at *this* piece. I've never seen coloured lace like this.'

'We used to buy the dyes. I can send to Sydney for some. They're expensive, but they might be worth it once business picks up and I have some spare cash.'

'We don't need to send to Sydney. I can make you dyes that colour.'

'Blue, like this, Jane?'

'Yes, it's easy. We'll have to trial a few and it depends on the fabric. Dandelions will give us yellow and we mix it with eucalyptus leaves from the blue gums down by the river and we'll find a greenish blue.'

'Is there no end to your knowledge? I can see you're beginning to get the idea.'

Jane clutched her hands to her chest, her eyes sparkling. 'I am. I am indeed. We could match the lace on the dress to the drawers, corset and petticoat. I reckon we could do anything.'

Twelve

As the sun breached the hills the cutters clambered back aboard the bullock cart. A different cargo for the docks this time. No timber, just men, the men Carrick had worked side by side and shoulder to shoulder with for the last two years. Though he'd be the last to admit it, he'd miss them and their rum-soaked antics. They deserved the send-off, though the town of Morpeth would take a week or two to recover. The cutters had drunk the place dry and got their money's worth.

He stood on the wharf as the steamer slipped out into the Hunter River. The voices of the cutters echoed across the water and the strains of Slinger's fiddle drifted mournfully in the night air as he serenaded them. Jojo and Blue responded in kind, their spoons clattering in a frantic rhythm against the hull of the ship. It would be a noisy and boisterous trip for the passengers who had the misfortune of travelling to Sydney with the cutters.

As the steamer rounded the bend and disappeared from sight, Slinger tucked away his fiddle. 'That's them sorted. Perhaps I'll join them later on. I like the company. First, we've got business.' He dusted off his hands, determination blazing in his eyes.

'We'll leave once it's dark. I don't want anyone questioning our plans. There'll be enough moon tonight to light the way. Go in, have a quick look, then back to Wollombi to pick up the gear and some supplies.' And the chance to see Roisin, and the lad, one more time before he headed back to Ireland.

Slinger and Carrick saw no one in the hours after they left the Maitland road. They made swift progress on horseback, without the bullock dray, and when the bush closed in and the hairs on Carrick's arms bristled, he knew they were close. The trees thickened and they muscled their way through the scrub, not wanting to hack at the branches and leave a path. With any luck they'd pick up a wallaby trail and it would be clearer. He reached up and the branch above him leapt away. His heart as good as stopped stone dead, then he laughed. 'Billy Boy what're you doing here?'

'Worried you might get lost, boss. Old Pella tell me you come.'

Slinger snorted, his hand slipping to his knife. 'And how would he know?'

'We hear you, Slinger. Giant wombats in the bush.'

Slinger growled deep in his throat and Carrick elbowed between the two men. 'Back off, Slinger. He's not out to hurt us.'

'I know that. It's them I'm going to hurt.'

'Cut it out.'

Billy Boy tossed his head and waved his spear in a good-humoured threat. 'Camp's up ahead. Old Pella there. He wants talk.' He threw Slinger a wide grin and took off ahead of them.

'I suppose we're going to have to get their say-so, are we? Think they own the bloody country.'

'Slinger, stop, now. You wait here. Make camp for the night.'

Billy appeared from nowhere. 'Not here. Up there.' He pointed to the caves dotting the sandstone cliff face. 'Hide the fire.'

'He's right.'

Slinger growled again and curled his lip. 'Thought it was you and me.'

'It is …' A black hand came down, covering Carrick's mouth and Billy shook his head, then lifted his hand and gestured for them to follow.

He led them through the fissure between two huge rocks, the walls of the narrow path littered with drawings of stick figures and handprints. The sun disappeared and the world became contained in the small space; even the ever-present birdsong of the bush vanished.

When they reached the top the path opened out into a wide-mouthed, low-roofed cave. Carrick tethered his horse, loosened the girth and unstrapped the saddle before making his way to the small fire burning in the centre of the sandy floor space.

'G'day, Old Pella.' Carrick inclined his head to the huddled figure wrapped in his possum blanket by the fire, and dropped his gear. The old man's eyes looked hollow with the skin drawn sharp across his cheekbones, although the gash on his head from the Paterson cutter had healed well.

'There's white men.'

What white men? Had someone beaten him to it? 'Cutters? Taking my tree?'

'Not cutters. Men walking, long steps. Digging up dirt. Disturbing.'

Not cutters. Surveyors by the sound of it. Rumour had it the land through the Yarramalong had come up. Surely he hadn't left it too late. 'We'll go and have a look.'

'Billy Boy take you tomorrow.' The old man dropped his head back onto his blanket and concentrated on the fire.

Carrick reached out and touched his shoulder. He didn't raise his head. 'You okay, Old Pella?'

'Old Pella good. What about the girl?'

'Roisin?'

The old man grunted and lifted his head. 'Who's caring for her?'

'She's good. Plenty of wood and lots of work.'

'Old Pella's goin' back tomorrow. He'll look out. Sleep now.' The old man dropped his head onto his arms and ended the conversation.

Carrick unrolled the canvas square strapped to his saddle and spread it out beside the fire. Slinger chucked his down beside him and opened the pocket on the side. 'I've hobbled the horses and I've got some rum. What've we got to eat?'

'Cold mutton, what else?'

Slinger snorted and took a swig of his rum. 'I'll stick with this.'

'I want to be out of here at sun up so go easy. Big day tomorrow.'

'I'll believe that when I see it.'

'You'll believe me, Slinger. You'll believe me.' Though if Old Pella was right and someone was scouting around they mightn't be doing a lot of cutting. 'We'll leave the gear here in the caves with the horses and go have a look-see.'

At first light they battled the heavy undergrowth again; above them the sky was barely visible. Down they went clambering, slithering and sliding until Billy Boy held up his hand and gestured to his ear.

Carrick stopped, picking out the trickle of water over rocks and in the distance a ray of light shining down, illuminating a small area of the forest floor.

'It's down there.' He shoved past Billy Boy, his blood surging with the thrill of the hunt. Slinger scrambled across the rocks and through the undergrowth, his curses peppering the air.

He could see it now, just the way Old Pella had shown him the first time. Tall and strong, dwarfing everything around it. Reaching for the sky. It would take twenty men, arms outstretched, to encircle the magnificent old tree. For a moment his heart sank. What right had he to bring down such majesty?

'What's your problem, Carrick? Looks like you've lost a quid and found sixpence.'

'It's grand. Perfect.' He gazed up in awe at the magnificent tree.

'If you don't take it someone else will.'

Slinger was right and now he'd paid off the team of cutters he needed the cash the tree would bring, needed it if he was going back to Ireland with money in his pocket. This time he'd do it right. Not the poor tenant farmer. Talking to Roisin had brought back the anger, anger he'd buried for so long he'd forgotten how brightly it burned. It was back now, fierce as ever, fuelled by the compassion in Roisin's eyes and the touch of the lad's hand in his.

Together he and Slinger ran their hands over the rough bark, tilting their heads back, staring up at the patches of blue sky barely visible through the entangled canopy of creepers and vines.

'It's the last one, Slinger. The last one for me. After this no more. I'm done with the cutting.'

'Keep your promises till she's down.'

'You'll take nothing down.' The words cut through the silence like a gunshot. 'Land's been granted. On your way.'

A scrawny man, his faced seamed by the years and weather, stood his ground, although his feet shifted in the leaf litter, his eyes sliding from side to side as if waiting for something, someone.

Carrick picked up the sound of scuffed undergrowth and then it was gone. He tossed a glance over his shoulder, locked eyes with Slinger and frowned. Slinger inclined his head in the direction of the creek and from the corner of his eye Carrick caught a woollen-clad arm and gloved hand holding a pistol, barely discernible through the trees. Not Billy Boy or Old Pella. Not any native wearing a jacket made of wool. Old Pella's white men sure enough.

The man sniffed the air, peered around and then his shoulders dropped, looking for all the world as though he was taking a stroll in the park. 'So you'll be on your way?'

Not a chance, not until he knew what was going on. 'You say the land's granted?'

'What business is it of yours?'

'Just curiosity. So we know to stay away.' Until the men moved on and then he and Slinger would be in and out so fast the idiot wouldn't know what had hit him.

'What're you doing here?'

'A bit of cutting up around the area.'

'Not anymore. Not this part—thousand acres all told. From the edge of the Wyong River right through the Yarramalong Valley floor and up to the rise.' He gestured to the hills framing the valley. 'No more cutting. I'm overseeing the property.' His bark of sharp, derogatory laughter echoed in the valley and faded until only the sounds of the birds and the rustle of the wind remained.

'Who's bought the land?'

'What's it to you?'

'Just curious. It's good land, especially with the river. Not much timber on it though.'

'Which is why you'll not be cutting this bugger down.'

'We'll be on our way, then.' Carrick turned, grabbed the sleeve of Slinger's chequered shirt and towed him down the track.

'What's the matter with you? Losing your nerve? We could've done with him and no one would be any the wiser. Taken the tree before they even knew he was missing.'

'Think, Slinger. Think and look around. There's two horses tethered over there, saddled. So there's another man around. Not a lot of gear. They're not planning on being here for long.' As usual Old Pella was right. How the man managed to know what was going on, or even travel so far, he'd never understand.

Slinger curled his lip. 'And you're telling me we couldn't take out two men?'

'Not when one of them has a gun trained on our backs.' And he had no intention of ending up behind bars. He was going home, back to Ireland. Behind bars after that maybe, though not before he'd done what he intended.

Slinger whipped around and froze as the barrel of the shotgun caught in the shaft of sunlight.

'Come on. Let's go. It's not a problem. Let them think we've gone. Billy Boy and Old Pella'll let us know when these fools have left and we can be in and out before they have time to do anything about it.'

They edged up the track.

'What d'you reckon they're up to?'

'Just like Old Pella said, someone's bought the land and they're marking it out, making it their own. You heard the bloke, he's the overseer.'

'Then who's the idiot with the gun? If they've got nothing to hide then what're they so tetchy about?'

'City folk want it all for themselves. This is my tree and I'll be havin' it. I've waited too long for this one.'

'She's a big bugger. How long do you reckon it'll take us to get it down?'

'Believe me now, do you?'

Slinger grunted. 'We'll get it down quick enough, a week, bit more maybe. It's the sawing'll take time unless we get some help.'

'I'm not for getting help. I reckon we go back to Wollombi, pick up the rest of our gear and some supplies, then come back in. Those two'll be gone by then. They're not cutters, they won't touch it, and we can get to it.'

'And when they come back and find the tree gone?'

'We'll be gone. You're going north and I'll be on my way to Sydney for a boat to take me home.'

'Might be easier just to put a bullet in them and bury them.'

'No, it wouldn't, you fool. Someone knows they're here and I for one have no intention of swinging. Not before I make it home. We'll go back to Wollombi, wait it out for a few days then come back and take another look, make sure they've gone before we bring the gear in.'

Roisin hurried down the street from the school, calling a morning greeting here and there and waving to some of the children as they headed for the school gate. People acknowledged her, glancing in her direction, nodding as she passed, greeting her by name as though she belonged in the town. It gave her a feeling of security and pride to be recognised as the local dressmaker.

And Jane, what a godsend. What luck to find someone with such skill. Quite why Jane hadn't set up her own business, Roisin had no idea. If Sydney had so many women running businesses then why couldn't Wollombi? Maisie and Elsie ran the inn and the General Store. With Jane's help she could imagine a whole emporium selling haberdashery, small items, buttons and silk, lace and bolts of material. And those wonderful ladies' fashion papers Mrs Winchester had shown her, available for people to browse through. Then the orders would come flooding in. She might even have to expand further. For the time being though she intended to concentrate on the business in hand. Mrs Winchester's evening dress was without a doubt her finest achievement. And now to make Lady Alice happy.

She ducked around the back of the street, running alongside the school, and knocked on the door of the storehouse. After a moment or two the heavy wooden doors swung open, bringing the stench of lanolin and wet fleece.

'Good morning.'

'Morning. What can I do for you?' A red-faced man with a purple nose, thick shoulders and a short bull-like neck, lumbered from behind a tower of baled fleece.

'Elsie, Mrs Sullivan, said if I called in you might be able to sell me some fleece.'

'Earmarked for Sydney. All baled and ready.' He sucked on his pipe, adding a whiff of damp tobacco to the already pungent air.

'Would you have any offcuts I could purchase?'

'Offcuts? Dags, you mean?'

'I need a small amount of fleece for a project I'm working on.' No need to go into explicit detail. It wasn't something a man, any man, needed to know about.

He sighed and sent a cloud of smoke wreathing around her face. 'Only the cleanings there.' He tossed his head at a stinking pile in the corner of the room. 'Help yourself.'

'I'll pay you for it.'

'We could sort it another way.' He took a step closer to her, the stench of tobacco, sweat and wet sheep making her gorge rise. 'I'll call in one afternoon after I finish up here.'

Call in. What was he talking about? Roisin bent down and picked through the smelly pile of offcuts, gathering several handfuls. 'I'd like this please.'

'It's all yours.'

She slipped the fleece inside the bag she carried over her arm. 'Please let me give you something for it.'

'Nah.' He sniffed. 'Now Carrick and his cutters have gone, you'll be a bit lonely like. Can't be having that.' He sucked on his pipe and sent a cloud of smoke swirling around her face, then reached out his hand.

She stepped back. What was he thinking? 'Let me pay you for it.' She shuddered, produced a shilling from her pocket and extended her gloved hand.

'Cheap at 'arf the price.' He wiped his hand over his nose and gave her a lecherous wink.

Surely the man didn't think … 'Well, thank you. Thank you very much.'

He grunted and sucked on his pipe again. 'What time do you open, then?'

'Open?'

'Open for business of a night time?'

'How dare you!' She turned on her heel and bolted down the street, her stomach twisting and her bag at arm's length to avoid inhaling the foul-smelling fleece and the equally foul insinuations the horrid man had made.

As soon as Roisin rounded the corner, Jane dropped her broom and came running into the street.

'Oh, Jane, I'm so pleased you're here. We have to talk. The most awful thing has just happened.' Nothing could be more important than the dreadful, smelly man in the wool store.

'Lady Alice is here already.'

'She's earlier than I expected.' Would nothing go right today?

'I think she's very keen. She was a little annoyed you weren't at home when she called. I've given her a cup of tea and she's waiting, tapping her foot and sighing.'

Roisin eased the pins from her hat and slipped her gloves off as she made her way along the flagstone path. She'd have to tread very carefully. Grace Winchester was lucky to have been granted such a perfect figure, and although she was sure she could help

Lady Alice, she wasn't sure how far she could push her. What would she say when she suggested padding her bosom?

Sucking in a deep breath, she shrugged out of her jacket and closed the door behind her blessing Carrick and the never-ending woodpile that kept the house cosy. Lady Alice sat perched in front of the fire, her fingers fiddling with the handles of the carpetbag resting in her lap. Her dress no doubt.

Dear God, please let the dress be a better colour than her other clothes. She could adjust it, remake it, just not change the colour, no matter what ideas Jane might have about dyeing lace with garden vegetables. And no amount of discreet padding would help.

'Good morning, Lady Alice. I'm sorry to have kept you waiting, I had to take my son to school.'

'Your son. How delightful, I didn't know you had a son.'

'He's a bit of a handful sometimes, but I wouldn't part with him for the world. You know what children are like.'

'Sadly, I don't. The good lord hasn't seen fit to bless me with children. I sometimes think I have left it all too late. I was hopeful the change in climate, the sea journey …' She lifted her shoulders then let them drop with a resigned sigh. 'I was hopeful that the country air might make a difference. It doesn't seem to be the case. I'm sorry, it is not something I should bore you with.'

Roisin set her hat on the table, then smoothed her hair. She could feel Lady Alice's gaze burning a hole in her back so she turned with a bright smile. The woman needed a large dose of confidence and she intended to provide it.

'The truth is I'm not attractive to my husband. I do not seem to have the vivacity that Grace has.' Lady Alice delved into her carpetbag and produced a bundle wrapped in an Indian silk shawl.

Roisin reached out and took the bundle from Lady Alice's lap. 'Why don't you show me your dress?'

'I can never compete with Grace, she is so ...' Her face flushed and she gestured helplessly.

Roisin lifted the bundle to the table. If the dress had something to recommend it she could work with that. Otherwise, she'd no idea what she'd do.

'I had the dress made in Sydney. I feel I have made a mistake. It is not a colour I'd normally wear.'

Roisin's heart sank. It would be another disaster. Just how many overskirts and embellishments could she attach to an evening dress? She unwrapped the shawl and gasped.

'You see what I mean. I fear I have been led astray.'

'Lady Alice, not at all.' She shook out the teal-coloured silk. 'It's delightful.' This she could work with. The colour was brilliant, like a peacock's tail. The scooped neck and the short sleeves were perfect. The ruching across the front had obviously been inserted to draw the eye away from Lady Alice's minute attributes.

'It seems wonderful in your hands, put me inside it and it is transformed into a brightly coloured sack more suitable for vegetables. I was swayed because it reminded me of home.'

'Not at all, not at all. I can help you.' And she could. A surge of anticipation traced her skin. She could do this and send another satisfied customer on her way.

'Would you be kind enough to step behind the curtain and slip it on? If you have any difficulties with the lacings I can call Jane to assist you.'

Roisin hid her smile. What a wonderful addition Jane made to the business. Her mind flashed back once more to the turbulent days at Maison Français. The laughing girls, the thrills and the fun. That was what Lady Alice needed. She'd turn this poor little brown mouse into a swan and let her sail forth and win her husband's affections. She rubbed her hands together. It was a challenge, but one she could rise to and the prospect left a satisfied glow inside her.

'Jane.'

'Yes, Miss.' She'd never cure Jane of her deference.

'Would you please assist Lady Alice? We have work to do.'

While Jane and Lady Alice disappeared behind the curtain, Roisin buried her head in her trunk, rummaging until she found a kingfisher-blue silk corset and a more decorous plain cream one. Both would be too large for Lady Alice; however, they would explain her thoughts. The black and red one she tucked back to the bottom, out of sight.

When Lady Alice appeared from behind the screen with her eyes downcast, clasping the skirt in her bunched fists, Roisin took a deep breath. 'Please relax. Drop your hands and stand still. I have to make a few tucks and pleats.' She tightened the dress around the waist and loosened the laces across the back of the shoulders, making the neckline gape painfully at the front.

'Oh no! That is just making matters worse.' Lady Alice wrenched away, clasping the yawning material to her scrawny chest.

'Please, trust me. Now turn to me. The carriage of your head is excellent; however, a little more padding here might …' She wisped her hand across Lady Alice's chest. 'Your waist is exquisitely slender, with a bit of artifice we can assure the décolletage will be all you would wish for.'

'I'd prefer a more flowing line and not too colourful, a grey perhaps, with the smallest amount of trimming.'

'No, no. The colour is perfect, it brings out the highlights in your eyes and flatters your complexion. I want you to stand very still, close your eyes and promise me you will not open them until I say so.'

Jane frowned at her and Roisin shook her head. All she needed was a moment or two and a large amount of trust. She dragged various remnants and offcuts of silk from the trunk. She'd much rather use the fleece, but the rotten stench still clung to her nostrils and to ask Lady Alice to put it against her skin would simply be too much. Balling the silk, she slipped it down the front of the dress and moulded it to the gaping fabric. Then she spun Lady Alice around and laced the back of the dress as tightly as she could. 'Don't open your eyes, not yet. Jane, can you fetch the glass please. Now before you look, Lady Alice I have to ask you to trust me and use your imagination.'

'My imagination is running riot. I have no idea what is going on, I feel like a stuffed Christmas goose.' Lady Alice smothered a giggle, the first Roisin had heard from her, and flashed her eyes open. Her cheeks pinked as she gazed in the mirror. 'Oh my dear.' A tear trickled down her cheek. 'I have bosoms.' She turned this way and that then threw her shoulders back. 'Big bosoms!' Her shrill laugh tinkled, filling the little room. 'You have worked a miracle.'

'Not a miracle, simply a bit of padding. Now this is very rough and doesn't fit you at all well. Given a bit of time I can make a corset that will fit you perfectly, and believe me, no one will know where the padding ends and you begin.'

Lady Alice ran her hands down to her waist. 'I'm a little lumpy.'

'You won't be. I have some fleece, which we'll insert in the corset. The dress is perfect and so are you.'

'Not perfect. A definite improvement.' The smile still hovered on her face and she stretched onto her toes, turning in front of the mirror.

'It's imperative that you stand tall and throw your shoulders back.'

'You sound like my governess. Please don't tell me she was right all along.'

Roisin's lips twitched and she slid her hand under Lady Alice's chin. 'It's all about your stance and the manner in which you hold your head.'

'An illusion.'

'Yes, I think you could say that.'

Lady Alice giggled again. 'My corset. Would it be possible to make it the same colour as the dress? I love this colour. It is like the wings on the ducks in the ponds in Ireland. Mallard ducks. It reminded me so much of home, I'm sure that is why I was drawn to it.'

'It's the perfect colour for your complexion.' Roisin unfolded the peacock-coloured corset and held it up. 'Something like this is what I have in mind?'

'Oh!' A dreamy look crossed Lady Alice's face as she ran her fingers over the pleated silk. 'It is simply …' She frowned. 'How long will it take? I have only a few days before we return to Sydney.'

'Jane and I will work on it and I believe we can have it ready for you in two days.'

Jane stared at her, eyebrows raised and Roisin flashed her eyes in warning. Yes, it would be hard work, but they could do it. She reached for a length of Jane's lace. 'We'll run two rows of lace here and it will sit proud and add to the effect. I'll need to take a few more precise measurements, if you can spare the time.'

'Of course, of course. I have all the time in the world.' Lady Alice grasped hold of the mirror, a secret smile lighting her eyes.

Wouldn't Lady Alice's husband be in for a surprise?

Thirteen

The time flew as Lady Alice's corset began to take shape and the final lace overskirt was sewn onto Mrs Winchester's dress. Without Jane's fine stitching and patient perfectionism Roisin would never have managed to complete anything. Poor Ruan, however, was left increasingly to his own devices, foraging in the garden, collecting treasures, attending school.

'Ruan, where are you?' Roisin peered through the kitchen window into the yard, then spotted his treasure box sitting on the floor next to the fire. She climbed the ladder to the attic and checked his bedroom. He was nowhere to be seen. She rushed outside and scanned the street. 'Elsie, have you seen Ruan?'

'After school. Not for a couple of hours.'

Her stomach performed a series of cartwheels. How could she have lost sight of the time and Ruan? He hadn't even eaten dinner. She'd sent Jane to deliver Mrs Winchester's dress and get a bit of fresh air after the late evening they'd had the night before. She'd spent the morning putting the finishing touches to the lace on Lady Alice's corset and Ruan had vanished.

Elsie frowned and gave a disappointed tut. 'The bloody cutters are back in town. Camped down by the brook. Bunch of rogues and scoundrels.'

Roisin's heart picked up a beat at the news. Not only would Ruan be safe, but Carrick was back in town and sooner than she'd expected. 'That'll be where he's gone. Ruan has taken such a liking to the man.' And so had she.

Elsie's mouth dropped open and her hand dampened Roisin's blouse when she laid it on her arm. 'Best go down and check. Ask Maisie first. Can't be too careful.'

'He'll be fine if he's with Carrick.' She made to return inside to her sewing. Maybe she could convince Carrick to stay and share tea with them. She still hadn't produced the meal of pickled cabbage and mutton pie she'd promised.

'You go find your boy and bring him back. Can't be too careful with those cutters. Go now. I'll keep an eye on your place.'

Maybe Elsie was right, she'd become just a little too free and easy with Ruan. He had to learn to tell her where he was going. Carrick or no Carrick. The caring nature of the people in the small town had lulled her into a false sense of security. After Ruan's escapade with the old Aboriginal man she'd kept him close to the house for a day or two; however, once she'd received the commission from Lady Alice and Mrs Winchester, she'd become too busy to worry.

She turned and headed across the street to the inn. The bullock dray was drawn up at the camp alongside the brook and even from a distance she could see the fire burning beneath the ever-present billy. No sign of Ruan, though.

Waiting for her eyes to become accustomed to the dark interior of the inn after the sunshine outside, she hovered in the doorway. Harry Kidd had his head down, deep in conversation with a well-dressed man at the bar, otherwise the inn seemed empty.

A shudder ran through her, a chilly finger tracing her spine, and she turned back to the welcoming sunshine, uncomfortable and unwilling to disturb the men's conversation.

She hovered a moment outside the inn, gazing across at the expanse of grass next to the brook. Then she spotted Ruan and Carrick hunched at the edge of the water. *Fishing!*

Elsie and her fearmongering. Of course Carrick would take care of Ruan, although who had managed to find whom would be impossible to guess, they seemed to have a sixth sense about each other's whereabouts.

She lifted her hands and waved. 'Ruan. Carrick.'

Carrick turned and waved back, making no effort to move. What did it matter? She was wasting time. Time she could spend on sewing. She had only two days to finish the corsets and everything required hand stitching. Carrick would bring Ruan home. She turned and made her way back up the street.

'Well, where's my boy?' Elsie stood in the middle of the road, hands on her hips.

'He's down at the brook with Carrick, fishing. You were right, the cutters are camped down there.'

Elsie narrowed her eyes. 'Why don't you come in and have a cup of tea. You and I need to have a little chat.'

'I'd love to, unfortunately I'm far too busy. That's why I lost track of Ruan. I can't afford to spend time taking tea, as much as I'd like to. I've only got two days to …'

Elsie blocked her way, her face a mask of concern. 'It's not a choice. You need to come inside and hear some home truths before it's too late.' Elsie's brisk, formal tone brooked no argument.

What was the woman talking about? 'Elsie, I'm sorry …'

'No apologies. No excuses. Come on.'

For goodness sake. She didn't want to put Elsie's back up, but she really didn't have time for socialising. She let out a sigh and returned to the store. 'Well, just a quick one, it's all I have time for.' Ten or fifteen minutes at most and then she'd plead work and leave.

'That's my girl. Come inside and sit down.'

Maisie was already waiting, elbows resting on the counter, staring into space. No wonder she couldn't find her at the inn. 'Maisie. I was down at the inn just now trying to find you.'

'Humph!'

Elsie pulled up a stool and gestured to the one next to her. Roisin sat down and tucked her hands into her lap like a schoolgirl waiting for a reprimand. What had happened?

Clearing her throat, Elsie poured out three cups of tea, added sugar, moved a cup in front of Roisin and then cleared her throat again.

'Oh, stop beating around the bush, Elsie Sullivan. Are you going to say something or am I?' Maisie glared across at Roisin, while Elsie pleated and unpleated the skirt of her apron.

'Looks as though it's going to have to be me. Roisin …'

Roisin lifted her head, waiting for the axe to fall. Were they going to tell her she had to leave the cottage? That Mr Martin had changed his mind about the lease on her house? Surely not. Not when business was just beginning to pick up. Maybe she owed too much at the store. She'd have enough to clear her debts as soon as she completed the work for Mrs Winchester. If not, Aunt Lil would lend her some money to tide her over, she'd said that from the very beginning. She simply hadn't wanted to ask and with the help of the money from the small jobs she'd had she'd managed to eke out the few pounds she'd brought from Sydney.

'… your best interests at heart.'

Roisin's head snapped up. She was so busy second-guessing Elsie she hadn't even heard what she'd said. 'I'm sorry. I didn't catch all of that.'

'Stay away. That's what we're saying. Treat them with a bit of distance. They're not to be trusted.'

Who were they talking about? The Winchesters? Surely the wife of the local magistrate could be trusted. 'Who?'

'Haven't you got a brain in that pretty head of yours? Carrick, Carrick O'Connor. He's the ring leader.'

'Carrick? What has he got to do with all this?'

'Have you listened to one single word we've said, or are you so besotted by his Irish charm that you can't see two inches in front of your nose?'

'I beg your pardon?' Roisin leapt to her feet, her face burning and her lips tingling at the memory of his fleeting kiss. So what if she was besotted by the man's charm, Irish or otherwise? It had nothing whatsoever to do with Elsie and Maisie.

'Clamber down from that high horse and listen. It's for your own good.'

Roisin lowered herself back onto the stool. 'Carrick is charming and he's a gentleman. Besides, Ruan is fond of him.' How feeble she sounded hiding behind her son. 'He's a friend of yours, too.' She glared at Maisie.

'That's different. He drinks at the inn. Same as they all do.'

Elsie pinned her with a beady-eyed stare. 'Do you or do you not want to make a go of this business of yours?'

'Of course I do.' Roisin schooled her mouth and swallowed the threatening pout.

'The likes of the Winchesters won't be calling on you if they find you, or that boy of yours, hanging around with a bunch of drunken louts and ex-convicts.'

'Carrick's not a convict. He's served his time, got his Certificate of Freedom. Besides, he was a political prisoner, not a convict.' At least that was the conclusion she'd come to after his drunken ramblings.

'Not for long if anyone catches him and his mates out. They've introduced licences for the cedar now and besides, it's their reputation you're taking on. You've got your own to worry about. Bunch of rabble rousing no-hopers, taking the law into their own hands. The brawl they had last time they were in town was the last straw. And there's the natives. The way he took to them Paterson boys just because they was havin' a bit of fun. Him and his cutter's justice.'

'And not only that,' Elsie chimed in, 'there's scandal around town and it's not the kind that's going to do you any favours.'

What was the woman talking about? There was always gossip around town and Elsie and Maisie were the prime instigators.

'I warned you when you moved in 'bout the reputation your place had and the way them girls had been drummed out of town.'

The leering inquiries from the man with the fleece sprang to mind. 'Exactly what are you saying, Elsie?'

'That some people think you and Jane are running a cathouse.'

'A cathouse?'

'You know, a house of ill repute.'

God, yes, she knew what a cathouse was. She'd spent most of her life living in one, though never been taken for one of the working girls, with the exception of Ruan's father. That had hardly put her in the bracket of a whore. She was set upon, raped. She certainly hadn't invited him. 'What a load of nonsense.'

'Look at it from everyone else's point of view. Two women living alone in a house, Jane hardly ever goes back to her own house these days.'

That was true enough. Not because they were entertaining a string of men, though, they were working every hour God sent. 'Jane's at home, now, as we speak. She delivered Mrs Winchester's dress this morning.'

'And then you've got Carrick and his sidekick there whenever they're in town, and what about the other night?'

And as far as she knew, poor maligned Slinger had never set foot in her house. Why did she feel it necessary to explain herself? 'What about the other night?' The other night the lamps had burned late over nothing more than lace and corsets.

'Even the Paterson boys were asking what the going rate was.' Maisie threw in for good measure. 'And my Harry's been asked all sorts of questions.'

'I can't believe you'd say such things. I thought we were friends.' Roisin scraped the chair back and stood up, glaring down at the two women. 'I'll ask you to stay out of my business, thank you very much.' Holding her head high, she marched out of the store and home. Interfering bunch of busybodies. What business was it of theirs?

Roisin slammed back into the house. 'Jane, Jane! Where are you?''

'Down here in the kitchen.'

She closed the door behind her. 'I am sick to death of those two busybodies sticking their nose in where it isn't wanted. They've as good as accused us of running a cathouse and apparently our prime customers are Carrick and Sling—'

Her face and neck flushed and she lifted her hands to her burning cheeks. Slinger sat, legs stretched out, dwarfing the chair at the end of the table, his lips twitching in amusement. 'Is that so?'

Jane smothered a laugh. 'Don't take any notice of their small-town tittle-tattle. They haven't got anything better to do. Did you find Ruan?'

'Yes, he's down at the brook, fishing with Carrick.'

'That's why Slinger's here. He came to let you know where Ruan was. They got back into town this morning.' Jane threw Slinger a dazzling smile, which as good as brought the poor man to his knees. Perhaps there was a smidgen of truth in Maisie and

Elsie's scuttlebutt, though goodness only knows how they always knew what was happening. She couldn't imagine Slinger discussing his feelings down at the inn. They'd give him a terrible time.

'Thank you for letting me know.' Come to think of it she couldn't imagine when Jane might have met Slinger. They'd both been so busy.

Slinger nodded his head and reached for his hat.

'Aren't you going to stay for a cup of tea?' Jane busied herself with the billy. 'It's as good as ready.'

'No I better be going. I'll have a look at that gate of yours as I promised.'

Jane threw her a sideways glance. 'I'll come with you and show you. Can you spare me for a minute or two, Roisin?' She untied her apron strings. 'I won't be long.'

'Of course.' It was the first she'd heard about a problem with the gate, but from the look on Jane's face she had no intention of letting Slinger out of her sight. 'Take as long as you need.'

Slinger stood aside to let Jane out of the back door, then followed her.

By the time they'd reached the path Jane had her hand tucked in the crook of Slinger's arm and they were meandering along the brook, in the opposite direction to Jane's house.

Roisin closed the door with a smile and poured herself a cup of tea. Jane deserved some attention after the terrible time Mick had given her and Slinger couldn't be all bad if Carrick trusted him. She hadn't got time to worry about Maisie and Elsie's gossip-mongering. She had two corsets to finish and it didn't look as though Jane would be back to help for a while.

No matter how hard she tried to put Maisie and Elsie's words out of her mind her thoughts kept returning to Carrick as she embroidered a series of tiny love knots onto Lady Alice's corset. What did they have against the cutters? Carrick had served his time, wasn't a convict any longer. He could come and go as he pleased. She swallowed back a laugh; she'd almost prefer it if he wasn't a freeman, then he wouldn't be able to return to Ireland. Someone must have been spreading rumours and stirring up trouble.

It was so wrong. She'd trust him with her life, trusted him with Ruan, which amounted to the same. What had Maisie said? *My Harry's been asked all sorts of questions.* By whom? The image of the man she'd seen deep in conversation with Harry when she was looking for Ruan drifted in front of her eyes. The same cold shiver traced down her spine and she put down her sewing.

The sound of Carrick's deep voice broke into her thoughts. 'One day we'll catch you some decent-sized fish and we'll have our dinner down by the river. What do you say to that, Ruan me lad?'

'I say yes, yes and yes.' Ruan bolted up the back steps. 'Can we, Mam, can we?'

'When the weather gets a bit warmer.' She stood up and smoothed her dress, her heart skipping at the sight of the two of them. Maisie and Elsie simply didn't know what they were talking about.

'Is there any tea in that pot? Fishing's thirsty work.'

'Of course, sit down. Ruan, go up to your room and get out of those dirty clothes. You're covered in mud. Jane won't be happy about the floor.'

'That'd be my fault. Splashing around in the shallows looking for tiddlers.' Carrick had such an easy way about him and Ruan scuttled off, keen to please. 'So Jane's become a big help to you, I hear.'

'I don't know how I managed without her.' Or without him. Just seeing Carrick sitting there at her table made all of Maisie's and Elsie's gossip seem unimportant. 'I wasn't expecting you back so soon and then when I couldn't find Ruan …'

'I told you the lad won't come to any harm while I'm around. Come and sit down and talk to me.' He rested his elbows on the table and stared at her as though she was the most important person in the world. A wave of heat swept up into her face and she sank down, frightened her knees might do something silly and she'd stumble. He kept staring at her. She didn't blink, didn't look away. A thin scar ran through his eyebrow—she'd never noticed it before, it was silvery white against the dark skin of his face.

The room fell silent apart from their breathing and she leaned forward, the heat inside her building, and then his lips touched hers. A momentary panic swarmed through her, but she allowed her lips to part and closed her eyes, leaning into his kiss. She didn't want him to stop, ever.

The scent of him made her mind spin, until there was nothing but his lips and the wonderful sensation of being close to him. He pulled away gently and smiled down at her.

'What?' Her breath came in shallow gasps.

'You.' Then a smile spread across his face again and he started kissing her until she was lost, dizzy, mindless. His arms tightened around her and his lips traced a path down her neck, her skin so over-sensitised she shivered and then she closed her eyes and refused to think.

His voice rumbled through her. 'You are beautiful.'

And realisation dawned. She'd never felt a man's lips on her skin before, never been held as though she was the most precious, fragile thing.

'Mam, Carrick …'

She jumped away from Carrick, her fingers touching her swollen lips, her gaze fixed on his face as he leaned back in the chair, smiling up at her.

'I forgot to tell you I found another treasure this morning.' Ruan skipped into the room.

'Did you now. And what would it be this time?' Carrick turned to Ruan and patted his knee.

'I think it's a button.' Ruan opened his palm.

'Show me.' Roisin held out her hand. 'Yes I think it is, too, and very similar to the ones on Elsie's coat. Why don't you go and give it back to her.'

Ruan scooted off Carrick's knee with a laugh. 'I knew that.' He took off down the hallway and disappeared.

'While he's busy I want to talk to you.' His voice held a serious note and she sat down, keeping the length of the table between them, unsure whether she could be trusted not to throw herself into his arms.

'You remember the tree I was telling you about?'

Of course she did, King Polai, the last tree he'd cut before he went back to Ireland, before he left Australia. She nodded.

'Slinger and I are leaving soon to go and cut it.'

She raised a hand to her chest to soothe the thump in her heart. So soon he'd be gone. Too soon.

'We'll be away for a few days to check things out, then back here to collect our gear before we take the tree. And then I'll be leaving for Ireland.' His gaze roamed her face as though waiting for her to speak.

What did he want her to say? That she didn't want him to go, that she'd miss him more than the very air she breathed?

'I'm going to get Slinger to bring the cedar back to Wollombi. To store it here till I return.'

Until he returned. Her heart took wings, caught in her throat. He would be coming back. 'And then?' She choked the words out, hoping against hope she hadn't misunderstood.

'I'm going to be building a house here, a house for you and young Ruan. While I'm away I'd like you both to be thinking about sharing it with me.' He raised his eyebrows in question.

How could he be so unsure? Didn't he know what her answer would be? She opened her mouth to speak but his finger crossed her lips.

'Don't be giving me your answer now. Think on it and tell me when I come back for the gear and bid you farewell.' He brought her hand to his mouth and kissed it, then covered her lips with his fingers. 'Take care, my love.'

When the door opened a gust of cold air swept in, replacing the space he'd filled only a moment ago. Goosebumps rose on the bare skin of her arms and she dropped her head into her hands.

'Where's Carrick?' Ruan skittered to a halt by the table, Jane just two paces behind him.

'He's gone,' she murmured.

'But he didn't say goodbye.'

Words deserted her, she didn't dare speak for fear she'd cry.

'He and Slinger had some business to attend to.' Jane stepped through the back door and into the breech, saving Roisin from having to answer. 'This tea's cold. Shall I make some more?'

Roisin shook her head and peered at Ruan sitting on the chair, his elbows propped on the table just as Carrick's had been. 'What's to eat? I'm starving.'

'I'll sort something out. There's bread and cheese and some of the stew we had last night.' Jane's reply circled in the air like some ethereal cloud too far above her head to be tangible.

'A man needs to eat.'

'What was that?' Jane offered Ruan a piece of bread.

'A man needs to eat, that's what Carrick said. That's why I'm going to learn to fish.'

She let the words swirl around her; she could think of nothing, nothing but Carrick and the look on his face and then she shuddered, feeling his lips on her skin again.

'Mam?'

She lifted her head.

'Can I?'

'Can you what?'

'See Carrick again tomorrow. You're not listening.'

She let out a long, slow breath and pulled herself to her feet. 'Of course you can.'

'They've left.' Jane frowned. 'Didn't Carrick tell you?'

'No, no he didn't.' He must have forgotten. Or maybe she had.

Take care, my love.

Roisin nursed the hot cup of tea close to her chest as she wandered down the hallway, a smile playing on her lips. When she and Jane had finally blown out the candles, the last stitches in Lady Alice's corset complete, it had been well past midnight. And despite Maisie and Elsie's warnings, there were no knocks on the door and the dirty old man from the wool store hadn't turned up. She hadn't, however, mentioned to Jane that Carrick had slept the night in the parlour, nor his promise to return. She'd no intention of doing that. She wanted to keep that memory like one of Ruan's treasures, hidden away so she could take it out in quiet moments and examine it, guard it.

The embers still glowed in the fireplace in the parlour. She placed her cup on the table and knelt, blowing gently. As the flames flickered to life she added another log or two and blew again, waiting for the thick dry timber to catch. Carrick had made such a possibility a reality. She was never short of wood. The shed was always half full and the pile outside replenished. Such a luxury to have the little cottage so well heated with one fire in the kitchen and one here. The nasty fingers of ice from the winter mornings rarely breached the walls.

Satisfied the fire would catch, she stood and brought the cup to her lips, permitting her eyes to wander to the box on the tabletop covered in blooms of teal that matched Lady Alice's corset. Half the pleasure was in the packaging, and with Jane's nimble fingers and artistic talent the box was as beautiful as its contents.

She lifted the lid on the box, inhaling the scent of the dried rose petals Jane had added, and peeled back the fine paper wrapping. Running the back of her hand across the satin, she admired the delicate embroidery framing the two ripples of lace below the bustline. Unable to resist, she took it from the box and held it up to the light to examine it. Not a stitch out of place. The tiny metal clasps down the front were evenly spaced and she knew the measurements would be perfect. Lady Alice would be thrilled, and so would her husband.

This additional pleasure in her business, knowing she was doing more for these women than she'd ever dreamed possible, made the job all the more enjoyable. And to think at first she'd thought to hide her corsetry skills and concentrate on simple dressmaking and alterations. How wrong she'd been. But then she'd been wrong about so many things before she'd settled in Wollombi.

Wrong in believing that she could never care for a man. Carrick had proved to her that love and caring could exist between a man and a woman. She hadn't been spoiled for love and Ruan's conception was not the way it was meant to be. When Carrick came back she'd tell him how much he meant to her. And maybe, just maybe he'd kiss her again. That little twist deep in the pit of her stomach tightened and twirled.

Smoothing the silky material, she lowered the corset back into the box and wrapped the paper over it, settled the lid and tied the deep-blue bow.

Lady Alice had said she'd send someone early to collect her corset. She'd asked for it to be wrapped in simple brown paper. She wanted it kept a secret. As Roisin tied the final knot in the string to hold the brown paper in place, a knock sounded at the door.

She straightened her skirt and patted her hair into place, then cast a quick glance around the room before turning to the street door. Before her fingers reached the knob the knocker sounded again, impatient, insistent, demanding. Surely she hadn't taken that long to answer.

'Open up.'

'One moment.' She swung back the door and her mind emptied.

'Do you intend to keep me standing here all morning?'

She scooted out of the way and held the door wide as the man barged past her into the parlour and raised his hand to the flames.

She couldn't say his name, couldn't squeeze even a breath between her lips.

Her heart gave one rapid thump and then seemed to stop. She went cold to the marrow.

'I am sent here like some lackey to collect a package for my wife. Hurry, girl, I haven't all day.'

She battled against the shock clogging her mind. Why had she let him in? She had to get him out. Had to deal with it herself. There was no one to turn to. He turned his pale eyes on her and the same icy shaft of fear pierced her. The familiar breadth of his shoulders. One had pinned her to the wall while his hands had groped beneath her petticoats. He still carried the ebony cane. There was no mistake. Bile rose in her throat and she forced it down, snatching a shaky breath.

He tapped his cane against his boot in his impatience. The vision of him raising it and bringing it down on her shoulders time after time was imprinted in her mind. There was no mistake. He rapped on the floor twice and his head came up.

The blood drained from his face, making the marks from the sun stand out on his nose. He recovered in the blink of his colourless lashes. 'Well, well. A pretty pass. It seems I have been searching in the wrong places.'

A sick giddiness overcame her and she reached for the table. He had recognised her, of that there was no doubt. She was stronger than this. She had to be. His gaze raked her face and his thin lips lifted in a sardonic grimace.

She couldn't have come so far, worked so hard to just give up in a moment. She'd ignore it. She'd give him the package he'd come for and tell him to—

The package. For his wife.

For a moment time stood still as she gaped at the man. His wife. Lady Alice? She moved on shaky legs to the table and picked up the box, holding it out in front of her like some talisman to ward off an evil spirit. For evil he was. Nothing would ever convince her otherwise.

He narrowed his eyes and reached out for the package. He was going to go. She wouldn't ask for money. It was a small price to pay to get him to leave. Just go. The words cleared the rising mist in her brain, brought her back to her senses.

'It seems you may have more than this,' he rapped his cane on the box, 'to which I am entitled.'

He hadn't called her by name, didn't know that she'd taken Aunt Lil's name. Was he toying with her? How foolish, of course she couldn't deceive him. She had to stand up to him.

'I have nothing else of yours, sir.' She dropped a small curtsy and slid the box across the table.

He ignored it and slammed his cane down on the tabletop. The sound reverberated through the room, through the house. Dear God, it might bring Jane running or worse, Ruan.

'Roisin. Imagine that I should find you here, though if I had paid sufficient attention to my wife's ramblings, I might have put two and two together. Of course one wouldn't find in Wollombi a seamstress who could work magic. Seamstress. Pah! Do she, and her fine friends the Winchesters, know that they are patronising a whore?'

'I am no whore, sir.'

Dankworth laughed, a cruel sound that sent shivers across her skin.

'I know otherwise. And can prove it.' He cast his gaze around the room as if searching for something that would indicate her whore-like status. Jewelled lights perhaps? A random piece of clothing, thrown in a fit of passion? The evidence of carousing, of liquor and the scent of debauchery. He failed and his lip curled. 'Where is my son?' He punctuated each word with a rap of his cane.

She shook her head. If she cried could she convince him Ruan had died? That he no longer existed? What in God's name had made her think she could hide from this man? She should have left, gone further, set sail for England, India, Ireland even. Anywhere. What a fool she was. And she'd invited Lady Alice into her home. *His wife!* Tried her very best to make her desirable, to please her husband. God forbid. *Dankworth, here in Wollombi!*

He stepped nearer. A fist of fear squeezed her innards and she gagged at the familiar smell of brandy and sour sweat; unwashed and dirty despite his fine clothing. In a moment she was back in the past. Back in the dark, rat-infested alley pinned against a wall. Begging, begging him to leave her alone.

His fingers dug into her arm as he pulled her close, so close she could see the twitch in his cheek muscles. His flat eyes icy with disdain. She'd thwart him. He would not have Ruan. Fury and malevolence rolled out of him, almost smothering her. She stared blankly at her scissors sitting on the top of the trunk. If she stretched out her hand she could almost reach them, then he'd die. And Ruan would be safe.

Her throat closed and her chest tightened. She kept her eyes on his and slid her hand across the top of the trunk. 'Let me go before someone comes. I'm expecting clients.' Her fingers brushed the handle of the scissors. If she could only reach them …

He jerked her chin up, his fingers biting. 'Where is he?' Spittle showered her face, the very spittle she'd rejected, spat back at him as he had taken her brutally against the wall behind Aunt Lil's. Caught her when she was least expecting it, walking hand-in-hand with her mother, laughing and singing. Her anguished cries played once more in her ears, mixed with the screams as the remembered pain laced through her.

Not again. He wouldn't hurt her again. She'd been young, unknowing, a mere girl, just shy of her fifteenth birthday. Not now. She'd lost too much at this man's hands and she wouldn't lose again. She drew herself up, standing on the tips of her toes, breathing deep until their eyes were level. 'You can't have him. He is not *your* son.'

His arm snaked around her waist, gripped tighter, squeezing the air from her lungs, forcing her to inhale another sickening gulp of his rancid odour.

'He is my son and I'll have him.' The vile man nuzzled her neck, and then dropped his voice until his foul breath dampened her skin and he whispered, 'Don't be so foolish, my dear. You have tried to run and hide, but I have found you. I'll always find you. And I have the law on my side. He is my son.'

His hand slid from her cheek to her throat and squeezed. She dragged her gaze away from the growing bulge in his trousers and prayed it was her imagination resurrecting those horrific moments. He'd taken her once, before she'd known better. It wouldn't happen again. For a moment the picture of Lady Alice rose in her mind. The corset she had wanted to woo her husband with. Why could they not produce a child of their own? There was nothing lacking in Dankworth. Ruan was the living proof of that.

'You will not have him.' Her fingers reached out, closer to the scissors.

'My dear,' his voice, almost cajoling, wrapped around her, a diamond python squeezing the very breath from her lungs. 'Don't be so selfish. Think what I can do for the boy. I can give him more than you ever dreamed. He is my heir. You will be well cared for. I want nothing from you other than my son.'

'He is not here.'

A pale-tinged eyebrow disappeared into his shock of strawberry-blond hair, so like Ruan's it made her heart shudder. She'd blotted out all memory of this man, blocked the vision of him, yet every day she looked at his mirror image.

The patter of feet. A cry and the door flew open. Ruan stood, a smile creasing his face, his hair on end from the night's sleep and dangling from his hand, a possum tail. 'Look, look, another present. I found it on the end of my bed when I woke. It's a possum tail.'

She stepped in front of Dankworth, shielding Ruan, the scissors forgotten. 'Go. Leave now. You are not wanted.' The imprint of the harshness of her words scored Ruan's face as if she'd hit him and his lower lip trembled. Why? Why in God's name had she spoiled him so? Why wasn't he a child who never dared to speak, never interrupted, and lived his life believing he had no right? It was her fault. She'd brought him up to be so confident, without that he'd be in no danger now.

'Young man.' Dankworth took a step towards him, the expression on his face half tender, half lascivious, one hand reaching out to stroke Ruan's hair. Cold dread raked her as Ruan's eyes sought hers in a mute plea.

'Go now. Go to Jane.' She glared at Ruan. What harm would a little hurt do now, compared to what might happen if Dankworth got his way?

Ruan stared at her, his wide eyes full of tears and his lower lip trembling, then turned and ran down the hallway. Dear God, let him find Jane. Let Jane have the sense to take him away. If only Carrick were here.

She slammed the door behind Ruan, turned and stood, arms outstretched. It was a futile gesture, yet it gave her strength. He could have her. Do what he would with her, but he wouldn't touch Ruan.

'Tempting, my dear, but unnecessary. He's mine and I'll have him. You are tarnished goods and do not interest me.'

She licked her lips, her throat dry as dust. She had no more words.

'The law is on my side. He is my son and I have every right to claim him.' His hand reached into his pocket and he withdrew a handful of notes and coins and threw them onto the table. 'There's a lot more when you hand over the boy.' He tucked his cane under his arm and grasped the box and stepped closer to her.

The fetid smell of sweat, or perhaps her own fear, enveloped her.

'Think on it and we will speak again now I know where to find you.' His backhanded slap sent her sprawling, her mind spinning, her legs no longer capable of holding her upright.

The sound of his retreating footsteps reverberated inside her head and her eyes blurred. Her thoughts reduced to nothing more than a jumble of confused and conflicting emotions. She closed her eyes and concentrated on the insurmountable task of dragging air into her lungs.

How long she stayed there curled in a ball, she didn't know. It wasn't until the cold wind worked its way into her consciousness that she dragged herself to her feet and closed the door. Would that it were so easy to shut out the past.

She staggered down the hallway, her hands on either wall for support, until she reached the kitchen. Nothing had changed. The room appeared cosy, the fire burned in the grate, the billy whistled on the hob, yet she was cold, so very, very cold. She clutched her hands around her shoulders and pushed against the back door. It swung free. 'Ruan. Ruan! Where are you?' Please let him be with Jane.

'Mam!' He flew across the yard, wrapping his arms tight around her waist. She clutched him close and let out a long, shuddering sigh and then held him away from her. 'Are you all right? Where's Jane?'

'I didn't get her. Carrick said I had to keep an eye out for you while he was away with Slinger.' He hugged her even tighter. 'Has the man gone?'

She groaned and placed one hand flat against the wall for support. 'Where did you go?'

'Who was that man? Why was he so angry?'

'He came to collect something. Something I'd made.' Something she wished she'd never become involved in. 'He wasn't happy with my work.' She hated lying to Ruan, but what else could she say?

He's your father, the most awful man who ever drew breath, the man who raped me and killed your grandmother. The only person I have ever wished dead.

'I like your sewing. You're very clever.' He led her to the chair by the fire. 'Shall I make you some breakfast?' Concern plastered his little face.

'Jane will be here in a minute. Go and get dressed. You'll be late for school.'

'I'm not going to school. I have to stay here with you.'

She started to shake her head, then stopped. No, she wouldn't send him to school. Not with Dankworth in town. She needed to keep Ruan close where she could see him. 'Thank you.' She gave a feeble smile as he stroked the hair back from her forehead, his small hand soft against her clammy skin.

The back door swung open and she jumped to her feet, sending the chair flying backwards. 'Jane!' Her legs began to shake.

She hugged herself tight, closed her eyes and rocked to and fro, willing away the memory of Dankworth's face.

'What happened? Oh my goodness. Sit down.'

She collapsed into the chair, her heart thundering, and buried her face in her hands.

'A man came. He didn't like Mam's work and he got angry.'

She lifted her head in time to see the frown cross Jane's forehead, a flicker of confusion in her eyes.

'Go and get dressed, Ruan. I'll make some breakfast.' Jane busied herself at the fire, pouring milk over the porridge and emptying the tealeaves from the billy. 'Go now, Ruan. Hurry up. I'll take care of your mam.'

Appeased, Ruan vanished, his feet pattering up the ladder to the attic.

Jane knelt at her side. 'What happened?' she hissed. 'Who was it?'

'Lady Alice's husband. Mr Dankworth.'

'And he wasn't happy with our work? It was perfect. Was he angry? Because of the corset?'

What could she say? She shook her head, more in despair than anything else. If she told Jane the truth then what would she think?

'Drink this.' Jane pushed a cup of steaming tea into her shaking hands. 'I'll see to Ruan's breakfast. So he can get to school.'

'No school. Not today.'

'He won't like that.'

'He says he's going to take care of me. Carrick told him to.' She gave a paltry smile, more of a grimace really. What she wouldn't give for Carrick to be here, to wrap his big, strong arms around her and hold her tight.

Dankworth's shadow hung over Roisin like a miasma, stripping the joy from her life. Dreams laced with dread and foreboding haunted her nights. If she glanced out of the window she saw shadows lurking in the frosty moonlight, only to discover it was the wind, the movement of the trees—an illusion. It didn't feel like an illusion.

When she slept she jolted awake twenty times a night with her heart hammering and her breath burning in her lungs. Wrapped in her quilt, she sat in front of the dying embers of the fire until the shaking stopped.

Was it him she'd felt watching her? Watching from the shadows. He'd be back. He always came back. The knowledge made her cold and queasy.

Even when Elsie presented her with the news that the Winchesters and their highfalutin friends had left the valley and returned to Sydney for the Governor's Ball, she still couldn't shake the sense of doom sitting like a lead weight in her stomach.

In the end she let Ruan go to school, insisting on accompanying him both ways. Her eyes constantly scanning the village for any sight of Dankworth, or worse, some henchman sent to do his squalid work. Searching the street as she'd done in Sydney. Looking over her shoulder, anxiety sparking at the slightest sound or footfall.

Without Jane, the work she had wouldn't have been done. She fussed over her like a mother hen, trying to make her eat. Roisin wasn't sick, though she might as well be. Dark shadows ringed her eyes and her cheekbones stood out like one of Ruan's skeletons. Even he was quiet, subdued, keeping the kindling pile high and stacking the logs in the basket by the fire. Somehow she had to get through this until Carrick returned. She couldn't keep running, and besides, she didn't want to. She wanted Carrick.

Fourteen

A gentle rain pattered against the shutter and Roisin rolled out of bed. As the days passed and Dankworth failed to reappear, she'd settled back into a familiar routine and finally slept the night through.

She stumbled into the kitchen and found the billy steaming on the hob. How long had she slept? Two plates and cups sat on the table half empty. She threw open the back door, her eyes still cloudy from sleep. Silence greeted her, an ominous, damp silence. Jane was nowhere to be seen. Ruan. Where was Ruan?

Then the squeak of the woodshed door as it swung crooked on the leather hinges. Ruan's high-pitched squeal broke the silence and her heart lurched into action, pumping blood back through her frozen veins, bringing her body to life.

'Come, Ruan. We'll find your mam.' The calm note in Jane's voice settled her and she stepped over the threshold into the dark interior of the woodshed. Out of the daylight, only a tableau of silhouettes greeted her. Jane holding Ruan's hand, the pair of them gazing into the darkest corner.

As her eyes adjusted, she picked out the crumpled outline of a body in the corner. 'Ruan. Come here.'

'Mam.' He turned and ran to her side.

'Thank goodness. I'm not sure what we should do.' Jane indicated the huddled bundle. Rheumy eyes watering, the old man's toothless mouth gaped then clamped shut against the tremors shaking his body. His skin was so dark, if it hadn't been for the white bone clasped in his hand and his eyes, Roisin wouldn't have known where his body started or ended.

'I think he's hurt, Mam.'

'You and Jane go inside, into the kitchen. Heat some water and find some blankets and we'll need tea and some food. Something soft. Soak a piece of bread in some milk.'

Another shudder traced the old man's body as though he was in the grip of some fever.

'Off you go, quickly now. Leave the door open to let the light in.'

As they left she took a step closer and a corpse-like grimace spread across his face. 'Carrick's lady.'

She bent over the pitiful, reeking old man, suppressing a shiver of revulsion as her stomach roiled from the stench seeping from his ragged clothes and old flesh. 'Are you sick?'

'Bit, missus, bit. Nothing bad. White man's sickness won't hurt Old Pella.' His pockmarked skin proved he'd survived the smallpox outbreak that had decimated the local native tribes.

'Can you stand?' She reached out her hand.

He ignored it and lumbered to his feet with a groan.

'Come inside, I have food and some tea.' She set off, hoping he'd follow. The dusty slap of his feet told her he had and she led the way across the yard to the back door.

He sank down onto the back doorstep and squinted up at the sky, searching for the sun to warm him. His trousers were ripped, and his tattered shirt left one shoulder and part of his skinny back bare, showing bruises and the clear imprint of a man's boot.

'Did someone hurt you?'

He lifted his bloodshot eyes and screwed up his face, then pointed to his head. Her whispered gasp moved the old man's hair as she leant over him. A fine line scored his head as though he'd been beaten with a long stick.

'Jane, can you bring me a cloth and some boiled water please, with a little bit of salt in it?' She sat down on the step next to him. 'What happened to you? Who hurt you?'

'Found me in the woodshed.'

'In my woodshed?'

He rocked slowly, his frail arms wrapped around his body.

'Who? Surely not Carrick.' He'd have called in. Told her he was here.

'Not Carrick. He's good to Old Pella.' He shrugged his bony shoulders. 'Blind Bunyip got Old Pella.'

Jane put a bowl down on the step beside Roisin and handed her a damp cloth. Roisin waved her away and dabbed at the blood around the slash across his head. The Paterson cutters hadn't been in town. Maisie would have told her if they'd taken to the old man again. *The Blind Bunyip.* What did that mean? 'It's not too bad. You'll be sore for a few days and you shouldn't be out here in the cold. Come inside.'

He shook his head. 'No good inside. I go there. Stay till Carrick comes.' He inclined his head to the woodshed. 'Keep him away.' He waved the white bone still clasped in his hand. The least she could do was make sure he was comfortable. 'Stay here for now and I'll bring you some food and blankets.'

She picked up the bowl and went inside. 'Ruan, go up to your bedroom. And stay there.'

'I have to go to school.'

'Not today. Stay at home today.'

'Mam!'

'Do what I say.' She followed her words with a tight smile. Since Dankworth's reappearance everything had changed. Just when she thought it was safe again something else happened. The memory of the shadowy figures she'd seen crossing the frosted earth flickered through her mind. She shuddered. *The Blind Bunyip!* Now she believed the natives' superstitions.

Waiting until Ruan had climbed the ladder to the attic, she busied herself breaking bread into the bowl of milk Jane had prepared.

'Did he tell you what happened?' Jane kept her voice low.

'Only that there was a blind bunyip.'

'Well blind or not it certainly did a decent job on him. He's been well and truly beaten.'

'He said he'd stay until Carrick returned. It's almost as though he's protecting us. I don't know what …' Her voice petered out and she sank down into the chair. 'You don't suppose …? Oh, God, surely not.'

Jane dragged up the chair next to her. 'It's time you told me what's happening.'

'I think I'm going insane. I see shadows where there are none. I hear voices, laughing, heckling. And just when I thought it was over—this.'

'You're worried. The man that came, he's worrying you. It's time to tell me, share your worry.'

'Maybe it is, Jane. Maybe it is. I didn't want to involve you.'

Jane reached out and clasped her hand. 'Roisin, I count you as my friend and I'd like you to think the same of me.'

'I do. I do. But you have had enough problems of your own. I don't want to …'

'Stop. You've turned my life around. Given me a job, a purpose. I've never been happier. You make everyone you touch happier. Look at Elsie and Maisie with their petticoats. What about Grace Winchester and her exquisite dress? And Mrs Blackmore—a turkey into a swan. You said those were her very words. And

Lady Alice, that poor miserable, cowering woman, proud to stand at her husband's side.'

'The biggest mistake I ever made.'

'How can you say that?'

'Shall we have a cup of tea? This is a sad and sorry tale.' Roisin forced herself to her feet, every bone in her body aching. Was it possible to feel like an old woman at the age of twenty-one?

'Let me.' Jane stood and indicated to the chair.

'No. Can you take this out to the old man?' She handed Jane the bowl of bread and milk. 'And give him this blanket. When you come back I'll tell you. It'll be easier if I'm doing something,' she said, her voice wry. If she didn't share it with someone soon, it would eat away at her until she shrivelled up like the frail man outside on the doorstep. She filled the billy and measured the tea.

Jane returned in a matter of moments and closed the door behind her.

'Is he all right?'

'He's stopped shivering. I can't get him to move. He insists he's staying until Carrick gets back.'

'I really don't see what Carrick has to do with all of this.' Roisin banged the billy with a piece of kindling and set two cups onto the table.

'Something, I have no doubt. Why don't you start at the beginning?'

Roisin sucked in a deep breath. Now that the moment had passed she wasn't really sure she wanted to talk to Jane. She snatched a breath and swallowed. 'Lady Alice's husband is Ruan's father.' There. Done before she lost the courage.

Jane's mouth gaped, literally gaped, open. 'He … I … the man who collected the dress and the corset? Who didn't like your work?'

'He didn't even look at it.'

'Does Lady Alice know?'

'I have no idea, but I also have no doubt she will soon if Dankworth gets his way.'

'What does he want?' Jane slurped her tea.

'Ruan.'

Jane set her cup down on the table and rocked back in the chair. 'Can you tell me everything from the start?'

'Dankworth is the reason I left Sydney. He discovered Ruan, realised he was his son and he wanted him. He said the law was on his side and he had every right to the boy.'

Jane's face blanched. 'He does. If he's Ruan's father.'

'He does not. He has no right. He raped me when I was fourteen, and beat my mother to death. He knew nothing of Ruan until he stumbled upon us in the street. He cares nothing for me. And nothing for Ruan. He didn't even know of Ruan's birth until then.'

'Then why would he want him?'

'That I don't know and I didn't wait to find out. The man is evil. He will not have my son.' She stood up and the chair clattered to the ground. A red haze of anger seeped into every corner of her soul. But for Ruan, she'd kill him, take a knife to him and happily hang for it. 'My mam walked down to Pitt Street to meet me after work. It was a balmy evening, the end of summer, the days getting shorter but still pleasant. We bought an ice cream on the way home.'

'You don't have to tell me, Roisin, you really don't. It's the past. Try to forget.'

She did have to tell the story. She'd held it inside her for so long it threatened to engulf her. She wanted the whole story out in the open. For too long she'd kept it bottled up, eating away at her like a canker. 'We took a shortcut through the lanes. There was a man standing at the end, a gentleman. I couldn't see his face, the sun was behind him. I could tell he was a gentleman because of his top hat and cane and patterned waistcoat. Some expensive embroidered material, embossed. The light glinted on the golden fabric in the weave. Mam's hand squeezed mine, clamped down so hard it hurt. That's when I knew she was frightened.'

Her hands shook and she placed them flat on the table, leaning against the rough timber, rocking backwards and forwards. 'She pushed me behind her and when he got closer and reached out to grab her, she shouted at me to run. I couldn't. I couldn't move. He grabbed at Mam, pawed her and laughed. I hear that laugh in my dreams even now, more now I've heard it again. He dragged Mam up against the wall. I tried to pull him off. I couldn't. He lifted his cane and slammed it down across my shoulder.' She wiped at the tears coursing down her cheeks. She hadn't even known she was crying. She shook her head, trying to rid herself of the sound of Dankworth's ominous laugh.

'Mam pulled him to her, lifted her skirts. I knew what she was doing. She wanted to keep him away from me. Offered herself. All he did was laugh. Then he threw her aside and brought his cane down hard, on her head, on her face. She curled into a ball and I ran to her side. Her face was a bloody mess. She kept telling me to run. I couldn't leave her. Then he hauled me up. Shouted he didn't want tarnished goods, he'd have me instead. And he did.

'He took me against the wall, then when he'd finished, straightened his clothing, tipped his hat and strolled away. Left us there. At first I was relieved, relieved he'd gone and it was over. Even when he was ramming into me, it didn't seem real. As though I stood outside myself and watched.' The words poured out of her, a flood of putrid loathing, bottled anger and sorrow, deep, abiding sorrow.

'I couldn't get Mam up. I couldn't leave her there; I didn't know what to do. Next thing I remember Aunt Lil came. They took Mam back to the house, the brothel where we lived. Aunt

Lil called the doctor. It was too late, he said. Mam never woke up, never opened her eyes. Three weeks later we buried her. Dankworth killed my mam.'

Through the window an eagle soared on a current of air. High above the earth, far away from the mess of her life. Perhaps Mam watched over her. She'd like to think she did. Liked to think Mam would be proud to know she'd fight the bastard, even now. She cleared her throat and turned. Jane sat, her chin in her hand, her face chalky and her tears leaving dirty track marks down her cheeks. 'I'm sorry, Jane. I didn't want to upset you. Once I started I couldn't seem to stop.'

She shook her head. 'No, tell me. Tell me it all. You have to get it out.'

Dear Jane, so right. Her strength was returning, the remembered anger stirring her sluggish blood. The telling had made her stronger. She needed to remember the pain. 'After Mam died I stayed with Aunt Lil, still went to work at Madame de Lolle's. Nothing changed, but everything had. It didn't occur to me I could be carrying a child. You'd think I'd have known. Lived all my life in a brothel, seen the girls come and go. It was Aunt Lil who picked it. I thought I was just growing older, getting bigger. She knew the signs. She didn't send me away. That's when I made my quilt, while I waited for Ruan to come, and afterwards, while I nursed him. I added all the scraps of silk left over from the work Madame de Lolle sent home for me to do, and from my mam's favourite dress. See, I couldn't go to work, not when I was showing. Other girls would have … Then Ruan was born. The moment I held him in my arms it didn't matter where he'd come from, how I'd come about him. He was mine. All I had in the world that was truly mine.

'I went back to work. Aunt Lil and the girls cared for Ruan, pampered him more like, spoiled him rotten. Even after all the sorrow we were happy. I knew Mam would want us to be happy.'

'And you never saw Dankworth again until the other day when he came to get Lady Alice's corset … Oh, God! Lady Alice. Does she know what kind of a husband she has?'

'I felt sorry for Lady Alice before I knew Dankworth was her husband, but now …' She lifted her shoulders, trying to relieve the weight of the memories. 'Dankworth didn't know about Ruan until we bumped into him on the street one day in Sydney. It wasn't until I saw Ruan and Dankworth together that I realised how alike they were. The same hair, same pale skin, but not the eyes, thank God Ruan doesn't have his eyes. Ruan has my eyes.' Not those opaque, milky eyes, almost like a blind man. 'He's not having my son.' Her horror turned to strength. Something good would come of all his evil. 'I'm done with running.'

Carrick led the three horses down to the brook and hobbled them. This would be the last time they would make camp before cutting King Polai. More than anything else he wanted some time with Roisin, and to see the lad. Tomorrow they'd begin the trek back into the forest and they'd take down the tree. In a week or two it would be done and he'd go to Sydney, cash in his accounts and take passage to Ireland. And after that? God willing, he'd return, to Roisin and the lad.

He pitched the tent and gathered some wood for the fire. Raucous shouting drifted from the inn down across the flats to the brook. It held no attraction for him. He wandered down to the edge. The clear, cool water lapped the bank and the mid-day sun chased away the winter chill. A splash and a flurry of water drew his eye. *Fish!* With a laugh he ran back to the camp and rummaged for a piece of line. There'd be bass or mullet, even eel around. He'd snag a couple and convince Roisin to come down and he'd cook them for tea. Just like he'd promised. Make it something of a farewell. Then once his debts were paid in Ireland he'd return and ask the lady for her hand, and if she'd have him, they'd settle in the valley, buy a few acres, build the home he dreamed of. He'd have enough put by if he was careful.

He moulded the piece of damper onto the hook and tossed it into the water, wedging himself in the fork of the roots of the tree. Shame the lad would be at school, he'd enjoy a bit of fishing. The lapping of the water and the sunshine made him drowsy. He was over the cutting, sick of the stench of sweaty men and the festering rot of the rainforest. It was the sun he wanted, the warm sun on his back and a warm lass in his arms. Just this one last job.

The thump to his gut knocked the air from his body, making him gasp.

'Carrick! You're here.'

'Woah, boyo, you'll be sending me for a swim if you're not careful.'

'When did you get back? I've been waiting for ages to see you. No one knew when you were coming.'

'Didn't know meself, lad. I'm here now.' He adjusted the line and handed it over. 'I'm looking to catch a fish or two for tea. Reckon your mam would like to come down here for tea?'

'She would! Have you caught any?'

'Not yet. Sit still and quiet and they'll come.'

Ruan settled between his feet, a fierce look of concentration on his face as he peered into the crystal-clear water. Was it the lad or his mam he'd miss the most? Both, for different reasons. Maybe he'd ask her to wait for him. Brigid would understand. She'd know she'd always hold that place in his heart, as would Liam. A picture of a flurry of healthy, strong boys, all splashing in the clear water of the brook, flashed in front of his eyes. That was what he wanted—a family with Roisin. He sighed and wiped his hands across his face, almost dozing in the sun, the lad still and calm against his legs. 'Caught anything yet?'

Ruan shook his head and placed his finger on his lips, then pointed to the clear water. A flash of silver, a tug on the line. Ruan tensed and snatched a breath as the line tightened. Then a shadow fell across the water and the fish disappeared with a tail flick, taking the bait.

'I lost him!'

The shadow shifted, throwing the light back across the brook; a loose rock splashed into the water. The hairs on the back of Carrick's neck rose, standing to attention. 'Aye that you did. Give me the line and run up to the inn and ask Maisie for some more damper.'

'There's still a bit left on the hook.'

'Do what I say. The fishes are hungry. You want enough for your mam for tea, don't you?' There was someone there. Watching. Best get the lad away until he found out who it was. Something nagged at him. Only he and Slinger were using the camp, no bullocky, no other cutters. 'Give me the line. Off you go. Quick as you can.' Ruan jumped up and took off across the open paddock to the inn.

Once Ruan had reached the fence, Carrick anchored the fishing line with a rock and stood. 'You want to come out and show yourself, or shall I be coming over to find you?'

The trees on the other side of the brook wavered and the silhouette moved. A man, tall, cane in hand, stood on the bank. 'Nice day for a fish.'

'Until you interrupted.' Shading his eyes Carrick squinted, trying to make out the face. A gentleman. Top hat. Pale breeches. High black boots, shiny. Never done a day's work in his life, he'd put money on that.

'That's no way to greet a man.'

His skin prickled. The man's laconic drawl snatched at his memory, but he tossed it away. Since Roisin and Ruan had arrived in Wollombi Ireland seemed so much closer. 'What do you want?'

'Just appreciating the sight of a man taking his time to relax.'

Carrick took a few steps to his right. He needed to see the face. That slow drawl and those clipped words tugged. He edged further along the waterline. If he could get the beam of sunlight off the man's face, he would be able to see him. 'Who are you …?' The words died on his lips as the sun slipped behind a cloud and the man turned back into the bush.

'Carrick, I've got it.'

He shook his head, turning to Ruan. Until he returned to Ireland it was the present not the past that was important. The thought of more fishing had palled, but the lad would be disappointed. 'Let's move along the brook a bit and try our luck there, nearer the bridge.' He picked up the line and followed Ruan as he gambolled along the water's edge.

'I hope we can catch five fish, then there's one each, and one for Old Pella. That makes six.'

'Old Pella?' What did Ruan know of Old Pella?

'He's in the woodshed. He's feeling much better. Mam says he has to eat otherwise his bruises won't heal.'

'Bruises, what bruises?'

'The Blind Bunyip got him. Attacked him in the night. Hit him with a stick. He was real sick. We found him in the woodshed. He said he'd stay till you got back.'

What was the old man doing out the back of Roisin's place? 'Right, well we'd better get a move on and find these fishies, then.' Had the bastard Paterson cutters been up to their tricks again? And then the penny dropped. 'How's your treasure box, Ruan?'

'Nearly full. I found a bird's nest the other day and another egg. And a while back a possum tail. All cleaned, not bloody. It's real soft.'

'Right.' Now the blown egg and the feathers, the snakeskin, all of it began to make sense. *Old Pella!* Just like an old bowerbird collecting bits and pieces that caught his eye and bringing them back to the nest. Carrick wasn't the only one who'd taken a shine to the lad.

By the time the light started to fade Ruan and Carrick made their way back along the path, six fat bass swinging from a piece of twine and Ruan's chest puffed out with pride.

'How will we cook them?'

'Well, now, that'll be depending on what your mam says.'

'We could ask Old Pella, he might know.'

'He might indeed. We'll see.'

It was like coming home, tramping down the street to the house where Roisin would be waiting. A man couldn't do much better than that. Maisie could keep her rum and Irish stew. A bit of fish and the company of a pretty woman would be hard to beat.

As they rounded the corner by the General Store, Jane spotted them and let out a screech fit to raise the devil himself. 'Your mam is ready to kill you, Ruan. Where have you been?'

'I've got tea and I found Carrick.'

'I can see that. Get yourself inside, quick smart.'

Ruan disappeared in a flash, up the back steps and into the house.

The shrill tone in Jane's voice set Carrick's teeth on edge. 'Jane, a minute.'

She turned and stood at the bottom of the steps.

'Is there a problem? Is Roisin all right?'

'She's fine.' She wouldn't meet his gaze, instead she peered down, picking at her apron. 'It's difficult to keep up with Ruan. To know where he is.'

'Boys.' He nodded, though he couldn't see the problem in the lad fishing down at the brook. 'Everything else all right? Ruan says Old Pella's taken a beating again.'

'He'll survive.'

'Was it the Paterson crew?'

'I don't think so. They haven't been in town. This happened a few days ago. Old Pella said he'd stay until you got back.'

'Where is he?'

'In the woodshed.' She turned away, wiping her hand over her face.

Whatever was going on? 'I'll have a word with him.' He shoved open the rickety door and peered into the gloom. 'Old Pella? You here?'

'You back. 'Bout time.' The ancient man heaved himself up and dragged his possum skin tight around his shoulders. 'Where you been?'

'You know where I've been. You were there. King Polai.'

'Days ago. Where you been?'

'Organising stuff for next time. To take the tree.'

Old Pella sniffed. 'Be better here.'

'What happened to you?'

'Blind Bunyip throwing his weight around. Watching. Been watching. Old Pella sent him away.'

Carrick scratched his head. Billy Boy was right. Old Pella spent all his time sleeping and dreaming his stories. 'Got some fish for tea. Going to cook it down at the camp. You coming?'

'With the boy?' He shuffled outside.

'With everyone if I get inside and sort it out.'

Fifteen

'Have you told Carrick about Dankworth?' Jane whispered as she loaded the basket with tin plates and mugs, a pat of butter, damper and some pickles.

'Ruan, go and get your jacket. It'll be cold when the sun goes down.' Roisin lifted her finger to her lips, shaking her head. 'No. I don't want to spoil the evening. Not the last one. There's nothing he can do.'

Jane waited until Ruan left the room, and then turned. 'What if he comes back?'

'Dankworth won't come back for a while. The Governor's Ball isn't until next week. They've all gone down to Sydney, that's why we had to have the dress and corset finished. Lady Alice told me they were all going and would stay for a few weeks.'

'And after that?'

'I've decided I'm not going to keep running. I'll fight him for Ruan. As I should have done in the first place.'

'It'll be his word against yours. What about Ruan's records at the church? When he was baptised?'

'Ruan wasn't baptised. They asked for the father's name. I wanted to forget. Not leave a tiny baby with the stain of the past. And besides, I don't hold with the church. What good did it do my mam?'

'I thought children had to be registered. They made it a law. Father Benson's big on that.'

'What he doesn't know won't hurt him. And Dankworth can't prove Ruan's his son. What man can?'

'What man can?' Jane repeated, brushing off her hands. 'You're right. We won't be worrying about it, then.'

But she did worry and she always would. Why did Dankworth want Ruan? He had a wife and surely they'd have children in good time. Lady Alice couldn't be much older than she was herself.

Jane smiled and tucked a cloth over the basket. 'I've got the plates and some pickles and damper ready for the fire. Let's go and see what Carrick and Slinger have planned.'

'Carrick *and* Slinger?'

A blush swept upward from Jane's lace collar, turning her face a pretty pink. 'Slinger said he'd be down there, too. He plays the fiddle, you know.'

'Does he now? And you'd be looking forward to seeing him again, would you?'

'Oh stop it. Let's have some fun.' She grabbed Roisin's hand and they ran down the steps.

It would be good to put all the worry behind her for an evening. There was nothing Carrick could do to stop Dankworth. He'd never asked about Ruan, about his father, no one had, not since that first time she'd lied to Elsie and Maisie. She'd no doubt she had them to thank for that. They would have told all and sundry she was a widow, that Ruan's father had died. Too late now to tell Carrick, and what difference would it make? Once he and

Slinger brought King Polai down he'd be gone, back to Ireland. When he came back, if he came back …

Basking in the glow of the fire, Roisin picked the last of the fish from the bones and put the tin plate onto the ground. The strains of Slinger's fiddle wrapped around them, a sad ballad of lost love and a forgotten homeland. Jane sat at Slinger's feet, her eyes never leaving his face. 'I'll not forget you, oh my darling! In the land I'm goin' to …' Her plaintive voice harmonised with the mellow notes Slinger conjured from his battered fiddle and weaved a special magic in the night air.

A fitting end. A farewell, Carrick had said. He sat across the fire from her with Ruan cradled between his long legs, his chin resting on the boy's head and his arms wrapped protectively around him. Ruan would miss him so much. The first man her son had ever truly known. He'd make a fine father, far better than Dankworth, no matter how much money and how many influential friends he had.

The memory of Carrick's ravaged face the night he'd told the story of Liam and Brigid still sent goosebumps trailing down her arms. She couldn't give Ruan up. Oh, she knew it happened, happened all the time. Children were adopted, taken in by families who had no children of their own. All the Irish lads and lasses fleeing the Famine left their families behind them. Sometimes it worked. They found new homes and happiness. It wouldn't happen to her son.

She lifted her eyes and met Carrick's smouldering gaze across the fire. Heat raced through her, scorching her skin. If only she could convince him to stay. She didn't want to wait for him to come back from Ireland.

'We should take this lad home.' Carrick eased to his feet, Ruan tucked close to his body, safe and secure as always.

Slinger lowered his fiddle into its case, his scarred, rough hands a strange contrast against the delicate neck of the musical instrument. Jane closed the lid, her fingers brushing his. There was no reason the night should be over for Jane and Slinger. He'd be back once they'd cut the tree, although as much as she hoped Jane would find happiness, she couldn't help being a little envious.

'You stay, Jane. I can manage.' The girl deserved some time and some admiration, and from the expression on Slinger's face he'd plenty to offer. 'Stay. Carrick will help me with Ruan.'

She tucked the tin plates into the basket next to Old Pella's latest offering: a sharpened bone, a fish hook, apparently. According to Old Pella, it would draw the fish like a magnet and no one would ever go hungry again. She let out a tiny sigh of pleasure—such a relief to know where all Ruan's treasures had come from and to know that the shadows she'd seen from the window were no more than the old man's patrol as he kept his blind bunyip at bay.

The native stories sparked more than Ruan's imagination; hers had run riot. All those wasted nights staring out of the window picturing someone in the shadows, watching and waiting. Carrick's arm slipped around her shoulders, cradling her close as the three of them wandered up the path beneath the canopy of stars, clusters of scattered diamonds thrown by an unseen hand.

'Shall I be carrying him up to his bed?' The lilt of Ireland in his voice and his fiery blue eyes stirred her blood, made her think back to the first time he'd pulled her into his arms, the touch of his hard body heating her skin, the flurry of sensations scalding her body.

'Yes, if you would.' Alone she'd have had to wake Ruan; he was far too heavy now for her to carry up the narrow attic ladder.

Standing in the doorway, she savoured the play of Carrick's strong muscles as he edged up the rungs, his body tight and taut, protecting her son.

Murmured voices drifted down to her: the creak of the bed and the rustle of blankets, sounds of comfort and caring. With this man Ruan would come to no harm. He'd give her son the space to grow and learn, to become strong, loyal, honest and loving.

Carrick eased back down the ladder and turned to her. Her cheeks grew hot and she swallowed, gulping down a breath. With his dark eyes intent on her face he stood motionless, leaning against the ladder, his head almost grazing the roof.

Sweeping her hand across her forehead she brushed her hair from her face. He moved towards her, raised his hand. She flinched, then her breath caught and her heart raced as step by step he backed her against the wall. The palms of his hands lay flat against the wall, not touching her, standing so close the heat of his body radiated against her skin.

A tangled cry slipped between her lips and she clamped her teeth.

'Roisin, my love.' His voice, low, almost broken, cut through her panic. This was Carrick not Dankworth. She stared into his face. Nothing like the face that had haunted her dreams and filled her with terror. She didn't want to live her life that way, running and hiding, jumping at every passing shadow. She wanted to live in the sunshine, know what it was to love and be loved by a man, and Carrick was the man she wanted, the man she loved with all her heart. Dankworth would not take that from her any more than she would allow him to take Ruan.

She snatched a breath as he murmured her name again and again, as if he wanted to imprint it on his mind, then lifted his hand to cradle her cheek. A long, low tug of lust curled in her belly. It was her choice. The past or the future—and she made her decision. She leaned forward and laid her cheek against his chest and his arms came around her, pulling her into his embrace, the base of his throat so close she could reach up and touch it with her lips. The man she loved by choice not by force.

She could smell him, the pungent scent of the timber and heat and man. His scent raced through her senses, feeding the heaviness in her limbs and the lightness in her head. The first man she'd ever wanted. Her treacherous body gave a wiggle of delight.

He raised her chin with his hand and bent down until his mouth rested against hers. 'I never thought I could love again. Never wanted to open myself to the pain of losing. You've stolen my heart, Roisin, and I'll not be the same again.' He breathed the words into her open mouth, turning her legs boneless, twisting her heart inside out.

'Will you have me when I return? Tell me.' He tightened his grip on her arms and pulled her close, so close his lean, hard body crushed against her, sending her pulse into a frantic spiral, filling her head with a rhythmic thud that drowned out all reason. A wave of heat stole the breath from her lungs as his lips roamed her face, awakening a hunger she didn't know she possessed, desires she'd never imagined.

From somewhere deep inside her came the answer to Carrick's question. 'Not when you return.'

His lips stilled, his eyes dark and questioning.

'Now, Carrick, before you leave.'

'Don't be tempting me, my love. It's not the time.' A sigh came from deep inside him and he dropped his gaze to her mouth, then removed his hands from her cheeks and shook his head.

She lifted her hands and cupped his face. The longing in his eyes was plain to see and behind that, deep into his soul, was the spirit of the only man she'd ever love. Sliding her hands into the thick hair at the nape of his neck, she stretched up onto her toes and brought his lips back to hers. His rumbling groan echoed against her breast, vibrated on her lips. 'Yes, tonight.' She murmured the words against his lips and his body stilled.

'And if I don't return?'

'You'll come back. To build our house. You promised me.'

A frown flickered across his brow and she smoothed it with her fingertips. It was time. The only time they had. Beneath her palm his heart beat steadily and his eyes never wavered.

'Wait, wait until I come back, then we will—'

She stilled his mouth with her kisses. She didn't want to wait, wouldn't wait. 'Tonight, Carrick, before you go. Leave me memories to cherish.'

He reached up and gently pulled the pins from her hair. One by one he removed them, letting her hair fall down across her shoulders. His eyes searched hers and she didn't look away, just stared deep into his blue, almost black, eyes. He trailed his fingers through her hair, sighing softly, then took her face between his hands.

'I want to be with you.' Even as she spoke his hands moved over her, as though he couldn't help himself. His body tightened, pressing against hers, telling her all she needed to know. There was no need for words. She couldn't think of right and wrong, of the future, of what might be, of tomorrow, there was only now. Need rose within her, strong and urgent, making her tremble as she wrapped herself around him, extinguishing the little niggle of fear inside her. Soon their skin would touch, their bodies communicate. It was all she wanted.

Roisin slid away from him, stretched out her hand and led him to her bed. His arms encircled her, his breath fanning her face, then his lips crushed against hers, his tongue darting and enticing. His hands slid down to her waist and he lifted her, cradling her to his chest as he laid her on her shimmering, silken quilt.

Goosebumps flecked her skin and her fingers trembled as she reached for the tiny buttons running down the front of her blouse.

'You're cold.' His lips curved a little, his eyes crinkling at the corners.

'Not cold.'

She let her hands fall to her side and he finished unbuttoning her blouse, sliding it from her shoulders, kissing her skin softly.

Their mouths met, sweet and hot. Even as her pleasure rose she sensed him holding back. His fingers, sometimes unsteady, skimmed over her as if he feared she might break. Then his hands were on her legs, sliding slowly up beneath her skirt. A flash of panic swirled inside her.

'Would you be wanting me to stop?' His fingers trickled across her skin. 'You tell me.'

And he kissed her so gently it made the tears trickle down her cheeks into her hair, damping the pillow beneath her head. She was here in his arms, in the arms of the man she loved. Her choice.

'I want you,' she murmured, then his mouth found her breast, making her body glow and prickle with anticipation. She had such a hunger for him, something she didn't know existed. Something greedy and desperate.

She pushed back into the familiar softness of her quilt and raised her legs around his waist. When he entered her a flicker of shock swept through her, making her hands fist on the quilt. She bit back a cry as the pain diminished and desire replaced it.

Her breath shuddered on a sigh and she turned her lips to the side of his neck and began to move under him. She rose and took him deeper, fell back and drew him into her again. Warmth simmered to heat and their skin grew slick. She arched beneath him and his long, full-throated cry ripped through her and the rage of his blood, the pound of his need became hers.

Basking in the afterglow, she lay wrapped in his arms half dreaming, a lazy sexual haze clouding her thoughts, while he traced his fingers over her skin as if he couldn't stop touching her.

'It breaks my heart that I must be leaving you.'

She buried her face against his shoulder and ignored his words. He'd come back, she knew he would. 'I love you.'

'And I you. More than you'd be knowing. I'll be returning, as soon as I make an end of it.'

'I know you will. You promised.'

'Aye and I keep my promises.' His lips skimmed her face and she drifted asleep, secure in the knowledge that above all else Carrick would keep his word.

When Roisin next awoke a shimmering path of moonlight lay across the bed, highlighting the planes and angles of his body, turning his skin to alabaster.

She ran her hand over his flesh, imagining the blood throbbing beneath, across his broad, deep chest to his shoulder, the raised, puckered scar strangely smooth, then down the sculpted muscles of his thighs. When he stirred and murmured her name she kissed him lightly on the lips and nestled in his arms.

So this was love. Not an aggressive assault in a back alley, or the sordid couplings she'd witnessed at Aunt Lil's. She didn't regret one second of the night and whatever the future might bring, she'd hold this memory close. Treasure it, let it strengthen her while she waited for his return, because he would. He'd come back to her once he had made his peace with the past. Rolling over, she moulded her body against his and closed her eyes. His arm snaked around her, pulling her into his embrace.

'If I die right now I'll die a happy man.' His words spoken in the stillness and dark of the world they'd created took her by surprise. He turned and gathered her to his chest and they slept away the night cradled beneath her silken quilt.

The frail light of the winter morning woke her and without opening her eyes she knew he'd gone. They had said their farewell and now she must wait. She could be patient.

She tucked the quilt around her shoulders and burrowed down and dozed, fixing every moment of the night firmly in her mind to be taken out and cherished like one of Ruan's treasures during the months that followed.

Ruan's squirming body landed on the bed with a thump. 'Mam, wake up. Wake up. Carrick has gone. Look, look what he left me.' She rolled over, her hand cradling her fluttering stomach, wondering if she, too, might have a lasting reminder. How she'd love that. Her lips curved in a smile as she imagined his face when he returned. 'What has he left you, another treasure?'

'His fishing line. Look, his fishing line. I'll practice every day and when he comes back I'll catch a hundred fish and we'll have such a party. I miss him, Mam. I'll miss him every day until he's back.'

'And so will I, my darling, so will I.'

Sixteen

Carrick slipped through the door and closed it firmly behind him. He'd known leaving would be hard but hadn't imagined it would be this difficult. Perhaps it was a coward's way out to leave with the memory of her welcoming body and loving smile. If he'd woken her and she'd cried he'd have come undone. He couldn't return until he'd cleared the stain from his heart; only then could he offer her everything she deserved. Revenge had sustained him for too long, burned a black hole in his heart as deep as the bastard's brand on his shoulder. Brigid and Liam's death had stripped the light from his life, from his very soul. Roisin and Ruan had given it back.

True to his word as always, Slinger stood ready down at the campsite. The horses were saddled and the two pack animals loaded with saws, axes, ropes and chains.

'Thought I might have to come and drag you out of bed.' Carrick slapped Slinger across the back and rammed his hat down hard on his head, then pulled the collar of his own jacket up against the biting wind.

'Told you I'd be ready. Besides, I want this finished. I've got me a nice warm bed waiting and an even warmer woman.' Slinger winked, tossed him the reins and mounted his own horse.

And how he envied Slinger. A week or so and he'd be back with a pocketful of money and the future free and clear. 'So you'll not be heading up to the Bellinger when we're through?'

'Someone's got to stay around and keep an eye on those two. Kill the scandal and make sure they're not wanting for anything. I'll think about Bellinger once you get back from your little jaunt.'

'And what makes you think I'll be coming back?'

'You'll be back.' Slinger belted his heels into his horse. 'Come on, let's get this job done.'

By the time the sun had risen above the hills they'd turned off the main track and were heading down into the valley. Old Pella insisted he and Billy Boy would be up at the caves waiting for them. With their help they'd be able to move a lot faster, get in and out sooner, while the bloody overseer and his mate weren't there. 'Doesn't look like anyone's been through since last time. Billy said he'd be keeping an eye out.'

'Can't trust the bloody natives, they're never where they say they'll be. Gone on one of those walkabouts, more 'n' like.'

'Old Pella told him we were coming. Wants to make sure we don't touch their special places.'

'Won't be their special places anymore. Not if the land's granted. That bloody overseer'll be in here and he'll take the tree before anyone can say *bleedin' redcoat*.'

'No one's taking that tree. It's mine. Besides, they haven't had time to get a crew together. We would've heard about it. If it were my land I'd take the tree, too, use it to build myself a home. Cedar's good for houses, keeps the bugs away.'

'It's also good for coffins. And no one cares whether the bugs stay away once they're six feet under.'

Sometimes Slinger could be a morbid bugger. Not coffins. He'd had enough of coffins and misery. Roisin would have her house even if he didn't make it back. 'No dray's come in. The bush is still too thick. We'll have to clear it so the bullocky can come through and get the timber out.'

'Have you told the bullocky you'll be wanting him?'

'Nah! Plenty of teamsters passing through who will do the job for a price. Wanted to keep it quiet. I reckon we'll be using someone else. If the land's been granted we're trespassing so we'll not be wanting anything or anyone to tie us to the place.'

'Bullocky's all right. He can't string two words together at the best of times.'

'Just because he doesn't say much doesn't make him a halfwit. He's a good bloke.'

'Could always take it out through Wyong, down to the coast. Might be better and quicker now they've clamped down on the licences.'

'I've got other plans.' He'd tell Slinger what he wanted done with the timber once the tree was down.

'Bloody dark in here. The canopy's as thick as all get out.'

'Nothing's been cut, that's why.'

'Nothing to cut.' Slinger threw aside a tangled vine. 'Why just the one, then?'

'Old Pella reckons it's because it's the king.'

'Blah! Load of rubbish. Will we make it before the light goes?'

'We'll make camp up in the caves with Billy Boy. Then get an early start in the morning.'

'I could eat the hind leg off a donkey.'

'Cold mutton and bread tonight unless Billy Boy's snagged a possum or two.'

When they reached Billy Boy's cave the light had turned grey and chilly, and a fine wind stirred the mizzling rain.

'Irish rain for you, mate.'

'Nothing Irish about this rain. It's not set in. Tomorrow it'll be fine. Check the sky.' Red streaks scored the clouds above the rock face, turning the sandstone to orange. 'I can understand why there's so many leaving the home country and coming here. They've got a better chance. No potatoes, no famine and no bloody rain.'

'Just the natives' fires, flood and bloody redcoats.'

'Redcoats will be gone soon. Most of them are handing in their commissions and heading for the goldfields, or they're being sent to Van Diemen's Land.'

'And good riddance to them.' Slinger tethered the horses and removed the packs, then clambered up into the cave after Carrick. He reached out to the remnants of the fire. 'No one's been here for a day or two. No sign of Billy Boy either.'

Carrick heaved a log under the overhang of the cave and brought it down with a crash, breaking the dead timber into small pieces, then crouched down and eased a packet of Congreves from inside his shirt. He lit the fire, hardly able to summon the patience to wait until morning. The sooner they started the sooner they'd finish. After ten years his patience had worn right through.

Slinger dragged the remains of the cold mutton from the saddlebag and offered him some. He shook his head. 'Tea first.' The thought of eating the cold, greasy mutton turned his stomach. He was getting soft. It didn't take long for a man to appreciate the comforts of home.

Pulling a flagon of rum out of his saddlebag, Slinger settled down, gnawing on a bone, more like one of the wild dingoes than a human. He wiped the fat from his mouth with the back of his sleeve. 'Once you've got your King Polai, then what?'

'I told you. I'm going home.'

'Why would you be doing that? Waste of bloody money if you ask me. You must have a fair bit stashed away by now. You could set yourself up right and proper. Or head off to the goldfields. Make a fortune if you've got some money behind you. And then there's Roisin. She'd help pass the nights. Help you leave the old country behind.'

'You stick with your affairs and I'll stick with mine. I've got business to sort out.'

'What kind of business?'

'The unfinished kind.'

'You're tighter than an emu's arse.'

'Here.' Carrick nudged the flagon of rum closer to Slinger. 'Get some of that into you, then get some sleep. Big day tomorrow. I want to be in there before the sun breaks.'

'Nothing else to do.'

Carrick unrolled his piece of canvas alongside the fire and lay down, covering his face with his hat. Ireland. Give it six months and he'd be there—less if he picked up a fast ship. As sleep claimed him, he waited for their faces to fill his mind, but all he saw was Roisin, her face in the moonlight, hair spread across the pillow. Fidgeting, he sat up and removed a stone pressed against his back. Smooth and round its colours flickered in the firelight. He spat on it, wiped away the dust, then rubbed it on his shirtsleeve and slipped it into his pocket. One for Ruan. Another treasure. Maybe he'd take him panning for gold, find a bit of real treasure. God he'd miss the lad. Was already missing his mam.

The grey misty dawn held the promise of a fine spring day. Good cutting weather. He stoked the remnants of the fire, stacked some more wood onto it and set the billy to boil. Excitement swirled in the pit of his stomach. He'd waited so long for this. Not just the tree, knowing it signalled the end of his time in Australia. All the waiting, all the planning. He'd finally have the bugger and he'd stick him. An eye for an eye, like the good book said. None of this turning-the-other-cheek rubbish. The bastard would die. Just the way he'd promised when he'd stood in the dock. He scratched at his shoulder then measured the tea into the billy, shoving his boot into Slinger's recumbent form. 'Oi! On yer feet. Time to make a move.'

'Fuck off.' Slinger dragged the canvas over his head and burrowed deeper, like a wombat hiding from rain. The empty rum flagon rolled across the ground. Carrick grinned. That'd make him work faster. He'd finished his ration in one night. No more grog till they were done. Tapping the billy, he stared at the leaves as they settled. Shame he'd not be here to teach the lad a bit about the bush, too. There'd be plenty of time when he got back. A man needed to know the way to survive, and the heritage of the country of his birth.

'On yer feet. Here.' The tea slopped over the edge of the tin mug as he thrust it into Slinger's hand.

'Okay! Okay! Give me a minute. You're bloody keen.'

'Stop whingeing. This'll line yer pockets for a year or four and buy some pretty ribbons for that girl ye're so keen on.'

Slinger took the tea, sipped it and rubbed his hand over his face. 'Where the hell did that rum come from? It's a shit load stronger than Maisie's usual brew.'

'Maybe you drank a load more. No more until the tree's down.' Carrick rolled his bed into a compact bundle and secured the ropes, then kicked over the traces of the fire. 'I'll saddle the horses.'

Following the wallaby tracks, they led the horses deeper into the valley. It was decent land; make a good grant, especially if it did front the Wyong River—give direct access to the coast—great for shipping cedar. Shame there wasn't any left. Boat from Sydney, smaller one down to the reaches of the Wyong River and you'd be there quicker than the days it took to travel to Morpeth, though the whole bloody world would know where you'd been and where you were going. No, he'd done it right. Taking the route over the mountain to Morpeth and keeping the stands a secret. He gave a harsh bark of laughter.

'Now what?' Slinger grumbled as he kneed his horse closer and ducked to avoid a low-hanging branch.

'Nothing much. Just thinking it's a top piece of land. Someone could do well here. Shame there's no timber left.'

'Reckon the stand we cleared belonged to this grant, too?'

'Aye, without a doubt.'

'Sure no one's been through here since we were here? The track seems clearer.'

'Don't think they have. Seen any surveyor's marks?'

'Nothing in the trees.'

'Keep yer eyes peeled for cairns.'

'For what?'

'The piles of stones they use to mark the corners of the grants.' Not that it mattered whether they'd surveyed the land or not. This was illegal whichever way it was looked at. It was private land now and they had no right to be on it. 'Give it another half hour and we'll be there.' Carrick pointed down to the valley floor. 'Creek's down there. Yeah. And look up.'

As he spoke the sun breached the hills and sent a swathe of light down to the valley floor. The tangle of undergrowth cleared a little as the track wound down to the creek. The thick branches of the huge tree supporting the ever-present tangle of vines cast shadows, interspersed with patches of filtered sunlight, across the uneven ground.

Carrick drew to a halt and dismounted. 'We'll leave the horses and the gear here and decide where to make camp.' He tethered his horse and moved up the bank. 'Slinger? You coming?'

'Someone's been here. On the bank, footmarks.'

'It'll be Billy Boy and his mates.'

'Billy Boy and his mates don't wear boots like these.'

As the words drifted up to him, Carrick's skin puckered and the hairs on his neck rose, making his skin prickle. He turned and ran his finger across his throat.

Slinger nodded, acknowledging his sign, and crouching low they crested the rise.

Above them the giant cedar loomed, a sentinel guarding the forest, its buttress roots stretching like fingers anchoring it to the land. He tipped his head back and followed the trunk into the canopy, the pink tips of the new leaves and beyond to the patch-worked sky. Only the occasional cry of a whip bird broke the church-like stillness of the place. Not a leaf stirred. The thick absence of sound niggled at his skin. He wiped the sheen of sweat from his face. Something was wrong.

A hand landed on his shoulder.

He jumped clear in the air and whipped around. Slinger grinned at him. 'King Polai got you, has he? Having second thoughts?'

'It's a magnificent beast, it'll break my heart to take it down.'

'You've said that before. Think of the money. If we don't take it some other bugger will. You're right, it's over two hundred feet. We'll have to peg it, build a couple of platforms, no way we can cut through that trunk low down. No chance of doing it in a week either, 'specially with no rum.'

Clambering across the buttress roots, Carrick reached out his hands and pressed his palms flat against the rough bark, spreading his pale and insignificant fingers wide against the dark-pitted bark. Step by step he measured the width of the trunk. The wood at the heart would be the deepest red, worth a fortune.

He continued sidestepping, counting as he went, craning up to the canopy. Beneath his fingertips the tree's heart beat fast, the sap flowing through its veins like blood through a man. It'd build a perfect home for Roisin and Ruan, down by the brook. He'd manage with less money, get back quicker.

Twenty spans and still not even halfway around the trunk, his foot caught and he slid, grappling the bark for purchase as he toppled backwards. Too busy counting, too busy imagining her breathing heart, a home and hearth. Damn it. His ankle turned and he slumped, letting his body roll over the roots until he settled in the leaf litter.

As his momentum stilled, he started to struggle to his feet when his fingers closed around—

He catapulted up, the muscles in his stomach tightening and loosening like a nervous fist. Wide, staring eyes. Slack mouth and the stench of voided bowels. His stomach heaved and he twisted away, willing the vomit back down his throat. 'Slinger!'

'Jesus fucking Christ. The bugger's dead.'

Carrick closed his eyes and forced some air into his starved lungs.

When Slinger prodded the body with his foot, it rolled and tumbled down the embankment. 'Christ, the smell.' He clapped his hand across his nose and mouth. 'The bugger's had it. Wasn't expecting it. No doubt about that.' He peered down at the corpse. 'Taken a bullet in his back.'

Willing his galloping heart to steady, Carrick skidded down the embankment. Shot in the back. Hadn't even known it was coming. Murdered by a sodding coward.

Slinger booted the body over and peered down at the waxy face. 'The overseer. The bloke that chased us off. Thought you said he wouldn't be back. It's the bloody natives. Billy Boy and his mates. He said it was a bad place.' Slinger paced up and down, throwing his arms this way and that, his face flushing first red then white.

'Slinger get yer act together—that's a bullet hole in his back. The natives don't use guns. It'd be a spear in him if they'd done it.' More importantly, why was the overseer alone? There'd been two of them last time, the overseer and the mug hiding behind the tree with the gun. He stood up and gazed around, the shock seeping away as he envisaged the scene. He wouldn't have been alone. No sign of a struggle. Not a fight. Someone he trusted or someone who'd followed him. There was no sign of horses, just the footprint on the creek bed.

Slinger stood with hands on his hips gazing down at the body. 'It doesn't make sense. Let's get the hell out of here. He didn't kill himself, so there's got to be someone else around. Come on.' Slithering and slipping, he toppled down the bank. 'You can keep your bloody tree. I want no part of it. It's bad luck. Bad place.'

Carrick settled the overseer on his back, his eyes roving the area. No matter who did it or how it happened the man deserved a burial. 'Slinger.'

Slinger had already untied the horses and started up the track. 'Are you coming or not?'

Carrick dragged himself to his feet, his thoughts spinning. 'If we're not going to take him out, the least we can do is bury him.' He needed to get out of the place, see the sky. Stop and take time to think. He bent down, closed the man's eyes and arranged his arms, settling them across his chest. They'd heard no gunshot; the man couldn't have been dead more than three or four hours. Sometime last night, or early this morning before the sun was up; any earlier and he'd be stiffer than a cedar split.

'Stay right where you are, gentlemen.'

Carrick's head snapped up. On the rise above him, almost invisible against the tangled growth, stood three constables in blue uniforms. The barrels of their guns trained on his chest. Slinger dropped the horses' leads and threw his hands in the air.

The hairs on the back of Carrick's neck settled. His body had known but his mind had ignored the warning. Too hellbent on the bloody cedar and years of planning to heed the signs. They'd fallen into the trap like a couple of novices. He scanned the faces of the three constables, recognising none.

'Carrick O'Connor, cedar cutter. Show us your licence.'

'Don't have one and I don't need one.'

'Weren't cutting,' Slinger gestured, his arms falling wide.

The red-faced, pockmarked constable stepped forward, his chest thrust out like a bumptious cockerel. 'Intending to by the looks of this.' He flicked his hand at the axes and crosscut saws on the packhorse. 'Apart from the cutting there's the small matter of the dead man.' He inclined his head towards the figure half buried in the leaf litter.

Slinger turned to Carrick. 'Dead man. What dead man? We ain't seen no dead man.'

There was little point in arguing the case. They'd got them stitched up well and truly.

'Well?' The constable edged closer and prodded Carrick's chest with the barrel of his gun.

Carrick nodded. No point in trying to crawl out of this one. 'We found him, down there under the cedar tree.'

Slinger drew himself up to his full height. 'We cut no timber and we didn't kill him. We found him.'

'You can tell that to the magistrate when you get back to Wollombi. He'll decide. If there's enough evidence, you'll be detained to await trial.'

'Magistrate.' Slinger twisted and dived into the undergrowth.

Slinger was behaving like a fool. Right out of character. The sight of the uniforms had turned him into a blithering idiot. They'd have more chance telling their story to the magistrate. There were no witnesses. And the constables had known about the murder before they did, otherwise they wouldn't have been here. 'Slinger, stop. We'll sort it out back in Wollombi. We've done nothing wrong.'

'Bloody constabulary. Give me cutter's justice any day. They're all as bent as a two-bob bit.'

The constable squinted over Carrick's shoulder then twisted around, searching the shadows, as if seeking guidance.

A bullet whizzed past and embedded itself in the tree behind him. He whipped around and it was the same as before: a woollen-clad arm, the gloved hand holding a pistol.

He rubbed his hand over his shoulder, his brand itching, as if trying to remind him how easy it was to be caught out and set up.

'Get a move on.' The constable prodded Slinger with his gun. 'Come with me. We're going to pick up the body. Evidence. Take it back to town. You.' He flicked his head at Carrick. 'Come here.'

Carrick stepped forward, with his hands out. The familiar weight of the cuffs locked around his wrists. The irony didn't escape him. He'd come full circle. Just when he was almost done he was back in irons where he'd started.

By the time the bedraggled party reached Wollombi darkness had fallen. One lamp burned over the courthouse and the constables led Carrick and Slinger around the back of the building, the overseer's body strapped across the saddle of the packhorse. The red-faced constable produced a large key and unlocked the chain looped through the handles. 'Your accommodation, boys. Down the end on the left.'

Slinger's eyes darted around the walled enclosure and back to the heavy metal gate they'd arrived through.

'Forget it.' Carrick headed into the darkened passageway, his cuffed hands in front of him. 'We'll not get out of here in a hurry.'

The moon shone through the high, barred window, where two cells marked the end of the short walkway. He stuck his head in the first: the outline of a single wooden board was visible in the shadows. Moving to the next door, he peered inside; it was the same set-up except for a small high, barred window facing the street.

'I'll take this one, Slinger.' At least with the window he'd see the passage of the stars and know what he was missing. He slumped down on the board suspended from the wall by two chains. The door to Slinger's cell clanged shut and the constable appeared in the doorway. He lifted the chain imbedded in the wall and locked Carrick's cuffs to it. 'They'll come off in the morning when I bring you some tucker if you behave yourself. Best just lie down and get some sleep, that way the chains won't give you too much grief.'

Carrick grunted. Not much he could do. Through the thick sandstone walls he could hear Slinger carrying on a treat. He might as well save his energy until they came up in front of the police magistrate. Bloody Winchester, the Sydney toff.

What were the chances of the system here being anything different to Ireland? Winchester's reputation preceded him, never mind the prejudiced behaviours of the town constables. According to the Paterson cutters, Winchester even employed an official scourge. Given the choice he'd rather stick with cutter's justice—hard but fair.

He settled back against the wall and drew his knees up to his chin. The wind howled through the window, working its way into his bones. At least this time he'd not be coming up against the might of the British army. Not that it mattered. If found guilty it would be back to Port Arthur at best. At worst the death penalty. Slinger, too. Poor sod. This was not a situation of his own making and yet here he was taking the fall. And they weren't guilty. He rubbed his shoulder up against the wall, the old scar itching as it always did when his skin contracted with the cold.

If he hadn't seen it with his own eyes, he'd not believe it. What was the overseer doing back there and who'd been with him the first day? Holy Mother of God, what he'd give to be able to ask the man some questions. Too late now. Dead men couldn't talk.

'Hey, Slinger.'

'Yep.'

'Any idea who the overseer was? Who he was working for? Who'd taken the land grant?'

'Nope. More interested in getting something to eat and drink than worrying about him.'

The door to Slinger's cell rattled as he hammered it to and fro. 'Oi, Where's our grub? We need rations. Food. You're meant to provide.'

'Quit your moaning. You'll get breakfast, until then put up with it.'

'Constable?' Carrick called.

'Now what?'

'Any idea who the dead man is?'

'Thought you'd know that.'

'Why would I know that, since I didn't kill him?'

'What about your mate?'

'Slinger. You know who the dead man is?'

'Me? Nope.'

Seventeen

A draught of cold air whistled around Roisin's legs and the door banged. 'Jane, would you drop the latch? The wind must have come up. The house is so warm, it seems a shame to lose the heat.'

'I thought it was closed. I'll check.' Jane left her tatting on the table and wandered off. 'I'll make a pot of tea while I'm there.'

'That would be lovely.' Roisin studied the last row of stitches, sighed and started to unpick them. Her mind wasn't on the job. Even if it was only a set of pillowcases, the least she could do was make sure the work was perfect. In the last two days she'd lost interest in everything. Knowing Carrick would be away for so long had left her with such a feeling of emptiness, and she hadn't anticipated Ruan's incessant questions about the cedar cutter. She found it difficult to have to keep saying *I don't know* and *I hope so.* Even Old Pella had vanished, disappeared goodness only knows where, tracking his blind bunyip more than like.

She re-threaded her needle and attempted, for the third time, to sew a straight line. Perhaps it was just that the more mundane, bread-and-butter jobs didn't fire her imagination. Not that she was overly keen on making any more corsets. Knowing she'd encouraged Lady Alice to wear something to entice her husband

and then discovering Dankworth was the man in question made her flesh creep and brought a bitter taste to her mouth. As though she'd in some way encouraged the vile man.

Not only that, if Lady Alice was barren, it made Dankworth's demands for Ruan all the more feasible. As much as she liked Lady Alice, she'd no intention of handing her son over to her. No matter what they could do for the boy. She'd rather he became a cedar cutter than a sadistic toff like Dankworth. At least the cutters had their own sense of justice and fair play. Ruan was *her* son. No one else's, although she didn't feel like that with Carrick anymore, not so possessive of Ruan. He spent so much time with him. It must be because he reminded him of Liam. The thought of Carrick losing his child and his wife still made her blood run cold.

'Roisin!'

Sighing, she put down her stitching. Jane's voice sounded strained. Perhaps the old man was back, sicker maybe, although the bruises seemed to have healed. Jane's compresses of arnica had worked wonders.

'I'm coming.'

'I'm all right.'

That was Ruan's voice and he sounded furious.

'Ruan!' She lifted her skirts and flew the last few feet into the kitchen. He stood in the middle of the floor, his clothes muddied and his hair standing on end. 'What are you doing here? Why aren't you at school?'

'I'm not going to school anymore.' The set of his shoulders squared and he turned to face her, his nose bloodied and his cheeks splattered with mud.

'What happened to you?' She reached out to pull him into a hug.

He shrugged her away and slapped at the cloth Jane held, thumping his hands on his hips. The anger radiating from his small body was heating the kitchen more than the cooking fire.

'Let me see.' She knelt down in front of him. He'd been fighting, no doubt about it. Perhaps it wasn't such a good idea for him to spend so much time with Carrick after all. The cutters always seemed to resort to their fists when things didn't go the way they planned.

He backed away from her, his eyes flashing. 'I'm fine.' She'd never truly appreciated how green his eyes could be, although she'd never seen him this angry. His whole body seethed with a barely contained rage.

'No, you're not.' She held out her hand for the cloth. Jane wrung it out and passed it to her. 'Did you fall over?'

'No!' He stamped his foot, eyes still blazing, then his lower lip started to tremble, giving him away.

What a fool she'd been sending him to school—swayed by Mr Blackmore and his wife's need for a new dress. He was too young. Too young to handle the other children. Just because he could read and write didn't make him capable of withstanding the horrors of the schoolyard. All those older boys teasing him. Her heart turned over and she wiped away the tear trickling down his dirty cheek. 'I'm sorry, my darling.'

'Not your fault.' He sniffed and turned his face from the cloth.

'Come and sit down, let me fix up your face.'

'I want to go.'

'Go back to school? We'll think about that tomorrow.' Had Dankworth called at the school? No, that was out of the question. Everyone in town she'd asked had confirmed the fact. The Winchesters, Dankworths and Martins were in Sydney for the Governor's Ball, otherwise she'd never have allowed Ruan out of the house on his own.

'Not back to school.' His voice caught and his little shoulders shuddered. 'To see Carrick.'

She frowned at Jane, who shook her head.

'Carrick? What has Carrick to do with this?'

'He's in the lockup. He's going to hang. I want to see him.'

The cloth fell from her hands. 'Don't be silly. Carrick's not in the lockup. He's away, cutting before he goes to Ireland. You know that, he left you his fishing line to look after until he got back. He'll be gone for months.' Probably even longer. How long did it take to get to Ireland and come back?

'He's not. He's in the lockup. Jimmy Brown's pa brought him in last night. He's got to go up in front of the magistrate.'

That would be a bit difficult since Winchester was in Sydney. 'They're just stirring you up, Ruan.' Children could be so mean. Once they found a weak spot they'd prod and pinch until … until something like this happened. 'Mr Winchester isn't even in Wollombi. He and Mrs Winchester are in Sydney for the Governor's Ball. Remember? I made the pretty dress for her.'

'They're back tomorrow and Carrick's going to hang. Jimmy's pa should know, he's the chief constable.' He flung away from her and wrenched open the back door. 'Carrick didn't murder anyone. I know.'

'Ruan, stop. Wait. Sit down and tell me what happened. I'm sure there's been some mistake. Let's go and sort this out.'

'This is men's business, Mam.' He stood tall and dragged his jacket straight. 'Slinger's in there, too.'

'Slinger?' Jane froze, despair marring her face. 'I'm coming.'

'No, I need you to stay here.' There'd be no stopping Ruan, she could tell from the set of his face. 'Jane, you stay here. Ruan can speak to Jimmy's father.'

She took her shawl from the chair and threw it around her shoulders. 'Please, stay here.' She stared imploringly at Jane, who had to be as anxious about Slinger as she was about Carrick; however, if there was a problem, she wanted to know she'd be able to send Ruan home and have someone waiting for him. 'Ruan and I will be back before long.' Of course they would. She'd take Ruan up to the lockup and prove Constable Brown's interfering son wrong and then they would come home and get to the bottom of this bullying nonsense. And after that, she'd have words with Mr Blackmore. What kind of a school was he running where his pupils were subject to such outrageous, malicious behaviour? Had the man no control?

Reaching out she took hold of Ruan's hand.

He snatched it back. 'I'm right. You'll see.' He took off at a gallop.

Slamming the door, she followed Ruan. She wouldn't allow herself to even contemplate the possibility he could be right. Carrick and Slinger were far too wily to be caught by the constables and for what? A hanging offence? Cutting, even without a licence, wasn't a hanging offence. A fifty-pound fine, not the death penalty. The more she thought about it the more she was convinced it was schoolyard jabbering and tittle-tattle. And besides, if there were any truth in the matter Elsie and Maisie would have been the first to tell her.

'Ah, so you've heard. Was just on my way to tell you.'

'I'll thank you to mind your own business, Elsie Sullivan.' She pushed past, glowering. The glower wasn't merited, but Elsie's words had deposited a stone of doubt in the pit of her stomach. Suddenly she had this horrible sense that Ruan's story might be true.

Carrick wouldn't kill anyone. She'd stake her life on that. The locals always blamed the cutters for anything that happened. Elsie and Maisie were the worst. Ever since Carrick's fight with the Paterson cutters he and his team had taken the blame, and look what those Paterson men had done to the poor old native. Just because the cutters chose to deal with their own problems without involving the law didn't mean they had no morals. For goodness sake, Carrick was the most honourable man she'd ever met.

As she marched up the road Maisie appeared on the verandah outside the inn. 'Roisin, Roisin!' She waved her plump arms, calling to her to cross the road.

Ruan ground to a halt and turned back to her. 'See, Mam, I'm right. Everyone knows.'

'We don't know, yet.' She grabbed his hand tight. 'And until we do we're not taking any notice of this drivel.'

'Carrick and his mate are in the lockup.' Maisie called across the road, just as Roisin reached the courthouse.

'Will you stop meddling, Maisie Kidd?' She tossed her head and crossed the grass on the corner of the road.

Ruan sighed and pulled his hand away. 'I told you, Mam. This is men's business.'

'If it's men's business then why did you come home first?' Ruan's eyes widened and she snapped her mouth closed. What had possessed her to say that? Bloody Carrick O'Connor. From the moment he had swept into her life Ruan had become, become … damn him. She grabbed hold of Ruan's hand again, wanting her little boy back.

Lounging outside the courthouse, the two constables followed her progress, their legs propped up, enamelled mugs in their hands and supercilious satisfaction splattered all over their reddened faces. She'd put money on the fact they weren't cradling tea in those mugs, and they accused the cutters of being desperate sots.

She marched up the courthouse steps. 'I want to see Carrick O'Connor.' No point in beating about the bush.

'And what makes you think he's here?' Constable Brown raised one wild eyebrow and the corner of his lip in a smirk.

'Jimmy told me,' Ruan piped up.

'Oh, did he indeed? I shall have to have words with my son. This is police business, not schoolyard chatter. Why should I let you see the prisoner? Not his next-of-kin, are you? Doxies aren't allowed.'

Ruan took a step forward, his little fists clenched and his jaw tight.

The reason for the fight in the schoolyard suddenly became clear. It hadn't only been Carrick Ruan was worried about, he had been protecting her. She could imagine the comments flying around behind hands. Elsie and Maisie right in the middle of it. Ever since Carrick had slept the night away in front of the fire. Never mind the other night. A mixture of pride and pain intertwined and tightened around her heart for her brave boy. 'So is Carrick here?' She slammed her hands onto her hips. If she had to wear the reputation, then she'd make the most of it.

Constable Brown took another swig of his drink and belched, leaving her in doubt about the contents of the tin mug.

'He is. And the answer's no. You can see him after he and his mate come up in front of the magistrate.'

'And when's that?'

'Two o'clock tomorrow afternoon, if Mr Winchester is back from Sydney.' A leer crossed his face and she clenched her fist as he ran an appraising eye up and down her body. 'Before you and Jane get too busy, so you should be able to make the time.' The red-faced, pockmarked constable let out a great bellow of laughter.

It wasn't worth putting him straight and the information didn't merit thanks. Obviously, the scandal about her and Jane was rife in the town. 'Come along, Ruan.' Keeping her head high, she stalked back down the steps. Ruan scampered after her, throwing half-formed questions revolving around doxies and Carrick, none of which she intended answering until they got home—if ever.

'Mrs Ogilvie, might I have a word?'

Roisin stalled in her tracks, her blood icy as she turned. *Dankworth!* Gripping Ruan's hand tight she swallowed and composed her face. The air grew thick and close and the sounds of the town retreated.

'Mam, you're hurting me.'

The pressure in her fingers registered and she relaxed. 'You go, Ruan. Go now, straight home to Jane.' She pushed him away. Thank God she'd had the foresight to ask Jane to stay at home. She might have guessed Dankworth would be involved somewhere.

'Do what your mother says, boy.'

Ruan turned and gawked at Dankworth, confusion painted all over his face. He was going to argue, and he opened his mouth to speak.

'Now, Ruan. Otherwise you won't be able to see Carrick.'

He frowned, narrowed his eyes, then nodded and took off down the road. She waited until he had reached the corner and turned back. Now was her opportunity. She had every intention of standing up to this man. She'd waited too long. He was not having her son.

'Mr Dankworth?' said Constable Brown.

'I would like a word.' He cast a derogatory glance at the two constables, who stood like statues bathed in a sea of rum fumes.

'Yes, sir. Right away, sir.' Constable Brown held open the door to the courthouse and stood back.

'A little privacy would be ideal. After you, Mrs Ogilvie.'

She cast one last glance down the street to ensure Ruan had gone home. He had. Maisie, however, stood on the verandah of the inn, her mouth gaping open. The scandalmongers would have a field day. So what? She didn't care.

It was cold inside the courthouse; she drew her shawl tight around her shoulders. How she wished she'd worn her green jacket. It made her feel courageous.

What did Dankworth want? Ruan, she knew that, but obviously he wasn't here to snatch the boy away. He'd sent Ruan home. Told him to go. She'd known from the beginning Dankworth would be back, though she hadn't expected him quite so soon. She had to stand up to him. Tell him no. She wouldn't hand over her son, not for anything or anyone.

He couldn't prove Ruan was his son and she wouldn't be intimidated. Some people might say she was mad or selfish or stupid even. Dankworth could provide for the boy, offer him chances and opportunities beyond her ability. At what price? The very thought of the life Ruan would lead turned her stomach.

Dankworth gestured to the chair in front of the desk and then circled the desk, running his long, bony fingers across the embossed leather surface. It was obviously Winchester's desk. Maybe the magistrate would help her, if she went to see Mrs Winchester and pleaded her case. Surely a woman would understand she couldn't lose her child.

He drew back the chair behind the desk and sat, legs stretched out in front of him, showcasing his highly polished black boots and his cane, tapping against them, beating the familiar, tedious tattoo.

'My dear.' His affected drawl made her skin crawl. 'I was rather hoping I would have the opportunity to be properly introduced to my son, but perhaps now is not the place or the occasion. He's a handsome little chap. Takes after his father.'

'He is not your son.' It was a pathetic attempt, but she couldn't help herself.

His ominous laugh echoed in the small courtroom. 'Apart from the fact he is the spitting image of me, I am capable of adding up time as well as the next man.' He rolled the cane in his hands between his legs. 'Let me see. The boy must be about to celebrate his seventh birthday. He's well grown. I'll give you that. He can't have lacked for sustenance.'

Seeing Dankworth sitting there, so at ease, so in control, didn't intimidate her, it toughened her resolve. 'No thanks to you.' The words were out before she could stop them. She clamped her teeth together.

He gave a throaty chuckle. 'So you acknowledge then that I have a responsibility to the boy. It is one I intend to fulfil. With the utmost diligence.'

'You're not having him.' She clenched her teeth, trapping the anger inside her, using it to sustain her. 'Nothing on God's earth would force me to hand him over to you. Over my dead body.'

'What about the dead body of your lover?'

Her head shot up. Her lover? She narrowed her eyes. The man was as slippery as an eel.

'Come, come, my dear don't be so coy. Everyone, even the good constable, knows Carrick O'Connor is your lover and I'll not have that murdering Irish insurgent anywhere near my son.'

'I don't know what you're talking about.' How did he know whether Carrick had been near Ruan or not? Dankworth had only been in town on the day he had picked up Lady Alice's corset, and Carrick had been out of town. When would he have seen them together? The local nosey parkers must have spread their stories far and wide.

'My dear.' The sleazy smile on his pale face made her knees tremble.

She clenched her hands into fists, her nails puncturing her palms. His odour—tobacco and brandy and the underlying sour stink of unwashed skin—caught in her throat, choking her.

'You hold his life in the palm of your hand.' He spread his fingers, the skin as white as milk, with nary a mark or blemish. Not like Carrick's hands, brown and scarred, rough and calloused, yet so comforting.

Why? How? The man was toying with her. 'Speak plainly. Why is Carrick in the lockup and what has it to do with you?'

'I am summoned to give evidence.' His oily, smooth voice sent a ripple of fear over her skin.

'Evidence?' Good God, she was sounding like a parrot. She clamped her lips tightly together. Let the man talk. *Murder!* How could Carrick have committed murder? Who? Slinger was with him. What had they done?

Dankworth tipped his head back, squinting out of the window at the dazzling blue winter sky. 'It's a beautiful day, is it not?'

The scream built slowly in her throat and she gulped it back. Nothing made any sense. She couldn't argue with the man if she didn't understand what he was talking about.

'Much brighter than it is in the forest. There's little light once you're deep beneath the trees. Difficult to see and difficult to know who is there and who is not.'

A cool, calm stillness descended on Roisin as a flurry of goosebumps trickled across her flesh. She ran the soft, silky fringe of her shawl through her fingers and waited, waited for him to continue, the knot tightening in the pit of her stomach.

'Of course, to be caught standing over the body of your victim is incriminating to say the least. Especially when three constables witnessed it.' He gave a dismissive snort as though he should hardly be bothering himself with such a trivial matter. 'Once a criminal always a criminal. His reputation does precede him.'

'Carrick has never murdered anyone. He has his Certificate of Freedom. He's an honest, upright man. He was transported to Australia for political crimes, not murder.'

'Immaterial, my dear, immaterial. He will hang.'

Her temper snapped. This man would not manipulate her. 'Not if I have anything to do with it.'

'And that is exactly why we are having this little conversation. You have it within your power to prevent this travesty of justice.'

The man was mad.

'The evidence I have against Mr O'Connor will see him hang. You have the power to prevent that happening.'

She leapt out of the chair; it clattered to the floor behind her. He would not toy with her. 'Speak your mind. I'll not listen to this nonsense.'

'Sit down, my dear.' With a laconic wave he indicated to the chair. 'We must deal with this in a civilised fashion.'

She ignored him, rested the palms of her hands flat on the desk and stared deep into his eyes. 'What do you want?' The tension knotted in her gut, a silken thread wound tight, gathering all her fear into a solid lump low in her belly.

'My son or your lover.'

Carrick drifted up through the swirling fug of his dreams and shifted to ease the weight of the chains. His brand burned as though it was seared into him yesterday. It was the dreams, always the dreams, the screams, flames and voices … Voices. Not screams. Roisin's voice, low and deep. This was no dream. She was here. Panic lacing her voice. He stumbled to the Judas door and pressed his face against the bars.

Ice spread through his veins. He rubbed at his eyes, blinked, slammed against the rusty bars, grazing the skin of his face. *The stinkin' murdering agent!* Gideon Dankworth. Here. Flesh and sodding blood. Not in Ireland. Right here. Lolling in a chair, shiny black boots, cane tapping. The patterned green of Roisin's shawl stabbed at the corner of his vision. He twisted, craning his head to see.

A slow smirk spread across Dankworth's face. 'My son or your lover.'

His son.

Carrick lurched against the door and sucked in a breath. *Her lover?* A load of stuff and nonsense. She'd no lover and if she did, he'd tear the bastard limb from limb. There was only one lover for Roisin and he was that man. *My son or your lover?* Ruan. Gideon Dankworth's son. A lie. All lies. Roisin would have told him if Dankworth was Ruan's father.

His heart started pounding like a bloody anvil. Why hadn't she told him? *Lying bastard!* This had to be some ridiculous plot to further his own aim. Not this time. He'd not catch him this time. He wasn't some wet-behind-the-ears fool now. Not like in Ireland. Sucked into Dankworth's devious plot to see the insurgents rounded up, accused of the fire he'd started. Accused of the destruction of property, insurgency then murders he'd not committed. He'd have him. If it was the last thing he did.

He grabbed at the bars, rattling hard. 'Come 'ere you murderin' bastard!'

A door slammed and silence fell.

For the first time since he'd left Ireland he didn't know which way his path lay. His plans were shot. He'd reached a fork in the road. One way led back to Dankworth, his past, the other to Roisin and Ruan. And straight ahead? That didn't bear thinking about.

Dankworth's voice hadn't changed, the cutglass accent, the lazy drawl. He'd recognised it down on the bank of the brook with the lad, he just hadn't believed it. He closed his eyes, seeing again the pale eyes sparking, the taunting glare when he'd lifted the torch to the thatch. The sadistic pleasure flickering as Dankworth sank the white-hot end of his cane into Carrick's shoulder. He'd never forget those eyes. They'd haunted his dreams for too long. Long after the pain from the brand. Pale eyes. Bone white. The orbs shimmering with a fierce intensity. Like a blind man.

Blind! Old Pella's Blind Bunyip.

It hadn't been the Paterson cutters. Dankworth had got to Old Pella. That's why he'd stayed. Stayed to watch over Roisin and the lad. While Carrick had been busy in the forest chasing his dreams. Why hadn't she told him? The lad couldn't be Dankworth's. Nothing so foul could produce such a treasure.

What was Dankworth doing here, in Australia? He belonged in Ireland. He could still see Dankworth's sardonic grin and hear the jubilant rap of his cane when the judge had sentenced him. Sent for seven years, to places beyond the sea. They'd escorted him from the courtroom in chains while Dankworth, flanked by his army of sycophants and redcoats, had grinned in pleasure. Now he looked more like a Sydney dandy—a politician, one of the English upper-class nobs who thought they ruled the world. He clearly couldn't crawl to the top of the heap in Ireland, so he'd come to Australia to lord it over everyone with cheap land grants and squatter's rights.

Land grants!

He dragged on his chains and moved closer to the barred window and let fly a harsh bark of disdain. 'Dankworth, you murderin' coward!'

Let him get his hands on the miserable worm. See those inhuman eyes show fear. It'd be worth hanging to know he'd rid the world of the godforsaken sadist. Let Brigid and Liam rest in peace. And Roisin—holy hell. Roisin. Ruan was Dankworth's son. The man had more than one debt to pay and he, Carrick O'Connor, would be calling it in, come hell or high water. 'Get back here, you halfwit!'

There were footsteps along the verandah; he clambered on to the hinged plank and pressed his face against the barred window. What he'd not give to get at the man.

'You can't prove anything.' Roisin's voice carried a high-pitched note; panic, fear. If the mongrel laid a hand on her … He tugged at his chains.

'It'd be obvious to anyone with half a brain.'

'And you'll be able to prove that in a court of law, will you, with the baptismal records and the like?' A note of defiance laced her voice now. Good on her.

'I don't need records.'

'That's just as well, because there aren't any.'

'I have my position in society, my connections. Who is going to take the word of a common whore?'

'I'm not a whore.'

'You'll have difficulty proving that, my dear.' The laconic drawl curled through the bars. 'Your reputation precedes you. There are many in town who will concur. Everyone knows you entertain the cutters. You and that other little tart.'

The tip-tap of heels signalled Roisin's departure. Not deigning to respond.

If Dankworth as much as touched her, touched his lad, he'd rip him limb from limb. He rattled the bars. A futile, meaningless action.

'Come back, you English pig!'

Not this time. Dankworth wouldn't touch Roisin, not while he had breath left in his body. He'd taken his family once; he'd not be doing it again. He banged his fists on the door.

It swung open.

Carrick lunged and fell, his nose grazing the toe of Dankworth's shiny boot.

'Where you belong. Grovelling. About time you accepted your place in life.'

Carrick swung aside and leapt to his feet, scarcely missing Dankworth's foot as it kicked out. 'You filthy murderer.'

'You'll have difficulty proving that in a court of law.'

'You were there at the tree before the constables.'

'Indeed I was. On my land as I had every right to be. Left my overseer to mark the boundaries, asked the constables to come and authenticate those boundaries and what did we find? You and your filthy cedar-cutting mate, standing over the poor man's body.'

'I'll have you if it's the last thing I do.'

Dankworth stepped closer. So close Carrick could smell him, smell the privilege. It didn't mask the stench of his lies.

'You killed an innocent woman and her child, and now you're adding another to your tally. Not this time.'

'You think you're going to get your own back by taking my son? Think again, you Irish scum. He's mine and I'll have him. No one in Ireland will care who bore the boy.' He rubbed his hands together, a dry, rasping sound that made Carrick want to wring his scrawny neck. 'He doesn't belong with you, you Irish peasant. Do you imagine I would let you touch my son? Say your prayers, tomorrow you'll be sentenced.'

Carrick lurched at him, but the chains held him fast.

Dankworth reached out and tore at Carrick's shirt, ripping the sleeve open, baring his skin. And then he laughed. 'Not only that, you'll go to your grave carrying my mark. No better than an animal.'

'May you rot in hell.' Carrick swallowed his useless words, and then very deliberately turned his back on Dankworth. The door slammed shut, leaving only silence and a terrible emptiness in his very soul.

Eighteen

Roisin stumbled down the steps of the courthouse, squinting into the bright sunshine. Sun that had no business shining. Her heart sat as heavy and black as the motives of that awful man.

His son or her lover? There was no choice. She wouldn't hand over Ruan or Carrick. Dankworth could bluster all he liked about swearing in court that Ruan was his son. She'd not give in to him. And how could he offer Carrick's freedom in exchange? How did he know who had killed the man in the forest? He wasn't even there. He was in Sydney at the Governor's Ball.

'Roisin, you poor darling. Come here. Is it true? Carrick did it? How's he faring?'

Interfering old biddy. Elsie was happy enough to slander the cutters when it suited her and now she offered sympathy.

'Not now, Elsie. Not now.' Her voice caught and she ducked around the corner. She couldn't cope with Elsie and her incessant questions and malicious tittle-tattle. Not now, not ever.

She slammed her fist against the front door, then tried the handle. It was locked. She lifted her foot and kicked out. 'Jane! Open the door.' Now she was locked out of her own house and where was Ruan?

After an eternity, the door opened a sliver and Jane's face appeared. 'Come in, come in. I'm sorry, I thought it was better to—'

She forced her way in. 'Where's Ruan?'

'He's here. He's safe in the kitchen with his treasure box. What happened? Is Slinger there? Are they all right?'

Roisin staggered into the parlour and collapsed into the chair. Then the shaking began. Her teeth chattered and her shoulders heaved until the tears fell, great gulping sobs beyond her control.

Jane's arms wrapped around her, pulling her face against her hip. Holding her tight. 'Let it out. Cry it out.'

How could she cry it out? Her heart was breaking and she was scared, so scared. Scared for Ruan and, holy God, scared for Carrick. Dankworth was evil. The devil incarnate. Why was he so determined to involve Carrick? What had he ever done to the man? As her mind spun, the sobs subsided, calmed by Jane's soothing pats.

'Let me get you a cup of tea. Then tell me.'

She shook her head. 'I don't want Ruan to hear. Not now. Not yet.' How would she ever tell him that sadistic excuse for a man was his father? What would he say? What would he think?

'I'll make some tea and give Ruan some biscuits and a drink of milk. He'll want to know about Carrick. He'll have to wait. Wait for a while. Is Slinger there still?'

Slinger. She hadn't even spared a thought for Slinger. Poor Jane. Nor for that matter had Dankworth. 'Slinger is in the lockup with Carrick. They'll come up before the magistrate at two o'clock tomorrow if Winchester is back from Sydney.'

Jane nodded, unable to mask the concern on her face. 'Tea.' She closed the door behind her.

Roisin let out a long, slow breath and wiped her eyes. She had to think. There had to be a way around this. Why was Dankworth even interested in Carrick? How could he know about the murder in the forest?

There was only one way: he must have been there. She sat up straight and stared out of the window, snatching at the elusive thoughts flitting through her mind. She had to think clearly. She stood up and threw off her shawl, pacing the floor. How could Dankworth give evidence against Carrick unless he knew something about the murder? Unless he had been there. His overseer, he'd said. Was he expecting Carrick and Slinger?

The door opened. 'Ruan's fine. Busy with his slate. I told him everything would be all right and you'd talk to him after you had your tea.' Jane put down the tray and offered her the cup.

She wrapped her fingers around the warmth and shivered. She was cold, so very cold.

'Now, tell me. Tell me everything.'

'Carrick is accused of murder.'

'And Slinger?'

'Just Carrick, not Slinger. I think they're keeping Slinger to give evidence.'

Jane's shoulders dropped and a tight smile crossed her lips. 'Mr Winchester is a fair man.'

'Dankworth must have been there.'

Jane's smile vanished. 'Dankworth. Ruan's father. Lady Alice's—'

'Yes. Dankworth.'

'How could he be? He's supposed to be in Sydney at the Governor's Ball, with Lady Alice and the Winchesters.'

'Well, he's back. And that's not all. He gave me an ultimatum. He said I have to choose between Ruan and Carrick.'

'I don't understand. What has Carrick to do with Ruan?'

'And that's what I don't understand either.' Roisin sipped at the scalding tea. None of it made any sense. Unless Dankworth had seen Carrick with Ruan and thought he was trying to take him. It was the only thing that made sense. She had to go and see the Winchesters. If she could speak with Mr Winchester, explain that it was her fight, her fight with Dankworth. Tell him Carrick was an innocent bystander, that he had nothing to do with her argument with Dankworth, and then at least there would be no question of choosing between her son and her lover. They were two totally unrelated events.

'Tomorrow I'm going to see Mrs Winchester and her husband. It's the only thing I can do.'

Convinced her heartbeat could be heard throughout the house, Roisin paced the luxurious jewel-coloured carpet in front of the fire at the magistrate's house, trying to settle her nerves. When the door flew open and Grace Winchester swept in, her determination deserted her.

'Ma'am.' She dropped a brief curtsy. Even if Mrs Winchester couldn't hear her thundering heart, the rise and fall of her chest must surely be visible. She had to appear calm and rational.

'Mrs Ogilvie. Roisin. I'm so happy to see you. I was intending to call upon you. We only returned from Sydney this morning. My dress was a coup, an absolute coup. I was the belle of the ball. I danced with the Governor, and his wife asked for the name of my dressmaker. I told her. Be prepared. She will call upon you.'

Unlikely. Not once Mrs Winchester heard the whole sorry tale of lies and deceit. It would be beyond her understanding. Even in Wollombi, her husband managed to shelter her from anything remotely unpleasant. Mrs Winchester inhabited a different world. Whatever had possessed her to think she could influence Carrick's case? 'I have come to ask for your help.'

'Why, of course. How can I help? Is it your son? Children often succumb to illnesses.'

Illness. If only it were that simple. Her life and this horrid, horrid mess, all of her own making because she'd run away, hiding behind a parcel of lies instead of standing and fighting her battles. 'It's about Carrick O'Connor.'

'The cedar cutter.'

'Yes, ma'am.'

'I was under the impression you intended to steer clear of him after the accusations regarding your business. Rumours spread like wildfire and it would be a shame to let …' She raised a perfect eyebrow and tipped her head to one side. 'How shall I put it? A misalliance jeopardise the future of your business and that of your son.'

Roisin chose to ignore the reference to Carrick and their relationship. That was more than she could deal with. There would be no relationship unless she could make Grace Winchester understand that the evidence against him was tainted, and tainted because of her actions. It was no fault of Carrick's. She should be standing trial, not him. 'Ruan is very well, thank you. He loves school. Mr Blackmore says he has a fine mind and his interests are well above expectation for his age.'

Why was she talking such nonsense, putting off the inevitable? Now. She must say it now. A man's life lay in the balance. Not any man. The man she loved. And love him she did, she had no doubt about that.

'I have not come here to talk about Ruan, ma'am, although it concerns him.'

The tone in her voice must have alerted Mrs Winchester because she turned from the window and gazed intently into her eyes, then nodded slowly. 'Come and sit down.' She gestured to the padded window seat and sat waiting while Roisin crossed the room. 'Now tell me.'

'I have not been truthful in my dealings with the people of Wollombi. My past is not as I portrayed it. I have lied.' There she'd said it.

Mrs Winchester smiled gently and patted her knee. 'We none of us dwell on matters in the past that we choose to forget.'

'When the past comes back to haunt me and an innocent man stands to suffer I can't remain silent.'

'I take it you are referring to the cedar cutter. I believe he is in the lockup accused of murder. Surely you don't intend to take responsibility for his actions.'

'Carrick O'Connor is innocent, of that I am certain.'

'How can you be? Were you in the forest? Did you see the murder committed?'

'No.' She shook her head slowly.

'Then how can you know he is innocent? And if he is, who is responsible?'

'I believe Mr Dankworth might be able to answer that question.'

'Gideon? The murdered man was acting on his behalf, protecting his land, his investment.'

'Mr Dankworth is Ruan's father.' There. It was done. The sound of her hammering heart and the blood pumping through her body reverberated inside her head. 'I'm not a widow as I claimed. Gideon Dankworth took advantage of me when I was fourteen. Ruan is the result. When he discovered Ruan's existence he demanded I surrender him. I refused, changed my name and fled Sydney.' She let her lashes fall, dreading the censor that would follow.

'And that is how you came to Wollombi?'

She nodded, letting her hands cover her face, wanting only to hide from the scrutiny. Mrs Winchester's gaze seared her skin and then her fingers reached out, cool and dry and lifted her hands. Why would she believe her?

'I think you'd better start from the beginning, my dear, because I can't at the moment see why, even if Gideon was Ruan's father, it has anything to do with the cedar cutter being imprisoned for murder.'

'Dankworth told me I must choose between my lover and my son.' Her shoulders shook and she gulped back a sob. She couldn't choose, wouldn't, and shouldn't have to. It was all so wrong, so very wrong. 'I believe he thinks Carrick is attempting to keep Ruan from him, prevent him from claiming Ruan.'

'If Ruan is Gideon's son, the man has every right to him.'

Roisin's heart sank. What a mistake. Of course Mrs Winchester would support Dankworth. They were the landed gentry, reputable members of society, friends for heaven's sake. How to make her understand?

'I was born in Sydney. My mother was a prostitute. I was brought up in a brothel. When I was old enough I was apprenticed to Madam de Lolle in Sydney, sewing for the girls, making corsets, undergarments, unmentionables. Men like to see women in pretty things.'

'A fact you have used to your advantage so very well,' Mrs Winchester remarked dryly. 'I should have put two and two together. Madame de Lolle calls herself a milliner; however, her real business is in corsetry, attractive corsetry, shall we say?'

'Dankworth was a frequent visitor to the brothel and I caught his eye. One evening when my mam and I were walking home, he attacked my mother and raped me. If it weren't for Ruan he wouldn't even remember. He had no interest in me. He didn't even know I was pregnant.' Or that his blows that night had caused Mam to die. 'Only when he bumped into me on the street several years later did he recognise Ruan as his child. I don't understand. He is married. He has a wife. Lady Alice will give him children. Why does he want my son?' Try as she might to maintain her composure, the tears poured down her face. She rummaged in her reticule for a handkerchief.

'My dear you are distraught.' Mrs Winchester gave her shoulder an absentminded pat.

Roisin opened her eyes and screwed her handkerchief into a tight ball. She'd see this through. She had to.

'Just think what Gideon and Lady Alice could do for Ruan.' Mrs Winchester cocked her head to one side and smoothed the velvet of her skirt. 'Would it be the worst thing that could happen? Why, Lady Alice is heir to her father's fortune. One day Ruan might inherit that fortune. Think of what this could do for the boy. What the Dankworths can do for Ruan.'

No! The word screamed and barrelled around her head. She'd wasted her time. Whatever had possessed her to think that Grace Winchester would be interested in the fate of the village dressmaker's son, or for that matter a cedar cutter?

'I suggest you go home, my dear and let matters run their course. I shall speak with Gideon on your behalf and I'm sure we can arrange something that would enable you to spend time with Ruan. Go home now. Nothing is as bad as you think. Rest assured Mr Winchester will deal with the cedar cutter in a fair and honest manner when his case comes up.'

Mrs Winchester rose to her feet and through a veil of tears, Roisin recognised her dismissal. Numb with fear and pain she stumbled to the door.

By the time the dray reached Wollombi the sun had dropped behind the hills. Roisin slid down and made her way home. Before she'd even reached the door it flew open and Ruan tumbled out. The breath returned to her lungs and she hugged him tight, more for her benefit than his.

He squirmed out of her arms. 'Mam, they let Slinger go.'

She knelt down and gazed into his eyes, absorbing the first good news she'd heard in days. She squeezed his hands tight. 'And Carrick?' She knew the answer. If Carrick were free then he'd be here right now, proving it was all a horrible mistake.

'Jane says they're going to decide about Carrick another day. And Slinger's going to stick around. I need to go and see Carrick.'

It was too much for a six-year-old boy to manage. He simply didn't understand Carrick's predicament. He couldn't call in and see Carrick whenever he felt like it. She had to speak to Jane, find out what had happened. Mrs Winchester wouldn't offer any assistance; in fact, she'd made matters worse by asking her.

For heaven's sake, Mrs Winchester believed Ruan should be with Dankworth. She threw a glance around the little house, tossing up the possibility of packing their bags and fleeing—where? Sydney? Dankworth would find her there. She had very little money left and Aunt Lil was too far away to help. Besides, she'd decided she'd fight Dankworth and she couldn't do that if she ran away. She must squash Dankworth's ridiculous idea once and for all. And perhaps in doing that she could help Carrick.

'Come and sit down, Roisin, you're all tuckered out. I've the billy on the boil.'

Jane led her like an invalid down the hallway. She was incapable of rational thought or reason, numb with disbelief. After Jane settled her in a chair and tucked her shawl around her shoulders, she stoked the fire and took the cups down from the mantelpiece. Ruan sat at the table, questions plastered all over his face. Jane must have told him to wait. He slid his treasure box closer, slipped the brass key into the lock and lifted the lid. Such a good boy, playing quietly and giving her time to recover, time to think, to make decisions. She couldn't hand him over to anyone, least of all Dankworth. How she wished she could talk to Carrick.

Jane placed the teacup in front of her and she wrapped her hands around it, allowing the warmth to seep into her frozen fingers. The steam coiled around her face and she inhaled it, closing her eyes and letting her thoughts drift for a moment.

'Look, Mam.'

She opened her eyes and smiled at Ruan. 'What is it, my darling? Something new for your treasure box?' Oh, God, if Dankworth took him would he be allowed this simple pleasure, or the freedom to run barefoot by the brook, or throw a line for a fish? A sob caught in her throat. She tried to imagine him dressed in clothes like a gentleman. A starched shirt frilled at the neck, his unruly hair tamed, plastered to his head.

'Old Pella gave it to me.'

She lifted her heavy head. Between his forefinger and thumb Ruan held a cork. 'I think it's from a bottle. Old Pella said to show you.'

'It's lovely, darling.' She sipped at her tea; it traced a path down her parched throat, bringing some sense of reality back to her crumpled body.

'You're not looking at it, Mam.'

She lowered the cup. 'I am, my darling, I am.' She placed the cup on the table and held out her hand, palm up.

Ruan dropped the cork into her hand. She gazed down at it. This was much more than a cork. It was a stopper, some sort of silver-topped lid, well worn. For no apparent reason her pulse began to race. No reason she could place until she lifted it between her fingers to the light.

This stopper was from a flask, not an old bottle, for the top was silver. She ran her finger over it, tracing the raised crest. And her heart stopped.

She let out a cry. The stopper fell to the floor.

'Mam! Be careful. You'll break it. It's a treasure.'

She dropped to her knees, scrabbling beneath the table, groping for the stopper. Her fingers wrapped around it and she lifted it close to her face, squinting in the half-light beneath the tablecloth. She ran her fingers over the top. Crawling on her hands and knees she heaved herself up, her head throbbing.

'Ruan, where did you get this?'

'I told you. Old Pella.' Yes, he had. And she hadn't taken any notice. 'He said I had to show it to you. Can I have it back?'

'No. No, you can't.'

'Roisin.' Jane's voice broke through her tumbling thoughts. 'Sit down.' Jane's hand was firm on her arm as she forced Roisin back into the chair. 'You're as white as chalk.'

She shrugged Jane off. 'Did Old Pella tell you where he found it?'

'In the forest. He said to give it to Carrick. I told you. That's why I need to see Carrick.'

He was right; she hadn't listened to what he'd said.

Beyond the window the light had faded to grey. The same grey as the morning when she'd found Carrick chopping the wood. Stripped down to his singlet, the light throwing shadows across his skin, across the scar on his shoulder. She ran her finger over the top of the stopper, tracing the letters, not feeling the cold silver of the stopper, instead the smooth raised skin of the brand on Carrick's skin.

'Mam.'

'Be quiet.' She had to think. She knew it. Why hadn't she realised before? Why hadn't she recognised it? The entwined initials. GD—Gideon Dankworth. The very crest atop an ebony cane that had thrashed her shoulders and broken Mam's skull. 'Where's Old Pella?'

'Dunno. In the woodshed. Can I have my treasure back?'

'Not for the moment. No. It's time you went to bed.'

'I'm hungry.'

'I'll get you some supper.' Jane, dear Jane, stepped towards the table, sensing her confusion.

'Move your treasure box so there's room for your bowl.'

Roisin glanced at Jane's face; her smile for Ruan barely concealed the frown etched across her forehead and the worry in her eyes.

What to do? Her thumb rubbed backwards and forwards across the top of the stopper. *GD—Gideon Dankworth.* 'Eat your supper and I'll take some soup out to Old Pella.' And ask him where he'd found the stopper. Jane must have read her mind because she pressed a bowl of soup into her hands and the next moment she stood in the fading light.

The door to the woodshed hung open and she waited, allowing her eyes to become accustomed to the darkness.

'Old Pella, I've got some soup. Are you here?' The silence clung to her like a shroud, then the pile of possum furs in the corner stirred and Old Pella's eyes appeared over the top.

'Missus.'

'Oh, thank goodness.' She squatted down, placing the bowl on the floor. 'I've brought you some soup. Sit up.'

He struggled upright and she passed him the bowl, then sank down on the floor next to him, enveloped in his smell of damp animal fur, wood smoke and old man. She let out a long, slow breath while he slurped his soup.

'Ruan gave me this.' She opened her clasped palm.

He twisted his face from the bowl and fixed his rheumy eyes on her face. 'For Carrick.' He went back to slurping his soup.

'Where did you find it, Old Pella?'

'With King Polai. In the forest.'

'Why does Carrick need it?'

'Blind Bunyip left it.'

'Blind …' Her words petered out. What was the point? So caught up in his Dreamtime stories, the old man could have found the stopper anywhere. He hadn't a clue what she was talking about.

Old Pella inclined his head, tipped the bowl and drained the remains of the soup, then smacked his lips and wiped the back of his hand across his mouth. 'Give it to Carrick. Carrick needs it.'

'But if you were there, tell me.'

He sat up a bit straighter and stared out towards the door, then leaned close to her ear. 'Bang!' She jumped, almost toppling over. 'Blind Bunyip killed him dead.'

Right, so now a bunyip had killed the man, not Carrick but a bunyip. It hardly seemed an improvement. 'Did you see him?'

'Old Pella there.'

One last try. 'Old Pella, what does the bunyip look like?'

'Told you. Blind, white eyes and the black stick. Rap, rap, rap on his boots.'

Boots. A shiver crossed her shoulders and then a surge of excitement. Pale eyes, boots and a black cane. There was only one person it could be. Dankworth, and if he was … Her heart lifted. If Old Pella had seen Dankworth in the forest, then Carrick may walk free.

'We have to take it to the courthouse, you must come with me and tell the magistrate before they sentence Carrick.' If nothing else it might stall the sentencing, give her time to speak to Carrick, show him the stopper.

Old Pella shook his head from side to side, his eyes wide with fear. 'No court.'

'Old Pella, you must. It will save Carrick. You're a witness.' The poor old man didn't understand how the justice system worked. Carrick couldn't hang for a crime he didn't commit. Not if there was an eyewitness to state otherwise.

'Useless natives can't.'

'You're not useless, Old Pella. We'll take it to Constable Brown and tell him.'

'You tell Carrick.' The old man struggled to his feet and tugged the blanket tight around his shoulders. 'Old Pella gotta go.'

'Me? No. I need you to come, too, Old Pella.' Why would they believe her? They'd say she was protecting her lover. Just as Dankworth had. How she wished Carrick were Ruan's father and not that evil man who soiled everyone he came into contact with.

Before she'd had a chance to protest, Old Pella slipped past her and merged into the gathering darkness. She stood for a while as the moon rose, watching the fleeting shadows. And for the first time realised there were no eyes upon her. There was no shivering dread. No tension, no sense of foreboding. When had it all begun? And why had it stopped now?

Clutching the flask stopper tight in her hand, Roisin made her way back inside.

'You should eat something.' Jane placed a bowl of soup on the table. How could she eat? The mere thought of food made her stomach rebel.

She closed her eyes, blocking out Jane and her sympathetic gaze, forcing her mind back to Carrick. She'd woken in the night, watched him as he slept, his body like alabaster in the beam of moonlight slanting through the shutters. She'd run her hand over his skin, across his chest. Heat rose to her face and a long, slow tug of lust snatched at her belly.

'Roisin, eat, eat now.'

'Not now, Jane. Not now. I'm trying to think.' Trying to concentrate on her memories, not her emotions, not the way her skin had danced and her soul had soared; she was trying to remember his skin beneath her fingertips. His shoulder. The scar. The brand.

A reminder not to tamper with the English.

There was no mistaking Dankworth's heritage. As English as the day was long. She ran her forefinger over the crest again. There were too many coincidences.

'Where's Ruan?'

'He's in bed. I said you would say goodnight to him when you'd talked to Old Pella. He's concerned. Very concerned about Carrick.'

And so was she. She turned the stopper over and over in her hand. What to do? She needed to talk to Carrick. What if she was jumping to conclusions? A thousand men must have the initials GD, but how many were so depraved they'd brand them into another's skin? The only link she had was the word of an old man who'd vanished into the night.

'Jane, I need your help.'

'Of course. Anything.'

'We need to play on some of the scuttlebutt in the town.' Would Jane do it? It was asking a lot, although she'd stood by her until now. She couldn't have asked for a stauncher friend. 'I need to talk to Carrick and I need to do it without Constable Brown listening in.'

A wide grin broke out on Jane's face and she batted her eyelashes. 'You want me to entertain Constable Brown. Prove to him the rumours around town about our cathouse are true.'

'We've suffered the scandal, we may as well use it to our advantage. It's asking a lot, I know. If we fail, your reputation would be in tatters.'

'Carrick's life is worth more than my reputation.'

'And mine.'

'What about Ruan? We can't leave him here. What if Dankworth turns up?'

'He won't and Slinger's outside keeping an eye out. He promised Carrick. Dankworth will be at the Winchesters'. Mrs Winchester will be telling him all about my visit and he'll be relishing her support. A legitimate way to gain custody of Ruan. Far easier than snatching him from under my nose.'

A cold calm settled over her. She would get to the bottom of this mess if it was the last thing she did.

Roisin shivered and glanced at Jane; she must be freezing. With her blouse pulled low on her shoulders and the lacy black and red corset forcing her breasts high until her nipples almost peeked over the top, Roisin doubted any man could resist her. Aunt Lil would snaffle her up in a moment. Her eyes shone huge in her rouged face and her lips puckered like an overripe cherry. She threw an outrageous wink and swung her hips. If it hadn't been for the fact two lives hung in the balance, Roisin thought she might enjoy the charade. 'At least I know I can always find a job.' Jane swayed down the road, twitching her skirt to display an expanse of leg above her sensible laced boots. 'Do you think he'll be interested?'

'You'll have to fight him off … Oh! I hope you don't. Are you sure you want to go through with this?'

'Believe me, if I have to fight him off, I'll manage. I did that for years with Mick before he shot through. This knee could stop a stud bull in its tracks.' She gave her skirt another swirl. 'That's the least of my worries. Now, you. What about you? Do you know where you're going?'

'Yes, I'll wait until you have the constable busy, there should be only one of them on duty tonight, then I'll slip through the courthouse into the corridor where the cells are. I don't need to get inside the cell, just to the door to speak with him.'

'Wait until you see me leave with the constable, then duck up the steps and through the door.'

Roisin settled behind the big tree shading the lockup, while Jane sashayed into the courthouse. Only seconds later she reappeared, leading a bedazzled Constable Brown by the hand, and they disappeared into the shadows.

Roisin flew across the expanse of open ground and in through the door. One lamp burned bright, illuminating the room where she'd spoken to Dankworth. To the right the door that led to the cells was closed. She nudged it open and slipped inside, pulling it closed behind her, throwing the corridor into darkness. Edging her way along the rough sandstone wall, she came to the first cell. The door was open. The second was not.

Carrick paced the floor, stopping to slam his chained hands against the wall every time his five paces took him to the back of the cell. How had it come to this? Dankworth here in Australia. His perfect opportunity and he'd wasted it buried in the forest chopping down trees. If he hadn't been so hellbent on chasing the almighty cedar and trying to accumulate enough money to seek revenge he might have taken more notice of what was going on in front of his nose. No amount of blarney could convince him that Dankworth was Ruan's father. Ruan's red hair came from Roisin, he had her eyes, not that startling green, but green all the same. A pig like Dankworth couldn't sire a lad like Ruan.

And he wasn't getting either Roisin or Ruan. Not taking his loved ones twice. Liam and Brigid were more than enough. He slammed his head against the wall, relishing the shaft of pain as it hammered in his temples. At least Slinger had got out of the place. If he was in any doubt, that fact alone proved Dankworth had his sights set on him.

He tossed his head. He'd not be thinking too hard about it. How could the bastard have got his filthy hands on Roisin? No wonder she'd run, chosen to escape the past, leave Sydney. It would stop here. Stop now. When he got hold of the maggot he'd beat the living shite out of him, end it all. Not only for Liam and Brigid. For Roisin and Ruan, too. He'd not stand for him touching them.

He sucked in a deep breath, inhaling the remembered scent of her, of her skin, her home, of warmth and peace. Linen and lavender. He lifted his head, absorbing the touch of her breath on his cheek as she'd murmured his name.

'Carrick.' The sound was more insistent. 'Carrick.'

He brought his head up and turned. His mind had deserted him, taken him away with the fairies. The constant dreams and mirages had to end.

'Carrick.'

He stepped closer to the door.

Through the Judas window her green eyes blazed. He reached up, touching her fingers. He had to touch her. Had to know she was real, that he hadn't conjured her from some addled part of his mind. 'Go away.'

She had to go, stay away from him, stay away from Dankworth. The bastard could argue with him now. She wasn't alone. He'd fight her battles for her. Brigid would want that. She would want to know he'd learned his lesson. He'd not fail twice.

She intertwined her fingers, small and fine, with his. 'I have to talk to you.'

'Leave, leave now before it's too late. Leave before you become embroiled in something you know nothing of.'

'I'm already involved. It's because of me.'

'Nothing to do with you. Old battles and old enemies.' He scratched at his shoulder. 'Remember the English pig who torched my darlings?'

She nodded, impatience glittering in her eyes, her hand curled in a fist held up to the grill. 'I remember, Carrick. I need to show you something.'

'It was Dankworth.' How could he make her understand? 'He wants Ruan. He'll take him as he took Liam and Brigid.' She'd no understanding of the depth of the man's corruption. Why hadn't she told him Dankworth was Ruan's father? He unlaced her fingers from his and her hand dropped.

'I know.'

How could she know? Know that Dankworth had killed the overseer. That he'd set him up from the start. Same as last time. Something glinted in the light. He squinted through the Judas door as she held out her hand, palm up.

'What is it?'

'Old Pella gave Ruan this.'

She forced it into his hand. He held it up in the shaft of moonlight shining through the window. A cork, a stopper. What use was that? The woman had taken leave of her senses.

'He found it. In the forest at King Polai. He said you must have it.'

'Too much rum. His brain's pickled.' He banged his head against the door and wrapped his fingers around the rusty bars, rattling at his cage. He had to get out.

'Carrick, I have no time. Constable Brown will be back. Give me your hand.' She unpeeled his fingers from the grill and traced them across the metal surface of the stopper. It was lumpy … no, something inscribed, raised.

'What is it?'

'Can you not feel the crest?'

He snatched away his fingers, the metal burning hot. *GD.* The letters he knew so well. The brand he'd carried since that fateful night. Dankworth's crest. She had to leave. 'Stay out of this.' Better he hang than Dankworth wreak his revenge on her and the lad.

'It belongs to Dankworth. I know it does. It's the same as his cane. The same as the brand on your shoulder.'

'Where did you get it?' Talk. Talk her out of it.

'Old Pella found it beneath the cedar tree. He said the blind bunyip left it.'

Carrick's hands fisted against the tide of rage and impotence.

'It proves Dankworth was there. Old Pella says he saw him shoot the overseer before you and Slinger arrived.'

A shout of laughter and a high-pitched giggle broke the taut silence, bringing him back to reality. He shook his head. 'What's happening out there?'

'Jane's entertaining the constable. We haven't long. I must rescue her.'

He groaned. Why couldn't she just leave him to sort it all out? 'So what if this is Dankworth's? I can't prove he was there and neither can Old Pella. He's native. His words won't stand in court.'

'If Dankworth is the man from Ireland, why does he want to harm you now? That's all in the past.'

'He wants Ruan.' He raked a hand through his hair. Maybe he didn't want to hear it. Too scared it would bring back the memories he thought he'd finally buried.

'I know he wants Ruan. That's why I left Sydney.'

'He believes I want his son. As retribution for him killing Brigid and Liam.' His mind spiralled out of control, lost in the insidious desire for revenge. Dankworth couldn't be Ruan's father. 'Is he Ruan's father?'

Even in the dim light he saw the colour flood her face.

'Is he?'

She nodded, just once.

A hand clutched at his heart, and twisted. 'Did you love him? Do you love him?'

'I hate him, with every fibre of my being. He raped me. Beat my mam to death.' A single tear tracked down her cheek, a pearl in the moonlight, and the breath returned to his body.

Between the bars he reached out and threaded his fingers through hers, knowing her pain. 'Can he prove he's Ruan's father?'

'No man can *prove* that. He says Ruan resembles him. He knows his age. He can work the numbers as well as any man.'

'Did you have the lad baptised?'

She turned her face away from him. 'I don't hold with the church—any church.'

Once her bland statement would have bothered him. Now? He doubted the truth that had sustained him for so long. How could there be a God if a man like Dankworth roamed the earth?

'Aunt Lil thought it better not to. She said the laws were new and there were lots of excuses we could give, so no one would need to know.'

'So there's no record of the lad's father.' No record of the maggot's claim on Ruan. 'Do you think he'll try to snatch Ruan?'

'No, he says he's going to swear to his paternity in front of a magistrate.'

'Roisin, this is important. Let me stand up for you. Tell them the boy is mine.'

'How could he be yours? I didn't even know you then. I was in Sydney, you were—where were you? See, I don't even know where you were.'

'Dankworth said he's going to talk to a lawyer?'

She nodded, that much was true. It seemed a million years ago she'd made the dresses and the corsets; how she wished she'd stuck with the likes of Mrs Blackmore and stayed away from the Winchesters and their fancy friends. And she thought it would be the making of her—well, it wouldn't. It would be the death of her. If anything happened to Ruan, or Carrick, her life would end.

'He'll be finding a magistrate in Sydney, so he can take Ruan from you.'

'Why? I just don't understand why.'

'Because the man's a monster, that's why.'

'No, that's not the reason. He wasn't interested in Ruan until we bumped into him in the street and he started hounding us. That's why I left Sydney. I didn't know what else to do.'

'Let me deal with it. I owe him one.'

'Carrick, I don't want you to do anything illegal, anything that could get you into trouble. It's my problem, not yours.'

'It *is* my problem. Dankworth is evil. He deserves to die. Do nothing. Stay away from him. Take Ruan and go—go back to Sydney, go somewhere he won't find you. Slinger will help you. Tell him to come and see me and I'll explain. I have money in Sydney.'

'I'm not leaving. I'll go back to see Grace Winchester, tell her—'

'Back?' What in heaven's name had she done?

'Yes. Back. I saw her yesterday. She said if Dankworth was Ruan's father then he had every right to claim him, and that it would be the best thing for Ruan, a wonderful opportunity.' Her breath snagged as she swallowed back a sob. 'That was before I knew about Ireland. Before I knew what Dankworth had done to you.' She snatched the stopper from his hand and clutched it tight. 'Old Pella has given me proof.'

'You will go nowhere near the Winchesters. Take Old Pella's godforsaken stopper and throw it in the brook. Go. Go now and leave Wollombi. Tell Slinger to take you to the Rose, Shamrock and Thistle in Morpeth and ask for Nell. She'll give you a bed for the night and then take the steamer to Sydney.' He'd find a way, find a way to get rid of Dankworth, even if it meant shooting him in the court in front of the magistrate. Now there was a thought.

'I'll be fighting this battle. Get Slinger to come and talk to me.' She scowled at him then opened her mouth to speak. He covered her lips with his finger. 'There now, leave it with me. I'll be keeping ye and the lad close to my heart.'

'He said I had to choose, choose between you and Ruan. I can't.'

He eased his fingers through the grill and caught a lock of her silky hair. 'And you won't have to, my darling. You won't have to.' He'd be choosing. There was no choice. The bastard would die this time. He'd die.

Nineteen

Roisin slipped back down the narrow passage and through the courtroom, pausing only to glance at the dock. The dock where Carrick would be sentenced. Sentenced for a crime he hadn't committed, all because she'd refused to succumb to Dankworth's demands. What good was that to anyone? Dankworth would still be free to pursue her. Even if she returned to Sydney, she and Ruan would have to live like thieves. She didn't want that.

Sentencing Carrick to Port Arthur or one of the other penal settlements wouldn't stop Dankworth taking Ruan, it would just make him more determined, make him think he could play with people's lives like wild cards in a poker game. She wouldn't give him the satisfaction. Surely Carrick understood.

Short of killing Dankworth, what else could Carrick do? She stopped, the breath snatched from her lungs. Did he mean to kill Dankworth? It was the only way she'd be free of him. How could he? He was locked in a cell. He wanted to see Slinger. What could Slinger do? They might live by the law of the cutter's justice in the forest, but that wouldn't stop the likes of Dankworth, it would only get Slinger into trouble. She had to go back and see the Winchesters, put the record straight. They couldn't imprison an innocent man. And she wouldn't allow Carrick to become a martyr. It was Dankworth who was guilty, not Carrick.

She slipped through the door and back into the night to find Jane lolling against the fence with Constable Brown, his legs astride her, his body pinning her. Laughing, Jane threw back her head, all the while keeping his wandering hands at bay. What now? They hadn't thought to plan their escape. Too hurried, too keen to see Carrick, and what good had that done? If she called out, would Jane be able to run away? Say her mistress was calling her. Roisin took a few more steps and turned, glancing back at Jane, still fending off the constable's advances.

A heavy arm wrapped around her, and a hand covered her face, stifling her scream. Her heart jumped into her mouth as she came to rest against the bulk of a body. She smelled cedar and rum, not sweat and tobacco.

Slinger!

He let his hand drop and motioned her to silence, then indicated she should wait. A splash of light from the inn ran across the road like a track.

Slinger stepped into it. 'Get your bleedin' hands orf my woman,' he hollered, vaulting the fence in front of the courthouse.

Constable Brown stepped back and dropped his hands as though he had a gun trained on him. Slinger's low, indecipherable words made the constable back off, then he grabbed Jane by the arm, gave her a hefty clip around the ears and marched her up the street, the perfect picture of an outraged husband.

The constable adjusted his breeches and slouched back into the courthouse. Once he'd vanished from sight, Roisin bolted, cutting around the buildings and in through her back door. Without bothering to check the house, she climbed the ladder to Ruan's room. He lay in a patch of moonlight, sleeping with the possum tail clutched under his chin. Light-headed with relief, she eased her way back down the ladder.

Moments later Slinger and Jane fell through the door, their laughter filling the tiny house, dispelling the last remnants of her fear.

'Did you see his face? It was a picture.'

'My hero.' Jane dropped a curtsy to Slinger, who bowed in a most impressive fashion and lowered his long, brawny body into a chair. 'Well? How did you get on?' Jane adjusted her blouse and rearranged her décolletage, oblivious to the disappointment on Slinger's face.

Now was not the time to tell Slinger what Carrick wanted him to do, especially as she'd no intention of following his instructions. She had a sneaking suspicion Slinger would want to carry out Carrick's words to the letter. Instead, she forced a smile.

'I'm going to present the evidence to Mr and Mrs Winchester tomorrow before Carrick comes up before the court.'

'You are?'

'Even after yesterday?'

She folded her arms and nodded at Jane and Slinger. If Carrick was determined to make some sort of a martyr of himself, she'd fight it with every fibre of her being. Doing what he wanted wouldn't solve anything. Dankworth wanted both Carrick and Ruan. He wouldn't get either.

The following morning Roisin dressed with care. Her emerald jacket was far too frivolous so she donned her slate-grey pelisse, squinting and turning in front of the glass. The colour did nothing for her, and besides, it sapped her courage. Today was a day for courage. She'd need every snippet she could muster. She tossed the grey aside and shrugged into her green jacket. If she failed … well … she couldn't contemplate it.

When she entered the kitchen she found Slinger lounging in front of the fire, a mug of tea in his hand and a broad smile on his face. Jane's cheeks glowed a pretty pink, enough to make Roisin envious. 'There's fresh bread and some of my raspberry jam if you'd like it.'

Roisin shook her head. 'No, nothing. Maybe tea.' She meant to be brave and she sounded like a shy, retiring pansy caught beneath the flagstones. Throwing back her shoulders she repeated, 'Tea.' Then settled her skirts and sat at the table, her head held high. 'A cup of tea, Jane, please, before I go.'

'To the Winchesters,' Jane finished for her.

'Yes, to the Winchesters. I can take Davy's dray again. He'll be going back to St Albans.'

'You'll do no such thing.' Slinger leapt to his feet, dwarfing the small room. 'Maisie's buggy is waiting outside all hitched up.'

'Maisie?'

'Yes, Maisie. I told her I needed a favour.'

'But you're one of the cutters. She thinks you're a bunch of troublemakers and we're a couple of whores servicing you and the Paterson crew.'

'Maisie blows a lot of hot air. I put her straight this morning. Now drink up and let's get this sorted.'

Whatever would Carrick say? Slinger was not doing what he wanted at all, although to be fair she hadn't seen fit to tell him what Carrick wanted.

'And while we're gone, Jane will pack up your belongings and keep an eye on the boy. If we need to leave for Morpeth, we'll be ready as soon as we return.'

He'd got everything covered and without a word from Carrick. 'Slinger I … I can do this on my own.'

'You might think you can, but you're not going to. I'll be waiting outside. Carrick would have my guts if he thought I'd left you to do this alone.'

Carrick would have his guts when he discovered that he was aiding and abetting her to do the very thing he didn't want to happen. 'But that's not what he wants.' She clapped her hand over her mouth.

'Sometimes a man doesn't know what he wants. This is what he wants. At least it will be when it works, so make sure you do your best. Are you ready?'

She nodded and pulled on her gloves.

'Have you got the stopper?' Jane asked.

She patted her reticule, all of a sudden unsure how something as simple as a stopper from a flask could solve any of their problems or prove a man's innocence.

As the buggy took off down the street, she snatched a glance over her shoulder. Elsie and Maisie stood out the front of the inn, flanked by Mr and Mrs Blackmore and a crowd of others. Even Billy Boy and Old Pella stood watching from the banks of the brook.

'They're all wishing you well.' Slinger threw her a lopsided grin. 'Can't have these Sydney folks running the show. This is Wollombi, we take care of our own.'

Not daring to speak, Roisin clamped her teeth firmly together and peered through a haze of tears. She could do this and she would.

It took an eternity to cover the few miles and when she caught sight of the magistrate's house, glaring down at her, all she wanted to do was turn and run.

Slinger's rough hand patted her arm. 'You'll be right, love. And if you're not, sing out. I'll sort the buggers out. We'll spring

Carrick and head for Sydney, or maybe even the goldfields. What do you reckon?' He winked and eased the buggy to a halt. 'Right now Carrick doesn't know his own mind. Too buried in the past. Believe me, this is what he'd be doing if he could think straight.'

With his words to buoy her, Roisin marched up the path to the impressive front door and knocked. A wisp of a maid opened up.

'I'm Mrs Ogilvie. I'd like to speak to Mr and Mrs Winchester.' The maid cocked a knowing eyebrow, smirked, then led her to the sitting room, where she'd spoken to Mrs Winchester so unsuccessfully only the day before.

Her courage deserted her as the sitting room door closed behind her. She paced the very same carpet as before, ringing her hands, pulling off her glove then replacing it, adjusting her hat and tucking a wayward curl out of sight. Out of the window in the fenced paddocks the cows grazed peacefully. There was nothing peaceful about her mood. Her thoughts tumbled and churned like a willy-willy.

'Mrs Ogilvie. Roisin, what a delight. I was so hoping I'd have the opportunity to speak with you, thank you.' Roisin froze as Lady Alice crossed the room, both hands outstretched as though greeting a long-lost friend. Thank her. Thank her for what? For providing her with a son? For handing Ruan into her care? She swayed, the very thought of it draining the blood from her head.

'Come and sit down. Goodness me, you're quite pale. Did you have a terrible journey? The road from Wollombi is a disgrace, all those holes. The jogging and the jiggling is enough to turn anyone's stomach.'

Lady Alice's words washed over her as she sank into the chair. She did feel a trifle disorientated. Was it any wonder her pulse raced and black spots danced in front of her eyes?

'I must thank you.' Lady Alice clasped Roisin's hand in hers and peered into her eyes. 'Thank you so much. You can't believe the difference you have made to my life.'

Made to her life. Difference. Of course, having a child, an heir, would make a difference, she supposed. Losing her son would make more than a difference. It would destroy her. She steeled herself to tell Lady Alice a son and heir would come to her only over her dead body. Oh, where was Mrs Winchester? Surely she could help, this was too, too difficult.

'If it hadn't been for my corset, I'd never have had the courage. I am quite a different person.'

Roisin let the air escape slowly from her lips and sneaked a quick glimpse under her eyelashes at this new, animated Lady Alice, whose mind was as far from sons and heirs as imaginable. Or else she was a consummate actress, as devious and two-faced as her husband.

'Why, I was positively fighting off suitors, my dance card full to the brim. I had the most delightful evening at the Governor's. I didn't even notice how quickly the time passed. Gideon was most put out when he finally arrived that I hadn't saved the last dance for him. He became positively attentive. You have, in a few masterful strokes of your needle, revolutionised my life, my confidence, and I doubt I'll ever be able to thank you enough. Ask Grace. She will vouch for what I say. And her dress. Oh!' She clasped her hands to her heart. 'It brought the house down. We have a list of people begging us to put you in contact with them. Both Grace and I are tempted to refuse and keep you all to ourselves. Would that be too awful? Too selfish?' She giggled inanely and preened in front of the mirror over the mantelpiece.

Lady Alice might very well change her mind when she heard about Roisin's reputation and Jane's antics last night. Roisin clutched the stopper in her hand, the silver edges cutting into her palm, anchoring her to this strange reality. While Carrick languished in gaol accused of murder, likely to hang, here she was discussing the merits of corsets and commissions. 'Lady Alice, I must speak with Mrs Winchester, or better still her husband. Are they available?'

'Why I'm sure they are. Shall I ring for tea for you? You still look a little peaky.' She reached out and pulled the velvet sash hidden behind a swathe of curtains.

Would that she could hide so easily.

'Oh, dear. I don't know where the girl is. That is one of the downsides of living in the country. I don't know how I'm going to manage. Gideon has his heart set on building up the property. I believe it is most suitable. Unlike Wollombi, the Yarramalong is just a few hours by cutter from Sydney. So much closer. Gideon will be able to fulfil his political functions, and of course we will need to maintain a Sydney house as well. Listen to me gossiping on like this. It doesn't seem that anyone is answering my call. I shall go and find Grace for you and rustle up some refreshments. The staff are usually far more attentive.' In a cloud of lily-of-the-valley, the newly corseted Lady Alice Dankworth swept from the room.

Roisin slumped into the chair. Gone was the mousey, downtrodden woman and in her place this vivacious, captivating stranger. What had she done? Lady Alice was hardly recognisable. Had a simple corset caused this, or was it more? Surely Dankworth must have told her about his plans for Ruan. He could hardly bring a child, his son, into their household without even mentioning it to his wife.

She let the air trickle slowly between her lips. She hadn't even thought how she'd tell Mrs Winchester. How to convince her that Carrick was not responsible for the overseer's death. Dankworth could have dropped the stopper at any time. One of the natives could have stolen it. How foolish. Old Pella had said he'd seen him, but Old Pella could barely see beyond the end of his own nose and besides, at the time, Dankworth was in Sydney attending the Governor's Ball with Lady Alice. He couldn't have been in the Yarramalong. The trip back to Wollombi alone would have taken him hours, even on horseback and thence to Sydney. He'd never have made it to the Governor's in time to escort Lady Alice to the ball …

Blood thundered in her ears. Only he hadn't been at the ball. He'd arrived late, barely in time for the last dance.

Roisin shot to her feet and paced across the thick carpet. He hadn't and what had Lady Alice said—*So much closer to Sydney, a matter of hours by cutter from Wyong.*

In the midst of her panic she almost missed Mrs Winchester's arrival.

'I'm sorry to have kept you waiting. Lady Alice said you were unwell. You seem positively heated. I do hope it is not a fever. Come sit down here with me.' Mrs Winchester patted the window seat. 'This morning mist can compromise the lungs. I recommend not venturing out until it has lifted. Did I tell you yesterday what a success my dress was? I have some wonderful plans for a spring wardrobe. I was hoping to call in and see you soon.'

She could not stand another moment of this social chitchat. She had to cut straight to the point. 'Mrs Winchester I'm here to discuss once more the matter of Carrick O'Connor and his arrest.'

'Of course, my dear, of course. I haven't had time to bring up the subject with Mr Winchester as yet. He has been so busy and I do feel Gideon should have the opportunity to speak. Lady Alice is such a frail thing and I'd hate to shatter her newfound confidence.'

'I would like to speak with Mr Winchester. A new matter has come to light and I believe it may impinge on the case.'

'Shouldn't this new evidence be brought up in the courtroom? That is the proper place for it. The hearing has been postponed until tomorrow, I believe.'

Tomorrow would be too late. She needed to speak to Mr Winchester before Carrick's hearing. 'There's more to this than I think Mr Winchester is aware. I believe it would be better dealt with outside the court. It concerns Mr Dankworth and Carrick O'Connor.'

Mrs Winchester tipped her head to one side and frowned. 'Oh. I see. Well?'

'I'm not sure if you are aware of the fact that Carrick O'Connor and Gideon Dankworth are not unknown to each other.'

Mrs Winchester's frown deepened and she sat down with a thump. 'Continue.'

'Carrick O'Connor bears a brand, on his shoulder, inflicted by Dankworth.'

'A brand? Don't be ridiculous. Men are not branded. That is for animals.'

She'd ignore Mrs Winchester's expression of ridicule. Not be browbeaten as she had yesterday. 'Not only that, Dankworth was responsible for Carrick's transportation from Ireland.'

Mrs Winchester's head snapped up.

That had got her attention. So she knew something of Dankworth's origins. 'They have a long-standing feud. Dankworth torched the house in which Carrick's wife and child were seeking refuge and then accused Carrick of inciting riot. That's why he was transported, as a political prisoner.'

'Oh no. I don't … I can't believe …'

'Dankworth saw Carrick with Ruan and believed he'd prevent him from taking Ruan, claiming him.'

'What nonsense. I fail to see how that may incriminate Gideon. Why would he want to see Carrick imprisoned again if the man has served his sentence? It seems we have two entirely unrelated incidents here. You are maligning the poor man, Roisin. I didn't imagine that would be the case. Why, if everyone in Australia harped back to their origins the country would barely function.'

'Dankworth told me I had to make a decision between my lover and my son.'

'Carrick O'Connor is your lover?'

She forced the flush beneath the collar of her green jacket and stared Mrs Winchester straight in the eye. 'I hope he will be my husband one day soon.' If he survived his trial and returned from Ireland.

'I still fail to see how the two are connected. Why would Gideon want Mr O'Connor to hang? What has he to gain from this?'

'I don't know. I only know Carrick did not kill the overseer and there is a witness who saw Dankworth commit the crime.'

'Oh.' Mrs Winchester's shoulders drooped and she slouched back against the chair. 'This puts a completely different view on the proceedings. I must call Mr Winchester. Who is this person? Where are they?'

'He is a native called Old Pella.'

'A native.' She gave a tight laugh. 'Well that's of no use.' She dismissed the possibility that a native could offer anything of value with a wave of her hand. 'He can't give evidence. Surely you know that. Natives are not permitted. Being heathens they can't take an oath. Whatever he claims, his words are worthless.'

Roisin swallowed her scream of frustration. Would she be stalled at every turn? No wonder Old Pella said he couldn't help. 'I also have this.' Roisin drew the stopper from her pocket. 'Old Pella found it at the base of the tree next to the body, after he had witnessed the shooting.'

Mrs Winchester sank back in the chair, peering down at her palm, the colour seeping from her face.

'It belongs to Dankworth. It has his initials as the crest. The same as those on the head of his cane.'

'I'm aware of that.' Mrs Winchester seemed to rally somewhat. 'However, this doesn't prove anything. It could have been found anywhere.'

'But it wasn't.'

'I think you better talk to Mr Winchester. Even though a native can't give evidence in a court of law, I'm sure Mr Winchester would, of course, be interested in talking to the man, unofficially. I'm certain there must be some simple explanation.'

Yes, there was. Roisin was in no doubt now that Gideon Dankworth had killed the overseer deliberately to prevent Carrick from claiming Ruan.

'There's a very simple explanation.'

Mrs Winchester's mouth dropped open. Roisin turned to the windows that led onto the flagstone verandah.

Lady Alice stood before them, tears streaking her face, clutching a scrap of white linen and dabbing uselessly at her swollen eyes. 'I hold myself entirely responsible.'

'My dear.' Mrs Winchester rose and led her to a chair. 'Now, now, please don't distress yourself, this is nothing of your making.'

Lady Alice pushed Mrs Winchester away, and gave one more swipe to her reddened face, trying hard to regain control. 'I can do no more than apologise to you, Roisin.' She dropped her head into her hands and rocked back and forth, keening like some bereaved wife, while Mrs Winchester patted her back and made soothing noises. 'I must ask you to believe me when I say,' she lifted her face and dabbed at her eyes, 'I had no knowledge I'd in any way be hurting you. You have shown me nothing but kindness and understanding. You have given me back my self-esteem and my self-worth and no matter what the cost, I can't see you suffer.'

A fresh bout of sobbing ensued. Roisin wanted to grab the woman and shake the story from her. She clamped her teeth and dragged in a deep breath.

'Believe me when I say I didn't know that this mad, foolish plan of Gideon's would come to anything. I have been so very wrong.' Lady Alice shooed away Mrs Winchester's hands and moved in front of the fire, determination etching her flushed face.

'I have no doubt that Gideon is behind this situation. His hand is written all over it. Roisin is right, it does go back to Ireland. Gideon Dankworth was my father's agent. My father owned several estates in Ireland, he was what the Irish termed an absentee landlord. He sold much of the food produced on the land to England. When the Famine came and times got bad it left the estate impoverished. The tenant farmers could not afford to pay their taxes or even support themselves. Gideon oversaw the clearing of the land. The removal of the tenants.

'Papa was not a cruel man and he was shocked and horrified by what Gideon had done in his name. Even though several of the tenants were accused and sentenced for burning their own homes and inciting riot, rumours were rife. Papa dispatched Gideon to Australia to escape the furore.'

Roisin's mind swirled as the pieces fell into place. Carrick was one of those transported for insurgency. It explained his relationship with Dankworth. It didn't explain why Dankworth would want Ruan. Why he suddenly, after six years cared whether he had a son and wanted to claim him. She sank down onto the chair by the window and waited to see if Lady Alice could offer any further explanation.

'Gideon returned to England, he courted me and I was taken in by him. He was a link to the past, a past that had been snatched from me by my father's illness, and I was no longer young. I'm under no illusion now that he married me for my father's money, for his estates. He could never inherit the title that would pass to our son and so would all the lands, on the condition I bore a son. That is where I failed. When Papa died my cousin inherited everything. Gideon didn't care what happened to me, I was of no use to him, and he returned to Australia. Then out of the blue he sent for me. He'd discovered some impoverished woman had given birth to his son and he thought to claim him and thus challenge my cousin's right to the title and estates. No one would know if the boy was mine. He simply had to ensure my compliance.'

'My dear, I'm certain you exaggerate. All marriages are difficult. I am sure …'

Lady Alice raised her hand to silence Mrs Winchester. 'If it hadn't been for my vanity, my desire to make Gideon want me, I'd never have come to you and asked for your assistance with my dress. Gideon would never have found you, never found Ruan.'

Roisin felt the weight ease from her shoulders. At least now she knew why he had pursued her, been so insistent about claiming Ruan.

'Oh, my dear.' Mrs Winchester dropped her head into her hands. 'I am so sorry. Would you believe me if I told you I knew none of this? It is I who have failed you.'

'Carrick? What about Carrick?' Roisin screeched the words. None of this would help Carrick.

Lady Alice sat down next to her and took her hand. 'You do not understand how obsessed Gideon is. When he discovered you and Ruan, he was determined to take the boy, not have him slip through his fingers as he had in Sydney. He spent days watching you, watching Carrick, waiting for the moment when he could spirit him away.'

She'd known all along someone was watching, but she had put it down to Old Pella and relaxed her guard. Dankworth wouldn't stop now. 'Where is Dankworth?' Her skin turned clammy and her stomach roiled. 'Where is he?'

Mrs Winchester turned to Lady Alice, who lifted her shoulders. 'I don't know. He was here this morning, said he would ride and then return for breakfast before he attends the hearing.'

Roisin jumped to her feet. 'I must go. I must go now. Ruan is alone with Jane.'

'I'm sure you have nothing to fear, Roisin. Gideon is a gentleman, he wouldn't do anything foolish.'

'Go. Go now,' Lady Alice said. 'I'll speak with Mr Winchester on your behalf. Go and find your son. I pray to God he is safe.'

Twenty

Roisin flew through the front door and down the steps. 'Slinger! Slinger! We have to leave now. Hurry.' She scrambled into the buggy.

Slinger gazed up at the house and ambled across the driveway as though he was enjoying a Sunday picnic.

'Slinger, please. Hurry!'

He jumped up into the buggy and tipped back his hat. 'If those toffs are givin' you a bad time, I'm more than happy—'

'Slinger just go, please! Dankworth is out riding and hasn't come home. Jane and Ruan are alone.'

Whether it was the mention of Jane or the panic lacing her voice, she'd no idea, but Slinger picked up the whip and brought it cracking down across the back of the poor horse and they took off up the road as though the angels of hell were after them.

Roisin clung to the sides of the buggy, bouncing and twisting with each and every pothole. Having listened to Lady Alice's story, she had no doubt Dankworth intended to snatch Ruan. He could have him in Morpeth in a matter of hours and Sydney not much longer after that and then, Holy Mary, onto a boat and heading back to England or even Ireland.

'What makes you think Dankworth'll make a move now?'

'He's got a lot to lose. He believes if he can prove he has a son he will inherit a fortune in Ireland.'

Slinger turned and threw her a bemused glance. 'And what's it to do with Carrick?'

'That I don't truly understand, Slinger. I can only think that Dankworth must have seen Carrick with Ruan and thought he'd stand in his way, prevent him taking Ruan.'

'A gentleman don't set a cedar cutter up for murder because he thinks he'll stop him getting hold of his son. Carrick wouldn't get a leg in. There has to be another reason.'

The buggy jostled and bumped along in silence. Slinger chewed his lip while she sat wringing her hands, trying to overcome the puddle of dread pooling in her stomach. 'Maybe it was because you were taking the tree from his land.'

'Nah. No need for that, he had the law on his side. We're illegal cutters, everyone knows that. That's not a hanging offence, though. Just a bloody great fine—more than those constables down at the courthouse earn in a year. There's more to it than that.'

He picked up the whip and licked it across the poor horse's back, trying to squeeze the last bit of speed out of the animal. Dankworth couldn't prove Ruan was his son. She clung onto the thought as tightly as her fingers curled around the edge of the buggy. With Lady Alice on her side he couldn't do anything. Oh yes, he could, a nasty voice reminded her. He could do whatever he liked. He believed he had some God-given right to manipulate everyone's lives.

'Ireland, you say.'

She turned to Slinger. 'Yes, Ireland. Dankworth was an agent for Lady Alice's father's estates. He got a reputation for cruelty for evicting the tenants and …'

'Dankworth's the English arsehole Carrick's intent on murderin'? The one who killed his wife and child, branded him and got him transported? Jesus fuckin' Christ. Beggin' your pardon.'

'One and the same.' She grasped the side of the buggy as they careered into a huge pothole. 'Carrick told you about Ireland?'

'You don't live and work with a man for ten years without learning some of his secrets, no matter how hard he might try to hide them.'

She could understand that. And hide them Carrick did. 'I believe Dankworth saw Carrick and Ruan together and thought Carrick was taking revenge, taking his son the way he'd taken Liam.'

'Jesus.' The whip came down with a heart breaking slash across the horse's back and it leapt forward, taking the bend over the bridge and slithering to a halt amidst a crowd of people outside the inn.

'What's going on?' Roisin gathered her skirts and leapt down from the buggy.

'No idea. I'll find out. You go and find Jane and Ruan.'

A nameless dread colonised her insides. She couldn't think, she wouldn't think. Not now. She flew up the road, forcing her way past the people crowded around the inn, scanning the throng for Ruan and Jane.

'Roisin, come 'ere.' It was Maisie's voice. She couldn't stop, couldn't turn back. All she could think of was Ruan. Dankworth would take him. With her sides splitting and her breath rasping she slithered to a halt. Elsie stood, barring her way. She tried to barge past the wretched woman, who stood like some stone carving refusing to budge. 'Get out of my way.'

'He's not there.'

Her heart began to thud in her chest, the answering echo beating in her head. 'Not there?'

'He's gone.'

'Where?' A sheen of sweat raced over her skin, hot then cold, and the nausea rolled up in one long, sick crest from her feet to her stomach and into her throat.

'I don't know. They're organising a search party down at the inn. Jane raised the alarm. He was playing out the back, searching for treasures. She was keeping an eye on him out the window. Next thing she knew he'd vanished.'

'It's Dankworth.' She gritted her teeth and fought back the waves of sickness.

'Dankworth?'

'Lady Alice's husband, he's taken him.' A scream tore at her chest, wanting to rip out of her, instead a long, slow keening sound built in her throat and a thundering noise roared in her ears as the ground spiralled up to meet her.

Her head throbbed and her vision cleared to reveal Elsie standing over her. 'What …'

'You took a turn. Haven't got time for that. On your feet.'

Feet. She couldn't even feel her feet. All she could feel was the great swelling lump in her chest. Her heart breaking. 'Ruan.'

Elsie grabbed her shoulders and eased her back into the middle of the road. 'You need to get down to the inn. Find out what's happening. It doesn't feel right to me.'

It wasn't right. She'd known from the moment Lady Alice had said Dankworth was out riding. Known in her bones Ruan would be gone. 'Why did I leave him?'

'It's too late for that now. Everyone's searching.' Elsie tucked her hands under Roisin's armpits and dragged her towards the crowd outside the inn. Surely there hadn't been that many people when she and Slinger had returned. The buggy still stood unattended in the middle of the street. A couple of the Paterson cutters were waving their arms, one of them standing on a barrel, then

Slinger moved through the crowd, towing Jane behind him, forcing his way to the back.

'Roisin. I'm so sorry I don't know …' Jane's face, ravaged by tears, peered up at her. 'One minute he was playing and the next he'd gone.' Jane tried to slip her arm around Roisin, but she shrugged her off.

'How could you? You knew. I told you.'

The tears tracked down Jane's face. 'Ruan wouldn't have gone off with him. He must have forced him, dragged him away.'

Roisin didn't care. Dankworth had Ruan, that was all that mattered.

A buggy skidded to a halt and Jane grabbed her arm and pulled her aside just before the wheels ran over her feet. Mr Winchester, hatless, his dramatic mane of silver hair flying in the breeze, and Lady Alice, her hand clamped over her hat, tumbled out. The crowd swirled around them. With an imperious wave Mr Winchester gestured them aside and strode up to the courthouse.

'Constable! Oi, Constable!'

'Quit your yelling, what's the problem?'

Carrick jumped down from the window and turned to the door, forgetting his chains, and landed in a crumpled heap. 'What's going on outside? Half the bloody town's out there.'

'Nothing to do with you. Least ways nothing you can do anything about. You're stuck here until the magistrate comes. Now quit your hollering.'

Carrick climbed back onto the bed and pressed his nose to the bars. Maisie and Elsie stood in the middle of the road. No sign of Slinger, that was good. He'd have everything under control. He was a good bloke, could be trusted in a pinch. He'd keep Roisin and Ruan safe. The Paterson cutters clustered around the big bloke, the ringie from the two-up game, as he clambered onto the barrel and spread his arms. Silence fell.

'Start from here and work your way around. We'll check the brook. Others out that way.' He waved his burly hands in the direction of the school. 'And anywhere else you can think of, anywhere a boy might go and hide.'

A boy? What boy? Where the hell was Slinger? 'Constable!' Carrick yelled at the top of his voice.

The keys rattled in the lock and the door swung open.

'Mr O'Connor?'

Carrick stared the toff up and down. His long white hair all awry and his face redder than one of Roisin's silks. 'And who'd be asking?'

'Winchester, James Winchester. Magistrate.'

Carrick opened his mouth to tell the sodding magistrate what he could do with his justice system, and then stopped when the keys in the man's hands rattled.

'Please lift your hands. I'm releasing you. I can see no reason to detain you. I would, however, request you stay within the town limits. You will be called when this matter comes to court. You might wish to assist in the search for the boy.'

'What search? What boy?' The fool fumbled with the key, taking his time. It'd be easier to rip the bloody cuffs from his wrists than endure this. 'What boy?' he repeated.

'Ruan Ogilvie. The boy's gone missing and we have reason to believe …'

'Me lad's missing?' He wrenched his wrists free of the open cuffs.

'We have reason to believe Gideon Dankworth may have taken him.'

Dankworth had done it again. Not a second time. He couldn't give a shit if he swung, he'd get Dankworth. Grind his bleedin' face in the dirt and take Ruan back. He elbowed his way past Winchester and out through the courtroom into the swirling crowd.

'Carrick.'

'He's out.'

'Good one, boyo.'

He pushed through and made his way to the barrel, where the ringie stood brandishing his arms, orchestrating the search, sending people in all directions.

'What's going on?'

'The dressmaker's boy's gone missing. Some say he's been snatched.'

'Where's his mother?'

The ringie nodded to a group of women clustered to one side. The green of Roisin's jacket stood out like a beacon as she sat crumpled on an upturned crate. She lifted her head and gazed at him, her eyes dulled with pain, tears streaking her bone-white face. He knelt beside her and took her freezing hands.

'Dankworth's taken him.'

'We'll find him.'

'I left him. Left him with Jane to see Mrs Winchester. I thought …'

'Where's Slinger?' He'd throttle the bloke when he got his hands on him. He was supposed to be looking out for her, looking after the lad, taking them away so this didn't happen. 'Why didn't he come to see me?'

'Slinger was with me. He took me to—'

Carrick shot to his feet. 'Slinger!'

He ran back to the ringie and held up his hand. The burly bloke hauled him onto the barrel and he scanned the crowd. 'Seen Slinger?'

'Nope. Useless good for nothing …There he is.' The ringie pointed to the back of the crowd where Slinger stood with two saddled horses and a grin from ear to ear. Jesus, the fool was enjoying himself. Carrick leapt off the barrel and returned to Roisin.

'We'll find him. You stay here with Jane.' He grabbed her in his arms and planted a firm kiss on her lips. To hell with the audience, let 'em think what they like.

She sank into his arms, her lips opening softly beneath his and the world retreated until there was nothing except her silken hair beneath his fingers and her arms encircling his neck as she rose on her toes to meet him.

'I'm coming with you,' she murmured and drew out of his arms.

'You can't, my love. Stay here.' He ran his fingers across the smooth skin of her cheek, catching the last of her tears. 'What if we're wrong and Ruan comes home? There has to be someone here.'

Jane unravelled herself from Slinger's embrace and took Roisin's arm. 'They'll be faster on their own. We'll stay here.'

Roisin's emerald eyes flashed a fiery warning. 'I'll kill him if he hurts Ruan.'

'You won't have to,' Slinger growled. 'There's two of us standing in line ahead of you.'

Slinger and Carrick covered the first thirty miles to Morpeth faster than any bullock dray, not resting for a moment. To hell with it. What good would the horses be if anything had happened to Ruan? The prick wouldn't have the satisfaction of beating him twice. And for once it seemed he had the law on his side. Whatever Roisin had said to the magistrate had got him released. He'd find out about that later. Right now finding Ruan was all that mattered.

Slinger drew up under a line of dripping gum trees.

Carrick's guts churned and tumbled. 'What's the problem?' All he could see was the glint in Dankworth's bloody eyes as he'd torched the thatch.

'What if Dankworth took the mail coach?'

He forced aside the swirling red mist and sucked in a deep breath. 'Then they can't be that far ahead. We'll go to the Rose, Shamrock and Thistle. Nell owes me a favour or two. She'll know if anyone does.'

'As long as he's still in town.'

'We've got to find the mongrel.'

'I reckon he'll be holed up with the boy. He isn't going to do anything to him. He needs him. He'll be aiming for the three o'clock steamer.'

Carrick swiped at the sweat trickling down his face. 'And how the hell would you be knowing that?' There were a million places Dankworth could have gone. Taken the Great North Road to Sydney. Gone back to the Yarramalong. Jesus, Morpeth was a long shot.

'You're not thinking straight. The boy's worth money to him, a lot of money. He's got to get him back to Sydney in one piece. Not only that, he's got to get Lady Alice to Sydney. Without her, his plan's shot.'

'Lady Alice? Who the hell's that? What's she got to do with anything?'

'She's Dankworth's wife.'

Carrick scrubbed at his eyes. 'What the bloody hell's going on?'

'You can thank her for getting you out of the lockup for a start, and it's how Roisin guessed Dankworth would take the boy. We haven't got time for this—trust me.' Slinger wheeled his horse around and dug his heels into the flanks of the exhausted animal. 'Come on. We've got another hour at least.'

When Carrick and Slinger entered the outskirts of the town the streets were alive with people heading to the docks, shopkeepers making the most of the hustle and bustle in town. They slowed and trotted into the courtyard of the inn. Carrick slithered from his horse, legs numb, and rubbed at his wrists, still screaming from the chaffing of the chains. He staggered through the door and wiped the dust from his eyes.

'And what would you be wanting?'

He rested his elbows on the counter, chin cupped in his hand and gazed across at Nell. 'A favour, Nell. A favour.' He didn't have the time or the inclination for the flirting and cajoling today.

'You used up all of those with them trunks.'

'You had no complaints. I need some help, Nell, and fast.' He wanted information and he wanted it now.

'Whoa. No.' She held up her hand. 'Not if you're in trouble again. I stay away from trouble. This is a reputable establishment.'

'I'm not in trouble, Nell; however, there's a little boy who may be. I need to know.'

She looked sideways at him, tipping her head and narrowing her eyes. 'Boy in trouble, you say?'

'Yes, Nell. In trouble. The lad's six, going on seven.'

'And he'll be travelling with his father.'

'No—aye.' Of course he'd travel with his father. What else would Dankworth say? That he'd kidnapped the lad?

'Well, which is it? Because that's the only little boy I've seen around here, other than those pesky buggers hanging around the stables, demanding a penny or two for doing bugger all.'

His heart gave a leap, sending blood coursing through his body, chasing away his exhaustion. 'And where d'you see him?'

'His father took him upstairs to wait. Poor little mite was bushed. Fast asleep in his arms, he was.'

'And they're booked on the steamer this afternoon?'

'Sold him the tickets myself. Fancy gentleman he was, too, with his shiny black cane and airs and graces. Not sure why he was travelling alone with the boy though. Think someone like that could afford a bit of help with the child.'

'Which room's he in?' His gaze slid to the open ledger.

She snatched back the book and closed it with a slam, trapping his fingers between the pages. 'I'll not be telling you that.'

'Come on, Nell.' He tugged at the ledger, then stared up at the ceiling. Upstairs. So close.

'No, I'll not be telling you 'cepting they're booked on the afternoon steamer. I've got me reputation to consider. You want to have a word, you can do it down there on the wharf like. No brawling in my inn. Know what you're like when your dander's up.'

Carrick clenched his fists and willed himself to relax. It would be easier on the wharf, easier to grab Ruan, let Slinger take him away while he sorted out Dankworth. He let his fingers relax. He'd waited so long for this moment, ten years. Revenge would be so very sweet. 'What time is it, Nell?'

'Two thirty.' She gave a sniff. 'Just clearing dinner before you came bargin' in interrupting.'

'And you're sure they're still here.' Supposing they'd slipped out and taken horses? He wiped his hand over his eyes. Ridiculous, no one in their right mind would choose a horse over the steamer. He'd be thinking he'd be in Sydney for breakfast. Well, he was wrong.

'Sure as sure. Haven't got the key back, so they must be.'

'What room?' That'd be the go. Up the stairs, whip the lad from under his very nose and take off.

'Not a chance, boyo. I told you, find 'em on the wharf. I've done enough. If people hear I'm giving away private information like that, I'll lose me custom.'

Sod her bloody custom and her reputation. There was a boy's life at stake. Not any boy, his lad. Ruan. 'Thanks, Nell.' He tossed the words over his shoulder and barged out through the door. It was light outside, just the distant rumble of the thunderclouds behind the hills. He couldn't miss him surely, a man with a boy. How many *gentlemen* travelled with a young boy, and no wife or servants?

Slinger slipped into step beside him. 'Well?'

'Holed up at the hotel.'

'Why haven't you …'

'Nell doesn't want anything happening on her premises. He's got tickets booked on the afternoon steamer. In broad daylight. Cocky bugger. Doesn't reckon anyone's going to stop him.'

'He's wrong there.'

'No one will question him. They'll only see his flash clothes, top hat and cane and they'll presume he's reputable. We won't have a leg to stand on if we challenge him. We've got to snatch Ruan away before he knows what's happening.'

'He'll claim Ruan's his son. The boy looks like him.'

'He hasn't got those bloody blind-bunyip eyes Old Pella keeps going on about. The lad's got Roisin's eyes. It's only his hair.' Hair the same colour as Liam's, the same colour as a million Irish boys, girls, men and women.

'Right, one step at a time, we'll see where it leads us. First we've got to find them. Over here.' Carrick led Slinger over to the wall where they'd get a decent view of everyone getting onto the steamer. They'd lowered the gangplank and the dock was a hive of activity, though the bloke at the end kept refusing permission to board. Had them all waiting in a line.

Carrick propped himself up against the wall. 'Right, while we wait you can fill me in on this Lady Alice.'

'Here's the short version. Roisin can tell you the rest of it when we get the boy back home.'

Roisin. Why couldn't she behave like any other woman and let a man sort things out? 'Get on with it.'

'I took her to see Mrs Winchester again. Lady Alice was there. Something about Dankworth needing a son to inherit her father's estates in Ireland.'

Holy shite. Lady Alice's father. The bloody absentee English landowner. Dankworth worked for him. The old man must have died. And Dankworth had an eye on his chances. Married his daughter. Didn't explain how he got to Australia though, unless … 'Did this Lady Alice say anything about how they came to be in Australia?'

'Something about insurgents and rumours. Nothing that made much sense to me. Probably means more to you. You'll have to ask her yourself.' Slinger's face crinkled in a grin. 'Right now I've got your back, mate. Now's me chance to repay the debt I owe you. We'll find the boy.'

'You owe me nothing.' Slinger and his fool ideas. So he'd saved the bloke from a bunch of punch-drunk redcoats and taken the rap. He'd spent so long in solitary, what did another bout matter? Hardly a debt worth remembering.

'Besides, I should've stayed with the boy. Not left him with Jane. Bad call on my part. Thought I'd be better with Roisin if Dankworth was around.'

He'd have done the same thing. 'Can't change anything. Just pray we've picked Dankworth's plan right.'

'Heads up.' Slinger's elbow hit him in the ribs. 'There we go.'

And the air sucked out of his lungs, more from relief than anything else. Ruan seemed no worse for wear, though none too happy. Dankworth had his hand gripped firmly around the lad's wrist, while Ruan twisted and turned.

'He doesn't want to be there. Let's go.'

'Wait!' Slinger grabbed hold of Carrick's arm.

'What're you waiting for?'

'Give it a bit longer.'

'I want me hands on the bastard now. Any idea how long I've waited?'

'Yeah and you'll end up back behind bars. Today we do it my way. You've called the tune long enough. I'm going to get Dankworth's attention, you're going to grab the boy and make for the horses; they're tethered round the back of the inn.'

'And what will you do with Dankworth?'

'I'll sort him out. Cutter's justice. Trust me. You get the hell out of here. I'll catch up with you when I know he's sorted. Besides, the lad'll be happier going with you.'

'No chance. I've waited too long for this.' Dreamed of it, planned it. The way his hands would slip around the bastard's throat and his eyes'd pop as he squeezed the very life out of him. For Liam, for Brigid and now for Roisin and Ruan.

'Who are you doing this for—yourself or Roisin and the boy?'

'For me own wife and child and the future.'

'And what good is it going to do Roisin?'

'The bastard deserves to pay.' What in the name of God was the matter with Slinger? 'Get off your high horse. He's mine.'

'Nah. You grab the boy and get him back to his mam. I'll sort the rest. Cutter's justice. I told you.'

'Slinger, I …'

'There he is.' Slinger pointed to the alley running from the stable yard behind the Rose, Shamrock and Thistle to the wharf and took off.

Carrick followed and he picked the moment Ruan spotted him. His eyes lit up like beacons. 'Carrick!'

Dankworth lifted his head and they locked eyes. In that second the little blighter broke loose and threw himself into Slinger's arms.

Carrick had waited for this moment for too long; it had sustained him through sentencing, transportation, the filthy coalmines and seven years of convict hell. No matter what Slinger wanted. He bunched his fist and let fly.

The smacking thud of flesh on flesh and the crunch of bone set his blood roaring. 'That one's for Brigid and this,' he grasped

Dankworth's jacket and pulled him close, lifted his knee and slammed it up, 'is for Roisin.'

The air whistled out between Dankworth's lips, his pale eyes glazed and his legs gave way.

'Carrick!' Slinger's strident tone permeated the red haze. 'The lad needs you.'

Slinger lobbed Ruan over Dankworth's crumpled body. Carrick snatched him up. Ruan's arms clasped his neck and his legs twined around his waist.

'I haven't finished with him yet. Hold tight.' He clutched Ruan, swung his foot back and landed a hefty kick in Dankworth's kidneys.

'Get the hell out of here.' Slinger dropped to his knees, cradling Dankworth's head in his lap. 'Go.'

Carrick turned and bolted. What he'd not give to stay and finish the bastard—kill the sod, but the warm, live body clamped to him was more important. Not a ghost, not the past, but his living, breathing lad.

Ever true to his word, Slinger had arranged fresh horses and they were saddled and waiting. Carrick set Ruan down, just for a moment, and leapt into the saddle. The ostler handed the lad up and before he had a chance to settle, belted the horse's rump.

'Good onya, Carrick.'

With Ruan clasped tightly in front of him, he dug his heels in and took off down the street, scattering the crowds gathered in the market place. It wasn't until they'd cleared the outskirts of the town that he slowed and turned to look behind him.

'Where's Slinger?' Ruan asked, leaning back against him.

'He'll be along soon. Let's get you home to your mam.'

Twenty-one

Roisin paced the footpath, her head splitting, her eyes so swollen from weeping she could hardly see straight. There was no sign of life, even the cutters' camp down by the brook was quiet. They'd searched every inch of the area until it was too dark to see the nose in front of their face and only then called it quits. Ruan couldn't have escaped their search, he simply wasn't there.

She knew, as only a mother could, that Dankworth had him and all she could do was pin her hopes on Carrick and Slinger. For the first time in her life she hoped Ruan was with Dankworth, because then they might find him. At least now, thanks to Lady Alice, Dankworth's reasons were clear. It made sense for her to stay at home, in case, just in case Ruan somehow managed to find his way back.

The inactivity sapped her strength, sending her mind into a useless, flat spin. She understood the sense of it, yet how could she do nothing when Ruan, her baby, was …

The memory of Dankworth's face when he'd seen Ruan still turned her blood cold. The way he'd run his hand over her boy's hair, the avaricious look on his face. She'd imagined he had some strange desire for Ruan, hadn't realised then it was greed.

'Roisin. Roisin.' Jane's voice wafted through the gathering twilight and she turned, her heart skipping a beat. Fired with a spurt of unexpected energy, she flew back down the path.

'Are they back?'

Jane shook her head. 'No, nothing. You must come inside and have something to eat. You have to keep your strength up.'

She shook her head. Jane meant well, but her stomach roiled at the mere mention of food.

'Tea, then. At least have some tea.'

'If I drink any more tea I'll drown.' She attempted a smile and failed miserably.

'Come along. I've stoked the fire.' Jane chaffed her hands. 'You're freezing. It's not going to help anyone if you take a turn.'

The fire in the kitchen roared and when the heat permeated Roisin's frozen bones, she took the mug of tea Jane offered.

'I'm anxious Carrick will do something stupid and get into trouble again. He's likely to kill Dankworth and then he'll be back behind bars, and no amount of treasures from Old Pella will save him.'

'You're making problems where there are none. Slinger's with him. They'll get Ruan back.'

'Slinger! He's more trouble than he's worth.' Her lips snapped shut. Her words sounded harsh, but she had no patience for niceties.

'Slinger won't let any harm come to Carrick. He owes him.'

'Owes him? What for?' Most times Slinger caused more problems than he solved. She forced herself onto her feet. Her sense of justice had gone out of the window. He'd taken her to the Winchesters', done the very best for her. There must be some good in the man if Jane was standing up for him.

'Carrick saved his life years ago in the mines and ended up doing a spell in solitary for him. That's how they became friends.'

Why didn't she know this? 'Carrick hasn't told me much about his life. He didn't even tell me the name of the man in Ireland. If he'd done that, told me it was Dankworth, none of this would have happened.'

'Oh, tush. Stop now. You can't keep searching for someone to blame.'

'I feel so helpless. I need to do something instead of sitting here waiting. It's the waiting that's killing me. I've made so many mistakes.'

'You've done the best you could for Ruan and look …' Jane waved her hand around. 'Look at this house and the business you've built up.'

'None of it will be worth anything if I lose Ruan.'

'You are not going to lose Ruan. Carrick and Slinger will find him. I know it.'

How she wished she could be so certain. She drew in a few steadying breaths. Jane was right, this hopeless complaining wouldn't help anyone. 'I'm sorry, Jane. You must be anxious. Worried for Slinger.'

The pretty pink blush rose to Jane's face again, the same as it always did when anyone mentioned Slinger's name. 'I am, though I know he'll be back. He made me a promise and I intend to make sure he keeps it.'

'He did, did he?'

'Aye, he did. He's giving away the cutting. He wants us to settle here in Wollombi so I can still help you.'

Roisin couldn't even think beyond this moment, never mind the future. 'That's wonderful. I'm so happy for you.' She took Jane's hand and squeezed it tight. It was the best she could do; she couldn't imagine being happy again.

'The cutters believe in their own justice. Slinger and Carrick will sort it all out.'

That's what concerned her. 'Having seen Mr Winchester release Carrick so quickly, I think I'd rather place my faith in the law.'

'Lot of good that would do, waiting for the law to catch up with Dankworth.'

'Winchester did the right thing. He took notice of the stopper, said he'd talk to the old man if he can find him. Where is Old Pella? I don't remember seeing him yesterday.'

'He'll be around somewhere.'

'He better be if Winchester wants to talk to him.'

The back door swung open and Roisin leapt to her feet, her heart pounding and her palms sweaty.

The old man unravelled his possum cloak and dropped it on the floor, stretching out his gnarled hands towards the fire.

'Winchester man came down to the brook to see Old Pella. Told him my story. He let Carrick go and find the boy. He's coming this way.'

Roisin frowned at Jane and lifted her shoulders. 'Carrick. He's coming this way?' Her heart picked up a beat, throbbing deep in her chest.

'Your treasure back soon.'

'You want some tea, Old Pella?' Jane laced a mug with sugar and pushed it across the table.

'Not today. Old Pella gotta go find Billy Boy.' He snatched a piece of yesterday's damper from the table and shuffled out, taking his stinking possum cloak with him.

'I hope he's right.' The first ray of real hope began to burn deep inside Roisin. 'I thought for a while I was going mad. After Dankworth first turned up I could feel someone watching. I thought maybe it was Old Pella, or that I was seeing shadows when there were none. Now I know it was Dankworth. He was watching. Watching Ruan, and me, and watching Carrick. Carrick posed a threat to Dankworth's plans and he decided the easiest thing would be to get rid of him.'

'Why not just shoot him, then? He shot his overseer.'

'Because then he'd run the risk of being accused. This way Carrick was the scapegoat. He'd got away with it in Ireland and he thought he'd do the same again. The man's mad. He thinks he can do whatever he likes. I feel so sorry for Lady Alice. She was so brave, going against him. It was almost as though she was relieved to get it off her chest. Her success at the ball restored her confidence so much. I can't imagine what her life must have been like with Dankworth.'

Jane shivered and reached her hands out to the fire. 'I don't like to think of being watched. And I don't like to think of any woman with a man who throws his weight around. I had enough of that with Mick. Let's forget about the past and remember what Old Pella said. Carrick and Slinger are getting back with Ruan.'

'You're right, and I might be hungry.' Roisin reached across the table and broke a hunk of damper from the little Old Pella had left and dunked it in her tea.

'Shall I make some more?'

'No, Jane you've done enough. More than enough, I don't know what I'd do without you.'

'I'm going to make some soup. They'll be hungry when they get home.'

If. She couldn't get past the if. And she couldn't stay inside the house. A giant fist had a squeezing grip on her heart. She picked up the chair. 'I'm going to sit outside.' Sit at the end of the alley, where she could see the road.

Settled in a frail patch of moonlight outside the General Store, Roisin sat and shivered. Almost twelve hours had passed since Carrick and Slinger had ridden down the road in a flurry of dust, more since Dankworth had taken Ruan. The courthouse was locked tight, and there was no sign of Maisie, Elsie or the cutters. Only a brooding silence, as though the whole town was holding its breath behind closed doors, waiting.

Roisin couldn't take her eyes off the road winding over the hill and disappearing into the moonlit line of trees. She'd never travelled that way, never needed to. Carrick had brought her trunks, Alfie Sullivan drove it twice a week bringing the mail and supplies, the bullock drays took their loads along it, whereas she had no idea what lay around the corner. The air was stiller than the grave. Not even a breath of wind in the trees. She squinted into the darkness, seeing clouds of dust, hearing the drum of hooves where there were none. Or were there?

She shaded her eyes, the muscles in her stomach clutched in an even tighter ball, and she pushed back the chair. She couldn't bear it, couldn't sit a moment longer. Moving to the centre of the road she started walking.

The blood buzzed in her head as she took one step after another, one foot then the next. The cloud of dust billowed, grew larger. Blood throbbed through her body, vibrating up from the soles of her feet to meet the tangled knot in her stomach. Her feet took on a life of their own, pushing her forward as she ran, ran down the road, past the cemetery, over the rise and down towards the millpond. And then her heart stopped.

Dust swirled in the silvery light and the drumming increased. She opened her mouth to call but no sound came out, her mouth was dry, her throat tight. Through the haze a horse appeared, its hooves beating out the tattoo in her heart.

'Mam!'

Her legs turned to jelly and she sank to the road.

His hand reached for the nape of her neck and drew her close, his soft cheek against hers. 'I'm home. Don't cry.'

Ruan's fingers wiped the tears, tears she didn't know she was shedding. 'Carrick rescued me. I'm home. Slinger threw me and we galloped nearly all the way.'

Then Carrick's arms wrapped round her, taking her weight, lifting her to her feet. She buried her face in his chest, with its cedar scent, musky and alive; the hard, fast beat of his heart against her cheek.

'We're here now. It's over.' His voice smooth and deep, potent as the rum he favoured, soothed. 'Come, let's go home.'

She didn't want explanations, didn't want to know what had happened. He and Ruan were here. That was enough.

Then he was kissing her, kissing her mouth. She clung to him as if they might drown if they did not hold onto each other. He became still, so very still, then his lips moved below hers and she felt him smile.

Ruan tugged at her hand. 'Come on, Mam. I need my treasure box. And I'm ravenous, real hungry.' He towed her along the road and Carrick fell into step beside her, leading the horse, his arm tight around her shoulders. The three of them moving side by side, step by step. Warmth replaced the cold stone of fear that had been lodged for so long in her chest and she smiled up at the man who held her heart in the palm of his strong, calloused hands.

'I told you that day after the Woodchop yer lad's as safe as houses with me. Did you not believe me?'

As they rounded the bend at the millpond the town came into view. It was no longer sleeping, and the street was full. Elsie and Maisie, the cutters, the Blackmores, Mr Winchester, everyone was crowded in a group in front of the inn, waving and calling. Then Jane appeared, her hair streaming and legs flying as she ran towards them.

'Carrick?'

'Yes, my love.'

'Where's Slinger?' Why wasn't he here? She hadn't even asked. She was so overwhelmed, she hadn't spared a thought.

'Don't be worrying yourself, he'll be along soon. He's just tidying up the ends. Slinger's a lucky man.' He winked at her. 'But I've got the luck of the Irish and I've got you.' He raised her hand and kissed it.

'Jane will want to know where he is.'

'Aye.'

He didn't want to speak to Jane. Didn't want to have to lie. Slinger was fine. He had to be. He'd waited, waited for over an hour outside Morpeth, and when Slinger hadn't appeared, he'd left as he'd promised, to bring back the lad. Slinger's words still niggled. *Cutter's justice.*

Jane slithered to a halt in front of them. 'Where's Slinger?'

'He'll be back in a day or two. Got some unfinished business.' He looked away, up the road, hoping against hope Slinger would appear. Finally he summoned the courage to turn to Jane.

Tears pooled in her eyes and her lips quivered. 'He's all right? Not hurt?'

'He's fine.' At least he hoped to God he was.

'I hoped he'd come back. He told me he would.'

'He'll be back, of that I promise you. Give him a day or two.'

It broke his heart to utter the words as she turned away into Elsie's waiting arms. It was no longer his story to tell. Besides, he didn't know the ending.

'Carrick?'

He buried his face in Roisin's golden-red hair, drew in her scent. 'It's over now.' He framed her face with his hands. Her eyes, shadowed yet steady, gazed up at him and in that moment everything changed. Revenge couldn't fill the hole in his heart, only Roisin and Ruan could do that.

The desire for vengeance that had fuelled his very existence, sustained him for so long, leached away, replaced by hope and the future, a future with her and Ruan. 'You mean everything to me. Everything.'

The love he had for Roisin was stronger than all the ghosts in Ireland. Better to honour Liam and Brigid's memory by giving up the misery, the recriminations and reprisals. Roisin had healed his need for blood, his need to strike back. He fingered the brand on his shoulder—that was Liam and Brigid's memorial, ever with him, not some cold granite lump on a grassy hillside he could no longer see. Time to move from the shadows into the light—the light that was Roisin, Ruan and their love.

'You are my home now, you and the lad. I want you so much I can scarcely draw breath. Will you have me?'

Her lips met his and clung, all the sweeter now he'd stepped into the light of her eyes and left the darkness behind.

Epilogue

THE MAITLAND MERCURY *WEDNESDAY 14th AUGUST 1855*

FATALITY ABOARD THE SS MAITLAND.

[BY TELEGRAPH.]

(FROM OUR WOLLOMBI CORRESPONDENT.)

As the steamer Maitland, which left Morpeth at 3.00 yesterday afternoon, was coming round Nobbys, one of the passengers, Mr GD Dankworth, a man of 31 years of age, was opening the gangway doors, when the vessel gave a lurch and he fell overboard. The engines were at once stopped and a boat lowered to search for him, but no trace of the poor fellow could be found. It is feared that he was struck by one of the paddle wheels, and sank immediately. His travelling companion raised the alarm and only three minutes elapsed from the time of his falling overboard to the lowering of the boat. It is believed the deceased was involved in an altercation on the wharf before boarding and may have become disorientated.

Mr Dankworth has been several years in the colony, and was a well-known Sydney figure and landowner in the Yarramalong. Great regret is felt at his death. He is survived by his wife, Lady Alice. Sadly, the Dankworths were not blessed with children.

[It will be seen by our telegrams that the body of the unfortunate man was found in Newcastle harbour on Sunday, and a verdict of found drowned was returned at the inquest held upon it.]

Historical Note

The Cedar Cutter began with photograph in my local Museum–three larrikins admiring a massive, felled cedar tree. Throw in an obituary I stumbled across on TROVE and the village of Wollombi in the Hunter Valley, the place I am lucky enough to call home, and this story started taking shape. The name 'Wollombi' is derived from the Aboriginal meaning 'meeting place'. The traditional owners are believed to be the Darkinjung, Awabakal and Wanaruah people although many others travelled hundreds of miles to visit Mount Yengo, a place of huge cultural and ceremonial significance connected to the Dreamtime story of the creation of the Earth. In 1833, after the completion of the Great Northern Road, plans for the village of Wollombi appeared in the NSW Government Gazette and by the mid nineteenth century Wollombi had become a thriving European community. Yarramalong is an Aboriginal word meaning 'the place of cedar'. The valley is now part of the Central Coast region of New South Wales. Timber cutters driving bullock drays from Wollombi and Maitland logged the area until it was permanently settled in 1856.

Competitive Woodchop competitions began in Tasmania, and quickly became a popular sport throughout Australia making an appearance at the Sydney Royal Easter Show in 1899. Every October, down on the banks of the Wollombi Brook, behind the Tavern, the Wollombi Woodchop is held. It is a more recent event so I have to admit to tweaking the timeline there, and in a few other places, to fit the fictional story. I take full responsibility for any errors.

Acknowledgements

Massive thanks are due to so many people…

Sue Brockhoff, Annabel Blay, Laurie Ormond and the entire team at Harlequin Australia. It is a pleasure and a privilege to work with you all. Also to my editor Alex Nahlous for her patient and insightful editing.

My wonderful critique partners Eva Scott, Ann B Harrison, Sarah Barrie and Joanna Lloyd who are there for me every step of the way. They listen to my mad ideas, read my dodgy plots and plans and without them my stories would never reach a conclusion.

And last but not least, thanks to the Wollombi locals, most especially 'wardrobe consultant' Lynda Marsh, Wollombi's own historian, Carl Hoipo, and Charles—I still can't make sense of those topographical maps!